Charlie had absolute faith in himself. The Royal Marines had taught him to kill and they'd taught him well. But then the politicians had sent them to fight a war on a bloody freezing rock in the South Atlantic and before it was over Charlie had vowed never again to risk his life for forty pounds a month. So Charlie went to America, the land of opportunity, and now instead of killing for Madam Thatcher he killed for Madam Masters. The work was easier and the pay infinitely better.

O'Toole was gasping for air. Charlie knelt beside him and jerked loose his watch and his ring. The two men's eyes met.

"Why?" the dying man whispered.

Charlie considered the question.

Why must Bernie O'Toole die this lonely dawn?

Fate he might have said, but that was unduly vague.

Power, too, might have been his reply, for that was closer to the truth.

Suddenly, absolutely, he knew the answer to O'Toole's question.

"*National Security*," he whispered in a voice as cold as eternity.

O'Toole's blue eyes widened, burned, then closed forever.

He understood everything.

Sinister
Forces

PATRICK ANDERSON

A Methuen Paperback

A Methuen Paperback

SINISTER FORCES

First published in Great Britain 1986
by Martin Secker & Warburg Limited
This edition published 1987
by Methuen London Limited
11 New Fetter Lane, London EC4P 4EE

Reprinted 1995

British Library Cataloguing in Publciation Data

Anderson, Patrick, *1936–*
Sinister forces.
I. Title
813′.54 [F]   PS3551.N377
ISBN 0 413 42340 9

Printed and bound in Great Britain
by HarperCollins Manufacturing, Glasgow

For Michael

PART I

Safe at Home

1

Matt Boyle awoke early on Inauguration Day, yawned contentedly, and glanced out his bedroom window to discover a world blanketed in snow.

"Oh no," he sighed. Boyle had two tickets to watch the Inauguration from a VIP grandstand. They'd freeze their butts off but it would be a good experience for Zeb. History in the raw. Now this sudden snow would make the drive into Washington a disaster.

Zeb stirred beside him, muttering, then opened his brown eyes wide. In an instant he was out of bed, his nose pressed to the window. He was a fair-skinned, wiry boy with elegant cheekbones, a mouth at once delicate and determined, and short, thick, straw-colored hair. After a moment he turned from the window, poised for the day's adventures. "Dad, can we go sledding?"

Boyle weighed history-in-the-making versus a monster traffic jam. "Don't you want to see the Inauguration?"

"We can watch it on TV."

Zeb was a child of television, suckled on the tube. What you saw on the screen was reality. The real-life event would be cold, crowded, and boring. The hell of it was, he was right.

"Okay," Boyle said. "But first, a good breakfast."

They dressed and went downstairs to the big country kitchen. Zeb mixed the orange juice, toasted the muffins, and set the table, while Boyle juggled coffee, bacon, and scrambled eggs.

Zeb wolfed down his food and rinsed the dishes while Boyle retrieved their sleds from the basement's junk.

Soon they were slogging through six inches of snow on the narrow road that curved out of the village, past a sign that proclaimed:

Harmony, Virginia

Pop. 317

Settled by Quakers in 1755

A Peaceful Place

They entered a field where two dozen men, women, and children confronted two glistening hills. Zeb joined the smaller kids who were navigating the gentler slope, for generations called the Little Hill. It warmed Boyle to watch them laughing and falling in the snow, so inutterably beautiful with their rosy cheeks and runny noses.

Howls came from higher up, as the village teenagers came shooting down the Big Hill. It seemed a Matterhorn, a hundred feet straight down. The sleds rocketed off the snow, sailed through empty air, barely missing boulders and trees. At the bottom, the sledders had to brake quickly lest they slide onto the road. It was a daredevil run and the teenagers gloried in its peril. Boyle guessed he'd been a teenager once, but all he could remember was that he'd had pimples and all the girls had been virgins.

"Hey, Boyle, let's see you try the Big Hill." It was one of his neighbors, a stockbroker named Clinton.

"No way."

"Have a shot of courage." Clinton handed over a silver flask. He was a beefy, red-faced fellow who sported an L. L.

Bean parka and a Hitlerian moustache. Boyle swigged his brandy gratefully.

"Well, we get us a new President today," Clinton said glumly. "You elected that turkey; you gonna work for him?"

"Not me. I'm writing a book."

"Must be hard to say no to the White House."

"Easier than you'd think." Clinton was a pain in the ass but his brandy was a blessing. Loving-kindness exploded in Boyle's gut and rose sinuously to his brain.

Clinton glanced about furtively and lowered his voice. "The *Times* says Webster'll have a bombshell in his Inaugural speech. Whatta you think? A tax cut, maybe?"

Boyle laughed. "Maybe a surtax on stockbrokers."

"Not funny," Clinton grumbled and swigged more brandy. "Listen, Boyle, Mimi's sister is coming next weekend. She's thirty-three, just divorced, and hot to trot. Be a pal, take her off my hands."

"Not this time," Boyle said.

The stockbroker scowled. "Face reality, man. There's ten million liberated women out there, waiting to humiliate you. Accept your fate."

Zeb raced up to them. "Dad, I'm going down the Big Hill," he exclaimed.

"No, son, it's too steep. You could get hurt."

Zeb's eyes flashed. He drew himself to his full four-feet-seven. *"Dad, I'm nine years old!"*

Boyle blinked against the dazzling morning sun, suddenly dizzy, seeing Cara, her eyes, her cheekbones, her fierce pride. What did you do with a child who hungered for challenge? Protect his body and break his spirit? Or let him learn the risks of this unforgiving planet?

"Please be careful," was all he could say.

Zeb hauled his orange plastic K-Mart sled up the Big Hill, yelling for the older boys to wait for him. Clinton passed Boyle the flask. "Kill it," he advised.

"It's one damn thing after another," Boyle raged. "Last summer it was riding his bike to the pool. Trucks drive fifty miles an hour on that road."

"You got it tough, pal," Clinton said. "Having to worry for two."

Zeb, a bright blur atop the Big Hill, waved and shot downward. Boyle's gut clenched like a fist. He remembered Cara making this same run, at dusk two Christmases before, emboldened by an afternoon's hot toddies. She'd flipped over at the bottom, banged her head on a rock, and wound up flat on her back, laughing joyously, even as her blood stained the snow.

He saw Zeb shoot off the ground, flying, landing precariously on one runner. He skirted some rocks and was airborne again, head high, blond hair flapping, eyes wide, as fragile as an egg. He whizzed past them, toward the road, even as a big yellow snowplow chugged into view.

"Zeb, stop!" Boyle yelled and started running after him. At the last moment the boy skidded sideways, sending a wave of snow skyward, and stopped ten feet from disaster.

Zeb leaped to his feet, pumping both fists over his head, as the other kids cheered.

"That's some boy you've got there," Clinton said.

Boyle wiped his eyes. "He's tough," he said. "Like his mother."

2

Father and son trudged home in midmorning to the big brick house that a prosperous Quaker merchant had built for his schoolteacher daughter a century and a half before. The house sat on a hill on the outskirts of Harmony, facing west to the gentle glories of the Blue Ridge. Washington, D.C., an hour to the east, seemed centuries away.

Zeb went to make hot chocolate while Boyle built a fire in the front room. He turned the TV set on at noon for the Inauguration but left the sound down during the various hymns and prayers. Finally, the new President, Calvin Webster, the war hero and politician who had been Boyle's boss, perhaps his friend, placed his hand upon a family Bible and in his gruff, no-nonsense voice repeated the oath of office.

"Look at that, son," Boyle whispered. "More power than you can imagine is passing, right now, from one man to another. Peacefully. Other countries do it with bombs and bullets, but we do it with votes."

"I *know*, Dad," Zeb sighed. He'd heard his father's democracy-in-action lecture before.

Calvin Webster stepped forward to deliver his Inaugural

Address. He was a bull of a man; he filled the TV screen, seemed to fill the world, as he gazed boldly into the cameras.

As Webster began to speak, Boyle settled into his big green sofa, professionally curious to see what line the speech would take. Had not fate intervened, Boyle would have helped shape this speech.

"My friends, the time has come to end the madness of the arms race," Webster boomed. "We must lead the world away from the threat of nuclear war and toward the blessings of permanent peace."

Boyle leaned forward, clutching his cup of hot chocolate, tense with interest. What the hell was he up to?

"I am today proposing a plan whereby we and the Soviets, with no risk to our own security, can achieve major reductions in our nuclear arsenals.

"I will soon designate one hundred of our nuclear weapons—a tiny fraction of our total nuclear stockpile—for destruction. If the Soviets agree to do the same, our weapons and theirs can be dismantled and used for peaceful purposes.

"I will propose that a joint U.S.-Soviet team of scientists monitor this process, so there can be no doubt that the weapons are in fact permanently and absolutely destroyed.

"This first round of cuts will only be a small beginning. But, given goodwill on both sides, there can be more and greater reductions."

"My God," Boyle muttered. This "deep cuts" disarmament plan was one he knew well. Back in 1982 a retired admiral had proposed it in the New York *Times* Magazine. Boyle had shown an advance copy of the article to Webster, then a newly elected governor. Webster read the article intently, then tossed it aside. "The country's not ready for it," was all he said.

But now Webster was President and gambling that America was finally ready to end the arms race.

The new President spoke on, passionately, outlining his plan in detail. He invoked the threat of a "nuclear winter" that scientists said might follow a nuclear war, as smoke from burning cities cut off the sun.

Matt Boyle suddenly realized that he had drawn his son close beside him. Boyle was a veteran of five presidential campaigns and not much surprised or impressed him any more. He was by profession an image-maker, one of the best. The rousing rhetoric, the slick TV spots, the cold-blooded manipulation of a nation's hopes and fears—all these were his stock in trade. Yet this speech left him breathless. For this wasn't illusion, pretty words, but the boldest action imaginable. Cal Webster was putting his political life on the line, and for no less a goal than to save the world. Boyle had known Webster for a decade, had managed three of his campaigns, had cursed him and fought with him and laughed at him, but now everything had changed and Boyle blessed him and hoped to God he could bring it off.

"Let us slay the nuclear dragon," Webster proclaimed, and soon he ended his speech. The crowd cheered, the Marine band began to play, and the TV commentators began jabbering wildly about Project Peace, as the new President had called his plan.

Boyle cut off the TV. He knew better than the reporters what was coming. Blood on the moon. A political free-for-all such as America hadn't seen since Woodrow Wilson lost the League of Nations fight.

Boyle heard shouts outside and glancing down the street saw his friend Jack Payne standing on his front porch, waving a big American flag. Boyle smiled at the sight. Jack was a bitter-end liberal who still had a faded McGovern sticker on his battered VW bug. Boyle knew where his friends the Paynes stood on the arms race, but he wished he knew how all those other people up and down his street, up and down a million American streets, felt about Cal Webster's proposal. He imagined them confused, torn between four decades of Cold War rhetoric and their own nagging, commonsense suspicion that things were out of hand, that the weapons themselves had become the enemy. To convince those decent, confused Americans that Cal Webster was right, that forty years of history must be undone—*that* was a challenge. It was Boyle's business, too, and his mind exploded with schemes and slogans and strategies.

Then he caught himself. He was out of it now.

"Dad, will Mr. Webster get rid of nuclear weapons?"

Boyle turned away from the window. "He said he'd try."
No false hopes in the Boyle home.

"It's so *dumb*. I read that we have enough bombs to blow
up Russia thirty times and they have enough to blow us up
thirty times. Why?"

"Grown-ups are crazy sometimes."

"No, Dad. Why?"

Boyle stared into his son's face. What could you say?

"Two reasons," Boyle said. "First, a lot of people honestly
believe that the more weapons we have the less likely it is
that we'll use them."

"But that doesn't make *sense!*" the boy cried.

"I didn't say it made sense. I said a lot of people believe it.
Reason two, powerful people make billions of dollars by
building and selling nuclear weapons and they'll fight like
crazy to go on making them."

Boyle sighed. "Now, how about lunch?"

The phone started ringing while they ate. Boyle let his
answering machine take the calls. After lunch he listened to
the messages. The callers were reporters, some of them
good friends of his, shouting that it was urgent that he call
them immediately. Boyle understood. The story of the year
had exploded out of nowhere and the reporters were scrambling to get a handle on it. Boyle could have told them a lot,
but feeding tidbits to the media wasn't his business any
more.

He turned the TV back on in midafternoon. The parade
was over and the announcer said the new President and his
staff had entered the White House. Boyle smiled as he imagined his old cronies waltzing through the White House, savoring the pot of gold at the rainbow's end, the power and
glory they'd dreamed of for so long. He thought of his friend
Harry Bliss, the new President's top man now, as happy as a
pig in clover.

When the phone rang again, instinct told Boyle who it
was. After a minute he went and played the message. The
familiar voice boomed out at him: "Matt, dammit, call me at

the White House right away. The boss wants to talk to you. We need you. Hurry!"

Boyle sank into a chair and stared into space. After a while Zeb spoke from the doorway. "Who was that?" he asked.

"Remember Uncle Harry?"

The boy nodded. "What did he want?"

Boyle reached out his hand and Zeb came and sat beside him. "I imagine they want me to come work in the White House. He called me a couple of months ago, not long after your mother died."

"Are you going to do it?"

"I don't know," Boyle said. "What President Webster wants to do is awfully important."

"Would you have to work in the White House?"

Boyle nodded. "That's the problem. I'd have to leave here early in the morning and wouldn't get home till late at night. We'd have to get someone to stay with you after school. Or else we'd have to take a house in Washington."

"Would I have to change schools?"

"If we moved into town, yes."

Zeb's lower lip trembled. The job that would crown Boyle's career would turn his son's life upside down.

"I won't do anything you don't want me to do, Zeb," Boyle said.

The boy's composure cracked. He huddled against his father. "I don't want to change schools," he said. "I don't want you to work in Washington. I want you home with me, just like it's been ever since Mom . . ." He buried his face in Boyle's shirt.

Boyle held his son tight. "Then it's all decided," he said. "I'll stay here and write my book and President Webster will have to struggle along without me."

Boyle touched the boy's soft yellow hair. "Now," he said, "how about you and me having another go at the Big Hill?"

The boy's eyes glistened in the soft afternoon light. "I love you, Dad," he said.

Boyle felt ten feet tall. "Love you, son."

The phone was ringing again as the two of them stepped out into a world of the purest, most dazzling white.

3

"Slay the nuclear dragon?" Serena Masters said scornfully. "Sell out your country is more like it!"

As the new President spoke on television, Serena paced about the vast, baronial hall, barely able to contain her anger.

Across the room, Charlie Trueblood was stretched out on a plum-colored Italian chaise longue, toying with a kitten that had wandered up from the servants' quarters.

"Let the cat be!" Serena snapped. "Listen to what this fool is saying!"

Charlie sighed and tossed the kitten aside. He was a tall, broad-shouldered, languid Englishman of twenty-eight, tanned and handsome, with shaggy, reddish-brown hair and disarming blue eyes.

"Why should I listen?" he drawled. "It's just more political blather."

"Blather be damned, it's treason!" Serena declared. "How they must be laughing in the Kremlin. This . . . this *charlatan* proposes to leave us naked before our enemies."

"More work for the faithful," Charlie said, grinning contentedly.

When Webster finished his speech, Serena snapped off the TV set and resumed her restless pacing. She was a slender woman who looked far younger than her fifty-three years. Her black silk gown flattered her hard, lithe body and her dark eyes burned with pent-up passion. Charlie thought her the most dangerous woman he had ever known and also the most desirable.

The room that she prowled like an angry lioness was the great hall of the castle her father, Garth Masters, had built in the wilds of North Georgia many years before. Dragon's Lair, he had christened it. Fires blazed in huge stone fireplaces at either end of the hall, which Garth Masters and his children had made into a unique museum of war and destruction.

Above one fireplace hung the machine gun with which Serena's older brother, Leo, had slain seventeen Japanese soldiers one morning in 1945 before being himself killed by a sniper. Above the other fireplace was the sword Napoleon had carried at Marengo. On display elsewhere were the .44 caliber Smith & Wesson revolver that Wyatt Earp fired at the O. K. Corral, gold-inlaid cannon from the eighteenth century, suits of armor from the Crusades, crossbows, gas masks, busts of Caesar and Alexander, and bookshelves bulging with volumes of military history. The walls were crowded too with photographs, including many of Serena with generals, admirals, and Presidents, for she had once served her country in high office.

On display on a platform in the center of the hall, highlighted by twin spotlights, was the most prized piece in Serena's collection, a huge mechanical dragon that had been created in the twelfth century for the amusement of the children of the ruling dynasty of China. The dragon was fashioned of tin, teak, ivory, leather, silver, and scores of precious jewels. It could raise its head, roll its emerald eyes, and shoot billows of fire from its gaping mouth. Serena's father had bought the creature for a song, years before, from a corrupt cousin of Chairman Mao. Serena kept the dragon in perfect working order and sometimes amused friends on the Fourth of July with demonstrations of its fire-spitting ability.

Soon after Calvin Webster finished his Inaugural speech, Serena's telephone began to ring, as she had known it would. "Yes, they want me now," she muttered as the calls poured in.

The callers were members of the Advisory Committee, executives of defense-industry conglomerates that received billions of dollars each year to construct atomic weapons, submarines, missiles, and other instruments of war. One after another, they denounced the new President as mad and his peace plan as treason, and finally asked, "Serena, what can we do?"

She sat curled on a moss-green sofa, a silver telephone nestled in her lap, reassuring the distraught executives, reminding them she could not talk openly by phone, promising to convene the Advisory Committee soon. Charlie, watching from the chaise longue, marveled that this slight, sly woman could so easily calm the blustering captains of industry. When she was off the phone he winked at her and asked, "So what's the verdict?"

She rose and faced him. "Our friends demand action."

"Political or otherwise?"

Serena lit a cigarette, threw back her head, and sent jets of smoke shooting toward the rafters. The gesture stretched the black silk of her gown tight against her nipples. "Whatever works," she said coldly. "Webster must be stopped. By political means, if possible. If not, your turn will come."

"I'll be ready," he told her. "There's never been a political problem that a bit of cold steel couldn't put right."

She wrapped her fingers in his hair and pulled his face close to hers. "You're so gloriously amoral, Charles."

"We're two of a kind, luv."

She studied his face. "And so handsome, too. You remind me of an actor—what's his name? He was in *Annie*."

Charlie cocked an eyebrow. "Albert Finney? But I'm younger than he is, and taller, and better-looking."

She smiled at his unabashed vanity. "You're a peacock, Charlie."

"No, sweet, I'm a professional killer, but that doesn't mean I have to wear bloody khaki all my life. Her Majesty's Royal Marines taught me to kill but they don't pay a living wage. So you got me."

"For my sins," she sighed.

He took her arm and squeezed it hard. "The whistle-blower," he said abruptly, with a passion that took her breath away.

"What about the whistle-blower?" she asked, knowing the answer.

"I want him."

"Why?"

Charlie's eyes glowed. "For practice." He loosened his grip on her arm. "We don't want me getting rusty, do we?"

"Very well. But I must think about the timing. The whistle-blower is of symbolic importance."

"Agreed."

She tucked her fingers lightly in the top of his jeans. "Now there's something I want," she said.

They coupled on the bearskin rug. As always he was awed by her ferocity; it was as if there was a demon inside her that would not be satisfied. She used him, taunted him, sucked him dry. Finally, glistening with sweat, she pushed him aside and reached for a cigarette. Charlie walked naked to the bar and opened a bottle of Louis Roederer Cristal, their favorite champagne. She threw down the first glass like water, then sipped the second moodily, gazing out the French doors at the slate-gray Georgia sky.

Charlie ran his index finger along the knobs of her spine. There was no fat on her, not an ounce. "Penny for your thoughts," he whispered.

Her thoughts, miles away, were not to be measured in pennies.

"Webster," she said bitterly. "He must be stopped."

4

Harry Bliss kept calling from the White House for a few weeks but he never got past Boyle's answering machine. Boyle was living a simple life that winter. During the day he worked on his book. When Zeb got home from school he would do his homework, then around five father and son would settle before a fire for a game of chess. Boyle was still the better player, although he contrived to lose about one game in three. His neighbor Clinton liked to boast that his son had never beaten him at chess, but Clinton had an ulcer and his kid was a mess.

Around six-thirty they'd fix dinner together. Boyle had been past thirty before he could cook anything more complicated than a fried egg, and he wanted Zeb better prepared to confront the women of the twenty-first century than he had been to deal with those of the twentieth. After dinner they settled down for TV or a movie on the VCR. Boyle intended for Zeb to know that the cinematic art could achieve higher peaks than the blood-and-vomit epics of the Eighties, so he brought home classics like *Shane, Gunga*

Din, The Gold Rush, and *Arsenic and Old Lace* for them to watch.

At bedtime, a negotiable hour, Boyle would read to the boy. They'd started with *Charlotte's Web* and progressed to *Huckleberry Finn, Gulliver's Travels, A Wrinkle in Time,* and the C.S. Lewis books. *Huck Finn* was Zeb's all-time favorite, which pleased Boyle immensely, for it was his favorite novel too.

Although Boyle was not returning the White House calls, he read the Washington *Post* each morning, eager for the latest developments on the President's Project Peace. There were front-page stories every day, but all that was really known was that the U.S. and Soviet negotiators were meeting in Geneva to see if the Kremlin would agree to President Webster's proposed first round of nuclear cutbacks. During these weeks of uncertainty and confusion, critics of the plan sprang up across the land, denouncing it as unilateral disarmament that would leave the U.S. defenseless.

Amid these attacks, public support of the plan was falling fast; Boyle, reading these stories, was agonized, for he could think of a hundred things the White House should be doing to shore up its support. But he wasn't advising Cal Webster any more.

One bleak Saturday in early March, Zeb went off to play with his pal Derek, who lived in a house on the other side of the village. Zeb and Derek had been Indians that winter, communicating by smoke signals. One smoke cloud meant "Come here fast" and two clouds meant "The enemy is coming." Boyle spent the morning chopping wood and had earned his first blister when the phone rang.

"Mr. Boyle?"

"Yes?"

"It's Dennis Womack, the manager of River Crest Farm, calling about your son."

Boyle froze. "What's wrong?" he demanded.

"Just a small problem. Your son and another boy were trespassing on the estate. I wonder if you'd come get them."

"You mean you're holding them?"

"Let me put it this way, sir. I could call the sheriff's office and charge them with trespassing, but that's not our policy. We just want to make sure the parents impress on them not to do it again."

"I'll be right over," Boyle said.

River Crest Farm was a thousand-acre estate, overlooking the Potomac, that an English actress had bought in the 1930s when she was involved in a celebrated romance with a California senator. The affair ended but the actress kept the estate and eventually retired there. When Boyle met her she was in her eighties, a tiny, delightful woman who told droll stories about "Willie" Maugham, "Winnie" Churchill, and the Duke and Duchess of Windsor. She'd taken a liking to Boyle's wife Cara and they had gone to River Crest for candlelight dinners several times before the actress died, as gracefully as she had lived, while taking tea one winter afternoon.

The estate had been tied up in litigation for several years, and all the while Harmony's preservationists were terrified that some greedy heir would subdivide the property into half-acre lots, which was happening with grim regularity elsewhere in Loudoun County as the Washington suburbs flowed westward as relentlessly as lava. Instead, to everyone's astonishment, the estate was bought by an Arab sheik for $10 million cash.

No one in Harmony had actually seen the sheik, but rumors about him abounded. It was said he had thirty-seven wives, eight of them American, and more oil than all of Texas, that he was spending an additional $5 million to remodel the estate, that he sometimes slipped in by helicopter to examine his property, and that he might someday use it as a summer retreat.

One known fact was that a ten-foot chain link fence, topped by barbed wire and punctuated by "No Trespassing" signs, had gone up around the property. Even more alarming, rumors soon followed that wild boars now roamed the estate, huge, horned brutes that feared neither man nor beast. Boyle thought the tales quite incredible, until one of the beasts somehow escaped and roamed free in the woodlands outside Harmony for three days before it was subdued, with drug-tipped darts, by terrified sheriff's deputies.

Strange business, everyone agreed, but still better than half-acre lots.

Boyle stopped his Toyota at River Crest's iron gate. A lanky man in jeans and a red windbreaker came out. "Mr. Boyle? I'm Womack. Follow me, please."

Womack opened the gate and led the Toyota past the gatehouse to a small cabin. The boys were inside, looking subdued. Boyle tried to look grave. "Well, what do you two have to say for yourselves?" he asked.

The boys stared at their wet sneakers. Finally Zeb said, "We were just looking around."

"Exploring," Derek added.

"Didn't you see the 'No Trespassing' signs?"

The culprits nodded glumly.

"How'd you get in?" Boyle persisted.

"Under the fence," Zeb said. Boyle had rarely seen a longer face; his son clearly had no future in crime.

"They showed me the place," Womack said. "I'll have it fixed."

"You boys were in danger here," Boyle said. "You still have your wild boars, Mr. Womack?"

"Yes sir. The sheik, they say he's real fond of them." .

The sheik is a madman, Boyle mused.

"I think you owe Mr. Womack an apology," he said.

"We're sorry," the boys chanted in unison.

"It's all right, boys. All we care about is your safety."

They shook hands all around, then marched to the Toyota. "The sheik ever come here?" Boyle asked Womack.

The Virginian frowned uncomfortably. "We're not supposed to talk about that," he said. "You understand . . . We have our orders. Mostly we deal with the lawyers."

"Sure," Boyle said. "None of my business anyway."

Womack led the way back to the estate's big iron gate. While he opened it, Boyle studied the new gatehouse. It was almost as formidable as those at the White House. These people were serious about their security. Boyle thought he saw someone move inside the gatehouse. He stared in unashamedly, hoping for a glimpse of some white-robed Arab prince.

He saw instead a tall, broad-shouldered young man with deepset eyes and a wide, sullen mouth. His cold eyes met Boyle's for an instant, then faded into the shadows.

The image, so unexpected, lingered for a moment, then was lost as they drove out the gate.

"Dad, are you mad?" Zeb asked.

Boyle had to laugh. "Yeah, because you desperados got yourselves caught. Do you really want to tangle with wild boars? You guys are nuts!"

"It was great!" Zeb declared. "We saw this gym they've built and an indoor pool and a shooting gallery. We watched this man target shooting."

"You mean Mr. Womack?"

"No, a young guy. He could really shoot, too."

"You boys stay away from that place," Boyle said. "Those people are crazy. Wild *boars?*"

He eased into the village and found the glistening black limousine parked in front of their house.

"What now?" Boyle sighed.

5

Harry Bliss heaved himself out of the White House limo. "Where the hell have you been?" he barked, by way of greeting.

"Visiting a sheik," Boyle said.

Harry hugged Zeb and asked him about school, but when the two boys raced away he was all business. "Look, you don't answer your phone, so I've blown half the day coming out here. Can we talk?"

"Sure. You got time for lunch?"

Harry shook his head. "Coffee," he said.

Boyle pushed open the front door and led the way into the house.

"Jesus, don't you lock your doors?"

"Not out here," Boyle said. "No need to. No crime."

They settled in the kitchen. Boyle made coffee while Harry fidgeted and chain-smoked. Harry was mostly gray now and grossly overweight; Boyle guessed running the world did that to you. Things had been different when they'd met, a few campaigns back. Boyle and Harry had drunk together and chased girls together and flimflammed the media together, and in the process they'd elected a President. Harry was the issues man, a sardonic young Rhodes Scholar turned kingmaker, and Boyle was the media whiz. They'd accepted one another as equals and that was rare. In Boyle's experience, the people around any candidate invariably spent more time backstabbing one another than trying to defeat the other candidate. Killer egos, out for blood. But he and Harry had been different. They'd been friends. Once, when the candidate went berserk, and threatened to fire Harry for some imagined foul-up, Boyle had said quietly, "If he goes, I go too." And the President-to-be had backed down.

But that was long ago. As Boyle sat down across from his old friend, he knew he wasn't really a friend any more. He was the President's Man now, and Boyle was just another item on his agenda. You could see it in his eyes.

"So how's it going?" he asked.

"Lousy," Harry said. "The Russians are stalling and we're getting cut to pieces. That's what I want to talk about."

"Wait a minute. Back up. Tell me how this got started. When I left the campaign, Webster wasn't talking about a big peace initiative."

"He kept it to himself. But he's been thinking about it ever since we showed him that *Times* article back in '82."

Boyle loved the "we." Harry hadn't even been in town that day. Soon he'd be saying, "When *I* showed him that article."

"We were afraid of leaks," Harry continued. "There were people at the Pentagon who'd have shot it down. So we had to announce it first, get it on the table, then go to the Russians, and they're taking their sweet time."

"The polls are bad," Boyle said. "You've lost your momentum. People are confused. You'd better push those damn Russians or you're in trouble."

"The Russians aren't the real problem," Harry said. "They'll come around. They've *got* to. It's in their interest as much as ours. Dammit, the verification is foolproof. No one can cheat."

"What's your goal, Harry? How far will you carry it?"

"As far as we can! Look, what do we need to destroy Russia? Maybe five hundred warheads. The same goes for them. Which means we could both destroy ninety percent of our stockpiles and be just as secure."

"Except for that last five hundred."

"Granted. But you've reduced the chance of war by accident or computer error or because some general goes bonkers. Plus, maybe we and the Russians start trusting each other. Maybe we work together to stop proliferation. *That's* the threat, pal. When every tinhorn dictator on earth has a bomb. Not to mention terrorists."

"You said the Russians weren't the real problem," Boyle said. "What do you mean?"

"I mean it's the arms people, the defense contractors, the people who *make* the damn weapons that I'm worried about. Listen, the military-industrial complex is alive and well and raising millions to beat us."

"Beat you how?"

"How do you think? In public opinion. In Congress. Cut off the money. Block the treaty. Impeach him. Whatever it takes. They're gearing up for a media blitz like this country has never seen."

Boyle felt his heart begin to pound. He'd feared this conversation for months.

"Matt, we need a media campaign like no White House has ever put on before. We've got to get people marching. Look, the boss wants you to come in and take charge of our entire media strategy, everything."

Boyle listened in wonder. Life was so strange. The one sure way to get whatever you wanted was to stop wanting it.

"I can't do it," he said.

"Why not?"

"Because it's an eighty-hour-a-week job and I've got a son to raise."

"You can do it in forty. You could rent a place in town. Or buy one. We could get you a good deal on a loan."

"Come on, Harry. How many hours did you work last week? Eighty? Ninety? I'm sorry, but I'm out of it."

"The boss won't take no for an answer."

"I can tell you five guys who can do the job as well as I could."

"So can I, but the boss doesn't want those guys. Look, you'll be Director of Communications. You'll draw a good salary. Win this fight and you'll be the hottest media guy in America. You can waltz out of the White House in a couple of years and make millions."

Boyle smiled sadly. "I don't want millions. I'm just trying to write a book."

"What is this book?" Harry demanded.

"The image-maker's art. The Confessions of Matthew Boyle. Turkeys I have elected to high office."

There was a time when they would have laughed about some of those turkeys. Once they'd joked about the book they would write about the politicians they'd known; its title would be *They're All the Same*. But those days were gone.

Harry's face darkened. "You mean like case histories?"

"People need to understand what a farce politics has become," Boyle said.

"People don't care. They enjoy it. Politics has replaced the circus in American culture. Matt, I don't understand you any more. I know you've been through hell, but you can't just sit out here in the boonies and rot. You're a kind of genius and this is the challenge of a lifetime."

Boyle hesitated, uncertain in the face of the other man's intensity. "I think that after I finish the book I'll open a small office. Media consulting, but not for political campaigns. Institutional PR. For charities, the Cancer Institute, the anti-smoking campaign. Things I believe in."

"Dammit, you believe in peace, don't you? Well, the boss has put his ass on the line for peace, so why can't you come help us?"

"Peace begins at home," Boyle said.

Harry caught his temper. "I understand how you feel about Zeb," he said smoothly. "But there are a hundred million Zebs out there, a world of them, and the boss is trying to keep them all from being incinerated one fine day."

"No, Harry. There's only one Zeb and he's only got one father. That's the point."

"Look, will you talk to him?"

Boyle shut his eyes. "I don't want to."

"*Will* you? Yes or no?"

Boyle looked out the window. Two huge balls of smoke were rising above the village. Two nine-year-old Indians on the warpath. In his imagination, Zeb's smoke signals exploded into a great mushroom cloud. What was right? What was wrong? He didn't know, didn't have the slightest idea.

"Okay, I'll talk to him," he heard himself say.

"Monday at ten?"

"I'll be there."

6

Bernie O'Toole was that most disaster-prone of creatures, an honest man.

Bernie was a stocky, stubborn, hot-tempered Irishman, an engineer by profession, who had gotten himself hired as a civilian "management analyst" at the Pentagon. The problem was that he never learned to play the Pentagon game.

He questioned cost overruns that other analysts accepted with a shrug. He had the radical notion that deadlines should be met and that airplanes that cost billions of the taxpayers' dollars should fly. He was increasingly in conflict with the defense contractors and skeptical of their promises and excuses.

"Lives are at risk," Bernie would angrily remind his superiors.

"Nit-picking," the contractors would respond.

Somehow the contractors, so many of whom were retired generals and admirals, always won these debates.

Bernie O'Toole simmered, biding his time.

Then one bright morning, high above the Utah desert, an FX-132 experimental fighter burst into a million pieces, a few thousand of those pieces being the remains of its young pilot.

A wild-eyed O'Toole went to his windowless Pentagon office on a Sunday afternoon and wrote a scathing, twelve-page memorandum to his superiors, reminding them that he had warned that a suspect microchip could cause just such a tragedy.

His memo was duly processed into the circular file.

Bernie wrote another memo, predicting more tragedies— "As sure as the sun will rise tomorrow"—and pleading that FX-132 tests be suspended.

O'Toole's boss called him in for a chat. He was a bird colonel, a rather charming fellow who was only months away from retiring and going to work for Hughes Aircraft. He patiently recited all the new assurances that Blue Sky Aviation had made about its beloved, incredibly profitable FX-132.

"If you believe that you'll believe anything," Bernie raged. He began thinking the unthinkable: an out-of-channels appeal to higher authority.

Another FX-132 exploded. Bernie saw the funeral on the evening news. A handsome air force major gave the widow a neatly folded flag to replace the husband whose mortal remains had been scattered over three counties. She wept and hugged her children. Jets roared overhead. O'Toole howled with rage. Why wouldn't they cancel those tests? It was slaughter.

Two days later Bernie read in the Washington *Post* of charges that Blue Sky Aviation had made secret, illegal contributions of $4 million to the party in power—this was a year before the election of Calvin Webster.

"The rotten bastards," Bernie muttered between clenched teeth. That night he drove to a 7-Eleven and called the *Post*'s Pentagon correspondent on a pay phone.

They met upstairs at Childe Harold, a bar near DuPont Circle. "Keep my name out of it," Bernie said. "My wife's pregnant again."

"Won't they know it's you?" the reporter asked.

"Maybe not," Bernie said.

The reporter's front-page stories forced the cancellation of Blue Sky's $3.8 billion contract for the FX-132 and also caused the Secretary of the Air Force extreme discomfort at his next news conference. "Find the bastard who leaked that story!" he roared to his underlings.

Bernie's guilt was suspected but could not be proved. Nevertheless, his job description was rewritten so that he was soon spending his mornings reading the newspapers and his afternoons working crossword puzzles. He was humiliated but how could he quit with another little O'Toole on the way?

Bernie began to gain weight and suffer headaches. He started jogging in the woods around his home in the rustic old "new town" of Reston, Virginia. It relaxed him.

Meanwhile, Governor Webster, campaigning for President, seized on the FX-132 issue. The voters, indifferent to decades of billion-dollar waste and mismanagement at the Pentagon, showed signs of indignation at the exploding FX-132s, particularly after one pilot's widow tearfully endorsed Webster.

One afternoon that summer, as Bernie O'Toole struggled with the *Times'* crossword puzzle, a colleague named Berg slipped furtively into his office. "Bernie, it's a disgrace what they've done to you," Berg whispered. "Do you know about the helicopters?"

The helicopters kept crashing, here, there, and everywhere, and the generals were striving desperately to hush up the carnage.

"Pilot error," said Comanche Industries, the contractor.

"Faulty design," insisted Berg. "Criminal negligence. I've got the evidence."

Berg's hands shook as he passed over the incriminating documents. "Don't get me involved," were his parting words.

"We are closet patriots," Bernie called after him.

He called his reporter. Another expose. "Flying Coffins," pilots had dubbed Comanche's choppers. The Secretary of the Air Force resigned and Governor Webster, furiously denouncing Pentagon mismanagement, surged into the lead for his party's nomination.

Before the first snow fell, Webster was the country's President-elect and Comanche had lost the $2.4 billion contract on its now disgraced and grounded helicopter.

What's more, Bernie O'Toole, the whistle-blower triumphant, had come in from the cold. His friend at the *Post* had written a long, glowing story, detailing Bernie's lonely struggle to save pilots' lives and taxpayers' dollars. There was talk that under the Webster administration Bernie O'Toole might be reborn as a bureaucratic David, empowered to smite the Goliath of Pentagon sloth and venality.

"O'Toole for President!" proclaimed bumper stickers in Bernie's Reston neighborhood.

7

One fine day in the late 1920s Garth Masters decided to build his dream house, or as it turned out, his dream castle. Because his empire was Southern-based—coal mines in West Virginia, textile mills in Georgia, pine forests in Mississippi, oil fields in Louisiana—Garth Masters had for some years dwelt in a many-columned mansion in the lush Atlanta enclave of Buckhead, but he had grown weary of the city's strife.

He therefore purchased a mountain in the wilds of North Georgia. There, aided by an abundance of cheap stone and even cheaper labor, he proceeded to build, high atop his craggy peak, a castle of a magnitude rarely seen since the Middle Ages. The result, Dragon's Lair, was barely completed when a challenge loomed. The Georgia Power Company, absentee owner of much of North Georgia, had decided to build a dam on a meandering river and thus bring electrical power to the natives and vast new profits to itself. The problem was that the dam would create a new lake that would inundate all but the peak of Masters's mountain.

He was more than willing to joust with Georgia Power,

which was controlled by several of his golf and poker cronies, but instead he decided that the proposed lake would be a blessing in disguise. The new lake would transform his mountaintop castle into an island castle, one surrounded by a mile-wide moat that would both enhance his privacy and remove the troublesome rednecks who dwelt in the lowlands. He therefore welcomed the dam, demanding only the right to name the lake, which became Lake Serena, in honor of his infant daughter.

It was there, in splendid isolation, amid the battlements and pinnacles of a medieval castle, that his two children, Leo and Serena, came of age. Their father, widowed soon after Serena's birth, directed their education, and their early years were idyllic.

The idyll ended with Leo's death at the hands of that Japanese sniper in 1945. The loss of his son plunged Garth Masters into a gloom that was only partially lifted by the U.S. atomic bombing of Hiroshima and Nagasaki later that year. Serena would always remember her father on the phone with President Truman, pleading for Truman to drop an atomic bomb on Moscow. "They'd do it to us, Harry," he argued in vain.

His son torn from him, Garth Masters began to groom his daughter to inherit the farflung family empire. The Masters family was of the Catholic faith, and insofar as Garth could not personally direct his daughter's education, he entrusted it to nuns he had carefully selected. Between her father and her religion, the watchful, dark-eyed girl grew up with a profound respect for authority. In her young mind, God, the Pope, and her father blurred into one all-wise and majestic figure. "Have faith!" her father told her again and again. "Faith can move mountains!" The nuns echoed this theme, assuring her that prayers, if strong and unselfish, were truly answered.

When Serena was twelve she hit upon a unique plan to demonstrate the depth of her faith. The nuns had often told her that one of history's darkest days came when a lustful Henry VIII had ripped England away from the True Church. Serena resolved to pray with all her heart and soul that King George VI would convert back to the Catholic Church. Her deadline would be Christmas Day; the return of England to the Church would be her Christmas gift to her beloved father.

She started praying in August, kneeling beside her bed for two or three hours a day, and by November she was up to six hours a day of fervent prayer. Some of the nuns began to worry about her.

The final weeks before Christmas, Serena prayed more or less constantly for the King's conversion, sixteen or eighteen hours a day, until she collapsed on the floor beside her bed, and then she prayed in her dreams. She was pale and feverish; she glowed, the nuns whispered, with a patina of saintliness.

On Christmas morning, Serena floated down the stairs to the library, where her father awaited her. She was giddy from lack of sleep; she moved in a dream. She did not even glance at the mountain of presents beside the Christmas tree. Rather, she marched directly to her father, who was contentedly puffing his pipe and reading the morning paper.

Serena's frail body was seized by elation—she heard angels singing hallelujahs—for she knew, with inutterable pride and absolute certitude, what the headline in her father's newspaper must be that fateful Christmas morning:

KING GEORGE VI RETURNS ENGLAND
TO CATHOLIC CHURCH!
COMMON PEOPLE CHEER;
POPE HAILS 'BLESSED MIRACLE'

In her fevered imagination Serena could hear the radio address wherein the King explained his miraculous conversion; she could picture him and the Queen and their two daughters setting off for Rome.

All these pious expectations filled Serena's mind as she peered at the front page of her father's newspaper.

To her astonishment, the headline did not concern the King's conversion, but a train wreck outside Macon. With a cry, she ripped the paper from her father's hands and began to search for news of the miracle in Buckingham Palace.

Nothing! Not a word!

Perhaps it was the time difference, she thought—that must be it! She switched on their big Philco radio and frantically twisted the dial, seeking bulletins from London, but all she found were Christmas carols.

By then Garth Masters was on his feet, demanding an explanation for his daughter's queer behavior. For the first time in her life, Serena ignored her father, as she sank to the floor in a swoon.

Weeks later, she told the head nun, "I prayed so hard, Sister, and my request was truly unselfish." The nun's sleek face hardened. "It's clear that your faith was not great enough," she declared.

Serena changed after that. To her father and the nuns, she was the same sweet, pious girl, but inwardly she knew she would never again be so trusting. Even God, she vowed, would not fool her twice.

Garth Masters had always told Serena that if she must marry she should marry for money—money and good bloodlines. At twenty she rejected his advice and married for love. Her choice was a handsome Georgia Tech football star who declared that he would not touch a dime of her father's money—he loved her for herself alone! His declaration at first seemed romantic, but after a few months of marriage she decided it was incredibly stupid. Why should they live in a shabby furnished apartment when they could live like kings? And while sex with Wally, as he was called, was an unexpected joy—nothing like the grim bondage the nuns had warned of—Wally soon ruined it by announcing that they should begin a family. That, Serena realized, was insane. It was horrid enough for two of them to be living in squalor without adding a howling baby to the mess.

So Serena left Wally and returned to her father. Six months of marriage had turned love to hate. She saw that her father was right, money was what mattered in life. There was no reason for a rich woman to marry unless she wanted children, and even that was debatable. Serena eagerly joined her father at the helm of Masters Enterprises, and they worked together to expand their already vast empire, particularly in the booming defense industry. It was at Serena's urging that her father bought a chain of newspapers which, although their profits were not great, would give them a pulpit from which to preach their single-minded brand of Americanism.

Unsurprisingly, Serena's political views were identical to her father's. Until she was twenty, he had shielded her from contact with anyone whose views were to the left of his friend and hero, J. Edgar Hoover. So total was his indoctrination that for years, whenever Serena chanced to meet even a moderate Republican, much less an out-and-out liberal, she regarded them with the same instinctive loathing that they, in turn, might have felt if confronted with a slave trader or an alumnus of Hitler's SS.

Garth Masters's death of a heart attack, which followed only hours after Dwight D. Eisenhower's speech warning against the growing power of the military-industrial complex, left Serena one of the richest women in America.

His death coincided with her growing interest in political affairs, for she had been outraged by the election of John Kennedy, whom she considered a traitor to his class and religion. She began writing a column for her newspaper chain and her acerbic style won her many readers. At a time of growing demand for women in high office, she was that rarest of birds, a lady hawk. In time a President named her his Secretary of the Army and she performed her duties with distinction. This led a later President to bestow upon her a most singular honor: Serena Masters became the nation's first woman Secretary of Defense.

She was a good Secretary—dynamic, dedicated, and much beloved by the military. She was also a lousy politician, still dwelling in the splendid isolation of her father's castle. The first reporters to visit her cavernous Pentagon office were stunned to see a signed photograph of one of the world's most notorious military dictators adorning her wall. Other reporters, joining her for dinner one night, were shocked when she told the waiter she wanted her steak "Communist

blood rare." She was in the habit of referring to the Prime
Minister of France as "that loathsome little toad," an epithet
that inevitably made its way into print.

In truth, reporters mostly liked Serena, because she was
smart, good-looking, rich, and sardonic, but it was their job
to report the outrageous things she said and did. Serena, for
her part, truly did try to modify her public pronouncements,
but time after time, in crucial moments, she couldn't keep
from speaking her mind. Eventually, after many firestorms
in the media, the President was obliged to call for Serena's
resignation, whereupon she denounced him as a "gutless
wonder" and returned to Georgia to ponder her future.

By then she had known numerous presidents and would-
be presidents, and she considered herself the moral and
intellectual superior of them all. Her destiny, she was convinced, was to be America's first woman President. She
imagined herself a nuclear-age Joan of Arc, rallying the Free
World from its torpor and leading it forth to slay the dragon
of international Communism.

But first she had to get herself elected. She had money,
energy, intellectual brilliance, powerful friends, and a hard
core of fanatical supporters. She therefore entered the presidential primaries, when the next election year rolled
around, only to discover the one essential quality she lacked:
She still couldn't keep her mouth shut.

Serena's press briefings became legendary among reporters.

"Would you ever use nuclear weapons, Ms. Masters?"

"Of course—and I'd use them first!"

"Is nuclear war winnable?"

"If you've got enough bomb shelters, why not?"

"Would you use women in combat?"

"I believe the Almighty made men superior fighters and
women superior thinkers—that's why I'm running for President."

And so it went. America's most expensive image-makers
could not keep her foot out of her mouth. Her campaign
collapsed after the third primary, whereupon the candidate

again retired to her island home to brood upon her future in an ungrateful world.

Serena reluctantly decided that she was too honest to be President, but that did not mean she was out of political life forever. She was only biding her time.

Her moment came when congressional investigations proved that major American defense contractors had paid hundreds of millions of dollars in bribes to foreign officials to persuade them to buy their airplanes.

Bribes of up to $10 million had gone to the Italian and Japanese prime ministers, to the West German defense minister, to the Royal Consort of the Netherlands (who needed the money to support his French mistress and their child), and to a large and unsavory assortment of Spanish generals, Saudi princes, African dictators, and Japanese gangsters who could somehow grease the wheels of commerce.

Before the scandal was finished, several corporate chairmen had been forced to retire and their companies had lost billions of dollars in canceled contracts.

The defense industry was bitterly competitive, but in the aftermath of the scandals its leaders recognized the need for collective action against its enemies in government and the media.

Seizing her opportunity, Serena convened a small group of top executives at her island retreat to discuss political action on behalf of the entire industry. This top-secret group, which called itself only the Advisory Committee, quickly elected Serena its chairman.

This committee was blessed with unlimited funds, and Serena made it her business to understand the post-Watergate campaign-finance laws, "reforms" that in truth had thrown American politics open to the highest bidder.

Working through a network of Political Action Committees, Serena elected dozens of compliant representatives and senators. She perfected the art of the "honorarium," whereby favored members of Congress were paid $5,000 or more to do little or nothing. At first, these statesmen-for-hire made speeches in exchange for their fees, but soon they were complaining that a speech was too much work. Serena then invented the "walk-through," whereby the congressman earned his $5,000 simply by strolling through an arms plant and waving to its employees. For those who disliked walking, golf carts were available.

With many members of Congress thus earning more of their keep from the arms industry than from the taxpayers, Serena proceeded to one of her most celebrated legislative achievements. Working with a friendly White House, she conceived and got legislation passed which guaranteed that the nation's top defense contractors not only would pay no taxes on their billions of dollars of profits, but that the government would give them hundreds of millions of dollars, on top of their profits, in "investment tax credits." It was a capitalist's dream come true: Instead of corporations paying taxes to government, government was paying taxes to corporations!

Despite these achievements, Serena and the Advisory Committee faced a mighty challenge in the unexpected election of Calvin Webster, a President who, as they saw it, was trying to put them out of business.

It was to meet that challenge that the Advisory Committee gathered in the great hall at Dragon's Lair one rainy Sunday in late winter. They were an impressive group of men. One had been an astronaut, two had been wartime "aces," and two had personally built small aircraft companies into vast, globe-circling conglomerates. They were men who had won all the rewards that the world's richest nation could bestow, and yet, as they sipped their cocktails before Serena's fire that evening, they were fearful, bitter, and ready to fight.

Serena, sensing their anger and their fear, spoke bluntly:

"Gentlemen, I need not dwell upon the peril that brings us together. A President has been inflicted upon us—by fraud, I continue to believe—who is committed not to arming America but to disarming her. The masses are too benumbed by drugs, sexual perversion, and Negroid music to know or care what fate befalls them. Even patriotic Americans—and let us never forget, they are many—are confused and leaderless."

"Damn well put, Serena," rumbled Blue Sky Aviation's CEO. "But what are we going to do?"

"I'll tell you precisely," she shot back. "We're going to discredit, defeat, and destroy this so-called Project Peace and its creator!"

"All *right!*" muttered the CEOs.

"We have a precedent," she continued. "Some years ago, the so-called 'nuclear freeze' started out with widespread popularity. But once we told the American people the truth about it, it was rather easily defeated in Congress."

She injected a cigarette into a jade holder, and Blue Sky's CEO leaped up to light it.

"It is never easy to defeat a President," she continued. "But we have our spokesmen, too. I am pleased to report that three former presidents and eleven former secretaries of state and defense, of both parties, have promised me they will work actively to defeat the Webster Plan."

"Damn fine!" declared Comanche's CEO.

"We will of course pay their expenses," she added. "Many millions will be needed to win this battle."

"Hang the expense," one of the men thundered.

"If we don't whip Webster, we're all out of business," another declared.

"Precisely," Serena said, her dark eyes aglitter. She proceeded to outline the many-faceted campaign she would direct against Project Peace. This included TV spots, telethons, rallies, newspaper advertisements, billboards, local citizens' committees, magazine articles, and anti-Webster leaks from the Pentagon.

"Finally," she said, "our Washington office has commitments from forty-seven representatives and twenty-two senators who are rock-solid for impeachment, and that's only the start. If we do our job, we'll not only defeat the Webster Plan but destroy Webster in the bargain!"

She paused, triumphantly, and all but one of the members of the Advisory Committee burst into applause. The exception was Skip Tybalt, the former astronaut who headed Excelsior Air, and was the only member of the group ever to question her leadership. They had been lovers once, one weekend in Acapulco, but Skip had tried to dominate her and Serena would not be dominated.

"Hey, Serena," Skip drawled, "before we go impeaching Webster, what do we know about the Vice President? We could be going from the frying pan to the fire."

Serena gave him her sweetest smile. "I'm so glad you asked that, Skip." She glanced around the table. "Gentlemen, I cannot go into detail at this time, but let me assure you that we have nothing to fear from Vice President Ben Remington. Should Mr. Webster be impeached, or otherwise vacate his office, we will have a friend in the White House."

Skip Tybalt noted, if the others did not, her casual phrase *or otherwise vacate his office.* Impeachment was a slow process at best.

"I'm sure we'd all like to know more about this," he pressed.

"I cannot say more at this time," Serena declared.

Tybalt muttered his displeasure, but the others were four-square behind Serena. She adjourned the business meeting and the group drifted to the terrace for drinks. In time, as the moon rose over the lake, the talk turned to Bernie O'Toole.

President Webster had that week named O'Toole to be Assistant Secretary of Defense for Management Control, from which lofty perch the plucky Irishman could raise holy hell with the generals and admirals whose "gold-plated" weapons systems and billion-dollar cost overruns he had so stubbornly resisted as a lowly GS-14.

O'Toole's elevation outraged the members of the Advisory Committee almost as much as Project Peace itself.

"The man's a creep," one executive raged.

"A worm . . ."

"A Red . . ."

"It isn't just O'Toole," Skip Tybalt said. "He'll encourage others like himself. These so-called whistle-blowers will come out of the woodwork. And every one could cost us millions of dollars."

Tybalt fixed his icy gaze on his hostess. "I trust you've considered this threat, Serena," he said.

"These things have a way of working out," she said with a devilish smile.

8

Bernie O'Toole did his jogging at the crack of dawn. He would ease out of bed in the first light, trying not to wake Myra, run four miles, come back and shower, then cheerfully scramble eggs for Myra and the kids. Bernie only had some yogurt, though, because he'd already lost twelve pounds and he was determined to get down to one-seventy-five before his swearing-in. By golly, an assistant secretary of defense shouldn't be a slob.

Bernie guessed he was the happiest, luckiest, most blessed man in America, with his new job and all the acclaim he'd gotten since his whistle-blowing exploits had been celebrated in the media. Best of all was the new pride that Myra and the kids had in him. One night that week he'd put his cheek against Myra's bulging white stomach and felt the baby kick. "His daddy's a hero," Myra said and her lopsided smile made the bedroom glow.

This Sunday morning, Bernie slipped out of the house, wearing the tomato-red Moss Brown ten-miler running suit that Myra had given him for Christmas, and trotted into a dull, misty dawn. At this hour, he almost always had the jogging trail to himself. The "new town" of Reston was a quarter century old now and afflicted with all the problems its denizens had hoped to leave behind in the cities. Drugs, delinquents, burglaries, car thefts, rape, murder—Reston had them all, homegrown. A couple of women had been attacked in these very woods where Bernie jogged. Still, he loved the place.

He was jogging contentedly, just starting to sweat, savoring the stark beauty of the winter pines, when he noticed another runner, a big, broad-shouldered fellow in a gray sweatsuit, with a stocking cap pulled low over his eyes, emerging from the morning mist.

Charlie Trueblood had planned this encounter with exquisite care. For three Sundays he'd watched O'Toole ramble past, always at the same time, always alone on this remote stretch of the trail.

As the Irishman drew near, Charlie's hand tightened on his knife. He loved knives. He was adept with most modern weapons, but he thought the knife the classic instrument of death. Man's first weapon had been a rock, used to pound his enemy's brains to jelly at close range. Next came crude clubs, tree limbs first, then the bones of animals. Soon after that, some forty thousand years B.C., came the first knives, fashioned from stone, then bronze. To kill with a knife, or indeed to be killed by one, was to enter the chain of human history.

When the joggers were a dozen feet apart, Charlie raised his left hand in greeting.

The genial O'Toole raised his in reply, high enough that Charlie Trueblood could, with the greatest of ease, slash the whistle-blower cruelly across the ribs.

O'Toole stumbled, stopped, groping at a wound that burned like the fires of hell. Thick, hot blood, a richer crimson than his jogging suit, stained his fingers. He watched uncomprehendingly as the stranger slashed him again.

Disbelieving, O'Toole raised his hands. "Please," he sobbed. *"My kids."*

Charlie ignored his victim's pleas. He thought only of the details of the job, the placement of the wounds, the perfection he sought. He could have killed this fool in an instant, with one perfect thrust, but elegance was not the need here.

The need, rather, was uncertainty, ambiguity. O'Toole's passing could not be clearly professional; that would raise too many questions. His death instead must seem the handiwork of the sort of third-rate thug who routinely raped and robbed in this failed paradise.

And yet—and this was the subtle touch, the challenge—for the imaginative, a taste of doubt must remain, enough to give pause to other bold bureaucrats, other would-be whistle-blowers.

O'Toole flopped onto his back, hugging his ruined gut, staring in disbelief at the stranger who had undone him.

Charlie eyed the jogging trail impatiently, unwilling to leave until O'Toole was finished. It would be foolish to let the dying man describe him to some jogger who might chance by. This was the only moment of true danger. If another jogger came, Charlie would have to kill him too.

Still, Charlie had absolute faith in himself. The Royal Marines had taught him to kill and they'd taught him well. But then the politicians had sent them to fight a war on a bloody freezing rock in the South Atlantic and before it was over Charlie had vowed never again to risk his life for forty pounds a month. So Charlie went to America, the land of opportunity, and now instead of killing for Madam Thatcher he killed for Madam Masters. The work was easier and the pay infinitely better.

O'Toole was gasping for air. Charlie knelt beside him and jerked loose his watch and his ring. The two men's eyes met.

"Why?" the dying man whispered.

Charlie considered the question.

Why must Bernie O'Toole die this lonely dawn?

Fate he might have said, but that was unduly vague.

Power, too, might have been his reply, for that was closer to the truth.

Suddenly, absolutely, he knew the answer to O'Toole's question.

"National security," he whispered in a voice as cold as eternity.

O'Toole's blue eyes widened, burned, then closed forever. He understood everything.

9

Boyle couldn't help laughing when he and Zeb stepped into the West Wing at a quarter of ten on Monday morning. Zeb was wide-eyed and even Boyle was momentarily awed. You always felt that jolt, entering the White House, delivery boys felt it and captains of industry too. The air was purer there and subtly intoxicating. You breathed deeply and you felt, however mistakenly, that you were suddenly one of the elect. Your ego puffed up, your soul cried out to the cosmos, "Hey, look at me, I'm hot stuff!" In extreme cases, you might suffer disorientation, delusions, severe dementia. The Kissinger Syndrome.

Daisy, Harry's secretary, greeted them. She was a plump woman in her early thirties who wanted nothing more than a husband and children, but had gotten caught up on the merry-go-round of politics. Now she had a job in the White House, and no time for courtship or marriage. Boyle had befriended her over the years and knew he could ask a favor.

"Daisy, you remember Zeb?"

Daisy embraced the boy. "Look how big you've grown!" she cried. "Oh, those eyes, just like your mother's!"

Zeb stood stiffly as this stranger hugged him. After a moment, Daisy released him, fearful that she'd done something wrong.

"Zeb has a school holiday today," Boyle explained. "I wondered if he could hang out with you while I see Harry and the President."

"Of course he can, Matt," the woman said. "We'll have somebody take him on a tour of the mansion. Would you like that?"

"Awesome," Zeb said.

Boyle found Harry Bliss behind the desk in his big corner office, simultaneously reading a memo, talking on the phone, smoking a cigarette, and gulping coffee. "Sit down," he barked, and pointed to the front page of the morning's Washington *Post.* "You see this?"

Boyle sank into a chair. "Yeah, I saw it."

"Hell of a thing. You go jogging and some bastard hacks you to death for your watch. In *Reston!*"

Boyle shrugged helplessly. When he read the story that morning, he'd thought of how many people hated O'Toole, how many billions he'd cost the big defense contractors. But you couldn't start thinking like that; it was too crazy.

"He'll see us in a minute," Harry said. "Things are hot this morning. We're expecting news from the Geneva negotiations. Look, have you thought this thing over?"

"Sure, I've thought about it."

"And?"

"I still don't want to do it."

"Is that what you're going to tell him?"

Boyle threw up his hands. "I honestly don't know. I don't even want to talk to him."

"That, old buddy, is irrelevant, since he wants to talk to you."

On cue, a light flashed on Harry's desk and he jumped to his feet. "Come on," he commanded. "The boss is ready."

Outside the Oval Office, Harry paused with his hand on

the doorknob. "Look, Matt, we want you back. I know how you feel about Zeb but I know something else, my friend. If you turn us down and we hire somebody else, you're gonna feel like the jerk of the century. Think about it."

· He pushed open the door to the Oval Office. Calvin Webster, poised behind his big desk, grinned and came marching toward Boyle, arms outstretched.

"By golly, Matt, it's been too long," Cal Webster declared and embraced his guest.

After a moment, Webster stepped back and looked Boyle in the face, still gripping the younger man's shoulders.

The President was a powerfully built six-footer. His broad, blunt face suggested strength, certitude. His hair was mostly gone and his bald head was tanned from endless hours of golf, tennis, and skiing. He was not the smartest or most likable man Boyle had ever known, only the toughest and the most stubborn. He had been fresh off the farm, seasoned only by a year in junior college, when he became the youngest American ace during the Korean War. For three years, when his contemporaries were enjoying college, Webster had blasted other men out of the sky.

He'd returned to civilian life at forty, made a fortune in insurance and real estate, and been bored to tears. He had, in truth, a profound sense of his own destiny, one that had possessed him over the skies of Korea and never let go. So he ran for mayor and was a good mayor and was still bored. Then he decided to run for governor. That was when Boyle had entered the picture, nearly a decade before.

"Matt, I've thought of you so often," Webster said finally. "You and Cara and Zeb. How is that boy?"

"He's fine, sir."

"I'll bet he's grown like a weed. Bring him to see me. The two of you can spend a night in the Lincoln Bedroom."

"That'd be wonderful."

"Kids are what this job is all about. You and I could have a quiet dinner and talk over old times. I'll tell you something. Jack Kennedy said the White House was a bad place to make new friends, so he'd stick with his old friends. He was right."

Boyle felt himself weakening, surrendering to Webster's

strength, his certitude, his rough charm. Boyle believed that Webster was many things but that ultimately he was a great politician, which was another way of saying he was a monster. Politicians of his magnitude consumed lesser mortals. They flattered your ego, dangled glittering prizes before your dazzled eyes, toyed with your ambitions, squeezed every last drop of juice or blood or energy or idealism out of you, then finally devoured you. And thought they had done you a favor.

Boyle had been there. He'd had violent shouting matches with Webster. He'd rewritten speeches ten times, making them progressively worse, to suit Webster's whims. He'd watched numbly as Webster reduced three secretaries to tears at the same time because of some lost document that he'd almost certainly lost himself. He knew what a cold, stubborn, demanding bastard Webster could be.

And yet the man was trying to make peace.

What mattered?

A son who needed you?

Or this charming monster who would devour you to save the world?

The President's phone rang. He seized it anxiously, listened a moment, then muttered, "Call me the moment you hear anything."

Then, smiling again, "Coffee, Matt? Decaf okay?" and to Harry, "I don't guess we'll be needing you." Boyle saw his friend's mouth tighten as he departed. Even the number-one boys got dumped on now and then. It kept them humble.

They sipped their coffee. Webster was relaxed, smiling. "I missed you on Election Night, Matt," he said. "You belonged there. I've always said there were three people I owe my election to. My wife Doris, Harry, and you. Not necessarily in that order."

"You did ninety-nine percent of it yourself," Boyle said. "The rest of us were just along for the ride." He meant it. Anyone who ever thought anything else about any President was a fool.

Webster ignored the compliment. He leaned forward,

eyes aflame. "I need your help, Matt. I'm in the fight of my life. We've got to destroy those nuclear weapons before they destroy us. Time is running out. Either I succeed or there'll be nuclear war by the end of the century. It's that simple. So I'm putting myself on the line."

He paused, waited.

"I know you are," Boyle said.

"It's hardball. The other side will spend a hundred million dollars trying to beat me. It's already started, the rallies, the ex-presidents denouncing me. It's the TV that worries me most. You know what it can do. Millions of people will believe their lies and distortions."

He stood up and paced nervously. "We can't let greedy men destroy the world, Matt. We've got to win this fight, here and now. We've got to make people understand that fewer nuclear weapons mean more security, not less. You're the one who can do it. I want you in charge of my media campaign. The strategy, the whole thing. What do you say?"

Boyle stared at the carpet. "Mr. President . . . when Cara was dying . . . I promised her . . ."

Webster sat down beside Boyle and put his arm around his shoulders. "She was a wonderful woman," the President said softly. "And I wouldn't hurt that boy of yours for the world. But we've got to think of all the Zebs of the world, millions and millions of them. If we don't stop this arms race, who will?"

"Mr. President . . . there are other guys . . ."

"I want the best. The one I trust. You."

Boyle felt drained, defenseless. "I just don't . . ."

"You could make your own hours, Matt. Maybe you should take a place in town. Georgetown, maybe. There are fine schools Zeb could attend."

How did you tell the President that your son was happy where he was and you didn't want him growing up behind bars in the battleground that Georgetown had become?

"Maybe if I talked to the boy," the President said. "If I told him how much I need you." He stood up, a man of action. "Can we get him on the phone? Is he at home?"

Boyle bit his lip. He thought Webster should leave his son out of it. But Presidents made their own rules.

"Actually, Zeb's down in Harry's office," he said reluctantly. "I brought him with me."

"Wonderful!" Webster declared. "Why didn't you say so?"

He murmured into a phone and within seconds Zeb stood in the doorway. He looked awed, Boyle thought, yet still self-possessed.

Webster hurried to the boy. "How in the world are you, son? Do you remember me?"

Zeb shook his hand solemnly. "I remember you," he said.

Boyle watched unhappily as the President made small talk with his son. He knew that small talk well. It was the foreplay that politicians engaged in before they went after whatever it was they wanted. Finally, with a glance at his Rolex, the President made his move.

"Zeb, I need your help on a very important matter," he said gravely.

Zeb gulped but did not speak.

"I've asked your father to come to work for me again. To help me make peace for the whole world. That's a pretty important job, isn't it?"

Zeb nodded, his brown eyes wide and unblinking.

"Your dad's a talented man," Webster said. "He can help me sell my peace plan to a lot of folks who aren't sure they trust me." He winked at the boy. "So that makes him mighty valuable, doesn't it?"

Zeb nodded again.

"But there's one hitch," the President continued. "You mean a lot to your dad, and he's worried about how much time he'd be away from you. So I'm hoping we can work this out, just the two of us. Maybe you and your dad can move into Washington, so you can come see me all the time. What would you say to that, son?"

Zeb bit his lip and stared glumly at his sneakers.

"What do you say, Zeb?" Webster asked, smiling broadly.

"It's up to dad," the boy whispered.

"Of course it is, but we both want you to say yes. Your dad would never do anything to hurt you."

Boyle was agonized. He thought it was outrageous of Cal Webster to put Zeb through this, yet he could not intervene. Webster was counting on the national mythology that no one ever said no to the President. In all the books and movies the hero always answered his country's call. Presidents counted on that; they had to.

Boyle spoke up. "Just tell us how you feel, that's all," he said. "Be honest."

Zeb looked at his father gratefully. "I want you to be home with me, like you have been since mom died," he said.

The President's mouth tightened. Boyle went to the boy, filled with pride. "It's all right, Zeb," he said. Then, "Mr. President, we'll talk it over at home and give you a final decision as soon as we can."

"Of course," Cal Webster said crisply. "It's wonderful to see you both."

"Thank you," Boyle mumbled, and abruptly they were out the door.

10

Boyle led Zeb out of the White House, back into the real
world of air pollution and traffic jams. They walked next
door to the Executive Office Building—the EOB, in Wash-
ingtonese—that bizarre and glorious Victorian pile that was
his favorite building in Washington.

"Where are we going?" Zeb asked.

"To see a friend," Boyle said. They wandered the EOB's
wide, gloomy corridors until Boyle found a door marked
"Office of the Vice President." A pert receptionist was lost in
a Lawrence Sanders paperback. Boyle coughed, caught her
eye, and asked to see the President's daughter, Jenna Webster. The girl eyed him with curiosity, whispered into her
telephone, and returned to a better world.

Zeb sat down and began leafing through a magazine while
Boyle paced the reception area, thinking about the Presi-
dent's offer, Zeb's plea, and his own maddening uncertainty.
What was right? He ached to be home, to sit by his fire.

But first, another love.

"Matt! Oh, Matt, is it really you?"

Jenna flew to him, arms outstretched. He caught her,

twirled her, beamed at her, oblivious to his son, the receptionist, and the scowling young Secret Service man who'd trailed her into the room.

Jenna pecked his cheek pertly, chastely, and grinned. "You look great," she proclaimed.

"You too."

"I started to call you, a hundred times. But I thought, no, when Matt's ready, he'll come. You always know what's right, don't you?"

Jenna was pink cheeks, dancing eyes, raven hair. She was champagne, bubbly and intoxicating. When they'd met she'd been a schoolgirl he teased and sent out for coffee. Later, when she was rebelling against her parents, he and Cara had been the special friends she'd come to for sympathy and advice amid the ups and downs of young love. Now she was a gorgeous young woman and he despaired of defining his feelings for her. All he knew was this glimpse of her made him feel warm, more alive than he'd felt for months.

Boyle gazed into her bright and lovely face and then felt two other eyes upon him. He turned and saw Zeb staring at him and Jenna in dismay. He stammered, "Jenna, you remember Zeb?"

"Of course," she said. She knelt and gave the boy a smile that would have melted any man, yet somehow left him quite unmoved. "It's so good to see you again," she said.

"Hi," Zeb muttered.

Jenna turned back to Boyle. "Matt, I want to talk to you both, but I have a meeting in twenty minutes I can't get out of. Would you like to take a quick walk? How's the weather outside?"

"Cool, but the sun's out."

"I'll get my coat."

Moments later, the three of them were striding down the long flight of steps from the EOB to Pennsylvania Avenue when they saw a black limousine stop at the curb. A handsome, jowly man with snowy white hair and a dramatic tan bounded from the car. When he saw Jenna he broke into a brilliant grin.

"Jenna, my dear, how are you?" he called, advancing toward them. "Do I know this gentleman? And this young man?"

She blinked at the man uncertainly. He was in his mid-fifties and there was something about him that seemed to inspire trust. His voice was gentle and he always appeared to be smiling, even when he was not.

"Mr. Vice President, these are my friends Matt and Zeb Boyle," Jenna said.

Vice President Benjamin Franklin Remington shook Boyle's hand and said, "So I finally have the pleasure of meeting America's premier media consultant? It's an honor, Mr. Boyle, and one that's long overdue. I'd like an opportunity to meet with you sometime—lunch, perhaps, in my office—to get your opinion on some ideas of mine."

Tourists had gathered around them, held back by Secret Service agents. The tourists squealed, snapped pictures, and begged for autographs, but Vice President Remington was oblivious to them. As Boyle stammered a reply, Remington dropped to one knee and shook Zeb's hand.

"And how are *you*, young man? Zeb, is it?"

"Yes, sir," the boy replied.

The Vice President reached into his pocket and extracted a red lollypop. "If your dad doesn't object, here's a treat for you."

Boyle didn't object and Zeb accepted the candy gladly. The Vice President stood up and faced Boyle again. "I'm serious about lunch, Mr. Boyle," he said. "I'm an amateur at politics, you know. I could learn a lot from a pro like you."

Boyle laughed. "I doubt that," he said. "But I'd be glad to talk with you."

"Excellent," Remington said, and with a final wave hurried up the steps to the EOB.

The others walked to the light at Pennsylvania Avenue. Boyle took Zeb's hand. He saw Zeb wince, for he thought himself too grown-up for such paternal care, but Boyle knew how many madmen were racing about Washington's streets and he feared them, even if his son did not.

"Where are we going?" Zeb demanded as they crossed the street to Lafayette Park.

"Just for a walk around the park," Boyle told him.

"I'm going to look at the statue," the boy said and sprinted toward the statue of Andrew Jackson.

"He's not very friendly today," Boyle said.

"He may be uncomfortable meeting a woman friend of yours," Jenna said.

Boyle frowned, perplexed. It had not occurred to him that anyone could object to Jenna.

"So how do you like the Vice President?" she asked.

Boyle shrugged. "Seemed like a decent fellow. How do you like him?"

Jenna shook her head. "He's *nice.* Very intelligent. Very pleasant to deal with. You can't help *liking* him."

"But what?" he demanded.

"But there's something strange about him."

"How so?"

"He's so distant sometimes. Like he wasn't *there.*"

Boyle laughed. "Your typical politician. Often, my dear, you discover there *is* no there there."

She ignored his humor. "We brief him every morning on the current issues and he smiles and nods and doesn't hear a word we say."

"So who is he listening to?"

"I don't know. One or two mornings a week he gets a call, precisely at ten. He takes it alone in his office and talks—or listens, really—for five or ten minutes. *That* seems to be who he listens to."

Boyle was mildly intrigued. "Old pals back home? Big contributors? The mob? Any clues?"

"I wish I knew. There's a rumor in the office it's a woman. But the thing is, Matt, Ben Remington is clean. We really checked him before daddy took him on the ticket. One wife for thirty-two years. A pillar of the Episcopal Church. No booze, no women, not even gossip. And a heck of a successful businessman before he got into politics."

"I never understood why your father picked him—he was a dark horse, wasn't he?"

"The darkest," she said. "But he's handsome and a great speaker and everybody was saying daddy was dull as dishwater and he needed a Vice President with some pizzazz. Plus, the Southerners wanted him. Plus, there was big money behind him. So we picked him. And he did a good job in the campaign. It's just . . . I don't know . . ."

"You wanted a woman Vice President," Boyle said.

Her eyes flashed. "I wanted daddy to win," she said. "I think he could have won with the right woman, but that's water over the dam now."

They had settled on a park bench. Jenna's Secret Service escort, a burly young man in a tan suit, perched on the next bench and peered at them over a *Wall Street Journal.* Across the park, Zeb was silently advancing on some squirrels.

"So how come you ended up working for Remington?" Boyle asked.

Jenna sighed. "Let's face it, a President's daughter is a problem. Anyplace they put me, somebody would yell nepotism. A job for the President's dizzy daughter. But, you see, nobody cares *who* works for the Vice President, because he's a fifth wheel. That was Harry's inspiration. So I'm Remington's issues coordinator. I learn a lot, and maybe in a couple of years I'll get a real job at State or somewhere. Maybe the Peace Corps."

Some Japanese tourists pointed a camera at them. Jenna stuck out her tongue and the Japanese scurried away.

"Tell me about you," she said. "What were you seeing daddy about?"

"He wants me to come back and handle the media for Project Peace."

"Are you?" she demanded. "You'd be so great!"

Boyle pondered the empty blue sky. "Jenna, God knows I want to. But I can't do it."

Her frown pained him. She was so young; dew still glistened on her. "Because of Zeb?" she asked.

"He's a factor. He lost his mother and this job would amount to losing me. It's not fair to him, no matter how I rationalize it. I look around and see how many people in politics don't know their kids at all. Zeb's at a wonderful age now. He's getting over what happened and he's reaching out to the whole world. He's into everything—chemistry sets, model airplanes, computers, Little League, chess, Dungeons and Dragons, you name it. Plus he wants a BB gun, which I have thus far resisted."

Jenna took his hand. "He comes first, Matt. Daddy can get somebody else to handle his media."

"I don't mean to sound noble," Boyle said. "It's not just for Zeb's sake. I've been in politics for twenty years and I'm sick of it. Burned out. I've elected two presidents and seven senators and God knows how many lesser scoundrels and it hasn't meant anything. Cara used to tell me to get out before I turned into a pin-striped shark—that was her name for politicians. I finally decided she was right."

He tried to smile. "Sorry about the speech. Tell me about you? Is your love life as complicated as ever?"

Jenna blushed. "My job doesn't leave much time. Plus I'm surrounded by a small army of Secret Service men, which doesn't exactly encourage carefree romance. I blush to admit it, but I've been seeing one of them on the sly."

"That giant over there?" Boyle glanced at the young man reading *The Wall Street Journal* on the next bench. To his amazement, he felt a pang that might have been jealousy.

Jenna smiled sheepishly. "Jeff's his name. It's against all their regulations."

Boyle laughed. "You're too much, Jenna, you really are."

"Just between us, I escape from them sometimes," she said.

"Escape? What've you got, a secret tunnel out of your apartment?"

"Something like that. A friendly neighbor with a back window."

He touched her hair. "It's hard for me to realize you've grown up. I still think of you as sixteen."

"I was sixteen when I got my first crush on you," Jenna said. "You were the dashing young genius who got Daddy elected governor. I was so jealous of Cara. Then I got to know her and I loved both of you."

They sat in silence until Zeb appeared. "I'm hungry," he announced.

"Son, maybe you could sit down and say a few words to Miss Webster," Boyle said.

"It's all right, Matt," she said. "I've got to get back to the office. Zeb, I hope you'll come see me again."

He stared back at her. "Maybe I will."

None of them noticed the tall, broad-shouldered young photographer who emerged from the West Wing gate. He wore a battered London Fog raincoat and had two cameras and a White House press pass slung around his neck. Halfway along Jackson Place he stopped and pointed a camera toward the park. His zoom lens caught one perfect shot of Boyle, Jenna, and Zeb before he hurried on.

In the distance, chimes tolled another noon. Jenna sighed and stood up. Then the cars started honking.

First one car's insistent *beep-beep-beep*, then others, in all directions.

"What is it?" Boyle demanded. His first thought, as it often was at the sound of unexpected sirens or news bulletins, was of nuclear war.

A pedestrian spoke to the driver of a car on Pennsylvania Avenue, then turned back to the park and began to wave his arms and shout.

Other people started to shout, as if in celebration, but Boyle noticed one man throw down his newspaper in anger. It was as if some strange outdoor drama was in progress.

Jenna's Secret Service agent was on his feet, scanning the park uneasily. More horns honked. "I'll find out what it is," Zeb said, and raced toward one of the men who was shouting.

In a moment Zeb ran back.

"They said yes," he yelled.

"Who?" Boyle demanded. "Who said yes?"

"The Russians," Zeb said. "They said they'd cut back their nuclear bombs if we would."

Boyle watched as the news spread. For every person cheering he saw an anxious, uncertain face. Then Jenna threw her arms around him. "He's done it," she sobbed. "We'll have peace."

Boyle held her close, unable to share her joy. He had been in Washington too long to think anything good would come easily. "I hope so, Jenna," was all he could say.

11

A few nights later Boyle and Zeb sat before the fire playing
Monopoly. Zeb had switched their nightly game from chess
to Monopoly when he realized he stood a better chance of
winning. He almost always won, because he cared more. He
instinctively pursued a cutthroat strategy, denying his father key properties, driving outrageous bargains, twisting
the economic screws as mercilessly as a young robber baron.
He was, Boyle thought, a born capitalist.

When Boyle was wiped out, and the game ended, they sat
on the rug before the fire. They had not discussed Zeb's
meeting with the President, so Boyle asked him how he felt
about it.

"Well, I *like* him," the boy said.

"Why?" Boyle asked. He was fascinated by the workings
of his son's mind.

"Because he's brave—he used to fly jets. But mainly because he's honest. I mean, he wanted to talk me into saying I
didn't care if you went to work in the White House. I didn't
like it, but I knew what he wanted."

Boyle got up and poked the fire. "Zeb, I have to give

President Webster a final decision about that White House job. You don't want me to do it, right?"

"Do you want to?" Zeb asked.

"I guess part of me thinks we could work it out. It would be a compromise. Maybe I wouldn't give the job enough time, maybe I wouldn't give you enough time, but I'd do my best. You learn to compromise in life, Zeb."

"You'd be gone all the time," the boy said. "Or else we'd move to Washington and I'd go to a new school where I didn't know anybody."

"I guess that's true."

"I don't *want* you to." The young robber baron's eyes filled with tears. Boyle took him in his arms.

He called Harry the next morning.

"That's great news about the Russians," he began.

"It's just a start. A lousy hundred warheads. They still don't trust us and we still don't trust them. Plus we've got three ex-presidents out barnstorming against us. Listen, it could fall apart in a week."

Harry skipped a beat. "So what have you decided?"

"I can't do it. I'm sorry."

There was a long pause.

"You stupid, stubborn, thick-headed Irish son of a bitch."

"It's my life, Harry."

"Okay, I'll tell the boss."

"Good luck. I mean that."

"Yeah, sure," Harry said. "Keep in touch."

He hung up. Boyle had to smile. That final "Keep in touch" shimmered with irony. They were in different worlds now, far out of touch. The train had left the station and Boyle wasn't aboard.

Boyle put his head on his arms, wondering if he'd done the right thing.

Probably he'd know, in a decade or two.

12

One blustery Sunday morning in early April, Jenna's jaunty Morgan skidded to a stop beside Boyle's home in Harmony. Boyle had been playing a few hands of poker with Zeb to pass the time, but he tossed down his cards and raced out to greet her. Zeb stayed behind, slowly picking up the cards.

Jenna wore a jacket with a fur collar and had a bottle of wine cradled in her arm. Boyle kissed her cheek. "Where's your armed guard?" he asked.

"I gave them the slip."

He led her into the house where Zeb greeted her morosely. Boyle gritted his teeth. He had been looking forward to Jenna's visit all week and he didn't know how to deal with Zeb's resentment.

Then, as he watched in wonder, Jenna turned all her charm on Zeb. Ignoring his sullen stares, she asked him about school, about his hobbies, about his friends until her warmth thawed him, broke through his wall of resentment.

"I'd love to see your room," she told him. "I haven't seen a boy's room in a long time."

"Do you like video games?" he asked, as he led her up the stairs.

It was not until Jenna had played three games of Space Invaders and solemnly examined Zeb's baseball cards and sticker collection that Boyle was able to retrieve his guest. The three of them drove into Leesburg, the county seat, for lunch. They bypassed McDonald's and Roy Rogers in favor of the Mighty Midget, a closet-sized carry-out where two elderly women served up hamburgers and homemade soup that no fast-food emporium could ever equal.

Boyle drove them out to Ball's Bluff for a picnic. A dirt road curved between tall pines and stopped beside a small cemetery that honored hundreds of soldiers who died on that wooded hillside in the first autumn of the Civil War. Boyle led them down to the Potomac, explaining how the Union troops in Maryland had attempted a surprise attack across the river, only to be pinned down by murderous fire from Virginians atop the bluff.

"Hundreds of men died here," Boyle said, "because their commander was a fool who looked across the Potomac, saw some wagons in a funeral procession, and convinced himself the Confederates were withdrawing from Leesburg. He sent his men across on rafts. It was slaughter."

Boyle caught himself just before he launched a tirade on the madness of war, civil or nuclear. They ate their lunch, then went for a walk along the riverbank, skipping rocks upon the water. When they arrived back in Harmony in midafternoon, Boyle and Zeb took Jenna on a walk around the village, all the way from the Quaker Meeting House to the Old Mill that once had served farmers for miles around and now was preserved as a historic landmark.

On the way back to Boyle's house, they stopped before a big Victorian dwelling with a wooden Indian on the porch and a dozen cars out front.

"Let's go in for a minute," Boyle said. "Some friends of mine are having a ceremony today."

"What kind of a ceremony?" Jenna said.

"You'll see," he said. Zeb had already run ahead of them.

"Their name is Payne. Jack and Sue Payne. He carves ducks."

"Carves *ducks?*" Jenna said.

"Yeah. Like the decoys that duck hunters use. There's a market for them. Jack used to be in advertising but he decided to hell with the rat race, and they moved out here. Sue's a potter, a wonderful woman. She was an angel when Cara was sick."

They stepped into a big, noisy room where twenty-odd people were talking and drinking beer. Several large dogs roamed about. Jack and Sue Payne greeted Boyle with hugs. Jack was reed-thin and bearded; Sue was a tall woman with long blond hair and a radiant smile.

"Glad you could come, pal," Jack said. "Who's this gorgeous person?"

"This is Jenna," Boyle said. He didn't say Jenna Webster, and if the Paynes or their guests knew this was the President's daughter they made no mention of it that afternoon. Boyle's friends in Harmony tended to be Libertarians, Anarchists, and the like, supremely indifferent to mainstream American politics. They were dropouts, most of them, writers and painters and lawyers who had once worked for corporations and politicians and newspapers, but had decided to trade security for freedom. Now they free-lanced, or operated small businesses, making half the money and having twice the fun.

Boyle and Jenna joined some people on the floor by the fire. Zeb was soon wrestling with Bruno, the Paynes' mastiff, who was the size of a young lion. A bearded fellow was angrily proclaiming that he intended to firebomb his neighbor's house. "It's the last time he'll call the dog warden on me!" he raged.

"Trouble in Harmony?" Jenna whispered.

"A little dispute about the leash law," Boyle explained.

There was talk of mysterious doings at River Crest Farm. "I heard a helicopter landed there last week, in the dead of night," declared a woman who farmed and wrote short stories.

"Was it the sheik?" someone asked.

"If you ask me, there isn't any sheik," said a pale young man, a beekeeper and would-be novelist. "Gangsters own the place. Whoever heard of a sheik with wild boars?"

"I heard they're building a huge bomb shelter there," said a sculptor who once had been an ulcer-ridden Washington lawyer. "And bringing in workmen from New Jersey."

"New Jersey!" declared the beekeeper. "What did I tell you? It's the mob!"

Later, when a golden sun blazed over the distant Blue Ridge, Jack Payne got to his feet. "Okay, everybody outside for the trial."

People groaned, grabbed their beers, and drifted out to the backyard. "What is it?" Jenna demanded. "What trial?" But Boyle only laughed.

Jack Payne came out last, carrying a television set in his arms. He stepped to the center of his circle of friends and dumped the set onto the ground.

"I charge you with the corruption of youth, the pollution of minds, the fomenting of idiocy, the debasement of taste, deceptive practices, grand larceny, and assorted other crimes against humanity," Payne pronounced. "What says the jury?"

"Guilty!" his guests cried.

"Then death to the one-eyed monster!" Payne shouted. He seized a sledgehammer and bashed in the picture tube. "No more boob tube—we'll read books now, and watch sunsets, and talk to each other."

He passed the sledgehammer on. Soon everyone was taking a turn battering the remains of the TV set.

"Your turn, Matthew," Payne called.

Boyle seized the sledgehammer and gazed defiantly at the shattered set. He felt wonderful, godlike; he wished they could maul every TV set in America. "Die, monster, die," he cried and pounded the cracked innards of the set like a madman.

He saw Zeb watching, wide-eyed. "Want a turn, son?" he asked.

Zeb looked truly fearful. "You're not going to bust *our* set, are you?" he demanded.

"I just might," Boyle vowed.

"Dad, you may not like TV, but *I* do," he said defiantly.

Boyle laughed and found Jenna. "You people are a little violent out here, aren't you?" she said.

"We're freedom fighters," Boyle declared. People were still smashing the set and howling with glee. Boyle said good night to the Paynes and took his party home. It was dusk now, and they were hungry. They hurried to the kitchen, where Boyle and Zeb teamed up to cook tomato sauce and pasta.

"Can I help?" Jenna asked.

"This is strictly a father-son production," Boyle said.

"You can do the dishes," Zeb added.

She made a face at him. "Thanks, kid."

Boyle stirred the tomato sauce lovingly, tasted it, and shook in more pepper flakes.

"Dad, you make it too hot," Zeb protested.

"It's supposed to be hot," Boyle declared.

"Dissention in the father-son team?" Jenna asked.

"The boy's tastes aren't fully developed."

"He makes it too hot," Zeb insisted, "then he drinks a lot of wine."

"How sharper than a serpent's tooth," Boyle sighed.

While they ate, Zeb told them an adventure story he was writing for a school project. "See, these two guys climb a mountain, looking for treasure, and vampire bats start chasing them so they jump into an underground river but there are piranha fish in it, so they get out and a grizzly bear starts after them and they're running down this mine shaft and they see a gold light at the end of the tunnel, that's the treasure shining in the sun, and what I'm wondering is, should there be a dragon guarding the treasure?"

Boyle sipped his wine thoughtfully. "Son, I would say that any adventure story worth its salt has to have a dragon. Would you agree, Miss Webster?"

"Absolutely."

"Maybe they'll kill the dragon and drink its blood," Zeb declared. "Maybe that's how they get the magical power to escape."

"Kill the dragon and drink its blood," Boyle mused. "I like
t. There might be a movie in it."

"Can I be excused?" Zeb asked.

"If you're finished."

Zeb stared at Jenna. "Will you come see us again?"

"If you want me to."

"I do—you're nice!" he declared, then rushed off to watch
ome new outburst of mayhem on TV.

"You were wonderful with him," Boyle said.

"He's wonderful."

"He's a good kid most of the time. He can be tough. I try
ot to spoil him."

"You haven't."

"It's a delicate balance. Where do you draw the line? You
know where I drew the line? No Fudge Rounds for break-
ast. We went to the mat over that. The old man got tough!"

Jenna laughed. "It was so nice at those people's house
oday, the way the kids mingled with the grown-ups."

"This is a good place for kids. That was why I couldn't take
he White House job. It would have meant uprooting Zeb at
a time when he needs stability."

"Harry was livid. Daddy too."

He shrugged. "You have to make choices. Coffee?"

"Please."

He poured two cups. "So how's everything?"

She smiled. "My job? My love life? My soul?"

"All of the above."

"My job is pretty dull. I'm tired of Ben Remington. He
von't listen to me."

"He's crazy then."

"My love life is zilch. Which is fine. This is no time for a
grand passion."

"Amen."

"You know who I wish you could talk to, Matt? My mom."

"How is she?"

"Not great. You know Mom, all she really cares about is
her painting. But a modern First Lady is supposed to have a
Cause. Plant flowers. Denounce drugs, whatever. Well,
Mom hasn't found her Cause. She'd rather die than make a

speech. But she's terrified that the media will say she's aloof or elitist or something and it'll hurt Daddy."

Boyle sipped his coffee. "She loves art, so they should build on that. Not anything fancy or highbrow, but let her visit schools and talk to kids and judge their art shows. It'd make nice visuals. If she went out every week or two, that'd keep the media happy. Just don't let anybody come in and try to make her something she's not."

"You make it sound so easy."

"Most things are. But people hire experts and form committees and screw them up. Your mother's lovely, just let people see that, in a natural way."

"I'll talk to her. She'll like that."

"That was always my approach," Boyle said. "Don't change people. Just go with their strengths. Accentuate the positive."

Jenna laughed and took his hand. "What was that story Daddy used to tell? About you electing a wife-beater to something?"

"That was no wife-beater, that was my candidate."

She plopped her chin on her hands. "Tell me."

Boyle sighed. "Once upon a time, my child, a candidate for governor got drunk and slugged his wife. She had him arrested. So, what is this candidate to do? Deny he hit her? Withdraw from the race? Apologize? Beg forgiveness? That was what the fainthearted proposed. But not Matthew T. Boyle. 'Let's calm down and take some polls,' sez Boyle. And do you know what Boyle's polls showed?"

Jenna's bright eyes reflected the candlelight. "I'm afraid I do."

"In a three-man race, my wife-beater commanded an astounding fifty-eight percent of the male vote. What's more, he had a respectable twenty-four percent of the female vote, with an unusual number of women undecided, God bless their downtrodden, guilt-ridden little hearts."

Boyle fished a cigar from his pocket and lit it on a candle. "Can't tell this sordid tale without a cigar, my dear," he said in his W. C. Fields voice. "Additional polls and focus groups proved that our candidate, who in truth was a mouse of a man, cowardly except when drunk, had only one thing going for him—*the voters of Massachusetts admire a man who slugs his wife!*"

Jenna laughed. "The slogan," she cried. "What was the slogan?"

"Wrote it myself, my dear, and we plastered it all across the state. FLANIGAN—YOU KNOW WHERE HE STANDS! We won going away. Flanigan's wife forgave him and he made a fine governor. He calls me every few months, hinting that he should run for President."

Jenna took his hand. "You're too much, Matt."

"All that was back in my wayward youth, when I consorted with politicians and other low types. More coffee?"

She shook her head. "I've got to start back."

They stood up. Boyle flipped on the overhead light and blew out the candles. "Back to reality," he said.

"I'll help with the dishes," she said.

"I'll get them," he insisted. "You've got a long drive."

In the living room, Zeb was asleep on the sofa, wrapped in an old plaid blanket. Boyle cut off the TV.

Jenna knelt and kissed the boy. "Good night, sweet prince," she whispered.

His eyes fluttered, opened, closed again. "Good night, Mom," he muttered.

Boyle turned away. Jenna took his hand and they went out to her car. The night was cool and he helped her put up the top.

Jenna turned to him. "Matt, I want to ask you a big favor."

"What?"

"The SPC dinner is next week. It'll be awful but I've got to go and I need an escort. I wondered if you . . ." She made a winsome little shrug.

Boyle sighed. The Society of Political Correspondents' black-tie dinner with several hundred self-important Washington journalists was his idea of the ultimate torture.

"For you, Jenna, anything."

Suddenly a car roared around the curve and skidded to a halt, its headlights blinding them. A burly young man with a sandy moustache leaped out and charged toward them.

"Dammit, what do you think you're doing?" he yelled at Jenna.

"Who the hell are you?" Boyle demanded. Even in the shadows, the man looked familiar.

"Don't yell at me," Jenna cried.

"Do you have any idea how many people are out looking for you?" the young man demanded.

"I don't really care," Jenna declared. "Matt, this rude fellow is Jeff Winnick, one of my protectors."

The Secret Service man continued to ignore Boyle. "Get in your car, Jenna," he snapped. "I'll follow you back."

"I'll leave when I'm ready," she shot back.

The young man stepped back, furious, and Jenna took Boyle's arm.

"Spoken like a President's daughter," he told her.

"I'm so sick of them. Particularly *him.*"

The two-way radio in Winnick's car crackled noisily. Boyle saw one of his neighbors at his window.

"Thank you for a beautiful day," she said. She kissed him and disappeared, into her little car, into the vast night.

Boyle went inside and carried Zeb up to bed. Then he stood by the embers of the fire for a long time, confused and sad, as if he'd opened a door that had better stayed shut.

13

One late April morning, as the full flush of spring went cartwheeling across the land, America awoke to an awesome and unprecedented sight.

In a score of states huge missiles, chained to the backs of flatbed trucks like nuclear Gullivers, were slowly moving along the highways toward destruction.

The U.S. government, like that of the Soviet Union, had chosen to surrender a hundred of its most vulnerable, least valuable missiles, Titan IIs and other big, land-based strategic missiles that had for years been mounted in fixed silos. Now these monsters, suddenly uprooted from their underground caverns, thrust into the sun, began the slow, silent journey across America toward the Tennessee Valley Authority nuclear plant.

These processions, escorted by federal troops and state national guardsmen, were greeted in a multitude of ways. Some Americans met the missiles with cheers, flags, and flowers; others watched silently, grimly, as they might the passing of a funeral cortege.

In Orange County, California, leaders of the John Birch

Society lay down in the paths of the trucks and shouted "Shame!" and "Treason!" at the soldiers who dragged them away.

In towns outside San Francisco, middle-aged veterans of the great antiwar rallies of the Sixties and Seventies flashed the "V" sign to the doomed warheads and joined hands to sing "We Shall Overcome" and "Blowing in the Wind" and "Give Peace a Chance."

In South Alabama, snipers halted one convoy for half an hour before they were disarmed and taken prisoner by army marksmen.

Throughout the Midwest, thousands of people fled their homes as rumors spread that the approaching missiles might somehow be triggered by Soviet agents.

At colleges across New England, the coming of the missiles set off beer parties, school holidays, and near-riots. One Yale student was charged with indecent exposure after he allegedly "mooned" the motorcade.

The progress of the convoys was reported on the evening newscasts, and these dramatic reports intensified debate over the wisdom of President Webster's disarmament program.

In city after city, ever larger and more impassioned crowds greeted the flying circus of ex-presidents, ex-generals, ex-Cabinet officers, and ex-CIA directors who nightly warned that the national survival was in doubt.

On Sunday mornings, in pulpits across America, hundreds of fundamentalist clergymen, well financed and well organized, invoked the name of Jesus of Nazareth as they shouted invective against a President who sought fewer, not more, nuclear weapons.

From her castle on an island in North Georgia, Serena Masters, plutocrat and patriot, sent forth the millions of dollars that fueled the anti-Webster, antidisarmament crusade.

Day after day, dozens of the nation's leading newspapers carried full-page warnings:

WHAT ARE WE DOING?
MUST AMERICA LIE HELPLESS?

STOP THE SURRENDER!
WRITE YOUR CONGRESSMAN!
SEND YOUR CONTRIBUTION!

Night after night, on television, slick spots selling dog
food, deodorants, and dental adhesives were preempted by
slick spots that portrayed an America being eaten away by
the cancer of appeasement while a bloodthirsty Russian bear
awaited its hour of conquest.

Amid this sound and fury, President Webster remained
silent, even as nightly polls showed support for his program
melting away.

Still, despite all the hue and cry, a hundred U.S. nuclear
warheads proceeded inexorably toward their destruction.

The missiles rolled on.

The critics raged.

The world waited.

While the world pondered disarmament, Zeb took the
plunge into Little League baseball, Pee Wee division.

Boyle was dubious at first. He'd heard about those victory-
mad Little League parents, and he didn't want his son exposed to that kind of inane pressure. But Zeb was determined, and when they went to the first practice the coaches
seemed like reasonable fellows. In truth, the immediate
problem wasn't the parents, but the players.

At the first practice, infielders collided and bickered, out-
fielders were beaned by fly balls, and batters didn't grasp the
principle that it was necessary to remove the bat from the
shoulder to address the ball. Still, in the weeks ahead, there
was progress. Some agile infielders emerged and one
chubby outfielder who could knock the ball a country mile.

Zeb proved to be one of the more promising of the Harmony Eagles, as they were known. He and Boyle had been
tossing balls and Frisbees in the backyard since he was a
toddler; the boy had good hands. He sought and won the
coveted first base slot, and demonstrated a good eye at the
plate.

When the Eagles took the field for their first game, against the hated Stumptown Tigers, Boyle made a chilling discovery: He had become one of those victory-mad parents.

It was a good game, that no one would deny. The Stumptown team, strapping farm boys, jumped to an early lead but, as Boyle and the other Harmony parents howled like banshees, the Eagles fought back. In the fifth of seven innings, Zeb singled with a man on third to bring the Eagles to within one run. He made some fine plays in the field, too, performing, in Boyle's biased view, like a young Lou Gehrig. Then, in the bottom of the seventh, with the Eagles still trailing by one run, they loaded the bases with two outs, and Zeb stepped to the plate.

With the count three and two, and all of Harmony screaming for a hit, Zeb popped up, into the glove of the Stumptown shortstop, who caught the ball, then raised his fist in triumph.

Zeb headed straight for the car, one of the unhappiest boys in America.

"I let everybody down," he said.

"You played a good game," Boyle told him. "Nobody gets a hit every time."

"We were awful," he persisted. "What if we don't win any games all season? What a bunch of jerks we'll be."

"You'll win lots of games," Boyle assured him, but in his heart he wasn't so sure.

14

Jenna hesitated in the doorway of the Vice President's office. He was hunched over the telephone, his back to her. "Yes, I agree, I agree," he was saying in his mellifluous voice. He scribbled in a leatherbound notebook as he spoke.

Jenna tensed with curiosity. Was this the mysterious caller who phoned Remington so often, who seemed to have the Vice President on a string?

With a final "I understand—I'll try to find out," he put down the phone, sighed unhappily, and tossed the notebook into his desk drawer. He locked the drawer, slipped the key into the pocket of his midnight-blue blazer, then noticed Jenna in the doorway.

"Come in, my dear," he called, flashing the bittersweet smile that men reserve for beautiful women half their age. "Sit down. What's our agenda for today?"

Jenna took a chair, all business. "You have the interview with *Cosmopolitan* this afternoon," she said. "We've prepared a briefing sheet."

She handed him some papers and he skimmed them rapidly. "I believe I know all my lines," he said with a grin. "I shall point with pride and view with alarm. I shall praise that peerless leader, your father, and I shall try to conceal from the readers of *Cosmo*, as I believe it's known, that I'm at heart an old fuddy-duddy. Now, how about a cup of coffee?'"

"Please," she said.

He poured the coffee himself. At his best, the Vice President had an unassuming, old-shoe quality about him. And yet he was very much the modern politician. Jenna had a keen ear for sex^{i}st remarks, for example, but you never caught Ben Remington using any offensive phrase. With his thick white hair, his deep tan, his gentle good looks, his sunny smile, he seemed the most sincere, approachable man in the world, typecast to be your family doctor or perhaps the perfect Vice President.

Yet something was wrong, something she could never quite put her finger on. He was distant, somehow melancholy, to a degree that was puzzling in a man who'd led such an active, successful life. She wondered if there were some problem in his marriage—Mrs. Remington was rumored to be "difficult"—but he spoke of his wife only in the most affectionate and glowing terms. Most of all, Jenna was troubled by the mysterious phone calls he took one or two mornings a week. They were starting to obsess her. Who was calling the Vice President and what was he—or she—saying to him? Or asking of him?

He made small talk until Jenna began to be suspicious. It was a trick her father used—he would give someone extra time, flattering them, softening them up, before making whatever pitch he intended to make. Finally, after she had declined a second cup of coffee, Remington said gravely, "Jenna, I'm worried about Project Peace. There's too much secrecy. The public is troubled, divided. I think your father should *do* something to shore up support—maybe go on TV more, or make a speaking tour, or bring this fellow Boyle in, if he's as good as they say. Do you have any idea what he's planning? I want to help him, if he'll only let me."

Jenna braced herself. It was a sore point. Determined to prevent leaks on his disarmament plan, her father was confiding in an absolute minimum of people, and the Vice President was not among the elect. It made for an awkward situation. Moreover, Ben Remington seemed to think she knew all her father's secrets, when in fact she did not.

"All I know is what's been made public," she said. "The first two hundred missiles are scheduled for demolition. Presumably we're negotiating for additional cutbacks."

"But when?" he pressed. "What progress is being made? How far does he intend to go? What's his timetable? What is the Soviet position?"

The Vice President's voice rose; he was suddenly breathless, his hands trembling. She'd never seen him so flustered.

"I really don't know any of those things, Mr. Vice President," she said gently. "He's so afraid of leaks . . ."

Remington sighed, shrugged, stood up. He seemed to be his genial, unflappable self again. "Well, time for my workout," he said cheerfully. He slipped off his blue blazer, hung it carefully in the closet behind his desk, and picked up the leather bag that held his gym clothes. He worked out three mornings a week on the Nautilus machines in the small gym in the EOB basement.

"I'll be back for my eleven o'clock meeting," he told her. "Acid rain, isn't it? So many problems." With a wink he was gone.

Jenna returned to her own office, more troubled than ever. What was it he'd been saying when she barged into his office that morning? He'd been talking to his mysterious caller and he'd said, *"I agree, I agree . . . I'll try to find out."* Twenty minutes later he'd been pumping Jenna, giving her the third degree, and he'd been terribly agitated, as if he was under some awful pressure, as if someone was forcing him to do something against his will.

Or was she just being crazy?

Jenna began to pace about her small office, with its one tall window facing on East Executive Avenue. Something else, some other piece of the puzzle, danced in her mind, just beyond her memory's grasp.

It came back with a jolt.

The notebook.

He'd been scribbling in a notebook when he talked to his

mysterious caller. Then he'd locked the notebook in his desk drawer.

And the key was in his blazer pocket, hanging in his closet.

Jenna shut her eyes and pressed her forehead against the wall. She had to see that notebook. It might explain who was calling, what they wanted, what was wrong. She thought she would go crazy if she didn't find out.

Yet she couldn't just walk into his office, steal his key, open his desk, and read his notebook—if she was caught, there'd be a terrible scene.

She argued back and forth with herself, curiosity versus caution, until abruptly she made her decision.

Gripped by compulsion, she opened her door, took a deep breath, and marched toward the Vice President's office. Who, after all, would challenge the President's daughter?

Irene would.

She was posted like a sentry just outside the Vice President's office, a tall, tough Tennessee woman of middle years, officially Remington's "executive assistant." That meant she'd been with him forever and she'd kill for him.

Irene looked up with cold, unblinking eyes as Jenna swept past her desk.

"I left my pen in his office," Jenna said.

Jenna shut the door behind her, raced to the closet, and fished the key out of the blazer. Her heart thumped madly. What had she done? There wasn't time to read the notebook now. Why hadn't she waited until Irene was away from her desk?

The door banged open. The older woman's eyes flashed fire. "Exactly what do you think you're doing?" she demanded.

"Found it!" Jenna said, forcing a grin and waving a ballpoint pen. The purloined key burned in the palm of her other hand as she hurried back to her own office.

What now? Jenna cursed her impulsiveness. She had the key but she couldn't use it, not with Irene alerted. Nor could she risk keeping the key longer than the hour Remington would be gone.

A copy! The answer was to make a copy, return the original key to his coat, and use her copy to get into Remington's desk later.

Jenna raced from her office and out into the corridor.

Irene seized her telephone and spoke into it furiously.

The young man who took her call was not far away, in the White House Press Room; he cursed her news bitterly, but nonetheless moved swiftly into action.

Jenna's Morgan was parked between two limousines on West Executive Avenue, the very private street that ran between the White House and the EOB. She was starting the engine when Jeff Winnick caught up with her.

"Where are you going?"

"To run an errand."

He jumped in and she roared past the gatehouse onto Pennsylvania Avenue.

"Make yourself useful," she said. "Where's a locksmith?"

"A locksmith?"

"To get a copy of a key. In a hurry."

"What for?"

"Jeff, do you know where a *locksmith* is?"

"Head toward Georgetown."

A few blocks past Washington Circle they found a tiny locksmith shop, squeezed between a deli and a liquor store.

"Wait here," Jenna said. She burst into the shop, causing little bells to ring above the door. The proprietor, a sad-faced old Italian named Calvari, was munching on a meatball sandwich.

"I need a copy of this key, please," Jenna told him. "I'm in a terrible hurry."

Calvari peered at her. "Don't I know you? You in pictures?"

"No, no. One copy, please, as fast as you can."

The old man examined the key. "Fancy," he declared.

"Can you *do* it?"

"Oh, sure. But you relax." He winked at her. "Make you even prettier."

Jenna leaned against the wall, wondering if she was crazy. When she got back to the office, three officials from the

Environmental Protection Agency were waiting to brief the Vice President. Jenna escorted them into Remington's office. She wondered if she dared replace the key while they watched.

Before she could act, Remington bounced in, his hair still glistening from his shower. "Sorry to keep you," he said cordially, and he shook each visitor's hand. He slipped his blazer from the closet and began searching its pockets. His face reddened.

"Something wrong, sir?" one of the visitors asked.

"I've lost a key," Remington muttered. He dropped to his knees and examined the closet floor. The visitors watched in amazement. Jenna made a quick decision. While no one was watching, she tossed the key on the rug beside his desk.

"Is that it?" she asked.

Remington whirled, spotted the key, and scooped it up. "How the devil did it get there?" he demanded.

No one voiced a reply. The Vice President sank into his chair, the key clutched in his fist. He was still scowling when the visitors finished their report on the menace of acid rain.

Charlie had watched from across the street as Jenna's Morgan pulled away from the locksmith shop. He was seething, to have been summoned so unexpectedly, unsure of what was happening, what the stakes were, what was needed. He hated to improvise; it was his passion always to control events.

He slipped into the shop so furtively that the bells above the door barely rang. The old man looked at him suspiciously.

"I'm with the Secret Service," he said, flashing a silver badge. "The girl who was in here—what did she want?"

Calvari grinned. "I knew I'd seen her. She was the Webster girl."

"That's right. Now tell me what she wanted."

"I don't tell you nothing. I think you're fake."

Charlie had neither time nor patience. He grabbed the old man's collar and slammed him against the wall. From his pocket he pulled the gleaming switchblade. He pressed its point to the locksmith's throat.

"Now, what was it she wanted?"

"She want a copy of a key, that's all," the old man whispered in terror.

"What kind of key?"

Calvari told him. Tears welled in his eyes as the knife pricked his neck. Charlie was indifferent to the old man's fear. His only reservations about killing concerned potential dangers to himself. What was the key to? What did the Webster girl know? What might this fool remember? Charlie's face, at the very least, and that was a risk Charlie did not intend to take. He made his decision.

"Go away," the locksmith begged.

Not the knife. Not so soon after the whistle-blower. He dropped the knife into his pocket and seized a small hammer off Calvari's workbench. The locksmith struggled helplessly as Charlie struck him once, with fierce and terrible precision, at a point just in front of the ear.

The locksmith died instantly but Charlie pounded him again and again, as a frenzied attacker might do. Finally, he let the body slip to the floor and moved to the cash register. He pocketed a few bills and scattered others to the floor. Then, with a quick glance up and down the street, Charlie left the locksmith shop, cursing the bells that jangled behind him.

15

"Good evening, this is a CBS News Special Report from the Tennessee Valley Authority's nuclear power plant in Oak Ridge, deep in the mountains of East Tennessee.

"Today, at this power plant, working under conditions of the utmost secrecy, a team of U.S. and Soviet scientists completed the historic dismantling of one hundred U.S. nuclear warheads.

"At the same time, at a nuclear facility outside Leningrad, a hundred Soviet warheads were dismantled by a similar team of U.S. and Russian scientists.

"I repeat: One hundred U.S. warheads, which could have destroyed most of the cities in Russia, and one hundred Soviet warheads, which could have destroyed most of the cities of the United States, have been destroyed—the weapons no longer exist.

"Later this evening, we are going to show you some extraordinary film we were permitted to take of the actual dismantling process, both here and at the Soviet nuclear facility. You will see the scientists isolating the fissionable nuclear material, and mixing it with nitric acid and other

hemicals to downgrade it from weapons-grade material to
orm oxides that can be used as fuel in nuclear power plants.

"Along with that film, we will have interviews with the
cientists who actually carried out the process.

"But right now we are going to switch live to President
Calvin Webster and a group of Americans he has gathered
with him for what promises to be a unique ceremony on the
grounds outside the nuclear power plant here.

"Let me say first that there is nothing wrong with your
television set. At the President's request, this ceremony is
being filmed in near-darkness."

The commentator's elegant face vanished and the nation's
TV screens seemed to go dark. Then dim, flickering lights
slowly came into focus. More than fifty men, women, and
children had formed a circle on the lawn outside the TVA
nuclear power plant. Each of them was holding a burning
candle. The light from the candles, as photographed by the
network cameras' night lenses, cast an eerie blue glow over
the shadowy figures.

The camera panned slowly around the circle. Some of the
faces it revealed were famous; others were unknown. Vice
President Remington was there, along with Cabinet officials,
congressional leaders, the Russian Ambassador, and a sprin-
kling of faces from the worlds of sports and entertainment.
Yet nearly half of those present were East Tennessee mountain families, black and white, residents of the area who
were the President's special guests.

Finally the camera focused on the determined face of
President Webster. He stood with Jenna on one side of him
and his wife Doris on the other.

"Good evening," Webster said, his face a ghostly blue.

Matt and Zeb Boyle were among the millions watching
the President on television. Boyle had turned his lights off,
the better to see the dark images on the screen. Already he
was awed by what Webster was doing. He had remained
silent for so long, while his critics assailed him, but now he
was speaking and at the same time creating a sense of
drama, of mythology, that was stunning. This was history in
the making, the global village united.

"We meet in darkness," Webster said, "yet at the dawn of a glorious new day.

"Today U.S. and Soviet scientists completed the dismantling of two hundred nuclear warheads.

"In this, we and the Soviets have truly done God's work—we have heeded the biblical admonition to beat our swords into plowshares.

"This is only a beginning. A hundred warheads is a fraction of our nuclear arsenal, or of the Soviets'. But the two hundred warheads destroyed today can be followed by thousands more in the months and years ahead."

A murmur of approval rose from the people around the President.

"When Project Peace began," he continued, "one issue was how to dispose of the fissionable material from the warheads. There were proposals that it be shot into outer space or dropped to the bottom of the sea. I felt, however, and my Soviet counterpart agreed, that if at all possible this powerful, destructive material should be used for peaceful, productive purposes.

"Thus, we instructed our scientists to convert the weapons-grade plutonium into fuel that can be used in nuclear reactors to provide energy. For many years, we Americans have paid vast sums of money for the production of nuclear weapons. Now, at last, some of that investment can come back to us.

"Moreover, many more billions of dollars will be saved, so long as we and the Soviets build no more nuclear weapons. These savings must be used to provide better schools, roads, housing, and medical care for our people.

"I am about to press a switch. The light that will shine forth comes from fuel that, until today, could have killed millions of people. Now its power will serve us, not threaten us."

President Webster reached out to a small platform that stood before him. Around him the candles flickered eerily in the deep darkness of the Tennessee mountains.

Suddenly the darkness exploded into brilliant light.

Ten powerful searchlights pierced the night, each

beamed upon an American flag that whipped in the night wind, high atop a pole in the center of their circle.

Old Glory burst into hundreds of millions of homes around the globe. In one of them, in the village of Harmony, Virginia, Matt Boyle drew his son close. "Remember this," he whispered. "Remember it for the rest of your life."

By June it seemed that the President had won his gamble. The dramatic ceremony at the TVA plant called forth a great outpouring of popular support. The polls showed a hard core of nearly twenty-five percent of the American people were still unalterably opposed to any disarmament, but the President had won over millions of the previously undecided, until fifty-five percent of the public solidly supported the peace initiative.

The White House moved quickly to consolidate these dramatic gains.

First, it was announced that the U.S. and the Soviets had agreed to the construction of two permanent nuclear conversion facilities, one in each country, where warheads would be dismantled in the future.

Soon after that, President Webster met with NATO leaders in Paris to announce new negotiations with the Soviets intended to reduce the number of nuclear weapons on European soil.

From Paris, the President flew to New Delhi, where leaders of Third World nations pledged to join the U.S.-Soviet moratorium on new nuclear weapons.

Finally, upon his return to Washington, the President called a news conference at which he revealed that he and the Soviet Premier had agreed to a second round of cuts, this time of two thousand warheads from each country.

"This is not a token or symbolic act," Webster told the nation. "This is a major cutback, by each country, of nearly ten percent of its nuclear stockpile. This is nothing less than the beginning of the end of the arms race."

Within twenty-four hours, the President's popularity had shot off the charts, surpassing the previous high that Dwight Eisenhower had achieved when he made peace in Korea.

On Capitol Hill senators and representatives who had straddled the fence on Project Peace were now scrambling to climb aboard the bandwagon. The far right's brave plan to impeach Webster was suddenly gone with the wind.

Matt Boyle watched these stunning developments from his home in the country with mixed feelings of pride, concern, and bemusement. As he viewed the news each evening he was sure that the President's beautifully orchestrated media campaign was the work of a top professional. His suspicions were confirmed when a political columnist revealed that Gabe Freeman, a New York media consultant, had been serving as an unpublicized White House adviser. Boyle knew Gabe and thought of sending him a note of congratulations, but somehow that note never got written.

The truth was that whenever Boyle thought about Gabe Freeman in the White House, doing the job he might have done, helping the President's historic program take flight, he grew profoundly depressed. What was he doing? Writing a book? Living in the past? Debunking the political process while others made history?

Harry's warning rang in Boyle's ears; he had been right. Boyle felt like the jerk of the year.

16

It had indeed been an Arab sheik who purchased River
Crest Farm, but not, as local rumor had it, to install a seraglio
into traditionally monogamous Loudoun County, Virginia.
Rather, the sheik had been acting as the agent of his old
friend Serena Masters, who wanted a base of operations near
Washington, D.C., that would provide her both luxury and
security. This River Crest Farm did, particularly with the
addition of chain link fences topped with barbed wire,
armed guards on patrol, and the fearsome wild boars that
were set loose on the thousand-acre estate.

She arrived at her new home by armor-plated Cadillac in
the dead of night, determined to intensify her political campaign against President Webster and his peace plan. Instead,
within weeks her campaign was belly up. The tens of millions of dollars she had spent on newspaper and television
advertisements, on speeches and rallies, on bribes and political contributions, all had been swept away in the face of the
President's dramatic demonstration that the nuclear monsters were paper tigers, easily torn asunder.

Political action had failed, the Advisory Committee was in

disarray, and defense industry stocks were plummeting. Thus it was that Serena, one gentle June evening, summoned Charlie Trueblood to join her for a talk.

Charlie was not far away; he had for several months made an old cabin, just down from the mansion, his base of operations. He strolled up at dusk and joined her on a veranda that overlooked formal gardens and a long hill that sloped toward the Potomac.

She had a bottle of Cristal on ice; he sent its cork shooting into the twilight and filled their tulip glasses.

"Cheers," he said.

"There's precious little to cheer about," she said.

"Webster's outmaneuvered us, eh?" Charlie said, with no apparent regret.

"He's a clever man. He has public opinion behind him, the Congress is spineless, and . . ."

"And we've been lumbered," Charlie said.

"No," she snapped. "We've lost a battle, but not the war." Charlie waited, smirking just a bit.

"You realize what is happening, don't you?" she said. *"We're disarming but the Soviets are not!"*

"Have you got proof of that?"

"Proof? Would anyone in their right mind trust the Soviets? They're murderers, criminals! We're throwing down our arms and they're just waiting to move in for the kill!"

Charlie slapped at a mosquito; all her millions could not keep them away.

"Come inside," she said impatiently. She led the way into a big, oak-paneled library. The room was decorated with suits of armor, swords, scimitars, crossbows, and other martial memorabilia that she had brought up from her Georgia castle. She had even brought her most treasured piece, the priceless Chinese dragon. Charlie beamed when he saw the dragon. He walked over and rubbed its bejeweled nose. "Well, how's old Puff?" He pressed a switch just under the dragon's left ear and a jet of flame shot from its mouth.

"Stop that!" Serena said. "Sit down, we have business to discuss."

She sank into an ocher wing chair; Charlie sat cross-legged on the floor, the bottle of Cristal at his side.

"I trust you understand what I'm telling you," she continued. "The political battle is lost. Therefore I have no alternative but to turn to you."

"I suspected you would," he said.

"You understand the Advisory Committee will not authorize your action."

"No, but they'll jolly well reap the benefits, won't they?"

"Time is of the essence," she said. "Are you ready to proceed?"

Charlie stood up, scowling, and jammed his fists into the pockets of his jeans. "I will be soon."

"Soon? How soon? Is there a problem?"

"A delay with the weapon," he told her.

"A delay? You'd better tell me more about this mysterious weapon of yours."

"No," he said sharply. "The less you know about it, the better. I should be ready to move in two weeks."

"And you're confident that . . ."

"I'm confident that I'll dispatch Webster in plain view of hundreds of witnesses and walk away a free man."

"Everything else is proceeding smoothly?" she pressed.

Charlie dropped his eyes. "One thing does trouble me," he confessed.

"What?"

"Webster's daughter, the one who works for Remington. She's suspicious."

"How do you know?"

"She stole a key to his desk. She may have heard him talking to you."

"That fool Remington!" Serena raged. "But does she know . . . ?"

"What we plan? I doubt it. But no matter how carefully I handle her father, her suspicions will be a threat to us."

Serena's dark eyes blazed with anger. "What do you propose?" she demanded.

Charlie shrugged. "I could remove her," he said.

Serena eyed him coldly, suspiciously.

He said, "But, of course, that would make the removal of her father more difficult, if not impossible. So, for the moment, we'll have to live with her suspicions."

"I trust you're watching her closely."

"Day and night," Charlie said. "Trust me."

17

When Thomas (Turk) Kellerman finished his tour as a Marine officer in Vietnam he stayed drunk for a few months and then went to work for the U.S. Secret Service. His motives were not wildly idealistic. There'd been a time when he'd dreamed of law school, of being another Clarence Darrow, but he'd left his ambition and idealism behind in some Asian jungle. His three years in the Marines, plus seventeen more with the Secret Service, would earn him a generous pension in his early forties. After the trauma of war, that sounded fine.

It happened that the U.S. had never harbored more would-be presidential assassins than in the early 1970s, and Turk was assigned to a special unit whose members infiltrated radical groups that were feared to be homicidal. He was sent to New York, where he grew a beard, dressed like a bum, and hung out in Washington Square. It wasn't long until an impassioned young woman, whose dirty hair and scruffy clothes could not quite conceal her elegance of face and body, began lecturing him on the evils of capitalism. He responded with manic enthusiasm, presenting himself as a disillusioned Vietnam veteran and munitions expert. The girl, whose name was Melanie, soon invited him to the loft she shared with three other girls and three young men. A fourth man had recently deserted their "cell" for graduate work in Medieval Lit.

Turk's military know-how impressed the men; his broad shoulders and dark eyes won the women. Soon he moved into the commune, whose members, he found, divided their time between group sex, psychedelic drugs, and vague talk of soon-to-be-launched "offensives" against the "imperialists." The women, he decided, were sincere, if naive. He was less generous about the three men, a fast-talking Harlem black who called himself Chairman Mo, a bitter West Virginia hillbilly, and a cold-eyed Chicago hustler. For all their talk of revolution, he thought those three were passionately concerned with protecting the status quo, wherein four guilt-ridden ex-debutantes were providing them with money, drugs, housing, and wall-to-wall sex.

Turk plunged into his role. He tripped on LSD with his new friends. He joined in some remarkable sexual acrobatics. He woke in the night screaming "Kill the Gooks." He even proved his revolutionary mettle by blowing up a mailbox on Delancey Street. That blow against the empire, plus a new supply of LSD, inspired plans for even bolder military action.

The most radical of the girls, a willowy Vassar dropout named Chloe, had dreams of fire-bombing President Nixon's limousine during his upcoming trip to the UN. Turk dutifully constructed a bomb, and the group drove one Sunday afternoon to some woods near Scarsdale to test the weapon, which was indeed awesome.

As the end of the charade grew near, Turk was not without regret. He had grown fond of Melanie, who once tearfully confessed to him a bourgeois yen for marriage and children, and he felt a certain pity for the other women. He knew, far better than they, how monstrous the war in Vietnam was; it had killed his friends over there and it had driven these innocents half mad at home. Still, they were plotting to kill the President, and such fantasies could not be tolerated, however high-minded the intent or inept the execution.

The joint FBI-NYCPD raid on the loft was, as Turk had feared, a fiasco. The raiders were late, loud, and disorganized. Dawson, the hillbilly, managed to scuttle across the rooftops and escape. It was only when the others were being led away that they realized Turk was allied with the lawmen, not with them. "Filthy scum!" Melanie snarled, head high.

The plotters were sent to prison, despite the best efforts of some of America's most expensive lawyers. Turk returned to Washington and a plum assignment on the White House detail. He bought a Corvette and a house in Arlington, and was considering marriage with a long-legged Pan Am stewardess named Sandi when one morning his doorbell rang.

"Who is it?" he yelled.

"Western Union."

The twang should have alerted him, but Sandi was on a flight to Tokyo and he was worried about her. He opened his door.

He caught only a glimpse of the rodent-like West Virginia visage before the acid burned into his eyes.

"Death to pigs!" the hillbilly howled, and made the mistake of pausing to savor his revenge.

It was a fatal mistake.

Pain such as Turk had never imagined scalded his sightless eyes, exploded in his reeling brain, and still he staggered forward, caught his attacker in an iron grip, and proceeded to strangle him dead on the front lawn as neighborhood children looked on in awe.

Sandi nursed him for three months, but eventually she left, not because he was blind, but because he was so angry. He didn't blame her.

He might have retired with full pension but retirement was no longer his goal. The Secret Service owed him something more, revenge. He demanded an office and a secretary. His superiors had no wish for a blind agent, but Turk was not an easy man to refuse. His case had been greatly publicized. Moreover, the concept of "rights for the handicapped" was emerging in Washington. Reluctantly, they gave Turk what he asked for, thinking they could ease him out later.

Day after day, Turk Kellerman sat in his tiny, windowless office being read to by shifts of secretaries. They read him newspapers and magazines, particularly crime reports and political news, as well as internal Secret Service and FBI reports, congressional testimony, medical journals, detective novels and "thrillers," books on behavioral science and psychosis, everything.

Not many people visited Turk at first, because he refused to wear dark glasses and his scarred face took some getting used to. But in time his colleagues came to realize that he was making himself the best single source of crime-related information in Washington, a human computer. Did you want to know the whereabouts of Lee Harvey Oswald's brother? Or the best source of Ruger mini-14 machine guns in Houston? Or the identity of the biggest drug dealer in Seattle? You could seek answers through official channels, but nine times out of ten Turk Kellerman was faster.

A year or so after he was blinded, one of the last great antiwar rallies was held in Washington. Amid the confusion an explosion rocked the office of a Southern senator, maiming a secretary. As soon as Turk heard of the blast he began calling other Southern senators, warning them not to open their mail.

By the day's end, four other letter bombs had been found. One was atop a senator's desk, minutes short of being opened by his own hand. Turk's quick action was the result of both research and intuition. He had for some time feared that American terrorists would imitate the letter bombs that were being used with such lethal skill in Europe. When he heard of the first explosion, in the office of an Alabama senator, he realized he was one of the Southerners who had filibustered against a "Black Pride" congressional resolution. That fact, plus the presence of dozens of black radicals in Washington, had been cause enough for Turk to sound the alarm.

It happened that the South Carolina senator who had

come so close to destruction was the chairman of the sub-committee that approved the Secret Service's budget. Thanks to his generous patronage, Turk was awarded a bigger office, more secretaries, and the title of Assistant Director for Protective Research and Analysis. He was, as much as any man in Washington's vast bureaucracy, set for life.

By then, Turk believed that his blindness had uniquely equipped him to protect America's presidents. His colleagues with 20/20 vision kept their eyes fixed relentlessly on the past. Sightless, he could look into the future. "Who wants to kill this President and how would they go about it?" That was the question, year after year, and Turk was sure that he could do as much to answer it as any man in the world. Time after time, in the years ahead, he was proved right. His warnings saved Jimmy Carter from a crazed PLO assassin and Ronald Reagan from a plot spawned by a disillusioned John Birch cell. By the 1980s Turk was, in the unsentimental world of law enforcement, a legend.

His personal life, too, prospered. For some years he slept with various of the adoring young women who read to him, as well as receiving discreet weekly visits from Sandi, now the wife of a Washington surgeon. Then one day he received a quite unexpected letter from Melanie saying that she was out of prison, working in Washington, and would like to see him. It crossed his mind that her motive might be revenge but he shrugged that aside.

The first thing he noted, when she entered his office, was that she didn't gasp. Most women did, the first time.

"Hello, Turk," she said, from the doorway.

"Sit down, Melanie," he said gruffly. "How was prison?"

"A lot like Vassar, except the food was better."

He felt her come toward him. He waited, wondering if she had a knife. It would serve him right, for his lapse into sentimentality.

It was not a knife, but a gentle hand that touched his ruined face. "Poor Turk," she said.

He stroked her hand, her face. Her cheekbones were as elegant as ever.

"I'm not much to look at," he said.

"You have such dignity," she told him.

They talked all afternoon; she had come to Washington to work for prisoners' rights. That night he found she had lost none of her sexual zest. "Making up for lost time," she called it. In time they were married and became the parents of twin girls.

All of which, if it made Turk Kellerman more inwardly serene, did nothing to lessen the scorn with which he treated young agents. Jeff Winnick groaned when he received a summons to Turk's office early that summer. Jeff was an earnest, uncomplicated young man, and he always felt helpless when confronted with the razor-sharp blade of Turk's sarcasm.

When Jeff arrived, the blind agent was sitting with his feet up on his desk, listening to a pony-tailed secretary read from a novel called *The Tears of Autumn*.

"Okay, doll, that's enough," Turk growled. "Sit down, Winnick."

Jeff sat.

"I hear Jenna got away from you the other day," Turk began.

Jeff stiffened, ready for the worst. "How'd you hear that?" he replied.

"Did she?"

"She slipped away from us and drove out to spend Sunday with a friend in the country."

"And you covered for her," Turk said.

"I didn't report it."

"Why not?"

"You know why not. The director would terminate her protection. He's threatened it once. At best there'd be a stink and at worst she'd be in real danger."

"You're sweet on her, aren't you?"

"I like her. I worry about her."

"Like her? You've dated her, in violation of regulations."

"It wasn't a date. She was going to a dangerous bar by herself so I went with her. It was protection."

Turk snorted in disbelief. "Who was it she went to see the Sunday she got loose?"

"Matt Boyle, the media guy who used to work for Webster. He lives out in Virginia."

"She banging him?"

"Dammit, she spent the *day* with him. They went on a *picnic* with his *son*."

Turk flashed a nasty smile. "Assume nothing, especially where sex is concerned."

"Thanks for the advice," Jeff said.

Turk leaned forward, scowling mightily. "On the sixth of this month, according to your daily log, you and Jenna drove from the EOB to a locksmith shop on Pennsylvania Avenue. Correct?"

Jeff was stunned. Did the man know everything? "That's right," he said. "She wanted to get a key copied."

"Why? What was the rush?"

"She wouldn't say."

"What did the key look like?"

"I didn't *see* it. I waited in the car."

"Was she upset?"

"Impatient. Nervous. In a hurry."

"Winnick, wouldn't you say it was unusual for Jenna to drop everything and rush to a locksmith's shop? What's the emergency? She can't get into her desk? The VP can't get into his liquor closet? No—she's *got* the key, but she wants *another* one. What for, you idiot?"

"I don't know," Jeff muttered.

"Did it ever occur to you that she'd swiped somebody's key and wanted to get a copy before they found it out?"

Jeff threw up his hands. "Look, if it's important I could press her. Or I could talk to the locksmith."

When Kellerman grinned, Jeff knew something bad was coming.

"Before you dash off," Turk said, "read this."

He nudged a paper across the desk. He had piles of them, neatly arranged. Jeff picked it up warily. A brief newspaper clipping related the death of Nicholas Calvari, locksmith.

"Oh my God," Jeff moaned.

Kellerman's sightless eyes were fixed upon him. "Your

report says you left the shop at 10:45. Someone found him at 11:02."

"They didn't catch anyone?"

"No leads, nothing. Just another senseless crime."

Jeff caught the sarcasm. "What do you mean?"

"I mean this stinks. Jenna Webster makes a mysterious visit to a locksmith and five minutes later he gets his brains beat in. Just a coincidence? Or was somebody after that key? Or after Jenna? You want to know something, Winnick?"

"What?"

"I don't believe in coincidences any more. Here's another senseless crime. I doubt if even you missed this one."

He took another clipping from the pile, this one on the murder of Bernie O'Toole.

"Sure, I remember it," Jeff said. "But what's the connection?"

"That's the question. A jogger who happens to be a whistle-blower gets his guts spilled by somebody who steals his watch. A locksmith who happens to copy a key for Jenna Webster gets his head banged in. Two random killings, three months and thirty miles apart."

"I don't see the tie-in," Jeff said.

"The tie-in is politics. I've got a theory. Washington's got a reputation for street crime, right? So say you want to get rid of a senator or a Supreme Court Justice, what do you do? Put a bomb in his car? Poison him? Not if you've got the sense God gave a flea. You just shoot him outside his house with a Saturday Night Special, then everybody says, 'Oh, horrors, another mugging!' Mugging my ass. I have a list of six unsolved murders in this city—muggings they said—that I know damn well were political. Assassinations!"

"You still haven't shown me a tie-in," Jeff said stubbornly.

Kellerman turned his ravaged face upward, imploring the heavens. "Tell me about your trip to the locksmith."

"She ran out of the Vice President's office. I caught up with her at her car."

"Did she know where she was going?"

"No. She asked me where a locksmith was. I told her to head toward Georgetown."

"Therefore, no one could have known in advance where she was headed. If anyone was after her, they had to follow you."

"That's impossible."

"Is it? Maybe somebody in the office saw the key missing, and followed her out, followed you all the way to the locksmith's shop, then went in after you left to quiz the old man."

"And then killed him? Somebody from the Vice President's office? Is that what you're saying?"

Turk chewed his cigar. "I'm saying that if you're so damn concerned about Miss Jenna Webster's well-being, you might get off your ass and start asking questions. This stinks to high heaven!"

Elsewhere, the star first baseman of the Harmony Eagles was having a rotten afternoon.

Zeb popped up his first time at bat and struck out with two men on his next time up. By then the Eagles were trailing the still-hated Stumptown Tigers, 6–2, in the Pee Wee division's championship game.

The game was being played on the Harmony field. Boyle, drafted to umpire, was stationed near first base, where he could sometimes whisper encouragement to his crestfallen son.

"Come on, hang tough," Boyle urged, as the Eagles took the field in the fifth.

"We can't win," Zeb said glumly. "We're too far behind."

"Sure you can," Boyle insisted. "Just one big inning. Show some hustle."

As if on cue, a grounder came shooting at Zeb—and shot between his legs for a double, scoring another run for the rampaging Tigers. Groans went up along the first-base line, where forty-odd Harmony fans were cheering their offspring at every opportunity.

Until now, it had been a great year for Zeb and the Eagles. After their opening-game loss, the Eagles had gone undefeated, including a revenge victory over Stumptown. The two teams tied for first place in the regular season, setting up this playoff for the Pee Wee championship of western Loudoun County.

In the bottom of the fifth, trailing by five, the Eagles loaded the bases with two out. The next batter, a pig-tailed charmer named Emily who could barely raise the bat from her shoulder, took two strikes, then chopped a slow roller to the mound. The Tigers' pitcher raced in, their catcher lumbered out—and to the delight of the Harmony fans, the two collided. The catcher struggled to his feet, grabbed the ball, and threw to first—but the ball sailed into right field. The right fielder's thoughts were elsewhere and the ball rolled past him to vanish in high weeds.

"Run, Emily, run!" chanted the Harmony fans, and a skeptical Emily was persuaded to circle the bases, whereupon the Eagles trailed only 7–6.

They held the Tigers scoreless in the top of the sixth and came to bat still behind by one. Two hits, two quick outs, and Zeb marched to the plate. By Boyle's calculations, his son was batting over .400 for the season, but he was zip for two today. No matter—Zeb slapped the first pitch past the shortstop into left field. Two runs scored, and Zeb, amid delirious cheering, tried to stretch his hit to a double.

The throw dribbled in, Zeb slid for the bag, and Boyle jerked his right thumb skyward. "Out!"

The hometown fans groaned. Zeb sprang to his feet. "I was safe a mile."

"You're out, son," Boyle said, and turned away.

In truth, the play had been close, and Boyle had lacked the audacity, or courage, to award the call to his son.

The Tigers came to bat in the top of the seventh, now down by one. They quickly loaded the bases with none out, and their star slugger, a lad with the swagger of a young Ty Cobb, stepped to the plate.

Over at first, Zeb Boyle grumbled to his father, "I was *safe!*"

"Play the game," Boyle shot back.

The Harmony fans watched joylessly as the young slugger blasted the first pitch over the left field fence—foul by inches.

Three balls followed, then another strike. With the Tiger fans howling for blood, the boy knocked a looping fly ball that sailed toward shallow right field. The runners set off at the crack of the bat, but Zeb was running too. He raced with all his might toward the outfield and at the last moment threw himself headlong and speared the ball before he crashed to the ground.

The base runners, blissfully ignorant that the ball had been caught, raced for the plate, as their frantic coaches implored them to get back. By then, Zeb had sprinted back to first base for the second out. He looked to second, but the second baseman was frozen, far out of position, seemingly hypnotized by this dramatic turn of events.

Zeb did the only thing he could: He dashed toward second just as the Tiger runner was charging toward it from the opposite direction. There was a mighty collision, a cloud of dust, then umpire Boyle roared "Out!"

The Harmony fans went wild. Zeb's triple play had nailed down the championship. His teammates lifted him to their shoulders, chanting "We're number one!" Players and parents piled in pickup trucks, staged an impromptu parade through Harmony's sleepy streets, and wound up at the coach's house for a swim and a cookout. Boyle basked in his son's reflected glory. After a couple of beers, he even had a few kind words for the Reverend Frye, the local representative of the Baptist religion, with whom he'd been at odds ever since the Reverend learned that his son had been exposed to naked females in *Playboy* at Boyle's house, courtesy of Zeb.

On the drive home, long past dark, Boyle could not resist moralizing: "Zeb, remember in the middle of the game, when you said you'd lost it? Well, you hadn't. You just had to keep fighting."

The young hero was having none of it. "Remember when you called me out at second?" he said fiercely. "Well, I was safe."

Boyle let it pass. A boy who could make an unassisted triple play deserved special consideration.

18

"I've got to talk to you."

"Why?"

"Not here."

"What is it?"

"Jenna, will you come on?"

Jeff hustled her out of the Vice President's office, out into the sudden heat of Pennsylvania Avenue.

"What do you want?" she demanded.

"To talk," Jeff said. "Privately."

He guided them up Seventeenth to H Street. Sometimes people gawked at Jenna, or smiled and waved. Sometimes she smiled back. She didn't know about the other agent, a friend of Jeff's, who was trailing behind them.

Jeff took them to the Class Reunion, a hangout of reporters and White House types. Jenna had first gone there with Matt Boyle, for whom long, liquid lunches at the Reunion had been an occupational hazard. The restaurant had closed once, then miraculously reopened, by popular demand. Jenna loved the place, so dark and crowded, with its larger-than-life photographs on the wall of Betty and Gerald Ford

cutting their wedding cake, of a solemn young Jimmy Carter
in his Naval Academy uniform, of a gloating Lyndon Johnson and an uneasy Hubert Humphrey on horseback at the
LBJ ranch, of a boyish Ronald Reagan in *Hellcats of the
Navy*. Sometimes Jenna wondered if those pictures were
supposed to be affectionate or satirical. Certainly some of
the most cynical men and women in America smiled at
them each day. But she liked to think they were affectionate,
a kind of White House family scrapbook. She liked to think
that even on the battlefield of Washington there came a
time, after enough whiskey had been drunk, or enough
years flown by, when everyone forgave everything, as families must.

It was three-thirty and only the hard core of the luncheon
crowd remained. Jenna winked at a Boston *Globe* reporter
with a walrus moustache who was knocking down Stingers
with a glassy-eyed congressman. Then she glared at Jeff.
"What's this all about?" she demanded.

He didn't speak until the waiter had brought their coffee.
"Do you remember the day I drove you to the locksmith
shop?" he said.

"What about it?"

"Why did you go there?"

"I went there to get a *key* made."

"What key? What for?"

"Why are you asking me these obnoxious questions?"

He seized her slender wrist. "Jenna, answer me!"

"You let go of me this instant!"

"All right," he said angrily, "but you take a look at this."
He slapped the Calvari clipping onto the table.

Jenna went pale as she read. "That poor man," she whispered.

"It happened just after we left," he said urgently. "I've got
to know if there was any connection. Whose key was it?
What were you doing? Could someone have been following
you?"

Jenna was sick of being bullied and sicker of her own
foolishness. To admit she had stolen the key would be bad
enough, even without Jeff trying to involve her in a murder.

She lifted her proud, delicate chin. "I needed an extra key to my apartment," she declared. "It couldn't possibly have been connected to that poor man's death."

"Jenna, for God's sake, tell me the truth!"

"Are you calling me a liar?"

"Yes, a lousy one."

"I hate you," she cried and rushed out the door.

Jeff, defeated, trailed after her. Across the street, his friend gestured. This time, at least, they hadn't been followed.

That evening, the first time Jenna called and got Boyle's answering machine, she politely left her name and asked him to call. Then she paced about her apartment for a half hour, growing more frenzied, thinking she might go crazy. She had to talk to someone and Matt was the best person. He knew Washington and he knew politics and he could make sense, if anyone could, out of this whole insane mess.

The trouble was, she wasn't sure if something terrible was happening, or if she was just being paranoid. What did she really know? That she was suspicious of the Vice President, for no very good reason except those mysterious calls he kept getting. And one day she had stolen a key from the Vice President and taken it to a locksmith for a copy and minutes later the locksmith had been murdered. Maybe it was crazy to see some dark plot there, but if it was, why was Jeff quizzing her about it? The more she thought about it the more anguished she became. When she called and got Matt's answering machine a second time, she found herself screaming.

"Matt, I've got to talk to you! Something terrible has happened. I'm afraid."

She seized control of herself. "If you call and I'm not here, it means I'm driving out to see you."

Jenna put down the phone. If she could slip past the Secret Service she could spend a quiet evening with Matt and Zeb. Matt had said something about a baseball game, probably that was where they were.

It was sheer chance that Charlie intercepted Jenna's call so quickly. He had been up at the mansion listening to Serena orate about her political plans. The prospect of power obsessed her; she couldn't stop talking about all she would achieve once Remington was in the White House. She would defeat the revolutionaries in Central America, of course, a few Marine divisions could handle that, and that victory would be only a prelude to action against Castro's Cuba. "We have the might," she proclaimed. "All that is lacking is the will!"

China was much on her mind, too, for she was convinced that the Chinese masses were poised to rise up against their Communist rulers. Charlie, it happened, had once spent several weeks in China as a military adviser to those tough old rulers, and he had detected no revolutionary stirrings, but Serena would not listen to him. Then she started asking him what he would do after he finished the Webster assignment. Charlie knew exactly what he was going to do: buy himself a Morgan Out-Islander, the world's finest sailboat, and set sail for the South Pacific. His was a high-risk profession and he intended to retire while he still had his health. But he wasn't prepared to tell Serena his plans, not yet.

When she kept on about it, Charlie grew annoyed. Serena had her charms but she didn't own him. He rose to his feet. "I think I'll stroll down to the cabin," he announced.

"Why? It's almost time for dinner."

"Some things to check, luv. Business."

He left her on the terrace and marched across the long, verdant lawn that sloped gently toward the Potomac. His cabin was down there, nestled in a grove of oak trees. The cabin had been restored to his specifications soon after he went to work for Serena. It might still appear rustic from the outside, but inside could be found some of the world's most modern weapons and communications equipment. Charlie opened the door, flipped on the light, and unlocked a steel cabinet that contained state-of-the-art radio equipment. Charlie had wiretaps on dozens of phones throughout the Washington area. In the past, to overhear wiretapped conversations, it had been necessary to venture very near the tapped lines and thus risk exposure. No more. The latest silicon superchips had made possible microelectronic taps no bigger than a thumbtack that would transmit every conversation from a given telephone or room to this isolated cabin, where they were recorded and awaited Charlie's pleasure. Checking the mail, he called it.

Thus it happened, because Serena had been boring him, that he chanced to hear Jenna Webster's anguished call to Matt Boyle not ten minutes after she placed it.

"Matt, I've got to talk to you. Something terrible has happened. I'm afraid." Then, moments later, she said she might drive out to see Boyle.

Jenna's words hit Charlie like an electric jolt. The girl had been suspicious of Remington before, but now she was calling a friend in hysterics, saying something terrible had happened, that she was afraid. What could have caused her panic? Charlie couldn't read her mind, but he thought he knew; he had a sixth sense about people that had saved him more than once. Jenna, he told himself, had somehow made the connection between her trip to the locksmith and the locksmith's death. How, he did not know, but he could imagine nothing else that might have caused her hysteria.

Charlie cursed bitterly. He was only weeks, perhaps days, from eliminating Webster—as soon as the damned weapon was ready. He couldn't let Jenna tell Boyle what she suspected, because he would surely tell her to go straight to the Secret Service or the FBI.

He could eliminate her, of course, but that would only create other problems. Charlie picked up his telephone, buzzed the mansion, and told the butler to tell Serena that he would be unable to dine. Then he walked to a nearby barn, and climbed into an anonymous Chevrolet. As he eased out the gate of River Crest Farm, a plan was forming in his mind.

Jenna felt better when she turned off the highway onto the narrow, winding road that led to Matt's little village. She had the top down and she savored the aroma of dogwood and honeysuckle in the night air, the magic of old barns aglow in the moonlight. Out here, the world seemed so tranquil, so timeless, that it was hard for her even to remember what fears, what wild imaginings had brought her speeding into the night. Probably she and Matt would have a drink and she'd tell him her story and they'd have a good laugh at her runaway imagination.

What she needed to do, Jenna abruptly decided, was to get out of Washington. Politics drove people crazy; they started thinking there was no life beyond the Beltway. She could quit her job with the Vice President and get one . . . where? Maybe with the Peace Corps. That would be fun. See the world. She smiled as she imagined the rich plains of Africa, tiny villages in the Andes . . . and then she saw the sign that said Harmony was two miles ahead and she suddenly asked herself, "What about Matt?" What indeed? Was this old friendship becoming something different? Or was that another of her wild imaginings? All she knew was that he was the most understanding friend she had and she wanted desperately to see him.

The big car came out of nowhere, its lights blinding her. It started to pass her on the narrow, winding road, but far too close, and she hit her brakes and swerved into the weeds beside the road. Jenna screamed as her tiny Morgan bounced into a shallow ditch and her head banged the steering wheel.

She was dazed, but when she saw the tall man looming out of the darkness she cried, "What's the matter with you? Are you crazy?"

A hand shot out. A cloth, soaked in a vile-smelling chemical, covered her face. As Jenna struggled, thinking for an instant of those fine, brave Secret Service men she'd eluded, she heard her attacker murmur, "No, dear, not crazy at all."

19

On Friday night, when Boyle and Zeb got home from celebrating the Eagles' great victory, Boyle was too tired to check his telephone messages, and when he got up Saturday morning he decided to hell with them. It was a gorgeous June weekend and he would shut out the world's demands and instead enjoy his son. They camped out on Saturday night and on Sunday treated themselves to a VCR triple-feature of *The Gold Rush* (Boyle's selection), *Raiders of the Lost Ark* (a joint favorite), and *Friday the 13th, Part II* (Zeb's choice, despite paternal grumbling).

Thus, it was Monday morning before Boyle checked his answering machine to see what callers wanted his time, advice, company, or money. He smiled as he listened to Jenna's first call—"Matt, it's me, please give me a call at home"—and then he was stunned, moments later, to hear her second—that she was afraid, that something terrible was happening, that she might drive out to see him.

He called her office but she wasn't there, and he got no answer at her apartment. He called her office again and left word that she was to call the moment she arrived. Boyle was worried but he didn't want to panic. She might have gone shopping or to the doctor or something, and not told her secretary. He'd give her another hour or two before he sounded the alarm.

He forced himself to return to his work. He'd been struggling for weeks with a chapter that used two campaigns he'd directed to dramatize how the media could be used to manipulate public opinion.

In the first campaign, his client had been an Alabama judge named Clearwater Todd who possessed a magnificent head of hair, the attention span of a squirrel, and an accent so thick that it was incomprehensible to anyone not a second-generation Alabaman. Boyle communicated with him by scribbled notes and sign language. Judge Todd was running for governor against the state treasurer, Harriet Love, who was honest, intelligent, happily married, and respected by all. She might have been elected in a landslide except for the unfortunate fact of her sex.

Judge Todd, at the outset, gallantly declared that he had no intention of using "Miss Harriet's gender" against her. He changed his tune, however, when the polls came in showing him ten points behind Miss Harriet. "Mistah Boyle, suh, if Ah lose this heah election to a woman, Ah'll hafta leave Alabam'," he wailed.

Boyle, inspired by a night's drinking with some bloodthirsty Birmingham lawyers, proceeded to develop what became known as "the World War III spots." Seizing on the indisputable fact that the governor was the Commander-in-Chief of the state's National Guard, Boyle filmed Judge Todd riding in tanks, grinning from the cockpit of a jet fighter, and otherwise committing every martial act possible, short of leading a raid on Mississippi. All the while, of course, the good judge was muttering gravely about the governor's solemn duties as "Commander-in-Chief."

Whether Judge Todd expected the Yankees, the Mexicans, the Russians, or the Black Liberation Army to invade Alabama was left unclear, but the World War III spots were a stunning success. From ten points behind, the Judge leaped to ten points ahead. The beauty of Boyle's strategy was there was nothing Miss Harriet could do to rebut it. She'd have looked silly trying to climb aboard a tank. She couldn't invent a military record. She couldn't *deny* the heroic role of the National Guard.

Boyle's World War III spots had simultaneously tapped two of Dixie's most potent emotions, militarism and sexism, and thereby sent Miss Harriet's campaign into a total and irreversible tailspin.

One night Boyle told Cara of his rout of Miss Harriet. Instead of praising his genius, she called him a "sexist skunk" and banished him to the guest room. In his gloom, Boyle began to see that the World War III spots had given him more power than he wanted, more than any one should have. The power had seemed wonderful at first. It was like inventing the ultimate weapon. But in time it seemed terrible too. Why should he, an outsider, a mercenary, have the power to elect Alabama's governor? His Alabama victory was, Boyle realized later, the beginning of his disillusionment.

The next year he ran a campaign for a woman; that was Boyle's second case history.

She was Barbara (Battling Babs) O'Brien and an inscrutable fate had made her the mayor of a once-proud American city. During her first term, Babs, who drank a bit, conducted herself in a manner that might at best be called inane and at worst psychotic. She was surrounded by crooks and incompetents whose highest goal in life was to keep themselves feeding at the public trough.

Boyle's job: Get this woman reelected.

He took the assignment reluctantly, not so much because Babs was an idiot, as because he thought her case was hopeless. Still, she offered him a lot of money, and he was intrigued by the challenge.

After taking some polls, Boyle met with his candidate and her sullen advisers and told her, "Madam Mayor, barring a miracle, you'll lose this election badly. You're a laughingstock. I think you should seriously consider not running again."

At that, Battling Babs threw an ashtray at him, her entourage howling its approval. As Boyle sought to escape, she suddenly locked him in her bony embrace and began to sob that only he could save her. Boyle used his advantage to get his fee up front, plus Babs's written agreement not to open her mouth in public unless he was first consulted.

With Boyle guiding her, coaching her, and approving every word she uttered, Babs held four news conferences in a month and not once did she make a fool of herself. The public was stunned. The polls got better.

Boyle could clean up Babs's election-year act, but he couldn't undo her bizarre record from years past. Nor did he try. One of his rules was "Don't change the candidate, change the context." Did Babs have a temper? Had she once slugged an elderly city councilman? Had she once tried to run over a black traffic cop who stopped her for speeding? Yes, yes, yes—but, in the world according to Boyle, that didn't make her nuts, it made her "feisty," "a fighter." His focus groups revealed that many people secretly admired Babs; she acted out their fantasies. The need was to redefine reality so that Babs's madness became her strength. The campaign slogan he chose for her was "O'Brien—A Fighter in Your Corner!" One TV spot showed an undecided housewife, musing, "I know she's hot-tempered . . . but, darn it . . . SHE'S GOT GUTS!"

Boyle's strategy worked to perfection. By muzzling Babs, by redefining her not as a hothead but as a fighter, he brought her from behind to a narrow victory.

Such was Boyle's record in two of his more celebrated campaigns; a record that made him much in demand among America's politicians. *Newsweek* called him a "miracle-worker" and his cronies at the Class Reunion loved to linger over his tales of Battling Babs. The trouble was, he had a conscience.

He knew all the rationalizations. He could say that his TV spots, however slick, were only another way that candidates put themselves in the best possible light, as candidates had always done. But Boyle increasingly believed that television was to politics what nuclear weapons were to warfare, a quantum leap, one against which there was truly no defense.

With enough money for television you could enter people's homes, invade their minds, and in endless subtle ways play upon their innocence.

It was a fascinating game, but only so long as you saw it as a game. The problems started when you started to think seriously about some of the clowns who were getting elected, and when you began to think that, in so many cases, television was being used to beguile people into voting against their own best interests. At that point, democracy became a sham and the image-maker was a hired gun.

Boyle thought the process was wrong. It was time to change the rules of the game, to stop the feel-good, fairy-tale spots, to demand that the candidates appear in person in their ads, to limit the amount of money spent on television.

Boyle's book would win him invitations to appear on "Good Morning America" and "Meet the Press" and other shows with an audience of millions. He was ready to crusade for new laws covering political TV ads, to testify before congressional committees, to go all the way, like an ex-drunk advocating Prohibition.

Boyle reforms! His old cronies would get a laugh out of that, but he didn't care. Boyle believed in Big Brother. Like Pogo, he had seen the enemy and it was us.

He wrote and rewrote all afternoon. He wished he could tell about the time Battling Babs, in her cups, had made a pass at him—he would sooner have had sex with a rattlesnake.

He was smiling at the vagaries of human nature when the phone rang. Hoping it was Jenna, he grabbed it anxiously.

"Mr. Boyle? The White House calling. One moment for Mrs. Webster."

Boyle was confused, until he realized it was Jenna's mother calling.

"Matt? It's Doris."

"Yes, Doris. How are . . . ?"

"Matt, you've got to help me. I don't know who else to ask."

"What's wrong?"

"It's Jenna. She's . . ."

Her voice broke. Boyle shut his eyes. All he could think was, Please God, no more tragedies.

"What *is* it, Doris?"

"Jenna's gone," the President's wife cried. "She's *vanished!*"

She broke into tears.

PART II

Looking for Jenna

20

One sun-drenched Sunday in the autumn of 1946 a stranger walked unannounced into Spearfish, South Dakota. He was a brawny, red-haired fellow in dungarees and a plaid shirt, the stuff of legend from the first.

Straight as an arrow he made his way to the Spearfish Baptist Church, interrupting the Rev. Ellerby's pieties to inform the startled congregation, "Brothers and sisters, I'm Jamie Boyle, a sinner come to repent!"

Here was drama such as Spearfish had rarely seen. "I'm out to make a new life," the stranger declared. "I need your help—and God's."

Having confessed himself a sinner, Jamie Boyle never got around to enumerating the specifics, so busy were Spearfish's Baptists in grasping this Heaven-sent opportunity for Christian charity.

"Welcome, Brother!" boomed the Rev. Ellerby.

"He's hungry," piped a deacon's wife.

"He's cute," murmured numerous deacons' daughters.

Soon the battle was on to see which family would minister to the mysterious stranger.

The prize went to Brother Henry Hardcastle, the chairman of the board of deacons, or rather to his wife and daughter. By midafternoon they had blessed Jamie Boyle with a home-cooked meal, a hot bath, clean clothes, and their guest room with its grand view south to the Black Hills National Forest.

The guest was up early the next morning, mowing the Hardcastles' lawn, cleaning their gutters, and making plans to paint the barn. His work on the barn, carried out with speed and skill, quickly won Boyle other assignments as a painter. He soon earned enough money to buy a second-hand Dodge and, over the protests of the Hardcastle women, particularly daughter Sarah, to move into a furnished room above the Busy Bee Bakery.

Boyle bought a rundown old house on the outskirts of Spearfish, fixed it up, and sold it for a tidy profit. That process was repeated many times over and the newcomer prospered in the postwar boom.

His fortune made, the ambitious Boyle wooed and won gentle Sarah Hardcastle, recently returned home from the University of South Dakota to teach the second grade and to find a husband. The latter was no simple matter, for Spearfish's most promising young men were drawn to the bright lights of Rapid City or even to such distant Babylons as Minneapolis and Chicago. Jamie Boyle, a hardworking, God-fearing man who intended to stick with Spearfish, was considered a suitable match for the winsome belle.

Still, despite Jamie's success, or perhaps because of it, he had his critics. His past, they pointed out, was veiled in mystery. He sometimes dropped vague hints of a boyhood in Boston, and of wartime service in the Pacific, but Jamie had a beguiling way, when details were sought, of winking and changing the subject.

Rumors soon abounded as to the furies that had driven Jamie Boyle (if that was indeed his true name) to the Spearfish Baptist Church that fateful Sunday morning. The generally accepted version was that Jamie had shot two men in a Boston fleshpot where women danced naked for money, then fled to Spearfish one jump ahead of the law.

Jamie Boyle, neither deaf nor dumb, found the rumors amusing but irrelevant. He was busy in those days, making money in real estate, dabbling in Republican politics, and raising a family. When his and Sarah's first child was born, the boy was christened Matthew Timothy Boyle, and everyone agreed that with his blue eyes and reddish hank of hair, he was the very image of his father.

Matt Boyle did not grow up, however, to be the image of his father. Jamie was an unbounded optimist, but Matt was haunted by a sense of unreality, of the fragility of things. Raised in comfort, he grew up hearing schoolyard taunts about his father: that he had killed two men, that he was secretly a Roman Catholic, that he had deserted from the army, that the FBI would someday haul him off to justice. For years, Matt lived in fear of the FBI's world-shattering knock at the door. No matter what you had, the boy believed, you could lose it in an instant.

He took refuge in books, devouring the tales of Twain, Poe, O. Henry, Tarkington, and Wilde. He thrilled to stories of courage, of loyalty, of sacrifice, and he loved to be surprised, confounded, at a tale's end. He didn't know much about "literature" but he adored drama, the shivers you got from a scary story, and the different, ennobling kind of tingle that came with a tale of heroism. It cannot have been pure coincidence that, later in life, Boyle became a storyteller himself. His medium was not the printed page but the television film. His heroes were his candidates, and he invented gripping, sometimes brilliant, vignettes in which they proved to be as wise and brave as the heroes of his boyhood books. It did not bother him, at least at first, that his candidates were not in reality always as good and true as his films suggested. The story was what mattered.

Matt went "east" to the University of Wisconsin, arriving in the heyday of long hair, sexual liberation, drug use, rock-and-roll, and antiwar protest. Matt joined in the fun, but with a certain reluctance. He felt silly with his hair down to his shoulders, he liked to concentrate on one girl, and he preferred beer to marijuana and jazz to the Rolling Stones. Moreover, although he hated the war in Vietnam, he doubted that the way to end it was to get stoned and stumble down Fraternity Row chanting "One two three four, we don't want your lousy war."

When Matt was a sophomore one of his professors ran as an antiwar candidate for Congress and he helped in the campaign. The professor lost but Matt was bitten by the political bug. More campaigns followed, until he emerged in 1972 as the Wisconsin coordinator of George McGovern's antiwar campaign for President.

McGovern was trounced and Boyle did not relish the experience. He decided that McGovern was a good man, but too liberal and too lacking in guile. Boyle resolved that his next candidate would not suffer from those disabilities. Thus, in 1975, when Boyle was out of law school and setting up his practice in Spearfish, he welcomed the advances of Jimmy Carter, a candidate with a glint in his eye and an elastic view of reality. Matt signed on with Carter early, gained the candidate's ear, and became a valued adviser on Plains States strategy.

The campaign was insane but it was an insanity Boyle understood. He was less emotionally involved than the Georgians (who were, in their hearts, refighting the Civil War) and he was therefore more objective, even more wise. He slogged through the madness like the only sober soul at a crazed bacchanal, and in the process he earned a reputation, a White House job, and even the first hints of a legend.

It was during the Carter campaign that Boyle's first marriage exploded. He had married Nadine in law school. She was a doctor's daughter, a cheerleader, a knockout. In the first flush of romance she'd been willing to follow Boyle back to Spearfish, but she grew increasingly bored there, particularly when he went chasing off with the Peanut Brigade. Boyle, for his part, was growing increasingly bored with Nadine. One weekend he arrived home worried and exhausted. The candidate was stumbling. The Georgia Mafia was blaming everyone but themselves.

The Carter campaign—or was it the candidate himself, ever smiling, serene, superior?—had driven Boyle to drink. The campaign plane, Peanut One, was a pressure cooker in

which candidate, staff, and media stewed, simmered, sometimes boiled over. When they escaped that airborne prison,
everyone went a little crazy. The candidate, it was said, took
his troubles to the Lord in prayer, but the rest of them
inclined toward hard liquor.

When Boyle arrived home that Saturday evening, he
downed some Johnny Walker, built a fire, downed more
Johnny Walker, put on a Billie Holiday album, and felt peace
engulfing him.

Then Nadine joined him.

Billie was singing "You Go to My Head."

Nadine started talking about a couple who'd moved in
down the street.

Boyle nodded gravely and kept listening to the music.

Nadine recited the biographies of the couple's several
children.

Boyle smiled falsely, his ears straining to hear Billie's
sweet music over his wife's inanities.

You go to my head, Billie sang, and her music did go to his
head, like wine, like love, like the dearest drug ever imagined, floating him away from the absurdities of politics and
the frustrations of marriage.

Nadine began talking about a new recipe for meat loaf.

With increasing difficulty, Boyle kept smiling and nodding.

She means well. She is a good woman. She is a great lay.

Nadine kept talking. Billie kept singing. Boyle kept smiling.

She wouldn't stop talking. Poor doomed Billie was pouring out her soul and Nadine the Homecoming Queen was
raving about instant mashed potatoes.

Suddenly Boyle sprang to his feet, wild-eyed, dangerous,
giving vent to frustrations that good-hearted Nadine would
never understand.

"DAMN YOU, SHUT UP! BILLIE HOLIDAY IS SING-
ING!"

His voice echoed for miles. Nadine, fearing for her safety,
sprinted from the house to take refuge with neighbors.

Boyle, unrepentant, started the record over.

He was not lonely for long.

The first time he visited Carter headquarters in Atlanta, a ripe Georgia peach told him, in her honeydripper drawl, "Sugahpie, ev'body's screwin' ev'body in this here campaign!" It was true, in more ways than one. Peanut One was a magic carpet, winging the saintly candidate and his sinful staff from city to city, day after day, and if a lad was so inclined he could assemble the jet-age equivalent of a girl in every port.

One Saturday night the circus was in Washington and Boyle, Harry, and some reporters were having a drink at Laredo, a noisy neo-hillbilly bar in Georgetown. Boyle, weary of political gossip, wandered to the jukebox, where a slender, sandy-haired woman in jeans and a cowboy shirt was playing Hank Williams and Ernest Tubb.

When the woman returned to the bar, Boyle took the stool beside her. She had a sleek profile, a bottle of Lone Star, and an air of total self-containment. Boyle was challenged.

"What's a nice girl like you doing in a dump like this?" he asked, being not perfectly sober.

The woman glanced at his image in the mirror behind the bar, a certain sparkle in her eyes. "I like the music," she said, with a telltale Texas twang.

"You alone?"

"Tryin' to be."

Boyle thought about that one. "You always dress like a cowgirl?" he said, blundering on.

"You always say dumb things to strangers?"

Boyle guessed it wasn't his night. "Excuse me," he said, and went to the men's room. When he returned she was still there. He climbed back on the stool. "My name's Matt Boyle," he said, "and I could waltz across Texas with you."

She favored him with a smile. "You like Ernest Tubb?"

"Ma'm, no one truly likes Western music who doesn't love Ernest Tubb," he replied.

"That's true," she said pensively.

"You from Texas?"

She nodded absently, as if the answer was self-evident, as indeed it was. "You?" she asked, with a flicker of interest.

"South Dakota." He never revealed the name of his hometown unless pressed. "But we always listened to the Opry on Saturday nights. That's how I know Ernest Tubb."

"Us too," she said. "I grew up in Pecos. My daddy's the vet there."

"What's your name?"

"Cara."

"Cara," he repeated. "What do you do, Cara?"

"For a livin', you mean?"

"Yes. For a living."

"I teach school."

"Like it?"

"Love it. Kids are nicer'n grown-ups. You a lawyer?"

Some instinct made him cautious. "Should I be?"

"I hate lawyers. My husband was a lawyer."

"I'm working in the Carter campaign," he confided.

She rolled her eyes.

"What're you, a Republican?" he protested.

"Mister, I'm a yellow-dog Democrat. I'll vote for that shifty-eyed prig of yours, but that doesn't mean I'll like it."

Boyle, who in his heart of hearts had begun to think of his candidate as a shifty-eyed prig, was awed by the woman's insight. Did all the world know? Just then, Harry came and seized him. "We've got a plane to catch, hoss," he raved. "Promises to keep and lies to tell before we sleep."

"Can I call you?" Boyle said to Cara.

"Call me what?"

Boyle was speechless. So many women had leaped into his bed that summer that he'd forgotten they could say no. Cara smiled at his befuddlement and touched his hand. "Most Saturday nights I'm right here," she said.

He returned to his magic carpet. The cities flew by and with them an endless parade of women, all fascinating at midnight, all forgotten by noon. But Cara stayed in his mind, like a Bob Wills tune, like an itch, like the right woman.

She was a type he knew and admired, what he called Tough Texas Ladies, TTLs. He'd spent time in Texas and he'd encountered plenty of classic Texas belles, girls who achieved stunning pinnacles of beauty, wealth, and blissful ignorance. But he'd also met, in the bars and barbecue joints of Houston and Austin, his first TTLs. They tended, like Cara, to be slender, rangy, small-breasted, shorthaired, taciturn, and utterly without pretense. They most often wore jeans, boots, and no makeup, seeing no reason to conceal their God-given freckles or hard-earned wrinkles. They were lean and mean, with sharp elbows and sharper minds. They thought men a necessary evil and were happiest in the company of other TTLs. They liked fishing, poker, cold Texas beer, Willie and Waylon, driving too fast with the top down, and sex at odd hours if they chanced upon a man who knew what he was doing. Boyle came to think of TTLs as throwbacks to the pioneer women who'd overcome drunken husbands and marauding Indians to tame a continent. They were rare gems, and Boyle, for all his failings, knew a gem when he saw one.

Three Saturdays later he rejoined her, same bar, same stool. For three hours they drank and talked and laughed and it was so easy. When he was leaving he told her he'd be spending the next week in Georgia.

"You ought to come down," he said, half-joking.

"Sounds like fun," she mused.

She met him in Atlanta and they drove down to Americus, where the Carter staff and the press corps were encamped at the Best Western. The fact that Cara moved in with Boyle in his little room overlooking the swimming pool caused little notice amid the chaos of the campaign. People were endlessly slipping in and out of other people's rooms. Now and then spouses arrived unexpectedly, causing confusion and/or violence. One celebrated TV correspondent was widely believed to have gone mad; he spent his days talking dirty to teenage girls and beating on the walls of the motel with a rubber hose. "Jimmy Carter did this to me," he would mutter darkly, his toupee slightly askew. Norman Mailer turned up that week, for a night of heroic drinking, and Ralph Nader and Warren Beatty and a woman who said she was the reincarnation of Marilyn Monroe and an ever-expanding army of crazies and conmen who, smelling a winner, sought Cabinet appointments or, failing that, to have their kinfolks sprung from jail.

"It's *bent*," Cara marveled. "It's crazier'n Texas. I love it."

She calmed him, gave him perspective. A chance remark of hers inspired Boyle to write one of Carter's best speeches of the campaign. When she said she had to leave, he begged her to stay, but school was starting and the kids in her class needed her or maybe she needed them.

After the election he moved in with her. She had a cottage on the outskirts of Harmony, the Virginia village where she taught. It was an hour's drive from the White House, and he had to leave at dawn to beat the rush-hour traffic, but he didn't care. As Carter was about to take office, he encouraged various of his followers, men and women who'd been living together without benefit of clergy, to make it legal. Cara said she'd be damned if she'd get married because some born-again Baptist told her to.

That summer, her point made, they wed.

Her cottage was cramped for two, but one of the finest houses in Harmony was for sale. "Let's buy it," Boyle said. "I can get a loan."

"I've got money," Cara said. It seemed that her father, the vet, owned a thousand acres of oil-producing West Texas prairie. Cara received two royalty checks a year; she had a drawer full of them, uncashed. They bought the house.

Life was hectic, yet magical. Cara was all he wanted. There was something elusive, unknowable about her that made her endlessly fascinating. Their sex was good, now and then spectacular, always comfortable. He realized belatedly what a solitary pastime sex with Nadine had been. With Cara it was a meeting of equals, taking became giving, he became she, two became one, in a union so absolute it was frightening. That was part of Cara's mystery, to be so fiercely self-contained, and yet some dark hot nights cling to him and whisper, "Boyle, I'd die without you."

She took him in hand, in various necessary ways. She wouldn't pick up after him, or live amid his accustomed frathouse squalor. One day she announced, "Boyle, I'm not going to feed you like a baby for the next fifty years," and began teaching him to cook. She started him on salads, and soon he advanced to chili, curries, pasta. Working together in the kitchen, washing this, peeling that, was a ballet; he loved the way their bodies touched and interacted, an unimagined intimacy as rich and subtle as sex. Sometimes, as they worked, she whistled softly, ballads of her own invention; he guessed that meant she was happy.

She liked to eat by candlelight. Happy light, she called it. One night she said, "We're going to have a baby."

Boyle gulped; he was past thirty but still uncertain about fatherhood.

"It happened New Year's Eve," she continued. "You rang the bell, Boyle."

"You're sure."

"No doubt about it."

"My God, that's great!"

"It's scary, Matt," she said, and took his hand. "Every day, teaching, I see how people mess up their kids. Good people. We're not gonna mess this kid up. What do you want to call him?"

"Him?"

"Trust me. Matthew T. Boyle, Jr?"

"Not in a million years. You got any family names we could use?"

"Leave my family out of this."

Cara was not close to her family. "They're a bunch of crazy Texans," she said, and the one time he encountered her family he realized she was right.

"The only person in my family who ever amounted to anything," Boyle said, "was my mother's great-grandfather, old Zebulon Vance, who was the governor of North Carolina during the Civil War. He was a hell of a guy."

"We'll call the boy Zeb then," Cara declared. "Because he's gonna be a hell of a guy too."

Once Zeb arrived, Boyle's happiness was complete. Later, when he looked back on those first years, it was always a summer evening, he was sitting in the chaise on their terrace, Zeb was playing in his sandpile or chasing Rags, their

Cairn, across the grass, and Cara was out in her garden, digging serenely, resplendent in cut-off jeans, an old bikini halter, and battered straw hat.

Now and then Boyle would gaze at this tableau and the truth would hit him like a freight train: *You are the luckiest man alive!*

It didn't matter that things were going to hell at the White House. Boyle saw it coming but there was nothing he could do about it. America was tiring of Carter's small-town piety and fancypants vocabulary and ratty cardigans and bizarre relatives and gutless policies. Sometimes Boyle wrote memos to the young Georgians who hovered near the throne, suggesting how Carter might shore up his sagging popularity, but they would only shrug and say, "He's not gonna change."

Boyle made the best of his four years in the White House. He cultivated the nation's top reporters. He became a serious student of the arts of polling and political advertising. He helped design Carter's TV spots. When the disaster of the 1980 election was past, Boyle hung out his shingle as a political consultant. Things were slow at first. Carterites were not in great demand. They held reunions each week in the unemployment lines. One girl who'd worked in Rosalynn's office was sighted selling hot buttered pretzels on Connecticut Avenue. Boyle rented an office in Georgetown, had long lunches with reporters, and waited for the phone to ring. One day it did. A friend at the *Post* reported that a popular Midwestern mayor named Calvin Webster wanted to run for governor and needed a media man.

Boyle was on the next plane.

Cal Webster roamed his office like an angry bull. "I'm running against a . . . *TV weatherman,*" he raged. "He's *pretty,*" he added, as if his opponent's good looks were an unspeakable perversion. "He hasn't got the brains God gave a duck, but he's ahead of me in the polls. Blast it, what am I supposed to do?"

Boyle asked questions and listened carefully. He soon decided that Cal Webster was a diamond in the rough, a politi-

cian of vast potential but one who needed a lot of help. The
man was not subtle, not brilliant, not cunning, not sophisti-
cated, but he exuded enormous strength. He had been a
success all of his life and he believed in success, believed in
himself, believed in America. In athletics, in the skies over
Korea, in business, in his race for mayor, he'd simply run
over whomever or whatever got in his way. His problem was
that you couldn't run for governor that way.

There was the problem of Webster's staff, which was over
its head in a statewide campaign; they tried to freeze Boyle
out, but eventually when Boyle put it on a me-or-him basis,
Webster coldly sacked his longtime chief of staff. There was
the problem of television. Webster's opponent, the TV
weatherman, used the medium easily. Webster, by contrast,
was uncomfortable before the cameras: He tried to cram a
dozen issues into every speech, a tactic that left his listeners
flabbergasted. Boyle, after a bitter struggle with Webster's
staff, wrote a series of speeches with each focusing on one
important campaign theme.

There was a related problem. Beneath his cordial exterior,
Cal Webster was a tough son of a bitch. Despite that fact, or
perhaps because of it, he liked to present himself as an Eagle
Scout, brimming with piety and platitudes. At first Webster
wouldn't budge from sweetness and light. Then, in a taping
session, Boyle goaded him, until Webster's eyes flashed, his
temper flared; Boyle almost got himself fired on the spot but
he got what he wanted on film, some of Webster's strength,
his anger, the fury that had made him a great warrior and
could make him a great political leader. Boyle quickly produced some powerful spots, only to have the candidate veto
them as "too negative." Boyle ran them anyway, on his own
authority. Webster fired him the next day, then rehired him
when the overnight polls showed that Boyle's tough-guy
spots had caused him to shoot up in popularity.

Guided by Boyle, Calvin Webster was elected governor.
He won big, so big that the political pundits had to start
including him in their lists of Possibles in the presidential
sweepstakes. Boyle's role in Webster's victory did not go
unnoticed and his business picked up dramatically. He

elected two representatives the next year and a senator the year after that. He entered a partnership with one of the country's leading pollsters and opened his own film studio in Washington. His fee was $50,000 to manage a campaign, plus expenses, and he generally took on two or three campaigns a year, plus some corporate filmmaking on the side.

As he moved around the country, from this campaign to that, he always had his eye out for a man he could make President, and he never found a candidate with more potential than Cal Webster.

The Reagan era came, and Boyle grumbled but prospered. Cara continued to teach school. Zeb started to ride a bike, to read, to be tall and confident. They spent a summer in France. Cara's royalty checks kept getting bigger and bigger. Boyle started to think about retiring at forty-five. Inevitably, Boyle knew he would be deeply involved in Cal Webster's presidential campaign, but once that was past he thought they'd go live in London or the South of France.

Joy.

Sheer, shimmering, undiluted joy.

Then it happened.

The thing he'd always feared.

Life's fragility.

Time's winged chariot hurrying near.

The FBI's knock at the door. The men in dark suits who came to take it all away.

It came in the late spring, just after Boyle blackmailed an old senator to win Governor Webster the presidential nomination. When he drove home one Saturday afternoon Cara was sitting at the kitchen table staring out the window. He'd never seen her do that before, just sit and stare.

"What's wrong?" he asked.

It was the first time he'd ever seen her face empty of emotion. Not joy, not anger, not pride, not amusement, not even fear. Just empty.

"I've got a lump, Matt. They want to cut me."

They talked to doctors, many doctors, who all said the same thing. They operated. Boyle told Zeb his mother was sick but getting better. His dark eyes drank it in; he slept with Cara when Boyle was away. Boyle tried to travel less but the convention was coming up, then the impossible leap to a fifty-state campaign. Cara said she was stronger. Boyle came home most weekends.

The poison spread. They operated again. The doctors grew more evasive. Cara took their treatments. When she lost her hair Zeb seized the scissors and hacked his off, "So I'll look like my mom."

Boyle quit the campaign. Cara quit the treatments. The hospice people came by daily, people who had embraced reality, saints. Cara's students visited after school in twos and threes. "Study hard 'n be good to your folks," she would tell them. The doctors gave her all the drugs she wanted; she felt little pain until the end. The hardest part was admitting the truth. "We can't lie, Matt, and waste what time we have," she insisted. They told Zeb his mother was very sick. Boyle spent most of his time at her bedside. They talked endlessly, telling each other things about their early lives they'd never shared before. Cara liked to recall her years at the University of Texas. She'd had a sorority sister who had big oil money and a wooden leg and a hopeless crush on Frank Sinatra. She'd get drunk and call him long-distance and once actually got him on the phone. "Frank," the girl had brazenly declared, "I'm nineteen and stacked and worth twelve million dollars and I've got a wooden leg and I can make your eyes bulge." To which Sinatra had replied, "Get on the next plane, sweetheart, I've been looking for you all my life."

Cara loved that story; she told it four or five times, too drugged to remember. She talked to Zeb a lot about the sort of man she wanted him to be; to Boyle she said gravely, imploringly, "Matt, when it's over, you mustn't spoil that boy."

"I won't, Cara."

"Don't be runnin' off and leavin' him all the time."

"I won't."

"Promise?"

"Promise."

They fought once, when she soiled her bed and he tried to

clean up the mess and she insisted on doing it herself, all ravaged, eighty-eight pounds of her. After they fought, they cried together, the only time that happened. That was the night she told him, "I'd stop it if I could, Matt. I'd take a handful of pills and be done with it."

"Whatever you want is all right," he told her.

"I *know*, honey," she said. "But I can't do it to Zeb, 'cause he'd have to live with it. So I reckon I have to go the route."

He turned off the presidential campaign, no TV, no newspapers, nothing. He didn't care. They played a lot of records in those last weeks. They started with the music they'd both grown up with and never really left behind, Jimmie Rodgers, Bob Wills, Hank Williams, Flatt and Scruggs, Bill Monroe. The simpler music of better days. They played rock, too, the good early stuff, the Clovers and Elvis's Sun Sessions and Jerry Lee and Chuck Berry and the Everlys. The Beatles, too: Side Two of "Abbey Road" until it almost broke their hearts.

Finally, as the end drew near, they turned to classical music. Cara died to Mozart. She was frail, feverish, all her pride and love still blazing in a body that had failed her. He summoned friends. She tried to smile, fought to stay, but darkness was sucking her away. They joined hands around her bed and sang hymns, "Amazing Grace" and "The Old Rugged Cross," and she trembled like a leaf and was gone.

They buried her on a golden October day. Jenna Webster came, and her father sent flowers, but it was mostly their neighbors in Harmony and the children Cara had taught.

A week after the funeral, two weeks before the election, Harry Bliss called. "We need you," he said. "It's too damn close."

"I can't," Boyle told him.

Webster won without him. Boyle watched the election-night news without interest. That world seemed far away. The idea for his book had come to him. He could write at home. His son needed him at home. Zeb had drawn into himself after his mother's death.

Boyle started his book.

Zeb slowly got better.

When Calvin Webster beckoned from the White House, it had not been hard to say no.

Then Doris Webster called and said Jenna was missing and he could not say no to her, to them.

21

Doris Webster, the First Lady of the Land, greeted him in a small, bright room that overlooked the Rose Garden. She tried gamely to smile, then collapsed in his arms. "Matt, Matt, I'm so afraid," she sobbed.

He had always liked her and never known her. No one had. Doris was an artist, gloriously apolitical, a graceful, elusive woman with porcelain skin, disheveled russet hair and long, paint-stained fingers. As far as Boyle could see, she and Webster had a good marriage, although their lives were largely separate. "I *do* vote for Cal," she would quip, but beyond voting she did little more than turn up on election night to smile nervously at the mob celebrating her husband's latest victory.

Doris was pleasant, sometimes witty, and always distant. Sometimes Boyle thought he saw glimpses of the real, inner Doris in her paintings, shadowy portraits of solitary, haunted women. Harry grumbled, "Why's her stuff so damn depressing?" But the critics approved and her pictures sold for $2,000 apiece.

Now she was huddled at one end of a small blue sofa, alone and frightened.

"Tell me what happened," he said.

"She just . . . disappeared," Doris said. "She slipped away from the Secret Service Friday night, and drove off in her car. They've been looking everywhere, all weekend, but . . . nothing."

Boyle groaned. "She called me Friday night," he said. "I didn't play back my messages until yesterday morning. She was upset about something."

"You'll have to tell Harry about her call," Doris said. "Maybe that'll help somehow. The Secret Service is reporting directly to him."

"What about the FBI?" Boyle asked.

"They aren't involved. Calvin doesn't trust them."

"The FBI not involved? They've got to be."

Doris Webster threw up her hands. "Matt, she told me she'd seen you recently. Did she say anything that . . . that might explain this?"

"I don't think so. She said she was busy with her job. That she wasn't crazy about the Vice President. That she didn't have much of a social life."

"She didn't say anything about going away? Or a trip? Or some new boyfriend?"

"No, none of that. Just that, you know, she resented the Secret Service protection."

"She didn't say anything about a key? About making a copy of a key?"

"No, nothing like that."

Doris put her hand over her eyes. "Oh, Matt, where is she? What could it be?"

Boyle was moved. Perhaps Jenna was just off on a spree but her mother was suffering, as mothers did. "I don't know, Doris," he said. "I'm terribly sorry about this. If there is anything I can do . . ."

She dried her eyes and abruptly took his hand. "There *is* something you can do," she said.

"What?"

"Look for Jenna. Find her for me."

Boyle was flabbergasted.

"I realize the Secret Service is looking for her," Doris explained, "but I don't trust them."

"Don't trust them?" he repeated. "Why not?"

"Oh, Matt, for a hundred reasons. Because they're bureaucrats. Because they have their own priorities. Because they're mad at Jenna for slipping away from them—embarrassing them. Most of all, because of Cal."

"I don't understand. What about him?"

"He's convinced himself that she's just off on a lark. He won't let himself imagine . . . foul play. He's so caught up in the disarmament program, Matt, that he just can't focus on anything else. He hardly eats or sleeps. And I'm afraid that if he doesn't take Jenna's disappearance seriously, the Secret Service won't either."

"Doris," he said, "I'm sure the Secret Service is taking this extremely seriously. They have to, if only to protect themselves. If anything happened to Jenna, heads would roll, and they know it."

She stood up, trying to compose herself. "I'm sorry, I thought perhaps you'd help me."

He was dismissed but he could not move. It was so strange that someone in her position could be so alone.

"I'll do anything I can," he said.

She forced a smile. "You'll find my little girl for me?"

"I'll try."

"I'm so glad," she said. "I feel better already."

Boyle didn't. He felt awful.

22

"Doris did *what?*" Harry roared.

Boyle glared back at his old friend. "She asked me to look for Jenna."

"We happen to have the Secret Service looking for her," Harry said coldly.

"I told her that," Boyle replied. "But she wanted someone she knew involved."

"Christ Almighty!" Harry raged. "All right, let's hear this tape you've got."

The two of them had met in Harry's office, along with Jeff Winnick of the Secret Service. They played the tape three times.

"She was sure upset about something," Winnick said finally.

"Oh, hell, that's just Jenna's melodramatics," Harry said. "She might have seen a mouse."

"She's gone, Harry," Boyle said angrily.

"If she started out toward Mr. Boyle's house," Winnick said, "someone might have seen her. That's as good a lead as we've got." He grabbed a phone and ordered a team of agents to start searching the roads that led to Boyle's village.

"I've got a question," Boyle said.

"Make it quick," Harry barked.

"Have you considered that Jenna's disappearance might be somehow political? A kidnapping?"

"Of course we've considered that!" Harry snapped. "Do you think we're idiots? But three days have passed and we've got no message, no demands, no nothing."

"That could still come," Boyle said. "Look, suppose you get a message that says, 'Mr. President, stop disarming America or we'll kill your daughter.' Then what?"

Harry's face reddened. "Our policy is we don't give in to blackmail," he said. "We don't negotiate with terrorists."

"Even if Jenna's life was at stake?"

"Especially if Jenna's life was at stake!"

"You've talked to Webster about this?"

"I've talked to the President about this, yes. But that's not what it is. I'm sure of it."

"What is it, then?"

"Look, nine out of ten Jenna's off with some boyfriend, having a great laugh about what jerks she's made of us."

"I don't think so," Boyle protested.

"Oh, hell, Matt, be realistic. You and I watched Jenna grow up. We love her. Okay, but don't forget the facts. Jenna's wild. Remember the summer after she graduated from high school? She disappeared, and turned up in Alaska on some save-the-whales expedition. The next summer, she's racing stock cars in North Carolina. Next it was skydiving."

"She was damn good in the campaign," Boyle grumbled.

"Yeah, but what happens this year? We put her over with the Vice President, not a bad job, but she's bored. So what does she do? Runs off, just for the hell of it."

Harry stood up. The others did the same. "Look, Matt, I want you to cooperate with Jeff here, but otherwise keep out of this. If anybody asks, we're saying Jenna is on vacation."

"Why haven't you brought the FBI in?" Boyle demanded.

"There's nothing the FBI could do that we're not already doing," Harry said.

"That's debatable," Boyle shot back.

"Look, the first thing the FBI would do is leak this to the press, to make the Secret Service look like jerks and themselves look good," Harry continued. "And we don't want this to leak. We want a nice quiet investigation, because we think Jenna's going to turn up in a few days no matter what we do. So why get egg on our faces?"

"I can't believe you're being so cynical when Jenna's life may be at stake," Boyle said.

"Don't get holier than thou," his old friend snapped. "Anyway, it'll leak in any event—you know that."

"Just don't *you* leak it, pal," Harry said. "The boss has enough problems. You want to cut him off at the knees?"

Boyle's temper flared. "You do what you think is best for the President. I'll do what I think is best for Jenna!"

He slammed the door behind him. It felt good.

As Harry Bliss took a call from Turk Kellerman, Jeff Winnick slipped out the door.

"Mr. Bliss, I think it's imperative that we bring the Bureau into the search for Jenna. At the very least, we need their lab facilities."

"I told you what the President said, Kellerman. He thinks that if we tell the FBI what's happened, somebody over there will leak the story."

"With all due respect, the President doesn't understand the problem. It's not a matter of us telling the Bureau. They'll find out. They don't miss much that's interesting. If they see they've been kept out, they'll damn sure leak, just to teach us a lesson. They've been doing it for years."

Harry grunted but did not reply. What Kellerman was saying made sense to him, but that didn't mean it would make sense to Cal Webster. Presidents, in Harry's experience, did not see the world like other men. They tended to see what they wanted to see, which was sometimes their greatness and sometimes their undoing.

"Mr. Bliss," Turk Kellerman continued, "Lyndon Johnson once said it was better to have your critics inside the tent pissing out than outside the tent pissing in. That's how it is

with the Bureau, believe me. I know a fellow over there, one
of their assistant directors, Saussy is his name, not a bad guy.
I could talk to him, butter him up a little, say we need to use
their lab, and maybe, just maybe, he'll plug up any leaks
over there."

"All right, go ahead," Harry said abruptly and hung up the
phone. He guessed he could fix it with the President somehow.

"Mr. Boyle!"
Jeff Winnick caught up with him on the sidewalk outside
the West Wing.
"We should talk, Mr. Boyle."
"We just did." Boyle kept walking. The agent fell in beside
him.
"We both want to find Jenna," the younger man said.
Boyle stopped and peered into Winnick's boyish face.
"Don't you think she's off on some lark, like Harry said?"
"No, I don't, Mr. Boyle. I'm scared."
Boyle examined the young man more closely. Jeff Winnick
was the sort of strapping young hunk who Boyle instinc-
tively disliked. Still, he seemed genuinely concerned about
Jenna.
"Come on," he said.
They found a coffee shop on Eighteenth Street and settled
in a table by the window.
"That was you who came to my house that Sunday night,
wasn't it?" Boyle asked.
"That's right."
"Mad as hell, as I recall."
"Jenna never really accepted the need for security," Winnick said. "I don't think she accepts that there's evil in the
world, or at least that it could touch her."
"She said she'd dated you," Boyle said.
The agent frowned. "That's a matter of definition. It's
against regulations for an agent to date a protectee. Natu-
rally, when Jenna found out about that rule, she had to break
it. We spent a little time together, but I always considered it
in the line of duty."

"Nice duty," Boyle said bitterly.

"Mr. Boyle . . ."

"Just Matt, please."

"Matt, if you'd just think about your conversations with Jenna. Did she say anything that might explain this?"

Boyle sighed unhappily. "I've thought and thought. She didn't mention any guys, except you. She didn't mention any trips, any places she wanted to go. She wasn't that crazy about her job but I didn't get the sense that she'd walk off and leave it."

"What did she say about the Vice President?"

Boyle shrugged. "Not much. That he didn't pay much attention to her. That she wasn't sure who he listened to. She said some outside adviser called him a lot."

"Did she mention a name?"

"No," Boyle said. "Look, what's this about a key?"

The young man frowned. "Who told you about that?"

"That doesn't matter. What's it all about?"

Boyle's question had only been a shot in the dark. Doris Webster had asked him about a key, then dropped the subject.

"I can't discuss that," the agent said.

Boyle stood up. "Then good-bye. You ask me to cooperate but you're holding out on me."

"Wait a minute," the young man said. "Sit down. Let me think."

Boyle eased back into his chair.

"This has to be in total confidence."

"Understood."

The Secret Service man tersely related the story of his and Jenna's trip to the locksmith and its fatal aftermath.

"My God," Boyle whispered. "What can it mean?"

"We don't know. It could be a coincidence."

"It sounds to me like she was snooping in Remington's office. That she was suspicious of something. Maybe trying to get into his files."

Winnick nodded. "I'd thought about that."

Boyle was getting excited. "When did you tell her about the locksmith's death?" he demanded.

"Friday afternoon."

"Then don't you see? It was that night she called me.
There must be something she wanted to tell me, or discuss
with me, that she wasn't willing to tell you."

"Maybe so," Winnick said. "But what?"

"I don't know," Boyle admitted. "Look, what are you people doing to find her?"

"Everything that can be done," the agent said. "We've got
dozens of men on the case."

Boyle sighed. "Well, I guess I'll be joining the search
party."

The young agent looked perplexed. "I honestly don't
know what you could do that trained professionals aren't
already doing."

Boyle stood up. "You may be right," he said. "But I promised her mother."

23

Serena was in her library listening to Mozart on her compact-disc player. The quality was magnificent; it was like being in the concert hall. She missed concerts, but she believed that at this crucial moment she should not be seen in public. Better for her whereabouts to be a mystery than for it to be known she was back in the Washington area. As she listened, she wondered idly what she could do, once she put Remington in the White House, to promote the study of classical music in the schools. Serena hated rock-and-roll. She thought it the perfect symbol of the mindless, animalistic decadence that had spread through America since the 1960s, sapped the national will, lost the war in Vietnam, and now threatened the survival of the Free World. Clearly, something must be done.

She frowned at the knock on the door, then smiled as Charlie entered. She thought him a remarkable young man. Of course, he was young, and arrogant, and uneducated, and she was not at all sure she could trust him over the long pull. But for the moment Charlie was a dream.

"Pour yourself a drink," she said.

He did, and raised his glass to her. "Cheers."

"Confusion to our enemies," she responded. Candlelight ɔarkled on her diamonds. He took her hand and kissed it. he beamed at him.

"You are a dear, Charles," she said. "But tell me about our work. Is there progress?"

Charlie poured himself more champagne. He'd read ɔmewhere about a man whose dying words had been, "I nould have drunk more champagne."

"I'm seeing the man about the weapon in a few days."

"The inventor?"

"Yes, yes," Charlie said. He paced about the room, glanc- ıg at the huge dragon, the suits of armor, the swords and .aggers. She'd never seen him so restless.

"Is something the matter?" she asked.

He whirled and faced her. "I've got the girl."

Her dark eyes widened. "The Webster girl?"

He nodded.

"Why?"

"I told you. She was snooping. Getting too suspicious of Remington. I had no choice. She could have blown the vhole plan."

"It's dangerous," she muttered.

"It's the lesser evil," he replied. "The interesting thing is, hus far there's been not a word about her disappearance."

"Which means?"

"It could mean they think she's run off for a holiday. Or, even if they suspect trouble, they don't want the country to ɔnow."

"But they're looking for her, of course."

"Of course."

"Where is she?"

"In a safe place."

"Answer me!" she cried.

"No. What you don't know can't hurt us."

Serena's hands trembled with anger. "What you pro- ɔose to do with her?" she asked.

Charlie shrugged. "Either we keep her or we don't."

"Obviously. But which do suggest?"

"She's no use to us dead," he said. "Alive, she might be of value, as events unfold. A bargaining chip, as they say."

Serena's face darkened. "She's pretty, isn't she? Is that what you want, Charlie, a plaything?"

Charlie noted her jealousy with amusement. "Say the word and she's gone."

Serena sipped her Cristal and licked her lips thoughtfully. "No, no, keep her for the present. I trust you'll find out what she knows."

"Of course."

24

Jenna had for three years rented an airy, rambling apartment atop a Kalorama Road townhouse. Her landlady, a salty, chain-smoking widow, lived below. Boyle knocked on her door and gave her his line: that Jenna had gone away for a few days, that there had been threats against her, that he wondered if she'd noticed any suspicious happenings. "I been through this already with the SS boys," the old woman croaked. "Who the hell are you?" Boyle flashed an old White House pass and for his trouble got smoke blown in his face but no leads. He next talked with Jenna's secretary, who was upset about Jenna's mysterious "vacation" but told him nothing of value.

Boyle inched home in the rush-hour traffic, purgatory along the Potomac, to find Zeb upset. "I'm doing a job for Mrs. Webster," Boyle explained. "It may take a week or two. Do you want me to get a baby-sitter?"

Zeb frowned. "I'll be okay," he said uncertainly.

That night, when Zeb was asleep, Boyle paced his red-walled, booklined study. He couldn't compete with the Secret Service at knocking on doors. So what could he do to help Doris, to help Jenna? What, what, what?

It came to him slowly, not an answer but a direction.

Boyle thought that his success in politics had not come because he was brilliant, for he knew he was not, but because he had an ability to focus intently on the big picture in his campaigns, the basics of winning and losing, while all around him people were losing their heads over details. In a campaign, he thought, or a war, or a marriage, or any endeavor, success came to those who could step back from the daily sound and fury and see the equation whole.

He had a nagging sense that Jenna's disappearance, terrible and all-consuming as it was, did not exist in isolation but was somehow part of a larger scheme. What, he did not know. But he had sensed for some time, even before Jenna vanished, that something was amiss in Washington. He had felt this despite his distance from the political scene, or perhaps because of that distance. Isolated events, barely noticed, began to gnaw at him, demanding recognition. The violence of the opposition to Webster's Project Peace unsettled him, this unyielding, bitter-end resistance of powerful forces to a policy that seemed to Boyle inevitable. Jenna's criticism of the Vice President, too, had echoed harshly in quiet chambers of his mind. And the death of the locksmith cried out for explanation. The times were out of joint. Sometimes Boyle could shut his eyes and see huge, vague, menacing forms moving about in darkness, but no matter how he tried, he could not make them out.

What in God's name is happening?

Boyle could not answer the question, but he knew it existed and that someone wiser than himself might hold the key. Thus, the next morning, fearful and ashamed, he dialed the office of Senator Ben Trawick and told a skeptical secretary it was of the highest urgency that he meet with the senator, a man who, Boyle well knew, had cause to despise him.

It had been more than a year since Boyle last saw Ben Trawick. Back then, the Webster campaign seemed to be faltering, out of gas. The primaries were over, the party

onvention was at hand, and Cal Webster was deadlocked
vith a golden-tongued Western senator who'd gained
round fast.

Two hundred uncommitted delegates held the balance of
ower, and there were increasing rumors that they would
ote as a bloc. Most were canny professional politicians,
oolly waiting to see which candidate would pay most dearly
or their support. Finally, as the political dust settled, it
ecame clear that Senator Ben Trawick controlled these
lecisive delegates.

Trawick had long been a shadowy force in national affairs,
nd it happened that Matt Boyle greatly admired him. Matt
vas a student of American politics; he knew of the days, not
ong past, when giants prowled the Senate: Kefauver of Ten-
essee, Douglas of Illinois, Russell of Georgia, Taft of Ohio,
ulbright of Arkansas, Johnson of Texas, men you might
lisagree with but had to respect, men who towered above
he landscape.

But the era of giants had passed, and the once-proud Sen-
te now was populated by pygmies, clowns, charlatans, and
ast-buck artists, odd characters who ranged from the harm-
essly inept to the dangerously demented.

There were exceptions, of course, and the most notable of
hem, trying to maintain some sanity, some dignity even,
mid the congressional bedlam, was Ben Trawick.

He was a throwback, the last of the giants. He had come to
he Senate young and stayed long, wielding immense power
rom behind the scenes. He never sought publicity or
tepped "out front" on the burning issues of the day, but
history would record that he was invariably right, and often
lecisive, on the great issues. In the Sixties, his quiet turn-
abouts had made possible Medicare and the civil rights laws.
Later, it was said that when Trawick broke with Lyndon
Johnson on Vietnam and with Richard Nixon on Watergate,
each President knew, immediately and absolutely, that he
was doomed.

Trawick was neither lazy, unambitious, nor excessively
modest, yet when friends urged him for decades to seek the
presidency, he always refused. No one knew why, except

that he had made the Senate his life. He owned an elegant estate in the Virginia hunt country, where his gracious wife presided, but when the Senate was in session he made his home in a tiny Capitol Hill apartment. He commanded a princely hideaway office, too, high in the Capitol, where for decades powerful senators of both parties had met each Wednesday afternoon for drinks, gossip, and horsetrading.

That spring, as Cal Webster struggled for his party's nomination for President, it became clear that these senators, thanks to the money and delegates they controlled, held the balance of power, and that they, as was often the case, were looking to Ben Trawick for direction.

Thus, one day in early summer, a rumor spread through Washington like fire across a dry and windswept prairie: Trawick was soon to announce his support for Webster's opponent.

The candidate and his staff, confused and heartsick, gathered in his office. Aides begged Webster to go to Trawick, to appeal to him. No, the candidate said firmly, he would never do that. Then, the staff agreed, some emissary must go to Trawick, to appeal, if not for his support, at least for his neutrality. The names of various elder statesmen and high financiers were suggested for this desperate mission. Finally, Matt Boyle, who had been unaccountably silent, shocked everyone by saying: "Let me talk to him."

Others protested that Boyle was too young to carry weight with Trawick. Boyle would not explain why he sought the assignment. "I think I can persuade him," was all he would say, even in a private talk with Governor Webster himself. But something in Boyle's manner persuaded Webster, and he was sent to confront Ben Trawick, on what was to be, up until then, the worst day of his life.

Trawick rose to greet Boyle in his hideaway office, where tall windows overlooked the Mall. He was a slender, courtly man in a dark suit, stooped by age but with bright eyes that had seen everything and remained amused.

"You've not been here before, Matthew?" he said. "It's the finest view in Washington, Harry Truman's balcony not excepted. Will you join me in a brandy?"

"No thank you." Boyle gazed out at the long green Mall, alive with tourists, unfolding like a magic carpet past the museums. A blood-red sun was poised above the Potomac.

Senator Trawick, brandy snifter in hand, lowered himself into a chair and nodded to Boyle to do the same. Quite effortlessly he took charge of the conversation. He praised Governor Webster. He told an ironic story about the LBJ campaign of '64. He seemed to have all the time in the world. Boyle found himself caught up in the old politician's magic; this was a masterly performance, like watching Louis Armstrong play trumpet or Ted Williams hit a baseball, an artist at the peak of his art.

In time, however, the senator paused, and Boyle's moment had come. "Senator, we all hope very much you'll give your support to Governor Webster."

Trawick sighed; he seemed genuinely aggrieved. "I fear that will not be possible."

"I know I'm prejudiced, but I truly think he'd be best for the country."

A smile crossed Trawick's canny face. "You'll forgive me, Matthew, if I say that reasonable men can differ on that point."

Boyle returned the smile. "Senator, would you forgive me if I say that Governor Webster would be honored to have you as his Vice President, or as his Secretary of State or first Supreme Court appointment?"

"Yes, Matthew, I'll forgive—and even forget—that impertinence, because you are young. I've lived a senator and in due time I'll die one."

"No harm in trying," Boyle said, stalling, not ready to take the plunge.

The old man sipped his Rémy Martin and waited.

So the moment of truth arrived. After a year of campaigning, a year of scheming and sweating and lying and dreaming, after all the handshakes and deals and rallies and primaries, after a king's ransom spent on television, somehow the process came down to this, the whim of one charming, inscrutable old man. Boyle gripped the arms of his chair.

"Senator, I'm sorry it's come to this," he said.

Trawick arched an eyebrow. Boyle produced a slip of paper and slid it across the desk. The older man glanced at the paper, which had only two words written on it, a name. Then he let it fall from his fingers and gazed into the amber shadows of his brandy.

For the rest of his life Boyle appreciated all that Ben Trawick did not say or do at that moment. He did not curse him, threaten him, order him from his office, plead with him, or ask his price. Instead, after a dozen seconds of silence, he said gently, "Would it suit the Governor's convenience if I announce my support for him at eleven o'clock tomorrow morning?"

"That would be perfect, sir."

"At what location?"

"He'll be glad to come to your office."

"Very well."

Boyle stood up. A union organizer had taught him a rule of negotiating: When you get what you want, leave fast, lest the other fellow change his mind. Still, Boyle hesitated.

"Senator Trawick, no one knows about this but me. And if it matters, I hate it."

Trawick, twirling his brandy snifter in his long fingers, looked amused, but did not reply. Boyle bolted from the office and ran blindly out of the Capitol, into the dusk, to throw up, sobbing and cursing, upon a bed of tulips.

Ben Trawick's eloquent endorsement, televised live the next morning, was a political earthquake; by sundown, all but a handful of the uncommitted delegates had scrambled aboard the Webster bandwagon and his nomination was assured.

Late that night, a radiant Webster summoned Boyle into his office. He embraced the younger man, something he'd never done before, gave him a cigar, and talked passionately of all he would do for America. "And you'll be at my right hand, Matt, all the way," he said.

Eventually the candidate asked, so very casually, "By the way, what *did* you say to the old reprobate?"

Boyle's head throbbed. "I'm sorry," he whispered. "I can't say."

"Very well," the next President said coldly.

Boyle recognized the look in his eyes. He knew that in some part of his heart Cal Webster would never forgive him, would always hate him for his secret, his pride. Like most politicians, he could tolerate almost any vice in the people around him except independence.

Boyle spent three days revising their TV spots. It was when he returned home that Cara told him of her cancer. He tried to believe it was coincidence, that there was no true link between the lump in her breast and the rot in his soul.

The story, which Boyle never told anyone, was simple enough. Years earlier, on a winter night when Cara was out of town, Boyle was seated at a dinner party next to a woman who'd once worked for Senator Trawick. She was a stubby, ill-natured woman who drank more than was wise among strangers. Boyle spoke of the senator, praising him, but the woman's comments about Trawick were caustic, bitter; Boyle guessed she'd been fired.

At the end of the evening the woman backed her car into a ditch and Boyle gave her a ride home. Curious, disliking her, he kept touching the nerve, saying what a great man Ben Trawick was. Finally, in front of her apartment house, all her bile and bitterness burst loose.

"You think he's so damn swell, ask him about Clay Templeton sometime," she raged.

"Who's he?" Boyle asked, sober, watchful.

"He's lover boy," the woman said. "The baby-faced drunk your great statesman has been keeping for twenty-six years. Why the hell d'ya think he never ran for President?"

The woman lurched into the rain, only to call Boyle in tears the next morning. "Please, please forget what I said last night," she whimpered. "I was crazy drunk."

He could imagine her, hung over, fearful that a vengeful senator would blackball her from any Washington job if he learned of her indiscretion.

"No one else knows," she went on. "I found out by acci-

dent. I've never told anyone, until last night, and you
mustn't either."

"I don't intend to," Boyle said coldly.

A few weeks later he made discreet inquiries, out of curiosity, he told himself, and was persuaded that the woman's
accusation was true. After that, he kept her secret, the old
senator's secret, locked away, all but forgotten, until one day
it became the key that unlocked the White House gates for
his candidate.

25

Now, a year and an election later, on another perfect summer day, Boyle returned to Ben Trawick, not because he wanted to, but because he thought him the wisest man in Washington.

He went there hating it. He thought that one moment with Trawick, when he slipped that name across his desk, was the only time he had behaved dishonorably in all his years in politics.

And yet, his blackmail had elected a President who was battling to end the arms race. Was it then so wrong? Or did the end justify his means?

Boyle knew the answer.

Wrong was wrong was wrong.

Once again the senator received him in his Capitol hideaway, with the sun poised above the green grass and marble columns of the Mall. The old man, a year more wrinkled, a year more wise, was as gracious as before.

"Sit down, Matthew," he said. "A drink?" His own oval of Rémy was already nestled in his long fingers.

Boyle shook his head. "Senator, let me say again, I'm terribly ashamed of what I did last year."

Trawick's hand fluttered, a gesture of dismissal. "I've been in campaigns," he said. "They seem like life or death. Perhaps I'd have done the same."

"I've often wondered what I'd have done if you'd thrown me out of your office. I'd like to think that I was bluffing, that I'd have done nothing . . . with the information I had."

"Perhaps," the senator said. "But I couldn't run the risk. The young man in question . . ." He stopped and smiled, lost in his memories. "I say 'young man,' although he was actually older than you. But he was young when I met him, an exceptionally handsome and charming boy, fresh out of law school, who came to work for me. A lovely boy, but destroyed by a weakness for drink and drugs."

Ben Trawick sighed. "In any event, Matthew, when you came to see me, the young man was dying . . ."

"Oh my God," Boyle cried. "I didn't know."

"I didn't think you did. But I had to consider the fact. At my age, I hardly fear scandal, but I couldn't risk whatever pain public exposure would have brought to him and his family. So perhaps all's well. My friend died in peace and your candidate became President. Now, what can I do for you?"

"Do you want to do anything for me?"

"Within reason."

"May I ask why?"

Another flutter of a blue-veined hand. "All things considered, you behaved decently."

Boyle lowered his eyes. "I never thought so."

"You got what you wanted for your candidate. You never came back for yourself. I've kept an eye on your career, Matthew. There are only a handful of men like yourself who know how to elect a President and who give a damn what sort of creature they elect. That makes you important to the future of our country. What can I do for you?"

Boyle glanced out the window, at the glorious sweep of the Mall, Washington's illusion, then back at the shrewd, flawed old man, its reality.

"Jenna Webster has disappeared," he said.

The senator waited, motionless. Perhaps he'd already eard. Boyle would never know.

"The Secret Service is looking for her," Boyle continued. But her mother asked me to help. I have a feeling that . . . don't know how to explain it . . . that it's part of some- ing larger. I want your advice, your help."

The older man took a Cuban cigar from its wrapper, owly, lovingly, and lit it; smoke rings rose like halos above is head. "Jenna Webster," he repeated. "A delightful, some- hat headstrong young woman, as I recall. She's been work- g for the Vice President, Mr. Remington."

"Yes, right on both counts," Boyle replied. "Senator, she alled me Friday night. Then she vanished. No word, noth- g."

"And what do you wish of me, in this matter?"

"I don't know. I think you see the big picture. I think omething's *wrong* in this city."

Trawick relaxed, nipping at his cigar. The room grew dim, uiet. Boyle waited patiently. Finally, the senator said, "I've een in Washington a long time, Matthew, longer than ou've been alive. I'd like to think I've gained a certain nderstanding of the place, and I've never known it more nsettled, more troubling than today. Your Mr. Webster, for ne thing, is playing a dangerous game with his disarma- ent program, perhaps more dangerous than he under- ands. The danger is not the Soviets, who have every reason o agree to his plan. The danger, rather, is that he is chal- nging some exceedingly powerful forces in our own coun- ry. Can the government control the arms industry? Or will he arms industry control the government? We'll know, I uspect, before this year is finished.

"So, the President proposes a bold program, and the Presi- ent's daughter is missing. Are those facts connected? Or ust other facts be added to the equation? Washington is a onfusing place, Matthew, but in time you see a certain rder to the political process. Not rules you can put into a ivics book, but you develop instincts, a sense of how things t together."

The senator's voice was soft, hypnotic, yet part of Boyle
was impatient, wondering where these reflections might
lead.

"There's an equilibrium here," Trawick continued. "Despite all the give and take, the passing 'victories' and
'defeats,' the city rarely gets out of balance."

The old man wet his lips with brandy. Rose-tinted dusk
embraced his quiet sanctuary. "It's my vanity, Matthew,
that when something goes wrong in Washington, something
serious, I can sense it. I've gotten to know the place the way
a man knows his own home, so that even in total darkness he
can move about with confidence. My wife and I once returned home after a trip. We had no sooner stepped in the
door than my wife said, 'Someone's been here,' and she was
right. In an instant, she had sensed, in a room cluttered with
antiques, one vase out of place. The burglar had moved it a
few inches, looking for a wall safe. It's that sort of sixth sense
that I fancy I've developed for the political landscape. Do
you understand?"

"I think so."

"Yes. That's why you're here, because you sense, as I do,
something out of place in Washington today. But what?
That's the question."

Boyle almost laughed. "I don't know the answer. That's
why I'm here."

"You must develop your own powers. Try to see it whole,
the entire equation, the vase that is out of place."

Boyle closed his eyes, summoning whatever muse might
dwell in this quiet corner of the Capitol. He tried to focus, to
see more deeply, but the creatures in the darkness remained
beyond his understanding. His mind ached with frustration,
tears seared his eyes. Where was Jenna? What was wrong?
With a cry, he buried his face in his hands. "I don't understand it," he groaned. "If you do, please help me."

The senator savored his brandy. "I'm an old man," he
whispered. "I feel breezes from distant doors. I feel my
powers fading. Use your own instincts. Trust yourself. Tell
me what you think, what you feel."

Boyle opened his eyes to the dusk; he smelled the old

man's cigar, his brandy. The room was eerie, an oracle's chamber, electric with possibility. Boyle was dazed, drifting outside himself.

"The Vice President," he heard himself say. "Something about him is . . . wrong."

The senator was lost in smoke and darkness. A clock ticked; a fire engine cried in the distance. "What is wrong about him?" he asked finally.

"Jenna . . . she didn't trust him. She said he wasn't there."

"The man came out of nowhere," Trawick mused. "Do you know what he was doing five years ago?"

Boyle tried to remember. "Five years ago he was still in business . . . selling computers."

"Yes. Five years ago Mr. Remington was a highly successful, and entirely apolitical, businessman. Then suddenly he became civic-minded, and with astonishing success. He formed commissions, issued reports, gained national publicity. He was the undistinguished first-term governor of a border state when your Mr. Webster unaccountably chose him for Vice President. Why?"

Boyle felt weak, confused, lost. "I don't know. He rescued a child, got all that publicity. I thought he was a fluke. A media creation."

Trawick chuckled. "A creation, yes. But of the media? Of himself? Or of parties unknown?"

"I don't know."

"Look back at our vice presidents. Bush, Mondale, Ford, Johnson, Nixon. All tested figures, party stalwarts, known quantities. Why? Because the vice presidency is a shortcut to the presidency, the joker in the political deck, and, with few exceptions, we've been careful with it. Yet your Mr. Webster, a shrewd and careful man, entrusted it to a man he barely knew. Why?"

"I wasn't there," Boyle said. "Jenna told me there was a lot of pressure. Remington was a new face. Attractive, articulate. The South liked him. He had big money behind him. It was a snap decision."

"I wonder," the older man said. He puffed angrily on his

cigar. "The man doesn't belong. He's not *right*. He's the vase that's out of place."

"What must I do?"

"Find out who created Ben Remington."

Boyle lowered his head. "But will that help me find Jenna?" he asked helplessly.

"I don't know, Matthew," the senator admitted. "You must discover that for yourself."

26

Jenna awoke in darkness. She lay on her back on a narrow, unfamiliar bed. The world before her was black and still. She imagined she was dreaming until she could no longer deny the truth: This might be her tomb. She lacked the courage to move, to explore her fate. She tried to force all thoughts from her mind, to sink into forgetfulness, but an image came racing toward her out of the darkness: the brilliant, blinding glare of an automobile's headlights, her own car sliding into a ditch, a man running toward her, a chemical-soaked cloth held to her mouth. Darkness then and darkness now, eerie and total.

She let her right hand slide across the rough bedspread. It moved cautiously through empty air, then touched solid wood. She groped and felt a chest. Emboldened, she swung her feet off the bed, sat up, and reached out with both hands. A lampshade rattled at her touch. "Thank God," she whispered. She fumbled for a moment, then found the chain and suddenly light exploded in her eyes.

Jenna found herself in a small, shabby room. A door led to a bath, another to a tiny kitchen. A third door seemed to lead out of the room. Jenna ran to that door, twisting its handle, beating against it, all to no avail. She prowled anxiously about the room, running her hands along the plaster walls, moving the furniture, until abruptly she realized what was missing: The room had no windows. No windows, no sounds, no hum of life or traffic. The awful truth seized her: She was underground.

She ran about the room in panic, searching here and there for some tool, some weapon, some avenue of escape, some ray of hope. She found food in the kitchen, paperback books in a bookshelf, a toothbrush and toothpaste in the bath, but nothing to ease her plight. Finally she lay on the bed and tried to think. She could only imagine that someone had kidnapped her to bring pressure on her father. What did they want? Money? No, there were easier ways to make money than by kidnapping a President's daughter. Their goal had to be political. To trade her freedom for that of imprisoned terrorists? Or even to trade her life for a halt in the disarmament program? If so, they were fools, and she was in terrible trouble. Jenna had seen the policy directives. The government did not negotiate with terrorists.

She realized, too late, that she had been a fool to play games with the Secret Service, to refuse to take seriously the danger she had faced; now she would have to pay for her folly.

She lost all sense of time. Her watch was gone, and the room contained no clock or radio. Hours passed. She paced, dozed, searched the room time after time, and finally, in desperation, forced herself to read a tattered copy of *The Godfather*.

She was half-asleep, unsure what day it was, when a·voice jolted her awake.

"Rise and shine, luv—company coming!"

The voice came from a small speaker above the door. Jenna perched on the room's one chair and waited. She had imagined this moment, had thought of attacking whoever entered, with a lamp or frying pan, but such action seemed preordained to defeat. Better to wait, to study, to move with guile.

She heard the scrape of a key. The door swung open. A
man stepped in, the same tall, broad-shouldered young man
who had seized her on the road to Matt's house. He was
grinning now, and holding a sack of groceries. He kicked the
door shut behind him.

"Hallo there," he said cheerily. "Brought you some good-
es."

A cocky grin lit his tanned, sensual face. Mahogany curls
cascaded over his ears. He wore jeans, Bally loafers, a polo
shirt, and gold chains around his neck. Jenna jumped to her
feet.

"Who are you? I demand that you let me go!"

"Call me Charlie," the man said agreeably. "I'll call you
Jenna—no use being formal, is there? I brought some things
—bread, milk, cheese, pastrami, ice cream. Beer, too. Make
me a list if there's anything else you fancy."

"Are you *English?*" she demanded.

Charlie smiled at her. "How'd you guess?"

He put the groceries away while she glared at him.
"Where are we? What do you want?"

He sighed. "I guess we'd better have a chat. How about a
beer?"

He opened two cans of Budweiser and handed her one.
He sprawled on the bed and she perched in the chair. When
Charlie grinned at her she almost screamed. "Damn you,"
she yelled, "I demand to know where we are and . . ."

"The where is easy, pet," Charlie said. "We're on a lovely
estate where no one will bother us. I'm right upstairs, although I'm not always there. The thing is, Jenna, there's
dirty business afoot in Washington, and you were sticking
your pretty little nose in it, so we thought you might be safer
here, till things sort themselves out."

"What 'dirty business'? And who is 'we'?"

Charlie shrugged. "I really can't tell you that, now can I?"

"It's my father's disarmament program," she cried. "But
can't you see you're wasting your time? He won't give in to
blackmail—he can't. Don't you know that?"

"Of course I know that."

"Then what do you want?"

"A bit of information."

"What information?"

"Why did you take the key from the Vice President'
coat?" Charlie asked.

Jenna's mind went reeling. The key, that damned key! "I
I tell you, will you let me go?"

"Maybe."

"I was curious, that's all."

"Curious about what?"

"The Vice President. I saw him taking notes, then lockin
them away. A diary or something. I wanted to see what said."

"Why?"

"I told you, I was curious."

"Stealing a key goes beyond girlish curiosity, Jenna. I
looks like you were suspicious of something and I'm wonder
ing what."

"Nothing, except the way he kept to himself. Look,
didn't find out a thing. Nothing came of it."

"But you had a copy of the key made."

"How did you know that?" she demanded.

"I'm a smart boy, Jenna. Don't let my good looks fool you
He winked. "Now this fellow Winnick, who went with you
get the key—what did you tell him?"

Jenna stared at him in sudden horror. "How did you kno
he went with me to the locksmith's shop?"

"I told you, I'm a smart boy."

Jenna went pale. "You killed him," she cried. "You fo
lowed us there and killed that poor old man."

Charlie frowned and sipped his beer. "Ah, Jenna," i
sighed, "so pretty and so troublesome."

"Damn you!" she cried and hurled her beer can at h
handsome, mocking face.

Charlie slapped the can aside. She leaped at him, scratc
ing at his face, but he quickly had both her wrists locked
one of his big hands.

"You mustn't do that again, Jenna. You'll only get yourse
hurt."

"You bastard," she shouted and kicked his shins. Char

yelped with pain and threw her down on the bed, where she lay sobbing.

Charlie leaned against the wall, rubbing his shin. "Jenna, you had better behave yourself, or else I might forget what a lovable bloke I am."

She was still sobbing, her face turned away from him.

"You're going to try to kill my father, aren't you?" she whispered.

"Ah, Jenna, Jenna . . ."

"You—you and whoever's behind you—you want to make Remington the President, don't you? I see that now. So why don't you go ahead and kill me and get it over with?"

Charlie sighed and went to the door. "Get some rest is my advice."

"You won't get away with it!" she shouted as he locked the door behind him.

27

It was after Zeb left for camp that Boyle decided to make a trip to Nashville. Camp was Zeb's own idea. His pal Derek was going, and Zeb decided to go too, lured by the prospect of nonstop swimming, tennis, boating, archery and, a modern touch, computer programming. Boyle had feared that Zeb would be homesick, but he soon found that he was the one who was unhappy. His big house was unnaturally quiet without a nine-year-old banging about. Boyle hurried to the post office early each morning, and on Zeb's third day away, his first postcard arrived. Scribbled across it was the message:

> "Dear Dad, Camp is great. I'm in a tent with five other guys. We fight a lot. Sorry, got to go to bed.
> Love, Zeb."

Boyle took comfort in the "Camp is great," and the next morning caught a flight to Nashville. He'd managed some campaigns in Tennessee and come to love its capital. Nashville was green and golden, big enough to be a center of politics, commerce, and music, yet small enough to retain the Southern warmth of yesteryear.

He flew to Nashville because he had decided to take Senator Trawick's advice and find out who had created Ben Remington.

He drove straight from the airport to the Nashville *Tennessean* and he spent the afternoon in the newspaper's library, digging through a mountain of old clippings that traced Remington's rise from BMOC at Vanderbilt to Vice President. The clippings, of course, raised more questions than they answered. That was why Boyle had a dinner date that evening with Jeeter Adcock, a political reporter for the *Tennessean*, whom he knew to be one of the most malicious, unscrupulous, and well-informed men in America.

Jeeter was a throwback to the golden days of Tennessee journalism, when reporters from rival newspapers went armed against one another. Jeeter had covered Boyle's first congressional campaign in Tennessee and unfortunately had loathed Boyle's candidate. Day after day, Jeeter had published distortions, half-truths, and outright lies about Boyle's man, and what he printed was not half so vile as what he said about the candidate to anyone who would listen. He accused Boyle's man—a teetotaling Baptist, happily married—of drunkenness, wife-beating, embezzlement from his church's building fund, and the seduction of boys from his Sunday school class. In remote areas of West Tennessee Jeeter would hunker down with tobacco-stained old-timers on the sagging porch of some crossroads store and grimly confide, "He's got a sister who's a thespian."

Boyle's man was soundly defeated, largely because of Jeeter Adcock's vendetta, but Boyle, taking the long view, kept on speaking terms with the reporter. They always had a drink together when Boyle passed through Nashville, and this evening they made their way to Printers Alley, the longtime center of good food, drink, and music in downtown Nashville.

Jeeter was a huge man, weighing over three hundred pounds, and he ate and drank on a grand scale, especially when an out-of-town political consultant was paying the bill.

They settled in a booth in a dark, quiet steak house and
Jeeter immediately ordered a fifth of Jim Beam, a three-
pound sirloin, and a huge platter of fried potatoes. When
Jeeter's dinner arrived, he pulled a bottle from somewhere
inside his coat and began to sprinkle a vile-looking green
liquid all over his food. "What's that?" Boyle asked. Jeeter
handed over the bottle, which proclaimed itself to be six
fluid ounces of Trappey's Green Dragon Jalapeño Sauce,
fresh from New Iberia, Louisiana. "The elixir of life!" Jeeter
declared. "Try some." Boyle dabbled a drop or two onto a
piece of bread and tasted it. Suddenly his mouth was aflame,
his eyes were blinded by tears. "Takes a little gettin' used
to," Jeeter conceded.

When Boyle recovered, he nursed a beer and they began
to talk, but about country music instead of politics.

Jeeter thought Hank Williams was the greatest musician,
the greatest poet, who had ever lived. "The Mozart of Mont-
gomery," he called him. Soon the two of them were arguing
bitterly about the relative merits of Hank Williams and Willie Nelson. Boyle, the devil's advocate, suggested that Willie
might be as great a figure in the history of country music as
Hank.

"You've got Jimmie Rodgers, Hank Williams, and then
Willie Nelson," Boyle declared. "There are other greats, but
those are the three innovators."

"Blasphemy," Jeeter grumbled.

"I'm not saying Willie is the poet, the *genius* Hank was,"
Boyle persisted, "but if you take everything together, his
songwriting, his singing, his guitar picking, the audience
he's reached, the old songs he's brought back, the *purity* he's
maintained . . ."

"Balls!" Jeeter Adcock roared. "Genius is genius and purity is for little girls." He grabbed a passing waitress to demand more ice, and Boyle eased into the subject of Ben
Remington.

"The thing is, Jeeter, the White House wants me to do a
documentary on Remington, but I don't feel like I understand the guy."

Boyle doubted that Jeeter believed that, but it didn't matter if the reporter felt like talking.

"Matthew, I've known our Vice President for thirty years, and we're talking about a man of unblemished virtue," Jeeter declared. "There are those who propose to kill him and start a new religion."

Boyle nibbled a French fry. "Nobody's that perfect," he ventured.

"The man is pure Horatio Alger. Rags to riches."

"Jeeter, are you telling me you haven't got anything on this guy?" Boyle said disbelievingly.

"I'm saying that this paragon only did two *slightly* unethical things in his life, and they made him rich."

"Explain."

"Ben went to Vanderbilt on a scholarship, didn't have a pot to pee in, but people liked him. He was student body president, number one in his class at law school, clearly a man of destiny. But then he made his first mistake."

"What was that?"

"He married Peaches Tidwell. Now some people wouldn't call that a mistake, her being the only offspring of the owner of Cherokee Insurance, but those people have never met Peaches. A man with his prospects who was out to marry money could have done a damn sight better. What I'm saying is, in the first big decision of his life, he showed rotten judgment."

"What's wrong with her?"

"You haven't met her? I guess they keep her tranquilized up in Washington. There's nothing wrong with Peaches, except she's a spoiled rich girl who never learned how to do nothing except drink, spend money, and copulate, and rumor has it she don't do the third one with any particular skill."

"So he marries this Tennessee belle. What happens? Other women?"

"Nary a hint of scandal. Pretty soon he's general counsel of Cherokee Insurance, and on his way to being chairman, as soon as his father-in-law kicks off. The trouble is, Ben's bored. He's too bright to be running an insurance company, which any nitwit can do, so he starts looking around for some likely investments."

"The computer company," Boyle said.

"Right you are. He buys a little company that's about to go under. The man has a Midas touch. He calls his computer the Little Colonel and aims it at the Southern market. Gets Opry stars to pitch it on TV. Makes it patriotic to buy the damn things. And his timing was perfect. Pretty soon the computers are selling like lemonade in Hades. Ben and his investors cleaned up—made twenty bucks for every one they invested. Then they go public with their stock. People were lined up for miles to buy in. Old folks with their life savings. So you can guess what happened."

"Refresh my memory."

"The bottom fell out. There were too damn many computers on the market. So Ben and his pals made millions, and the little people who bought their stock lost their shirts."

"So next he turns to politics?"

"Not right away. He had to be dragged in. The thing is, Ben don't have fire in his belly. He likes being rich, singing in the choir, playing golf, and don't much like hard work, which politics is from time to time."

"But he got drafted?"

"I give Peaches the credit. She figured it'd be nice to be the First Lady of Tennessee, so she bitched and hollered until he ran to shut her up."

"Okay, Jeeter, here you've got a middle-aged business-man, good-looking, more or less honest, but no fire in his belly. And not all that great a governor."

"Ben spent a lot of time on the golf course. Nope, nobody was hailing him as the pride of the New South."

"Yet this man gets to be Vice President," Boyle said. "What I want to know is how. I've known smarter men, tougher men, who've tried to make that leap and landed on their faces. Why Remington?"

"Well, your Mr. Webster had something to do with it," Jeeter drawled.

"Sure he did. But Remington had changed, before that. He took off, went national, went into orbit. How?"

Jeeter, ignoring the question, lumbered off toward the men's room. When he returned he was carrying a chess pie and two plates. "Dessert," he explained.

Boyle tasted the pie, a Tennessee specialty; it was heavenly. "Why Remington?" he repeated between mouthfuls.

"Well, it was that little black girl, wasn't it?" Jeeter said with a wolfish grin.

Boyle nodded. "That little black girl."

"You know about her, I reckon."

"I know what was in the papers," Boyle said. "And I saw it on the news when it happened."

Boyle had spent an hour that afternoon reading and re-reading the *Tennessean*'s story about Ben Remington and the little black girl. The banner headline: REMINGTON SAVES GIRL FROM RIVER. The photographs. The breathless prose. A five-year-old girl had fallen into the Cumberland River. Passersby had looked on helplessly. Then Governor Remington had chanced by, driving across the bridge; he stopped his car, saw the drowning child, stripped off his coat, and plunged into the deep and dangerous waters. A television cameraman had raced up in time to film him emerging from the river, the girl safe in his arms.

It was beautiful, incredible, the stuff of legend, and it made Remington a national celebrity overnight. He was fawned over by Johnny Carson, canonized by *Time* magazine, and awarded a medal at the White House. His ghost-written, inspirational book, *Paths of Courage,* topped the bestseller list for three months. The next year, "Draft Remington" committees sprang up like mushrooms across the South. The rest was history. When Calvin Webster won the party's nomination that summer, he chose the handsome, white-haired Tennessean as his running mate.

It was an inspiring story. The trouble was, Boyle didn't believe it. Boyle was in the business and he knew that miracles didn't happen.

Boyle finished his chess pie. "What about the little girl, Jeeter?" he said.

The reporter poured himself more bourbon. "What about her?" he replied. "Ben saved her. Our boy's a hero."

"It stinks," Boyle said. "It's too good to be true."

"It's on film," Jeeter said.

"I *saw* the film. I *still* don't believe it."

Jeeter showed his crooked teeth. "Welcome to the club. Hell, we figured maybe he fell off the damn bridge by mistake. But, the thing is, he did it. What's your alternative? That somebody tossed the kid in the river so Ben could be a hero?"

"Did anybody check that out?"

"Lemme tell you something. We sold more papers that week than any time since the Kennedy assassination. We *like* that story. Reminds me of thirty years ago, we had a reporter we sent out to cover the State Fair every year. He'd always get drunk and come back with a story about the little blind girl who won the blue ribbon for her angel food cake. There wasn't any little blind girl, you understand—he made her up —but what a hell of a story! Well, Remington jumping off the bridge is a hell of a story, too, and we're not gonna knock it."

Jeeter led Boyle down the alley to a club called The Carousel where a jazz trio was playing. They bellied up to the bar and Jeeter ordered a double brandy.

"Who's behind Remington?" Boyle demanded.

"Nobody," Jeeter said.

"Impossible. I'm in the business, Jeeter. Somebody smart is calling the shots. Reagan had his California cronies. Kennedy had the Irish Mafia. Who does Remington have?"

"Nobody," the reporter repeated. "Not in Nashville, anyway. He's a lone wolf. Remember, he ain't stupid."

"No, but he's not *that* smart," Boyle said. He thought a minute. "What do you mean, not in Nashville? Has he got somebody somewhere else?"

Jeeter grinned. "You're not as dumb as you look, boy. Well, there have been rumors."

"Of what?"

"Ben flies his own plane, you know. They say that sometimes he just takes off, into the wild blue yonder."

"Where to, Jeeter?"

The reporter downed his brandy and yelled for another. "Some people say Georgia," he told Boyle.

"Georgia?"

"Course, he might be going fishing. Some right good fishing over in North Georgia."

North Georgia. A memory flashed in Boyle's mind, then
faded into darkness. When he tried to pump Jeeter Adcock
some more, the newspaperman yawned. Outside, as they
waved for a cab, Jeeter said, "You know, for a fellow who's
maybe gonna do the official White House documentary on
old Ben, you don't seem real fond of him."

Boyle had to laugh. "Like you said, Jeeter, I'm not as dumb
as I look."

28

The next day Charlie arrived with a pot of vegetable stew. "Made it myself," he announced. She tried to detain him, but he said he had no time. "Back soon," he promised. "Enjoy!"

Jenna ate a bowl of stew and drank a glass of orange juice. She felt not so much fearful as profoundly depressed. She didn't know how many people were involved with Charlie, or how capable they were, but she was convinced that somehow they were planning to kill her father, make Remington President, and scuttle the disarmament program. They'd kidnapped her because she was suspicious of Remington. But why hadn't they killed her? The murder of the locksmith proved Charlie would kill without a second thought. Perhaps they thought she might be more valuable alive. That was her only edge, her only advantage: They wanted her alive.

Escape, she thought. All her brains and strength and guile must be directed at that one goal.

She finished the stew, washed the bowl, and sat down on the bed, thinking of Charlie, his vanity, his potential weak-

nesses. Suddenly she felt giddy. She was flying, spinning, out
of control. She'd felt that way once at a fraternity party
when a boy had stuck a vial under her nose and told her to
inhale and foolishly she had; she'd gotten a whiff of amyl
nitrate and gone into orbit, a leaf in a storm, terrified, and
she felt that way now. Then, as abruptly as it had come, the
storm passed. She lay on the bed, drained, trembling. The
stew, she thought, he put something in the stew, some drug.
It all seemed wonderfully funny. She started to laugh and
then she was unconscious.

Charlie returned in a few minutes, wiped Jenna's brow,
took her pulse, then slapped her.

"Can you hear me?" he demanded.

She moaned and he slapped her again. "Can you hear
me?"

Her eyes fluttered. "Yes," she whispered.

"Will you tell me the truth now?"

"Yes."

"Have you been working for the Vice President?"

"Yes."

"Were you suspicious of the Vice President?"

"Yes."

"Why, Jenna?"

Her pale skin glistened with sweat.

"Why, Jenna?" Charlie repeated.

"He was . . . strange . . . got phone calls every morning . . . not know who . . ."

"You were suspicious because he received mysterious telephone calls?"

"Yes."

"Do you know who the calls were from?"

"I . . . no . . . don't know."

"Tell me the truth, Jenna. Who called him?"

"Not . . . sure."

"Who do you think?"

"Maybe . . . a woman."

"How do you know?"

"Not sure . . . heard him say it . . . on the phone."

"Jenna, who did you tell about this woman who called?"

"Nobody."

"Are you certain?"

"Talked to Matt . . . but . . . don't think . . . didn't tell."

"You told Matt Boyle you were suspicious of the Vice President but you didn't mention the woman. Is that correct?"

"Yes."

"Did you mention her to Winnick, the Secret Service man?"

"No."

She slipped back into unconsciousness. Her raven hair fanned out atop the pillow. "Jenna, be a dear and get up now," her captor said.

"So tired."

"I know you're tired. You can sleep for a long time. But first you must get up."

"Can't."

"Yes, you can," he said, and helped her into a chair.

"I want you to write something for me," he said.

He gave her a pen and a postcard and told her what he wanted her to write. When he was satisfied he helped her back to the bed.

"You get some sleep now," he said. "You'll feel better in the morning."

"Sleep," she muttered.

He spread a blanket over her, then pushed a wisp of hair back from her eyes. Such a lovely girl, he thought. More's the pity.

The next morning Boyle drove to East Nashville and tried in vain to trace the black girl Remington had saved from the river, but she and her mother had vanished. "I think maybe they done moved to Florida," was the hottest lead he found.

Boyle's next stop was a local television station, where he viewed the unedited film of Remington's rescue of the girl from the river. Despite all his suspicions, Boyle found the film moving—it seemed a moment of sheer heroism.

As he left the station, a burly man in jeans and a leather

jacket called his name. "Boyle? I'm Bobby Crump, the one that shot the Remington footage. A buddy of mine called and said you was asking about it, so I figured I better see what's in it for me."

Boyle nodded agreeably. "Good to see you, Bob," he said. "How about some lunch?"

They walked to a nearby tavern and ordered beer and barbecue. Boyle kept the cameraman drinking and talking while he sized him up. It didn't take long. Bobby Crump was a hustler, down on his luck.

"Listen, I had plenty of offers after I shot the Remington story. I coulda gone to New York or the Coast. But my wife, she had to stay in Nashville. Now the bitch has run off with a guitar player and I'm stuck here."

Boyle nodded sympathetically. "That Remington footage is fantastic," he said. "I may want to use it in a documentary. You'd be paid, of course."

"How much?"

Boyle shrugged. "A thousand?"

Crump laughed nastily. "Five," he said.

"It's a fine piece of work," Boyle said. "Tell me how you got it."

The cameraman belched. "How about another round first?"

"Sure," Boyle said.

"Boilermakers, maybe."

"Just beer for me," Boyle said.

The waitress brought the drinks. Crump gulped his boilermaker. "Not much to tell," he said. "I was a block away, on another assignment, when I heard people yelling down at the river. I got down there about the time Remington hit the water and I shot it all, exclusive. Three minutes on the network that night. By-lined."

"You didn't see the little girl fall in?"

"Naw, she was in the drink when I got there. I figgered she was a goner. Him too, the crazy fool. Listen, Boyle, you wouldn't need a good cameraman up in Washington, maybe some free-lance work, would you?"

"I might, Bob. Let me think about it."

They wound up in Printers Alley with Boyle buying the cameraman many more drinks. Boyle had missed his plane, because he thought this cheap hustler was getting at something, in his own sweet time.

An oafish, drunken grin spread across the cameraman's face. "You don't trust old Ben, do you?"

Boyle shrugged.

"Look, I need a break, so I'm gonna tell you something I never told nobody else. You repeat it, I'll call you a damn liar. You follow?"

"Sure."

Crump fixed his half-closed eyes on Boyle. "I was tipped onto the Remington story—the famous rescue."

Boyle never blinked. "What do you mean?"

"I got a call. Some guy says be outside the union hall— right at the end of the bridge—at three o'clock. They'd been having trouble at the union, brawls, guys packing guns, so I figured it was worth a look. So at three I'm parked at the end of the bridge when the kid goes in. Johnny on the spot."

"That's some coincidence," Boyle said.

"Ain't it?"

"What do you make of it?"

"Me? I'm just a hick cameraman. You're the big political genius. But, since you ask, I figure no politician is gonna risk his ass without a camera around."

"Any idea who called you?"

"Nope."

"Did anything happen at the union hall?"

Crump's smile made him uglier. "What do you think? See, Boyle, I kept quiet at first because I didn't want to screw up my big story. Later on, I figured that someday old Ben's gonna run for President, and maybe my information might be valuable—you know what I mean? But, hell, I meet you and I figure you're a smarter man than I'll ever be, so I'll tell you about it. See, all I want is a break. Can you help me, up in D.C.?"

"Maybe so," Boyle said. "Call me next week."

29

It was cool in the Oval Office but the Secretary of State was sweating. Cal Webster's fury did that to people. Harry Bliss, watching, was pleased, for he thought the Secretary of State was a fool. A senior partner in a distinguished Wall Street law firm, a man who had held high posts in three administrations —and a fool. Where did these people come from?

"You have no explanation for this, Mr. Secretary?" the President said coldly.

"I . . . we . . . my people say . . ." the Secretary stammered. It was amazing, Harry thought, how a President's scorn could turn these high muckety-mucks into squirming schoolboys.

"I don't care about what *your people* say," Webster raged. "*You* met with the Soviet Ambassador this morning—what did *he* say?"

The Secretary mopped his brow with a silk handkerchief. "He denied there was any problem, sir," he mumbled.

"At which point I trust you told the sucker he was lying," President Webster declared.

"I . . . ah . . . stressed that we had information to th contrary."

"Very diplomatic, Mr. Secretary," the President said bi terly. "And what did *he* say?"

"He continued to deny any change in Soviet intention Mr. President," the Secretary of State said lamely.

"By damn!" Webster shouted, pounding his fist into h desk. "Mr. Director, perhaps you'll refresh the Secretary memory."

The Director of Central Intelligence suppressed a smil He was a thick cold slab of a man, but formidable, and h hope of himself becoming Secretary of State was the wors kept secret in town.

"Mr. President," he said gravely, "we have informatio from satellites and on-site sources, that more than a hundre trucks, bearing Soviet missiles to their deactivation cente suddenly turned around yesterday morning and returned t their points of origin. This casts grave doubts on the Soviet intention of carrying through with the second phase of di armament."

"Mr. Director," the President said, "would the Kreml leaders be aware that we would know immediately if a hu dred missile-bearing trucks suddenly returned to the bases?"

"Absolutely, sir."

"And if this were caused by some innocent reason—som logistical problem—would you say they would hasten to i form us, lest we grow anxious about their intentions?"

"No question about it, Mr. President."

"Therefore, would you say they don't give a damn wha we think, because they've got some Godawful power strug gle in progress?"

"That is my conclusion, sir."

"Thank you," Webster said. "Now, would you please giv us your best guess on what is happening in the Kremlin?

"Gladly, Mr. President. There seems to be a small bu influential faction in the Soviet Union consisting of senio military men and old-line party officials who've opposed th disarmament process from the first and now have gained th upper hand, at least to the extent of postponing or delaying the second round of dismantlings."

"Mr. President," the Secretary of State said, "I might note that we and the Soviets have some ten days remaining under the terms of our agreement before the second round of missiles must be destroyed."

"Nine days, to be precise," the CIA Director said.

"Where are *our* thousand missiles, Mr. Director?" Harry Bliss interjected.

"All but a handful have reached the conversion centers," the CIA Director said.

"In other words," Harry pressed, "we have a thousand nuclear weapons—some ten percent of our arsenal—out of commission, while the Soviets are returning theirs to their bases? Is that correct?"

Now it was the CIA Director's turn to sweat. "Technically speaking, that is correct, sir. But of course these are our oldest and least potent weapons, and our national security is in no way diminished."

"By damn, my political security is diminished," the President raged. "If this leaks, we'll have a political earthquake. We've got to find out what the Soviets are up to. We've got to let them know we're mad as hell. So you two get off your duffs and be back here at ten in the morning with a plan for action. That's all!"

The CIA Director and Secretary of State scrambled out of the Oval Office. The President sighed loudly. Dusk blurred the Rose Garden. "A drink, Harry?"

Harry poured two mild scotch and waters. They sipped in silence for a while. Finally the President said, "The worst of it is how little control I have. Who knows what's going on in the Kremlin?"

Harry said, "The worst-case scenario would be that the hardliners win the Kremlin power struggle. Then they'd accuse us of some violation and pull out of Project Peace."

"Whereupon I'd have to denounce them," the President said. "Congress and the media would be in a dither. So, for that matter, would all of Europe. The Soviets might move into Eastern Europe. I'd have to retaliate. Anything could happen."

He sighed again. "All because of two or three fools in the Kremlin who think I'm a capitalist warmonger. What a world."

There was a rapping at the door, then one of Harry's secretaries scurried in. "Excuse me, sir, but I thought you'd want to see this right away."

Harry glanced at the postcard, then broke into a grin. "Well, here's a bit of comic relief," he declared, and handed the card to the President.

Webster read the message aloud: "Dear Mom and Dad, I'm fine. Just needed some time to think. I'll be in touch soon. Love, Jenna."

The President leaned back and roared. "By God, a *postcard*. Addressed to 'Mr. and Mrs. Calvin Webster, 1600 Pennsylvania, Washington, D.C.' Isn't that just like her?"

"I imagine the FBI will want to examine the card," Harry said. "To make sure it's authentic."

"Will the cloak and dagger never end?" the President groaned. "It's *Jenna*, out for a lark!"

"One other thing, sir. Matt Boyle's been nosing around, looking for Jenna. He talked to her landlady, then flew down to Nashville, quizzing people about the Vice President."

"What is *wrong* with that guy?" the President demanded.

"The thing is, sir, apparently Mrs. Webster asked him to . . . ah . . . check into Jenna's whereabouts."

The President's face reddened beneath his tan. "Well, we know her whereabouts now, don't we? I'll speak to Mrs. Webster. You take care of Boyle. I'm sick of that guy. I don't want us having anything more to do with him. Do I make myself clear?"

"Perfectly clear," Harry said.

30

On Boyle's first morning back from Nashville he hurried to the Harmony Post Office and found Zeb's second postcard. It reported:

> "Dear Dad, Camp is still fun except I have to walk 1/4 mile to breakfast, lunch and dinner. I am taking a shower every morning and evening and the same with my teeth.
>
> Love, Zeb."

Have to work on the boy's syntax, Boyle reflected as he walked back home. Then he called the White House.

"Matt, I'm sorry, he's in a meeting," reported Harry's secretary, Matt's old friend Daisy.

"Ask him to call me as soon as he can, Daisy," Boyle said. "Tell him it's urgent."

Boyle had no doubt that his call was urgent. He was more convinced than ever that Jenna's suspicions about the Vice President had somehow led to her disappearance. And now the cameraman's confession that he'd been tipped off to Remington's rescue of the little girl persuaded Boyle that

Remington's entire rise to national fame was tainted, somehow manipulated by shadowy forces. Once Harry understood, he had the power to take a closer look at the Vice President, to put some heat on him.

But where was Harry? Boyle paced, fussed, fumed for an hour, then called again. "I'm sorry, Matt, he's still tied up," Daisy told him.

"Did you tell him it was urgent?"

"*Yes*, Matt. He's just so busy."

Boyle settled down with the Washington *Post*. When he reached its Style section he was startled to see Jenna's picture. The White House Press Secretary, the story said, had "scotched" rumors that the President's daughter Jenna had mysteriously vanished from the Washington scene. The "First Daughter," the Press Secretary said, was en route to Florida to visit friends. Her parents had heard from her and, contrary to reports, were in no way concerned about her absence. "If you know Jenna, you'll understand," the spokesman had concluded with a wink.

Boyle didn't believe a word of it. What the hell was going on? Why hadn't Harry returned his call. Boyle paced, tried to read a magazine. At four he called again.

"I'm *sorry*," Daisy said. "I gave him the message, both times. I said it was urgent. Honest."

"Daisy, tell him it's about Jenna."

There was a long silence. Daisy was overweight and overworked, a sweet kid. He'd given her flowers on her thirtieth birthday. Finally she said, "Matt, I shouldn't say this, but you've always been good to me. Harry won't return your calls, no matter what it is."

The finality of it sank in fast. He'd been there himself, at the top of the heap; sometimes you cut people off and there wasn't a thing they could do about it except hate you.

"Okay, Daisy," he said. "Thanks much."

Turk Kellerman, sightless and serene, rocked gently in his chair while Jeff Winnick reported on his trip south.

"The postcard is mailed from Savannah, so we figure she's driven down I-95, right? Turk, there are three *hundred* gas stations off I-95, and we've checked them *all*. A pretty girl in a Morgan, probably with the top down, and nobody remembers her."

"She might have gotten bored with the Interstate," Turk said. "Cruised the back roads. Bought her gas there."

Jeff rubbed his eyes wearily. "We're starting on those. We're checking motels. We've got men working house to house around the post office where the card was mailed. Nothing. What the hell is going on?"

The blind man shifted heavily in his chair. "One of two things," he said. "Either a pretty girl with a famous face can drive a sports car to Florida without anybody noticing her or . . ."

He lit a cigarette and flipped the wooden match unerringly into the wastebasket in the corner.

"Or what?" Jeff demanded.

"Or the postcard was a fake."

"But the handwriting analysts . . . they said it was her writing, no sign of coercion."

Kellerman blew a perfect smoke ring for others to admire. "Listen, the new drugs they've got, you could throttle your mother and never stop smiling."

There was a knock at the door and Elton Saussy, Kellerman's friend from the FBI, stepped into the room. He was a tall, pockmarked, cadaverous man in a cheap suit who spoke with the unlettered drawl of North Florida. His close friends called him "Swamprat." Kellerman discounted Saussy's redneck style; experience had taught him that no one rose to the top at the Bureau without finesse and an instinct for the jugular.

"It was a miracle they found it," Saussy declared, sinking into a chair. "The state boys were flying over a national forest, looking for marijuana, when they saw something glittering, way the hell back in the woods."

"What are you talking about?" Kellerman boomed.

"Jenna's car. Somebody ditched it in the woods in West Virginia. When the state boys figured out who it was registered to, they called us. I hauled ass over there and what I found was a dent on the left front fender, like she'd been forced off the road."

"No, no," Jeff moaned.

"It gets worse," Saussy said. "I put the car up on a rack and went over the chassis, inch by inch. And guess what I found?"

"What?" Jeff demanded.

Saussy pulled from his pocket a metallic object the size of a hockey puck. "This."

Jeff groaned. "A homing device," he said. "A beeper."

Saussy handed the device to Kellerman, who stroked it with his fingertips. "Japanese?" he asked.

"Yeah," Saussy told him. "The best. If you've got the right receiver, you can pick this baby up for five miles."

"How long had it been on the car?" Kellerman asked.

"Judging from the dirt, three–four weeks."

"Well, that's that," Kellerman said. "Somebody planted this on Jenna's car a month ago. Somebody world-class professional. That's how they followed her and Jeff to the locksmith's shop. And the other night they followed her, grabbed her, and dumped the car in West Virginia. In such a hurry that they left this little jewel behind."

"Probably figured the car'd never get found," Saussy said.

"Or that by the time it was found it wouldn't matter," Kellerman added. Pieces of the puzzle danced elusively in his mind. To him, Jenna was only part of the equation. *Who would want to kill this President and how would he do it?*

"So what do we do now?" Jeff asked.

Kellerman exhaled two plumes of smoke. His ruined eyes were twin holes burned in the toughest oak. "We report to our masters," he said.

When Kellerman finished his report, Harry Bliss cursed bitterly, then said, "All right, what you're saying is this: Jenna's been kidnapped by the kind of foreign agent, or professional criminal, who would use a homing device. We've had no message or demands from the kidnapper, but you think she's alive. The postcard was a fake, intended to throw us off. The kidnapping may be somehow connected with her trip to the locksmith shop and the murder of that old man. But you have no idea who's behind this or what they want. Correct?"

"Correct," Kellerman muttered. Jeff Winnick gritted his teeth. He had a theory on who was behind this but he was fearful of speaking out until he had evidence.

Harry fiddled with a chain of paper clips he had linked together. "I want you men to remember one thing. The President is in the midst of delicate negotiations with the Soviets. I'm concerned about Jenna, but I'm also concerned about this mess blowing up in our faces at the worst possible time. You can have all the manpower you want, but keep this quiet, unless you can show me an urgent reason for going public. Okay?"

Kellerman had started to rise when Jeff spoke up. "There is one other thing."

Harry glared at him suspiciously. "What?"

"The key," Jeff said. He hadn't intended to speak up, but he couldn't help himself. Now he felt as if he were walking on the thinnest of ice. When very junior agents were included in White House meetings, they were expected to speak only when spoken to.

"What about the key?" Harry demanded.

"We've never known why Jenna went to the locksmith that day. But I think Jenna had become suspicious of the Vice President and wanted a key to his desk or his files."

Harry Bliss laughed mirthlessly. "Suspicious of Ben Remington? Look, he's harmless."

"There's something new," Jeff said.

"What the hell do you mean, new?" Kellerman roared.

"After Jenna returned from the locksmith shop," Jeff continued, "she and Remington met with three officials from the EPA. A briefing on acid rain, I think. I talked to the EPA fellows this morning. Something strange happened in that meeting."

"Get to it!" Harry snapped.

"The Vice President came back from working out to meet with them. He'd left his coat in the closet behind his desk. He started searching its pockets. He got very upset—he said he'd lost a key. He looked everywhere, even got down on his hands and knees, searching the floor. Then, suddenly, Jenna said, 'Is that it?', and there was the key, on the floor, beside the Vice President's desk. Except one of the EPA officials told me he doesn't think the key was there before; he thinks she tossed it there while they were all watching Remington grub around on the floor."

"So what are you saying?" Harry demanded.

"That when Remington went to his workout, Jenna grabbed the key from his coat, hurried to the locksmith shop to get a copy, but didn't get back in time to replace the original in his coat. So she tossed it on the floor, and got away with it, except that she ended up with the Vice President suspicious of her, even if he couldn't prove anything."

Harry said, "Okay, maybe Jenna did steal the key—she's nutty enough. But what's your bottom line? That the Vice President had her kidnapped, to teach her a lesson?"

"I don't know the bottom line," Jeff admitted. "Except that I'd like to question the Vice President about the key. Maybe there's some explanation. If not, we rattle his cage a little."

"Listen, fellow," Harry said, "if you start asking the Vice President questions, two things will happen. Number one, he'll throw you out of his office. Number two, he'll start bitching to his cronies and the whole thing will wind up on the front page of the Washington *Post*. And we don't need that particular problem right now. You men get on with your investigation. And Kellerman, I'm holding you responsible if any young hotheads on your staff cause me any problems."

Jeff saw red. "Dammit, Jenna's been kidnapped," he yelled.

"I know that, Sir Galahad," Harry said coldly. "So why don't you go find her?"

As they marched out of Harry Bliss's big West Wing office, Jeff was furious. He decided then what he must do, that very night.

When Jeff arrived back in his office, he had a message to call Matt Boyle. He did so reluctantly.

"I've got to see you," Boyle began.

"Why? I'm busy."

"I've found out something important."

"Where are you calling from?" Jeff demanded.

"A pay phone."

"Okay, what is it? Be specific."

"It concerns the Vice President," Boyle said. "But I can't explain it over the phone. I have to see you."

The young agent frowned. He didn't trust Boyle, but they were moving in the same direction. "Come by my office tomorrow afternoon," he said.

"Tomorrow afternoon?" Boyle yelled. "Jenna's missing. This could be life or death. How about tonight?"

Jeff was uncertain. "I'm busy tonight," he said. "I'll be tied up until late."

"How late?"

"Late."

"There's a Little Tavern on Wisconsin Avenue in Georgetown that stays open all night. I'll meet you there, anytime you say."

"I'll try to be there around two," Jeff Winnick promised.

"I'll be there," Boyle said.

Harry saw the President that afternoon. They talked about the Russians and the latest polls and a Cabinet member whose wife was playing around. The President kept coming back to the Russians. Nobody knew what was happening in the Kremlin power struggle. Russian roulette, the President joked bitterly. Harry had never seen Webster so short-tempered, so frustrated. He was a brave, blunt man, a man who wanted all the cards on the table, and that was his limitation, for in this game there were no cards, no table, hardly even a game, just echoes and rumors, mirrors and masks, and the specter of tragedy beyond all imagining.

Halfway through the meeting, Harry made up his mind. He wouldn't tell the President about Jenna's car and the beeper and the certainty that she'd been kidnapped. What could he do except worry? He was already half crazed by the Russians, why worsen his pain?

A girl had once moved in with Jeff Winnick and moved out in a few weeks with the comment: "I'm too old to live with a Boy Scout." The specific problem had been that Jeff wouldn't let her keep marijuana in his apartment, but he recognized that her angry words had reflected a general truth. He *had* been a Boy Scout—an Eagle Scout, in fact—and even as a grown man, tended to be trustworthy, loyal, helpful, friendly, and all the rest of the Scout Creed, right down to brave, clean, and reverent. Jeff thought that if he had any serious flaw as a law-enforcement officer, it was that he could never truly understand the criminal mind. The idea of stealing, of lying, of cheating, of *breaking the law* was as foreign to him as to Gulliver's noble Houyhnhnms. If Jeff Winnick so much as jaywalked, he felt more guilt than many a mass murderer.

Thus, late that night Jeff was sweating, his innards churning, as he approached the sign-in desk at the Executive Office Building. The guard greeted him with the anxious smile of one who would welcome company on a long, boring night. Jeff, for his part, hesitated to sign the check-in sheet; he feared his hand might tremble.

"I hear them Orioles lost again," the guard volunteered.

Jeff muttered something about them needing an out-fielder who could hit. He'd played baseball himself in college, and been president of the FCA, the Fellowship of Christian Athletes. Now his voice seemed a dry croak, a giveaway.

Why am I doing this?

He was doing it for Jenna. For whatever guilt he might feel for this transgression, it was far less than his guilt for letting Jenna elude him. She had been his responsibility and he had failed her, perhaps because he was half in love with her, no matter how ridiculous that might be.

"Burning the midnight oil, are you?" the guard said.

"Got to check a couple of things," Jeff said. "Won't be long."

He wrote in his name and the time; his hand did not tremble at all.

With a casual wave, he started down the shadowy corridor the Vice President's suite.

His key admitted him. To enter was not the problem. Soft ght filled the reception room; the rest of the suite was dark d silent. He went to Jenna's office and turned on her desk mp. If questioned, he would say he had come to check her apers once again, a flimsy story but all he had. The problem as that he intended to go farther, into the inner sanctum, nd he had no excuse for that intrusion. Nor was he sure hat security he might offend; if he was dealing with people ho used homing devices to seize a President's daughter, othing was certain except peril.

He sat at Jenna's desk, listening, until he could wait no nger. He slipped through the darkness, clutching a flash- ght the size of a pen, until his passkey opened the Vice resident's door. The big office was quiet as a tomb. Jeff ased across the rug to Remington's desk, sat in the swivel hair, startled to hear its squeak, and searched his key ring r a key for the desk drawer. Across the room, gold and lver fish darted about in Remington's aquarium, mute, immering witnesses to his crime.

He found the key and the drawer slid open, revealing a lutter of papers and small objects. A blue address book aught his eye. He wondered if it might contain Rem- agton's most private numbers. A fast search of the other esk drawers revealed no better hope, so he slipped the ddress book into his pocket and hurried back to the relative afety of Jenna's office.

He sat at her desk, beneath her John Lennon poster, read- ng through the names and numbers recorded there in the ice President's neat script. He could not risk copying the ttle book, nor could he take it with him—his entry that ight was on record, and he could not afford to have a theft iscovered. Some of the names he recognized—senators, elevision celebrities. Sometimes there were simply initials, wo letters, or even one. He went through the book, A to Z, opying down names and numbers, not sure any of them neant anything, and then he noticed something written on he inside back cover of the book. Not a name, an initial, but

put differently than all the other initials: "Ms. M.," followe
by a number with a 404 area code.

Jeff's mind ached for a connection. A woman in Georgi
half-concealed in the back of the book. Some name, som
memory, from months past called to him in vain.

Jeff froze as he heard footsteps out in the corridor. Whe
they had died away he quickly returned the notebook to th
Vice President's desk, locked the desk, locked the office, an
returned to the guard's desk at the front door.

"Did I tell you them Orioles lost again?" the guard said o
parting.

Jeff got into his car and drove toward Georgetown. H
wanted to find out what Boyle knew, if anything, but h
intended to tell him nothing. The last thing the Secret Se
vice needed was an amateur screwing up its investigatio

Even in the middle of the night, Georgetown's street
were crowded. Jeff found a parking place beneath som
trees on O Street, two blocks from the Little Tavern, an
paid no attention to the car that pulled past him.

Nor did he pay attention when the tall, loose-limbe
young man hurried his way on the brick sidewalk.

Charlie seethed with anger. This summons, like the one t
the locksmith's shop, had come too fast. He felt himsel
losing control. He wanted no confrontation with the Secre
Service. And yet he had no choice.

He came abreast of Jeff Winnick and lashed out with hi
knife.

Jeff was an athlete in the peak of conditioning. His bod
reacted instantly, even before his mind understood th
threat. His left arm deflected the blow, although the knif
bit deeply into his flesh. The two men were joined in a gor
embrace. They bit, butted, pounded, and fell to the side
walk, struggling for their lives a hundred feet from the glar
of Wisconsin Avenue. Neighbors, accustomed to shouts an
brawls, slept on.

Boyle sat at the counter in the Little Tavern, sipping a
of rancid coffee. The longer he waited, the greater was hi
despair. What was he doing, running off to Nashville, then t

Georgetown in the middle of the night? If Harry wouldn't talk to him, he should tell Jeff everything he knew and then let the Secret Service find Jenna. What could he possibly accomplish by himself?

Soon, as he waited, his thoughts were of Cara. It often happened like that; out of nowhere he would be day-dreaming about her, some joke they'd shared, some trip they'd taken, some image of her, holding Zeb or working in her garden. He thought that some part of his mind was always focused on Cara. He was thinking of the way she went to the hospital four times a year to give a pint of blood. Boyle, who hated needles, had never fully understood it, but he said that she didn't need the blood and someone else did —it was that simple to her. His memory skipped to another image, of a time he and Cara and Zeb had gone skinny-dipping, down by the dam outside of Harmony, and he was lost in that memory when the Little Tavern's door crashed open.

Boyle leaped to his feet. Jeff Winnick, his shirt soaked in blood, stumbled toward him. Boyle embraced him, kept him from falling. "Who did it?" he demanded.

"Ms. M., Georgia," the agent gasped.

"She stabbed you?" Boyle asked in confusion.

"Ms. M. Address book. Find her."

He sank to the floor. Boyle knelt beside him. "Call an ambulance," he yelled at the cook, who was frozen behind the counter.

Boyle tried to stop the flow of blood but the young Secret Service agent was unconscious when the first ambulance arrived. Then dozens of people were crowded into the tiny restaurant. Boyle made a quick decision and, before anyone could question him, slipped out into the night.

31

"My goodness, Major, you look awful," declared Professor Seymour Lamb, with a high-pitched giggle. "Hit by a truck?"

Professor Lamb was a rotund, pink-cheeked man in his forties.

"Tripped on my basement steps," Charlie said.

Charlie's left hand was bandaged and his face was cut and bruised. There were other bruises the professor could not see, beneath the uniform Charlie was wearing. It was the uniform of an officer in British army intelligence and he looked quite splendid in it.

"I'd think a fellow in your line would be more careful," the professor said. "Well, Major . . . ah . . . Pitt is it?"

"Pitney-Boyce," Charlie said, with a clipped and quite convincing Oxbridge accent.

"Ah, yes, Pitney-Boyce. Well, shall we proceed?"

As he led the way from his farmhouse to his barn, Professor Lamb launched a monologue on laser beams. He taught physics at the University of Maryland and was accustomed to a captive audience.

"I like to think that three of the great men of this century re the godfathers of our little weapon," he said coyly. Think you can guess them?"

Charlie's smile hurt his mouth. "Three great men," he epeated.

"If you know anything at all about modern science you ould guess the first one," Lamb said.

Charlie's ribs ached; he was thinking how he would like to rottle this fool.

"Albert Einstein," the professor said. "The theory of stim-lated emission was a by-product of his theory of relativity, ack in 1917. What happens if an excited electron is hit by a hoton? Stimulated emission happens. Sounds racy, eh? All means is an intense, coherent beam of light. The word aser comes from Light Amplification by Stimulated Emis-ion of Radiation. L-A-S-E-R. Clever, eh?"

Lamb led the way into the modern laboratory he had stalled in the old barn on his farm in rural Maryland. Char-e looked around, grudgingly impressed.

"Yes, clever," he said.

"But stimulated emission was only a theory until, oh, 1960 r so when the second great man entered the picture. I oubt you'd guess this one, Major Pitt."

"Pitney-Boyce," Charlie said frostily.

"The second godfather of the laser was none other than Ioward Hughes, the so-called bashful billionaire. A bit of an dd duck, they say, but a giant in the defense industry. He uilt a research laboratory in Malibu, California—out where he movie stars live—and a fellow named Maiman used a uby rod to produce the first laser. After that, it was Katie ar the door. One invention after another. You could use asers to measure the distance to the planets. To cut dia-nonds. For eye surgery. To burn away tooth decay or tat-oos. To replace needles in record players."

Professor Lamb paused to fire up his pipe. Charlie gritted is teeth and waited.

"But burning away tattoos isn't what excites your govern-nent or mine, is it, Major? Of course not. What our govern-nents want is the ultimate weapon. A Death Ray. Zap,

you're dead. The Pentagon was putting money into las
research as far back as 1959, and the Russians weren't f
behind. There were rumors in the Sixties that the Russia
had tested a laser weapon in their border war with Chi
and blinded Chinese soldiers. No proof, but it scared t
blazes out of the Pentagon."

The professor puffed contentedly on his pipe. "You se
Major, the problem has always been size. There's nev
been any doubt that a laser beam could kill a man, but i
always been assumed it would take a weapon as big as
cannon. You *can* have a laser cannon, for shooting dov
incoming missiles, but for your combat soldier it looked li
the laser would never replace the trusty old rifle. The 'r
gun' was just for James Bond and the science fiction write
or so they thought, but that's where the third great ma
comes in—care to guess?"

Charlie smiled his most sardonic smile. "You, Professor

The professor actually blushed. "Nonsense, Major, I'm ju
a soldier in the trenches of science. No, I mean a truly gre
man."

"Ronald Reagan," Charlie said.

The professor's grin melted. "How'd you know?"

"How many great men are there?" Charlie shrugged.

Lamb pouted. "Well, what happened was, Reagan too
office in '81 and told the Pentagon they'd be getting an ext
$36 billion to spend on national defense. Well, the Pentag
panicked—they didn't know *how* to spend that mu
money. But the White House wouldn't take no for an a
swer, so the Pentagon dug up every old wish list, eve
crackpot scheme that'd ever been proposed."

"Indeed," Charlie said.

"My proposal, needless to say, was not a crackpot schem
although there were those who'd called it that. But I'd b
lieved for years that the laser could be miniaturized. Wh
with the new technology, integrated circuits, silicon supe
chips, there had to be a way. And one day I got a call fro
Masters Aviation, 'Professor Lamb,' they said, 'how mu
money do you need to revive your laser project?' Holy
ledo, I'd almost forgotten the project, but I said, 'A millio

'Are you sure that's enough?' they said, so I said, 'With infla-
tion, maybe two million.' "

Dr. Lamb surveyed his gleaming new laboratory. "The
two million was well spent, Major," he said. "There were
difficulties, but I've overcome them. We have our weapon.
The only question is how the weapon can best be applied."

Charlie lit a cigarette. "Quite."

"I didn't realize the Pentagon had such an . . . intimate
relationship with British Intelligence," the professor said,
his eyes narrowing.

"We're thick as thieves."

"You understand what we have here is a weapon that can
be held in one hand and can kill a man instantly. The only
drawback now, in its present state, is that you have to shoot
the fellow through the eye. The intensity of that jolt is like a
thunderbolt, short-circuits the brain. And leaves no clues.
Any doctor will say the victim died of a stroke, cerebral
hemorrhage. I've been thinking, Major Pitt, about that Castro. Our CIA has been after him for decades, with exploding
cigars and poison darts and nonsense like that, but here's a
weapon that . . ."

"You're sure about the doctors?" Charlie asked.

"The what?"

"The doctors would say it was a stroke."

"Oh, no doubt about it. Ruptured blood vessels. Death in a
matter of seconds. Happens every day. No reason to suspect
foul play."

Charlie puffed intently on his cigarette. "Interesting," he
said.

"You understand, Major Putney, that there's much more
to be done. I'll need staff, more laboratories, a budget of, oh,
twenty million, to get started. I can revolutionize modern
warfare."

"Pitney-Boyce," Charlie said. "I'm sure you'll get what
you deserve. May I see the specifications?"

Lamb's eyes narrowed again. The Englishman had been
vouched for by Masters Aviation but something about him
troubled the professor. "Will you understand them, Major?"
he demanded.

"Try me," Charlie said. The professor handed over a thick sheaf of papers and blueprints. Charlie understood enough for his purposes. When he finished reading, he said, "The demonstration."

The professor opened a cabinet to reveal a wall safe. He twirled the dial, unaware that his guest was memorizing the combination. With great care he extracted from the safe a small, gleaming tube the size of a flashlight battery. "Isn't it a beauty?" he asked.

Charlie held the device in his hands while the professor lovingly explained its triggering mechanism. "It's as easy as pie," Lamb declared. "All you need now is a housing of the sort you described to me."

"Yes," Charlie said. He opened his bag and took out a camera, an old Nikon F with a 200-millimeter lens and a flash attachment. The laser fit perfectly.

"A camera?" the professor said with astonishment. "But that's perfect. You can just pretend to be a . . ."

"The demonstration," Charlie said.

Dr. Lamb led them around the barn to a henhouse. "I thought we could test it on one of my hens," he said with his toothy grin. "Then I'll have her for dinner. Destroy the evidence, so to speak."

A plump red hen stared stupidly at Charlie. He aimed the camera at one of her glassy eyes from a distance of six feet. When he tripped the shutter the hen gave a shrill cry and fell dead.

"Lovely, lovely," the professor crooned.

"Something larger," Charlie said.

"Beg your pardon?"

"I want to test the laser on something larger than a chicken," Charlie said, with great deliberation, as if speaking to a half-wit. "You have pigs, don't you?"

The scientist's pale blue eyes bulged. "I . . . yes . . . but . . ."

"Professor, after all Albert Einstein, Howard Hughes, and Ronald Reagan have done to create this weapon, surely you can sacrifice one pig to the cause."

Lamb frowned, unsure whether the Englishman was joking. "Well, yes, I suppose . . ."

"Let's go."

The professor sighed and led the way over the hill into the next field. He huffed and puffed as they reached the crest. Lard-assed fool, Charlie thought.

A dozen pigs were at leisure in the shade beside a small pond.

"Your choice," Charlie said. "A year's worth of ham sandwiches there."

"I don't care," Lamb grumbled.

Charlie aimed the camera at the largest pig, an insolent, rust-colored fellow; the beast eyed him indifferently. Charlie pressed the shutter and the pig's head sagged abruptly and he rolled onto his back.

"I'd have thought you people had animals of your own," the professor snapped.

Charlie smiled. "But not such lovely surroundings." He gazed about contentedly. Not another house, not another soul, could be glimpsed for miles, only green rolling hills.

"Well, is the slaughter complete?" Professor Lamb asked bitterly.

They started back toward the barn. "I trust you appreciate the need for absolute secrecy in this matter," Charlie said.

The professor reddened. "I haven't told my colleagues about this project, my wife, no one," he declared.

"That's a good fellow," Charlie said.

They came to a woodpile beside the barn. Charlie stopped walking. Some crows flew over. "Dr. Lamb," Charlie said.

The professor turned, a dozen feet away. Annoyance was etched on his soft pink face.

Charlie raised the camera. "Smile for the birdie," he said.

Dr. Lamb's innocent face registered surprise, then horror, in the instant it took Charlie to fire.

Two days later, Charlie relaxed in bed with coffee and the morning's Washington *Post*. The shocking murder in Georgetown was still front-page news. Police now said the investigation was focusing on an unidentified man who met the dying Secret Service agent at the Little Tavern.

Charlie cursed. That damn Winnick had been so bloody strong. He wouldn't go down. So who was this "unidentified man" he'd met and what might he have told him? It was another maddening loose end to be tied up, lest the whole scheme unravel.

By contrast, Professor Seymour Lamb's death was briefly reported on the obituary page. Noted scientist found dead at Maryland farm. Professor had worked on military research. Cause of death, a stroke, perhaps brought on by chopping wood on a hot afternoon.

Charlie smiled. The weapon was a success. He was ready to proceed.

32

Boyle had written Zeb asking for more details about camp life and he was rewarded with the third and longest of his son's epistles: "Dear Dad, It rained and we built a bridge out of toothpicks. The guys in my tent are Mark (dumb jerk), Paul (smart but silly), Harry (fat but funny), Pete (real cool), and Marty (nice but homesick all the time). Send $10— HURRY! Love, Zeb."

Boyle sent the money out of appreciation for the postcard. He thought the boy had the beginning of a literary style; he knew world-famous journalists who did not express themselves with such precision.

Zeb's postcards were the only bright spot in the gloom that overcame Boyle in the aftermath of Jeff Winnick's murder in Georgetown. For days, Boyle agonized over the meaning of Jeff's last words: *Ms. M. Address Book. Georgia. Find her.*

Who was Ms. M.? Was Georgia her first name? Was Jeff saying that a woman had attacked him? How could Boyle find her, knowing so little about her?

He asked himself a hundred times why he didn't turn over

what little he knew to the Secret Service and be done with this mess.

But he couldn't. Harry Bliss had cut him off from the White House—he'd be damned if he'd call and beg to speak with Harry again. Moreover, Jeff had been his only contact at the Secret Service and Jeff was dead now—his final words had been to command Boyle to "find her," whoever she was.

That night at the Little Tavern, when Jeff was unconscious, the first ambulance had arrived, and police sirens were wailing outside, Boyle could have stayed and been a good citizen and told what little he knew to the police. But that had not been his instinct. Rather, his instinct had been to flee, to go it alone, and in that instant he had crossed some personal Rubicon. He had been an Insider once but now he was an Outsider; if there was any way he could help Jenna, he thought it would be by trusting himself and his own instincts, as Senator Trawick had urged him, and by acting alone.

One of the questions that puzzled him was what Jeff had been doing so late the night he was killed—why couldn't he meet Boyle until two in the morning? It happened that Boyle knew a police reporter for a suburban paper who sometimes moonlighted by writing speeches for various of Boyle's political candidates. Boyle called the reporter and the next day he called back with an answer: It had not been made public, but starting at 12:30 A.M. that morning Jeff had spent more than an hour alone in the Vice President's office. "Nobody knows why," the reporter said. "He had access to the VP's office, of course, but it's weird that he'd go there in the middle of the night."

To Boyle, the midnight visit did not seem strange at all; it confirmed his suspicions. Jenna had tried to get into the Vice President's desk and that, he was convinced, had led to her disappearance. Now Jeff had followed in her footsteps and paid with his life.

The address book that Jeff had spoken of, Boyle thought, must be the Vice President's address book. Ms. M., or Georgia, or whoever she was, must be someone listed in the book,

me friend of the Vice President's, someone of such ur-
ency that Jeff would speak her name with his dying breath.
But who was she?

He puzzled over that question for days and then an an-
wer came to him out of nowhere one night as he lay in bed
alf asleep. He was thinking back over what Jeeter Adcock
ad told him about the Vice President, and he remembered
hat Jeeter had said about Remington making mysterious
ights to North Georgia. Suddenly it struck him that "Geor-
ia" might not be a woman's name but the state of Georgia.
nd it was then that the name of Serena Masters burst into
is mind.

Serena Masters! She was one of those inane figures from
he political past who'd not seemed so funny at the time, a
ast-talking, high-stepping lady hawk who'd talked herself
ut of a Cabinet post and then mounted a doomed campaign
or President. But where was she now? Boyle had not seen
er name in print in at least a year, maybe two years.

He knew that her conglomerate had its headquarters in
tlanta. And he remembered, from some long-ago maga-
ine profile, that she'd been raised at a bizarre castle somewhere in North Georgia. At that, Boyle sprang from bed and
onsulted an atlas to find that Ben Remington could indeed
ave flown a small plane from Nashville to North Georgia for
ecret meetings with Serena Masters.

To what end? Boyle didn't know. But he did know that
Masters controlled vast amounts of money, and in his experi-
nce there weren't many questions in politics to which the
ltimate answer wasn't money. He began to think, too, of
hat island she lived on, in splendid isolation. He was seized
y the idea that Jenna was a prisoner there. By dawn he was
acking his bag and calling the airlines to find the next flight
o Atlanta. There was one out of Dulles at ten-thirty that
norning and Boyle decided he would be on it.

He drank some coffee, thought about the uncertainties
head, and on the spur of the moment walked down the
treet and found his friend Jack Payne, clad only in an old
athing suit, mowing his lawn.

"Jack, I need to ask a favor."

"Sure, pal. Name it."

"I want to borrow a gun."

Jack looked him up and down. "I thought you were Mr Gun Control." It was an old joke between them. Boyle had worked for gun control for years, while Jack, who'd been mugged twice when he lived in Washington, was an outspo ken advocate of the right to bear arms. "Hell hath no fury like a liberal who's been mugged," he would say.

"I'm serious Jack. Can you help me out?"

Payne went into the house and returned in a few minute with a small revolver. "You know how to use it?" he asked Boyle shook his head.

"Well, there's not much to it," Payne said. "The hard par is deciding who to shoot. Sometimes that's not so hard."

He gave Boyle a brief lesson on how to load and fire th revolver. When he was finished, Boyle put the weapon in hi pocket. "Thanks, pal," he said.

"Listen, Matt, is there anything I can do?"

Boyle shook his head. "I've got a trip to take, and it migh be rough."

"Be careful, buddy," Jack said, and hugged him, and ther Boyle hurried back home.

When he reentered his house, he saw Zeb's postcard lying on the table by the door, and he read it again and smiled and he asked himself: What the hell are you doing flying of to Georgia on a wild goose chase with a loaded gun? Who are you going to kill? Have you lost your mind?

He threw himself into a chair and sat for a long time and when he got up it was to call the airline and cancel hi reservation. Then he had another idea, a better one, h hoped, and he called an Atlanta reporter he knew named Sid Lester. Les's exposes had sent three congressmen and two governors to prison—he wasn't someone you wanted t have working against you.

Some years earlier, Les had come to Washington to re ceive a Press Club award for one of his exposes and he'e gotten himself arrested while stumbling around a part of Fourteenth Street where white men didn't go unless the wanted black women, hard drugs, or an early demise. He'c been thrown in the drunk tank and had given the police a false name—too late he'd realized that this arrest could end his credibility and, in effect, his career.

In desperation he'd called Boyle, who was then working in the White House. It was a tricky, dangerous situation. Boyle wanted to help the reporter but he didn't want to involve the White House in a nasty influence-peddling case. It happened, however, that Boyle had gotten to know the D.C. mayor's chief political fixer, a man who hungered for political respectability after years as a bagman. In particular, he yearned to be invited to a White House state dinner, which he viewed as the very pinnacle of political status.

Thus, over breakfast one morning, a deal was struck: The fixer got his invitation to a state dinner, and the reporter was sprung from the D.C. jail. "Boyle, I owe you a big one," had been Lester's parting words.

So now, rather than go rushing off to North Georgia, Boyle called Lester at his Atlanta home and told him he was looking for Serena Masters.

"Isn't that a coincidence?" the reporter said. "I've been looking for her too. She's flown the frigging coop."

"What do you mean?" Boyle demanded.

"Serena's been real quiet for a couple of years," Lester said. "Other people run her company—I hear she calls in once in a while, but that's all. She's been up on that island of hers. I get rumors about corporate heavies flying in and out of there. But nobody knows what she's up to."

"So she's living on the island?" Boyle asked.

"She was, but about three months ago I got a report that she'd left. Just by God vanished! I drove up there and the locals said one night boats went out to the island and loaded up and from the boats the stuff was put in trucks and the trucks drove off, nobody knows to where. The lady vanishes."

"Les, are you sure nobody's on that island? Somebody hiding out there, maybe?"

"I went to the island. There's a couple of guards there. I laid some long green on 'em and they let me look around. Believe me, there's nobody there."

"So where is she?" Boyle asked.

"I don't know," Les admitted.

Boyle hung up the phone in frustration. He had saved himself a pointless trip to Georgia, but only to confront more uncertainty. What did he really have on Serena Masters? Only that she might possibly be the Ms. M. that the dying Jeff Winnick had told him to find. Or she might not be. In any event, her whereabouts were a mystery. It was, finally, her very silence, her invisibility, that convinced him of her complicity in whatever was happening. She had for a dozen years or more been one of the most outspoken women in America. He remembered Sherlock Holmes's case of the barking dog that didn't bark. Serena Masters, silent and invisible, was a barking dog that didn't bark, and he knew he had to find her.

33

Jenna lived in a dream, floated between anger and despair. She tried to read, to plot, to hate, to remember, but reality was slipping away from her, a memory, a blur in the shadowy past. In her windowless room there were no days, no nights, no time, no news, no voices, nothing. It was worse than death because death at least would be sleep, peace. She cursed Charlie, her captor, yet awaited his irregular visits. How many days had she been entombed? Ten? Twenty? Sometimes she sobbed, sometimes she slept, sometimes she schemed, and always she knew that she must be her own salvation.

She lay in limbo, half asleep, half dreaming, when he knocked and entered; she turned her head away.

"Brought you some books. Good stuff. The new Ludlum."

"I hate Ludlum," she said bitterly.

"Well, there's others. How's about coffee?"

Jenna sat up. "Yes, coffee," she muttered, sullenly brushing back her hair. Then she noticed his face. "What happened to you?" she demanded.

"A little accident. Not to worry."

Not to worry, indeed. The bruises on his face were a ray of hope, a reminder that he bruised, bled, could die.

"What time is it?" she said. "What day?"

"Wednesday afternoon. Sixish."

"I'm not even sure what month it is," she said. "I'm losing my mind. Is that what you want?"

He returned from the kitchen and knelt beside her. He didn't touch her; he never had. "I want you healthy and happy, but I have to keep you a little longer."

"I'm going *crazy,*" she wailed. She threw herself back on the bed and her tears were real, not calculated.

The water boiled and Charlie mixed two mugs of instant coffee. "Drink it, you'll feel better," he told her.

She held the mug between her hands, taking warmth; her hair tumbled down across her blotched face. "I want to see the sky," she sobbed. "The sun. The stars. Trees. Flowers. People. If you want to kill me, kill me, but don't keep me here like a rat in a trap."

Charlie tasted his coffee. He was tired. His broken ribs ached. When he looked at Jenna he felt sorry for her, and a little angry at her, for getting herself caught up in this mess. Was it his mistake to have taken her alive? Was he only postponing the inevitable? Or might she yet be useful?

"We're a fine pair," he muttered.

She looked up suspiciously. "What?"

"I'll tell you what," he said impulsively. "Drink your coffee. Freshen up a bit, if you like. Then come upstairs to Chez Charlie. We'll have us a splash of bubbly and a bit of dinner."

She gazed at him with disbelieving eyes. Charlie winked and strolled out, leaving the door open. *The door open!* The parting of the Red Sea could not have stunned her more. Jenna hurried to wash her face. How pale she was, how haggard. She pinched her cheeks for color and then she began to brush her hair, firmly and methodically. A great surge of hope rose up inside her. There was no hurry, she told herself. The night was young. Anything could happen. He was, after all, only a man.

Outside her door a round metal staircase led to a trapdoor that opened into a snug cabin with a huge stone fireplace. Jenna stood up, saw sunlight pouring through a small window, and with a cry she raced to the window. It was barred, all the windows in the cabin were barred, but that didn't matter, because she could see the setting sun, majestic green trees, clouds, birds, the sky, a world reborn. Tears scalded her eyes.

"Take me outside," she whispered.

"Sorry, can't do that," Charlie said crisply. He opened a bottle of champagne. The bottle was clear glass, enclosed in a golden cellophane wrapper. "Try this," he said, pouring two glasses. "Make you forget your troubles."

"What is it?"

"Louis Roederer Cristal. The champagne of the czars. That's the reason for the clear glass, so the poor blokes could see if anybody was trying to poison them. Cheers."

Jenna sipped the champagne. Its icy bubbles tickled her nose. "It *is* good," she said.

"Take it slow now," he warned.

Charlie settled cross-legged at one end of a long white sofa. He wore jeans and a flowered silk shirt, and she saw the bandages across his ribs.

She took the far end of the sofa, one arm outstretched, savoring the champagne, smiling moodily, thinking. She had gotten this far, this wonderful first step into the sunlight, how then could she complete her escape? She tried to see this scene as he might see it. She ached for her freedom, but he was only killing time, resting his battered body, amusing himself with a pretty girl. Better, then, to be pleasant than to plead her cause. Charlie was young and handsome and full of himself. His weakness would be that of all men, vanity— vanity and its brother, sex.

"It's nice here," she said. "Where *are* we?"

Charlie shrugged amiably. "An estate in the country. Living like kings."

She was glad he wouldn't tell her precisely where they were; that could mean he intended to free her.

"I saw a big house, up the hill. Who lives there?"

"A very rich lady."

"Your employer?"

"For the moment."

"What do you call yourself, Charlie? A soldier of fortune?"

"That has a nice ring to it."

"How did you follow me?" she asked. "How did you know where I was going?"

Charlie laughed good-naturedly. "Listen, in the U.S. today, any phone you use, any room you enter, any person you talk to, can be bugged, and most likely is. Plus it's easy to put a beeper on somebody's car, if you feel like following them. Don't ever assume you have privacy—assume the opposite, particularly if you're the President's daughter."

"Particularly if you ignore the Secret Service," she said bitterly.

"Hey, cheer up, nobody's safe these days. I was on a job once, we sent an easy chair to the Polish Ambassador, told him it was a gift from his chums in Russia. We put a bug in the stuffing, you might have guessed. So he put the chair in his conference room, just like we wanted, but the trouble was that the Ambassador was prone to what you'd call flatulence, so all we got was two hundred hours of Polish farts."

Jenna laughed despite herself, and Charlie grinned at her. "Tell you what, I'll build a fire, to brighten things up."

He expertly started a small fire in the huge stone fireplace.

"It's a beautiful fireplace," Jenna said.

"Some Quakers built this cabin, solid as a rock," he told her. "This was where they cooked."

"This seems a strange place for you."

"I'll be gone soon enough. Once I finish the job I'm on, I'll buy the boat I want and set sail."

"Set sail for where?"

"Around the world. I've never understood how people could live in cities when there's a Caribbean, a Riviera, a South Pacific. Places where the sun's hot and the drinks are cold and the women are beautiful."

He refilled her glass. Their hands did not quite touch. "I sailed to the Virgin Islands once," she said. "I loved it."

Charlie ambled into the kitchen and returned with some

mixed nuts. "How about dinner?" he said. "You fancy a curry?"

"That sounds wonderful. Can I help?"

"Keep me company," he said.

She sat on a stool by the kitchen counter, sipping the champagne, while he made chicken curry. Once, as he moved about, stirring this, tasting that, a big, serrated kitchen knife lay on the counter, within her grasp, and for an instant she was poised to seize it, to plunge it into him. But she did not. Because she feared he was watching, waiting, testing her. And because, even if she surprised him, he was stronger, faster, and she might ruin everything.

Charlie served Indian beer with the spicy curry. They ate at a small table beside one of the barred windows, watching a languid summer sunset, talking of this and that, and abruptly Jenna knew where she was.

The sunset told her, the light, the pastels in the west. She had seen that sunset before, the same hills and shades of gold, and she knew she was not far from Matt Boyle's little Virginia village. It all came to her with perfect clarity: At Matt's friends' house that spring, there'd been gossip about Arabs buying a nearby estate; indeed, she'd been driving past that mysterious estate the night Charlie seized her. Jenna's heart beat boldly; she knew something Charlie didn't know she knew, and in her desperation that knowledge was like a dagger in her grasp.

"Tell me about you," she said. "Where did you come from? How did you get from there to here?"

They switched to brandy after he cleared away the dishes. Jenna was relaxed, light-headed, expectant.

"You probably never heard of the place I grew up," Charlie said. "A pit village in Yorkshire, the north of England. The important thing was that my dad was the local barber. All me chums' dads worked in the bloody mines, but my dad clipped hair and sometimes he kept an old magazine or two around the place. I started reading his magazines, even a book or two, when I could put me hands on one, and I found out a secret that my chums never knew, that there was a big world out there where people didn't muck around in coal

mines. I started dreaming of the sea. I'd see these pictures of
royalty in their yachts and that looked good to me but I
couldn't puzzle out how to get my first yacht. So I joined up
with Her Majesty's Royal Marines. And I got lucky. I was a
big, healthy bloke, so they took me for the Red Berets."

Jenna laughed. "All I ever heard about was the Green
Berets."

Charlie snorted his disdain. "A bunch of girls," he said
"The Red Berets are the real hard boys. The cherry tops, we
called them. I was 2 Para. The parachute regiment. The
best. Bloody killers, when we got the chance. But we never
got ourselves assigned to the South Seas. They sent us to
Norway instead—arctic warfare training, they called it. Two
years of freezing our arses off."

Charlie laughed and lit a cigar from one of the candle
that glowed between them. "Then came the Falklands war
and a sweet little war it was. Do you remember it? Your TV
called it a 'comic-opera war.' As if us and the Argentinian
were down there singing Gilbert and Sullivan to each other
Is that what you thought?"

"I . . . I didn't know much about it. I guess I was in col
lege then."

"Oh, it was lovely when we sailed out of Portsmouth with
the bands playing and the girls all waving their hankies. 'Get
this tub moving,' we told the captain, 'we want to bang
them Argie bastards.' Well we landed but instead of a fight
we spent a week in the mud, shivering and starving and
getting trench foot.

"Then comes the good news: We're moving south to at
tack the Argies at Goose Green. Action at last! What's more
the scuttlebutt was that it would be a piece of cake. You see
the main Argie base was way across the island at Stanley
Goose Green was a sideshow. We could have let it be, except
that back in London the politicians were getting impatien
for a victory."

Charlie smiled into the darkness. "So off we march fo
Goose Green, mighty pleased with ourselves. Our CO, H
Jones—short for Herbert, it was—was walking two feet o
the ground. Somebody told him this was going to be the firs

real battle the British army had fought since Korea. March-ing into history, we were, and H loved it. A good fellow. Tough. Stood up for his men.

"The first night we marched seven hours, loaded down like mules. At three in the morning, we reached a place called Camilla Creek House, where we spent the rest of the night, four hundred of us, shivering and freezing, but happy as pigs. Then at dawn we got our little surprise.

"Some of the boys were listening to the news on BBC and what do they hear but a report out of London announcing to the world that 2 Para was five miles from Goose Green.

"Do you follow me, Jenna? We're making a surprise attack and some filthy politician in Whitehall, trying to suck up to a reporter, announces our raid to the whole bloody world, including the Argies.

"There was a BBC bloke with us, and H grabbed him by the collar and yelled, 'If any of my men die because of this, I'll charge the BBC with murder. Write that down and send it back to London.'

"H had us disperse and dig in, because we had to think the Argies would shell us or attack by air. Well, lucky us, they didn't, but what they did was to reinforce the hell out of Darwin and Goose Green. Helicoptered men and supplies in.

"The next morning we started forward and got ambushed, pinned down by machine fire on open ground, as we were advancing on Darwin Hill. A lot of men dead and wounded. Shells and mortar coming in. Bloody *napalm* for a time. The Argies had cover and plenty of ammo. H told a chap named Wickham-Smith to take a ledge, but he lost three men and came back. So what did H do? Grabbed his submachine gun and dashed up the gully toward the gun that had us pinned down. And got shot through the neck for his trouble."

"How terrible," Jenna said.

"We gave him morphine, transfusions. We called in a chopper to take him out, but it got splattered. Finally H was dead. There was a kind of hush. We're still pinned down, shells falling all around, but we were all in a trance. My whole life changed, right there. Like a flash I realized,

'Charles, if H can die, anyone can die, even you.' And then next thing I realized was that it was the bloody politicians, tipping off the Argies that we were coming, who had killed H, and all the other men we lost that day. And I said, 'Charles, you're going to get out of this hellhole in one piece, and then there'll be some changes made.' "

Charlie puffed at his cigar, holding it at a jaunty angle.

"What happened?" Jenna asked. Caught up in his tale, she had for a moment forgotten her own plight.

"Oh, we outflanked the Argies. Killed all we could and captured the rest. We surrounded Goose Green the next day, four hundred of us, dog-tired, and twelve hundred Argies surrendered to us. Marched out and sang their bloody national anthem and threw down their weapons. Oh, it was a famous victory. They handed out medals like gumdrops when we got back to England.

"But yours truly, he'd decided to opt out. It's not that I don't believe in killing. I do. Men have been killing since the first monkey picked up a rock and bashed some bloke who'd stole his banana."

"But don't you think it's wrong to kill?"

"It's wrong to *be* killed. Killing is as natural as breathing. How long have people been on this earth? Ten million years? A long time, fighting and killing and dying, pathetic little creatures, a bunch of ants scurrying around, each one thinking how God-Almighty important he is. Well, we're not important. We're just meat."

"Poor forked animal," she murmured.

"What?"

"That's what Shakespeare called man," she said. "In *King Lear,* I think. Poor, bare forked animal. But he felt compassion for us, not contempt."

"Well Shakespeare was an actor or poet or whatever he was, but I'm a soldier and I tell you we're just meat waiting to rot. The only question is do I get you or do you get me."

Charlie grinned and poured himself more brandy. "So, armed with this pragmatic philosophy, young Charles turned in his red beret and set forth to seek his fortune, knowing that a lad who's handy with small arms and explosives never starved in the good old U.S. of A."

Jenna's words leaped out unbidden: "You're going to try to kill my father, aren't you?"

Charlie frowned at her. "Don't spoil it. Drink your brandy."

"But it's wrong!" she cried. "Don't you see? You saw people die for no reason in the Falklands and that's what my father wants to stop. Pointless wars. Senseless slaughter."

"No, you've got it wrong. Your father wants to stop *nuclear* wars, because they'd kill the rich along with the poor. He can tolerate dirty little shooting wars, colonial wars, the kind that kill poor sods like me. Your dad is just another politician to me."

Jenna burned with anger. "All right, he's just another politician. But he's powerful. Do you really want to risk your life trying to kill him? If you want money, you've got it. Let me talk to him on the phone. I guarantee you a million dollars, or whatever your price is."

"Promise 'em anything, eh?"

"My father keeps his promises. Why risk your life when I'm offering you a sure thing?"

Charlie sighed. "I don't doubt you mean it. But once your boys had me all bets would be off. Let's hang this madman, they'd say. I'm in too deep to change sides."

He yawned. "Now, it's time for Cinderella to return to the basement."

Jenna felt herself starting to panic. To return to that underground cell would be like death. "Wait," she said.

"Finish your brandy," he said. "I don't mean to rush you."

She took his hand. "Let me stay here."

He frowned, as if he didn't understand.

"Let me stay up here with you," she said. "Why should I be down there and you up here, both of us alone? Why not a little warmth before . . . before whatever happens?"

Charlie's smile was more gentle than she'd ever seen before. "Scrry," he said. "But I do appreciate the thought."

She drew back her hand. "Why not? Are you gay?"

His smile became a grin. He clutched his heart. "Oh,

Jenna, you do know how to hurt a fellow. No, it's girls I fancy."

"Then why do you say no."

"For one thing, you'd put a knife in my back if you got the chance . . ."

"I don't *have* a knife!" she protested.

"No, but the idea of it would spoil things a bit, wouldn't you say?"

"That's all in your head."

"It would be unprofessional. I shouldn't have had you up here for dinner—you see what it leads to."

"But you enjoyed it."

"Who wouldn't enjoy dinner with a bright girl like you?"

"Then why not enjoy the whole night?"

"Damn it all, because . . ."

She finished the sentence for him. "Because you may have to kill me."

"Yes. Sad to say."

"All right, I accept that. But the fact remains that I'd rather be up here tonight than down there going crazy in that awful little tomb. *I* can handle it, Charlie, why not you? Are you afraid your 'rich lady' will find out?"

"No, I'm not afraid of that. But I don't fancy going to sleep afterwards and not waking up."

"Do you think I'm crazy enough to try to kill a professional killer? I want to live, Charlie, and there's always a chance that you may think about my offer—that my father can pay you more than your 'rich lady' can. I might save both our lives, Charlie. Think about it. What have you got to lose?"

"I'd be taking advantage of you. It'd be unprofessional."

"That's ridiculous. You're willing to kill me."

"That's business. Sex is personal."

"You're a romantic, Charlie. A good time is a good time. Don't you find me attractive? Are you afraid I know judo or something? What are you afraid of, you big, tough soldier?"

Charlie's handsome face knotted into an uncharacteristic pout. She was lovely and yet somehow, against all logic, frightening. Was he in control or not? Could this slight and desperate girl be a threat to him? Her proposal was cold-

blooded, and yet she could have not looked more beguiling
as she smiled at him in the shadows. The night burned with
promise. What, indeed, was he afraid of?

"Have some more brandy, Jenna, and let me think."

34

The news that the Russian missiles had been returned to their bases instead of progressing to the demolition centers soon leaked out in Washington. An opposition senator first proclaimed it on the Senate floor, shouting and waving papers toward the press gallery. Unnamed Pentagon officials confirmed the report, and soon the White House was besieged by reporters.

The White House Press Office announced that the President would meet with reporters at two that afternoon. As the hour approached, Calvin Webster paced the Oval Office in frustration.

"You've got to put our troops on alert, worldwide," Harry Bliss insisted, for the third time.

"Mr. President," the Secretary of State protested wearily, "the situation in the Kremlin seems delicately balanced. If we invoke a military alert . . ."

"Those sons of bitches have broken their word," Harry raged. "They've screwed us. We've got to cut our losses."

"Restraint, Mr. President," the Secretary pleaded.

Calvin Webster kept pacing.

"Ten minutes, Mr. President," the Press Secretary called. Muttering to himself, Webster sat down at his desk, grabbed a notepad, and began to scribble furiously. The others watched in silence.

The last photographers were lined up at the White House security checkpoint.

The tall, good-looking young photographer called Wes Hillman was in line behind a veteran New York *Times* photographer. The *Times* man put his bag on the table, walked through the metal detector, and suddenly red lights began to flash. Three guards whirled in his direction. "Lordy me," he moaned, and fished a wad of keys from his pocket. He passed through the second time uneventfully. One of the guards was digging through the canvas bag that held his extra cameras, film, batteries, and other apparatus.

"Better fire off a round for me, George," the guard said, nodding to the long-lensed Nikon the photographer wore round his neck.

George rolled his eyes. "Mac, you've known me twenty years. If I'd ever wanted to hide a gun in my camera and do in a President, there's two or three I'd have shot before this one."

"Gettin' late, George," the guard said.

The *Times* man sighed and clicked his camera twice. "Wasted film," he said.

"Good security," the guard said.

The photographer called Wes Hillman heaved his canvas bag on the table. The guard eyed him carefully—Hillman had only been on the White House beat six months or so, and thus was still suspect. The guards all distrusted photographers; there were too damn many of them running in and out of the White House, long-hairs, radicals, drug-users, Vietnam veterans, foreigners, all sorts of crazies. The guard noted the cuts that had not quite healed on the photographer's handsome, boyish face.

"Been in a fight?" he said.

"A lover's quarrel," Hillman said with a smile.

The guard picked up one of Hillman's cameras, opened it,

and peered through its lens. Hillman ambled through the metal detector and returned to the table, where the guard was still poking through his camera bag. He had studied the security process carefully, in a score of checks like this, and he knew it was cleverly done. They had no set routine which you could anticipate and easily evade. Sometimes they passed you in thirty seconds and sometimes they spent ten minutes tearing your gear apart. Sometimes they used a dog and sometimes they didn't. Some of the high-and-mighty reporters protested, said they were being harassed, but Hillman knew better. These boys were doing their job as best they could. As security men, they were caught in a cruel dilemma: They could trust no one, yet they could not adequately search everyone who was admitted into the President's presence—and a strip-search was what was needed if you wanted 100% security. So they did their job the best they could, knowing that out of all those reporters and photographers and dinner guests and visiting firemen who saw the President each day, inevitably one, someday, would be an assassin.

The guard returned Hillman's cameras to his bag, glaring at him suspiciously. "What's that outfit you're with?"

"The Goode News Bureau," Hillman said with an easy grin.

The guard shook his head sadly. Where did all these characters come from? "Okay, go on, go on," he growled.

The photographer hurried toward the White House.

A half hour later, when the President entered the East Room, the waiting reporters dutifully rose to their feet. The photographers, unburdened by this ritual, eagerly began snapping Cal Webster's picture. Webster quickly waved the reporters back into their chairs—to have them stand when he entered genuinely embarrassed him—and said, "It is my duty to confirm reports that the Soviet missiles have been returned to their points of origin. We're concerned about this, but nothing irretrievable has happened. The Soviets still have three days to destroy those weapons, according to our agreement. As best we can determine, their action relects a strong disagreement within the Kremlin high command. We hope they'll make the sensible decision and carry out the dismantling as scheduled. If they don't, we'll take appropriate steps to protect our interests. I'll take your questions now. Carrie?"

A pert wire-service reporter leaped to her feet. "Mr. President, several senators are calling for an immediate U.S. military alert. Would you comment?"

"I don't believe that's called for yet. It would be a dramatic gesture, but our security is more than adequate."

"But Mr. President, aren't you face to face with the failure of Project Peace and of your own political credibility as well?"

Cal Webster gripped the podium, his face set in anger. "My political standing isn't the issue," he declared. "The issue is the future of the world, and I'm still optimistic about that."

The skeptical questions kept coming, and the President stuck doggedly to his guns. Off to the side, Harry bit his tongue, furious, thinking *You stubborn SOB, why didn't you call the alert?*

On a platform at the back of the room, the photographer called Wes Hillman focused a long-lensed Nikon until Cal Webster's image was brilliantly clear. His face, his eyes. Then he waited, tense, for the perfect moment.

A famously combative woman reporter from Des Moines came close, in her rambling question, to accusing the President of the United States of incompetence, if not outright treason. Webster's eyes bulged, he pounded the lectern with one big, hamlike fist as he shouted his reply: "Not only do I not think . . ."

Bam! went the fist on the lectern.

Two dozen of the best photographers in the world saw the moment, the perfect moment, the glimpse of the real man, angry, frustrated, powerful, his eyes cold, his jaw jutting forward, and they clicked off picture after picture.

Wes Hillman touched the shutter of his Nikon, adding one more click to the hubbub.

". . . and furthermore, I think the Soviets respect my position," the President told the lady from Des Moines.

"Thank you, Mr. President," a reporter in the front row called, thereby ringing down the curtain on the show.

The President, looking relieved, beat a hasty retreat.

In the back of the room, Wes Hillman was smiling. His dry run had gone to perfection. Next came the real thing.

35

Peaches Remington, the Vice President's wife, was overripe. Boyle had seen pictures of her, blonde and vivacious in her debutante days, but now her face had grown puffy and her body thickened. She had a hoarse whiskey voice and she talked too loud, as if everything she said was very funny or important.

"The First Lady asked me to see you," Peaches said. "But she really didn't explain why."

They were sitting in the bright drawing room of the Victorian mansion in Northwest Washington that was the Vice President's official residence.

"Doris and I have been discussing a documentary on the role of the First Lady," Boyle said. "She wants you included if we do it."

"She's such a dear. But you don't want *me*, Mr. Boyle. To be Second Lady of the Land is Dullsville. Please, don't get me started."

"But you've been active in . . . volunteer work, haven't you?"

"I do the minimum. My choice is either to spend my time

going to teas and cutting ribbons or to have my husband and his staff hate me for not doing my share for the cause."

Boyle flashed his most disarming Irish grin. "But, Mrs. Remington, are you saying you *dislike* being Second Lady?"

Her face hardened. "Mr. Boyle, some thirty years ago my husband married me for my money, which was an eminently reasonable thing for him to do. I kept my part of the bargain by being a reasonably loyal wife and by bearing him three healthy children. He kept his part by becoming a successful businessman and a pillar of the community. He even got himself elected governor, which was a thrill I hadn't counted on but must confess I enjoyed.

"But, Mr. Boyle, it was implicit in our arrangement that we remain in Nashville. I happen to love the city. It has Vanderbilt University, the Belle Meade Country Club, the Swan Ball, cheap and reliable help, and a never-ending succession of scandals involving the very best people. I adore Nashville, and I despise Washington—that is my situation in a nutshell."

"But you might be First Lady someday," he said.

Peaches threw up her hands. "Good Lord, that'd be leaping from the frying pan to the fire. Don't you see, if your husband is President, and you love him, you spend all your time afraid that some lunatic will kill him. And if you don't love him, you still have to attend all his speeches and sit there with an adoring, Pat-Nixon smile frozen on your face, all the while wishing he'd shut up, so you could go have a drink."

Boyle laughed. "I agree with you about Nashville," he said. "It is a wonderful city. We have a mutual friend there."

"Oh? Whoever could that be?"

"Zelda Gittings—I knew her in college."

"*You* know *Zelda?* Why she's practically my dearest friend. She divorced Floyd, you know."

"So I heard."

Peaches beamed. "Well, this calls for a celebration. How about a martini—specialty of the house. And do call me Peaches—I'll call you Matt!"

"Wonderful," Boyle said. He hated martinis. He thought gin the most dangerous of drugs. Still, it had its uses.

The martinis arrived in a pitcher. Boyle encouraged Peaches to talk, about her husband, about politics, about anything. Harry Bliss had sent the Vice President on a fact-finding mission to South Korea, and Peaches seemed to have nothing better to do than to spend the afternoon drinking and talking with Boyle. In time her voice began to blur. Boyle charmed her, flattered her, and when the moment was right asked, "Did you ever expect your husband to become Vice President, Peaches?"

"Are you serious? My husband likes his golf, his bourbon, his hunting. He was never eaten up with ambition, like so many of the politicians we met. But after he pulled that child from the river everything changed. Everything was politics—he just went into orbit."

"Were you surprised when he saved the little girl?"

"Surprised is not the word for it," Peaches said. "I would be less surprised if you sprouted wings and flew like a bird. I know my husband, Matt. He is a *very careful person*. If he saw you in the river, going down for the third time, he might wave good-bye, or call the fire department, or appoint a committee to study the problem, but he would *not* leap into the river himself, at risk of life and limb, believe me!"

"But he did."

She sighed and refilled their glasses. "Yes."

"So what happened?"

"Matt, I have lain awake many a night pondering that question, and I have arrived at three possibilities. One, temporary insanity. Two, that I don't know Ben as well as I think I do. Three . . . well, three would be that something strange is afoot."

"Strange? Like what?"

"I have no earthly idea. Sinister forces?"

Peaches flashed a wicked smile and he had to grin back at her. Any Nashville belle who remembered that bit of Watergate trivia—General Haig's infamous suggestion that some "sinister force" had erased 18 1/2 minutes of the Nixon tape —was not without her charms.

She led him out to the terrace. Peaches wasn't walking terribly well but she was happy.

"So after he saved the girl it was all politics," he said.

"Morning and night. Plotting, traveling, scheming."

"Who advised him?"

"Nobody. He's self-made, like Mr. Gatsby."

"Peaches, somebody had to help him. Smart politicians pay political consultants millions of dollars, hoping for the sort of success your husband had."

"Oh, he met with people. But have you ever seen the retards who run Tennessee politics? A bunch of ex-firemen whose grand vision is to stuff two ballot boxes at once. Give them two years in office and they'll parlay it into five years in the state pen, every time."

Peaches blinked her eyes and put her glass down unsteadily. "Goodness, I do believe I'm dizzy. It must be the humidity."

Boyle went to her. "Is there anything I can do?"

She smiled up at him. "You are a dear. No, just give me a minute."

It was the moment to strike. "Peaches, does your husband know a woman named Serena Masters?"

Peaches turned deathly pale. "I do believe I'd better go in," she said. "Be a dear and help me."

He took her arm and she led him into a tiny, booklined library. "Shut the door," she said. "The servants give you no privacy. I believe they're all spies for somebody."

She dropped onto a small sofa and pulled him down beside her. "I'll be all right in a moment," she whispered, and blinked her eyes coquettishly. "Matt, I'm going to trust you, I think you're a good man. I'm frightened. And it all has to do with Serena Masters."

She clutched his hand, and he responded with his most sincere gaze. "I'll help if I can," he vowed. "Tell me what you know about her."

Peaches sighed and said, "Ben has his faults but he's never been a womanizer. But after he saved that child, he started making mysterious trips. He'd climb into his Learjet and sail into the wild blue yonder. Well, I employed a private detec

e and eventually he found out that Ben was flying to a
tle private airport near Clayton, Georgia, which is the
solute middle of nowhere. From there he'd go to that
zarre island where Serena Masters makes her home—
ther like the Bride of Frankenstein, I've always thought.
ell, it might have been politics or it might have been sex—
hough I, for one, do not consider her the slightest bit
tractive—so I confronted him. 'Ben,' I said, 'why are you
eaking off to see Serena Masters?'

"He went white as a sheet. He started blubbering. It was
litics, he said, but he wouldn't explain. He begged me to
ver mention her name to anyone. Well, it didn't make any
nse to me, but the next thing I knew all those Draft Rem-
gton committees sprang up like toadstools and before you
uld blink an eye my handsome but otherwise harmless
sband was Vice President of the United States."

She began to tremble. "It scares me to death. I think
rena Masters is a dangerous woman. Ben's afraid of her.
e calls here sometimes—I'm not supposed to know, but I
tened outside the door. What is the woman up to? I think
e's got her hooks in Ben somehow. I'm afraid she'll make
m do something terrible."

"Like what?" Boyle asked.

Her eyes sparkled, suddenly hard and shrewd. "Well, if
e has her hooks in him, if she thinks she can control him,
en she'd want him to be President, wouldn't she?"

Boyle nodded reluctantly. "Yes, I guess she would," he
id.

36

One of the joys of life in Harmony was that Boyle did
worry about crime. His friends in Washington lived behi
bars and double locks, but Boyle never even locked
house at night. Harmony's citizens sometimes drank to
cess, smoked forbidden weeds, parked their cars in ille
places, ignored the leash laws, and committed sins of t
flesh, but they were not much given to theft or violenc

Boyle, however, had begun to see the world differen
Dangerous men were abroad and if he was going to contin
his search for Jenna he'd best protect himself. Thus, he s
to Zeb one Saturday morning, "I think we should start lo
ing the house."

Zeb looked up from a crossword puzzle, a new enth
asm. "Why?"

"I've been gone a lot lately. The world's full of cr
people. Wouldn't you feel better with the doors locked

Zeb shrugged. "Pete and Billy," he said.

"Huh?"

"Pete and Billy. Four letters. That's all it says."

"Rose," Boyle said. "Look, what about locking the doo

"Would it make you feel better?"

"Yes, it would make me feel better."

"Okay with me then. Do we have any keys?"

"Oh hell," Boyle grumbled. A search failed to uncover any keys to the various locks that supposedly protected the house. "I'll have some made," Boyle vowed, and headed off to the post office.

It was a glorious summer morning and Boyle walked the half mile to the post office. Off to his left, past the houses, the fields were green and golden, and beyond them the Blue Ridge was wreathed in mist. He greeted various dogs and neighbors along the way. At the post office he paid his respects to the postmistress, a formidable woman who knew everything about everybody, but mostly kept it to herself, and she rewarded him with a telegram and a package.

He tore open the telegram first. It was from Jeeter Adcock, who'd gone along as a reporter on the Vice President's Asian junket. Boyle had talked to Jeeter at length before he left. He didn't tell Jeeter everything he knew, but he told him enough to arouse his curiosity and enlist his aid. He also gave Jeeter a couple of questions to ask the Vice President. The telegram related to one of those questions: ASKED POINTBLANK. DENIES EVER MET MADAM M.

Boyle sighed. So now Remington was denying he'd ever met the woman his wife said had masterminded his political career.

Boyle tore open the package as he started the walk back home. It was postmarked Washington but had no return address. Inside he found a pile of legal documents. Boyle frowned, leaned against a car, and began to study the documents. As best he could make out, they pertained to the rather tangled corporate ownership of an obscure Washington news bureau. It made no sense at all until finally he spotted the name of Masters Industries on one of the documents. Then the documents began to make a lot of sense but one big question remained unanswered: Who had sent them?

Some thirty-odd miles away, across the Potomac River,
Turk Kellerman spent that hot Saturday afternoon at the
Maryland farm where Professor Seymour Lamb had met his
untimely death. He had only belatedly learned of the professor's passing. He had fallen behind on his obituaries and that
morning had summoned a young woman to read to him.

A surprising number of the people whose deaths were
noted in the Washington *Post* had once worked for the FBI,
CIA, DIA, DEA, BTF, or other of the alphabet-soup agencies
that supposedly promoted law and security in America.
Ninety-nine deaths out of a hundred were perfectly normal.
Still, over the years, Turk had sometimes spotted an unlikely
suicide, an unexplained accident, an untimely disappearance that upon investigation had led to foul play. Obituaries
were a kind of hobby for him; there were many he read for
simple, nostalgic pleasure. When minor actors died, somewhere in the Southern California desert, he savored the lists
of their films, trying to remember the ones he'd seen, at
what Saturday matinee or drive-in with what lusty teen
queen of yesteryear. He cherished old songwriters, too, not
the Cole Porters and Richard Rodgerses, but obscure fellows
named Harry, who died in their eighties, having written six
hundred songs, the best known of which was "Chattanooga
Choo Choo" or "The Lady from Twenty Nine Palms" or
some other gem, dimly remembered.

The girl read him the obit of the man who wrote "There
Will Never Be Another You" and then raced through six
paragraphs on the passing of Professor Seymour Lamb. Suddenly bells went off and Turk was yelling for her to read that
one again, while he pondered the professor's age, his de-
fense-related research, and most of all the detail about chopping wood. Within minutes he had Saussy coming to take
him to rural Maryland.

They met Dr. Bagley, the county medical examiner, at the
farm, and the medical examiner led the way to the place
where Professor Lamb had died.

Turk loved the breeze and the sun and the sound of birds
and the smell of trees and flowers and manure, miracles he
had ignored when he had sight. Now he had a sort of radar,

the "facial vision" some blind people develop, so that he "saw" things by the way the wind blew and the way sounds came back to him. He felt the barn looming before them.

"He was right here by the woodpile," Bagley said. "Flat on his back. A hunter found him. He'd been chopping wood and just keeled over."

"The ax was nearby?" Turk asked.

"Still in his hand," Bagley said.

"Cause of death?"

"Stroke. Might as well call it suicide. The temperature was in the nineties."

"Curious," Turk said.

"How so?" the medical examiner asked, wiping his brow with a grimy handkerchief.

"Did you know the professor, Doctor?" Turk asked.

"Knew him to speak to."

"What sort of shape was he in?"

"Physical? Piss poor. Thirty–forty pounds overweight."

"Would you say he was the sort of man to chop wood on a hot summer day?"

"I'd say he was a nutty damn professor who might do any fool thing. I figure he got tired of working in his lab and came outside for a break. Decided to swing his ax a little. And that's all she wrote."

"His lab? Where's his lab?" Turk demanded.

"Didn't I tell you?" Saussy asked, his face more mournful than ever. "He'd built him a lab in the barn. That's what he was doing here that day."

"What the hell was he working on?" Turk demanded.

"I don't rightly know," Saussy admitted.

"Doctor, do you know anything about his work out here?" Turk asked.

"Not a thing," Bagley drawled. "What's more, I don't think you ought to be making mountains out of molehills. Folks do keel over in hot weather. Hell, that same day the professor died, one of his pigs died too. A big, healthy animal, just dropped dead."

"Where?" Turk demanded.

"Where what?"

"Where did the pig die, dammit?"

"Over the hill, down by the pond. But what the . . . ?"

"Take us there!"

"Jesus H. Christ," the medical examiner grumbled, and started lumbering up the hill.

"Right there," Bagley said, when they reached the pond. "Right there under that oak tree is where Mr. Pig went to his reward."

"In the shade?" Turk asked.

"In the shade."

"No blood, no signs of violence?"

"I told you, he just keeled over, like the professor. Is that so damn preposterous?"

Turk turned his big, sightless face toward the doctor. "Dr. Bagley, do you think the pig was chopping firewood too?"

Bagley spit on the ground. "I'll be leaving now, gentle men."

"Hold on," Turk commanded. "What killed the pig?"

"I don't do pigs, mister. Just people."

"Where's Mrs. Lamb?"

"She flew to Paris, France, I understand, to ease her grief."

They walked back to the farmhouse, where their car waited. "Good day, gents," the medical examiner said, and drove away.

"God in Heaven, why didn't I read that obit the day it was published?" Turk groaned. "Come on, we've got to get into that lab."

"We've got no warrant," Saussy reminded him.

"Damn you, get us in there," Turk yelled. "Pick the lock. Kick down the door. But get us in!"

37

he rain began on Sunday morning, beating down relent-
essly until the day was a dreary indigo haze. At noon Charlie
t a fire to hold back the chill. He kept busy all afternoon,
udying maps, listening to tapes, experimenting with the
niny new toy that was his weapon, but in the early evening
e put work aside and brought Jenna up to join him.

"What a wonderful fire," she said, standing before it grate-
ally, hugging herself.

"It's nasty out," he said. "How about a spot of bubbly?"

"Please."

She had been upstairs four times now since she'd first
oldly offered to trade sex for freedom from her basement
ell, and she'd learned much about her charming, calculat-
ng captor during those visits. He was as vain as she'd ex-
ected, and his greatest vanity was that he, the son of a pit
illage in the coal-mining country, was a gentleman, a pro-
essional, an "honorable assassin" as he'd once had the au-
lacity to say. Yes, Charlie admitted, he would kill her ("re-
nove" was his preferred word) if his professional duties thus
lemanded, but no, he would not be an "animal" and "take

advantage" by having sex with her while she was his pri
oner. Had her situation been less desperate, Jenna migh
have laughed—this was clearly a psychopath's code c
honor, which would permit him to cut her throat but not t
make love with her.

Still, his vanity worked to her advantage, for she had go
ten her visits upstairs, to his warm, cozy cabin, without pay
ing the price of unwanted sex. Unspoken rules had evolvee
They put aside the roles of captive and captor, outwardly
least, to eat and drink and talk as equals, as man and woma
His outsized ego made this charade possible, she thought, fo
if part of him surely understood that she loathed him, ar
other part liked to think she found him irresistible. So Jenn
smiled, listened, learned, and did nothing to bruise h
bloated self-image.

She knew now that he had an apartment in Washington, i
Foggy Bottom not far from the White House; he boaste
sometimes of the many girls he took there. She ha
glimpsed, there in his cabin, the elaborate communication
gear and the expensive cameras, although he remained ev
sive about whatever plot he was caught up in. Thus, on th
rainy Sunday evening, after he had poured champagne an
put an old Eric Clapton record on the stereo, she wa
stunned to hear him say, quite casually, "I saw your dad th
week."

Jenna tried not to show her excitement. "How is he?"

"Looks fit as a fiddle," Charlie said. "Maybe not in suc
good political health, though."

"What do you mean?"

"The Russians pulled out on the disarmament deal. Th
Senate's up in arms, saying your dad should put U.S. troop
on alert or bomb Moscow or whatever. Your old man's tryin
to be patient and reasonable, so the wolves are howling fo
his blood."

"Poor daddy," she said, genuinely moved. Then sh
added, "Where did you see him? On TV?"

"No, no. In the flesh. I was his guest at the White House
you might say."

Charlie grinned at her, self-satisfied, full of himself. Sh

-ied to imagine him in the White House and she remem-
-ered the expensive cameras scattered about the cabin.

"You're a photographer," she said. "You saw him at a news
onference."

Charlie's eyes hardened. "Very good, Jenna. You don't
miss a trick."

Jenna stared angrily into the fire. "There were always too
many reporters and photographers running in and out," she
aid. "All the security people said so. Hundreds of them,
rom obscure little papers and news bureaus."

"True," Charlie said.

"But," she continued, "the Secret Service checks all their
backgrounds."

Charlie smiled. "There are people who investigate backgrounds and there are people who invent backgrounds, and
ometimes the people who invent them are more clever
han the people who investigate them."

"They've always been suspicious of photographers," she
persisted. "They check them closely, anytime they're going
near the President. It's so obvious that someone would try to
hide a weapon inside a camera."

"They do indeed," he agreed. "They make photographers
walk through a metal detector and they poke around in your
camera bag and look inside cameras. It'd be the devil to
smuggle a gun past those blokes. Still, not impossible."

"I've talked to Secret Service men about it," she said.
"They know you can kill a President, if you're willing to
trade your life for his. But most people aren't that crazy. You
aren't that crazy, are you?"

Charlie laughed. "Nope, I prize my life too highly to go
trading it away. The thing is, though, what if a fellow slips up
close to the President with a weapon that can kill without
being detected?"

"I don't understand."

"Of course you don't. But that's the challenge, isn't it? Just
to take out a President, if you're not particular how, that's
duck soup. Look how often he meets with people in the Rose
Garden, or takes off from the White House lawn in his helicopter. And all the while, traffic moving past, not a hundred

yards away. All you need is a van with a missile launcher, and
maybe a heat-seeking missile. You'd drive past, pretty as you
please, and lob your missile in.

"But that's crude. Messy. What you'd expect some bloody
Arab to do. So, let's imagine a more subtle approach. Say a
fellow's got access to the President. And say this fellow has
got a blowgun or a deathray or whatever, and he fires it and
the President keels over. No bang-bang, no blood, just a
middle-aged man keeling over, like a stroke or a heart attack. So there's a lot of confusion and the doctors poke over
him and all the reporters run to file their stories about this
horrid development. Meanwhile, the fellow with the secret
weapon, he just drifts away with everybody else."

Charlie poked the fire. Jenna saw suns, worlds exploding.
"It's the perfect crime," he said.

"You'll never get away with it," she exclaimed.

He cocked one eyebrow in feigned dismay. "Me get away
with it? Who said anything about me? I thought we were just
speculating, for goodness' sake. Now, how about a spot of
dinner?"

They ate before the fire, listening to the steady beat of the
rain on the roof, talking of this and that. She tried to be
charming, to cover up her earlier outburst. He seemed con-
tent enough. After dinner he brought out a bottle of brandy;
he seemed to have nothing better to do than to drink and
talk.

"You ever met the Vice President's wife?" Charlie asked
her abruptly.

"Yes, I've met her."

"Peaches. Isn't that a fine name for a grown woman?
What'd you think of her?"

"I felt sorry for her."

"Your friend Mr. Boyle went to see her the other day."

"Matt, went to see Peaches Remington? Why?"

"Looking for you, I suspect."

"Looking for me?" The night was suddenly ablaze with
light and hope.

"Oh, yes, he's quite dogged. Everyone else thinks you're
off on a lark, but Mr. Matthew Boyle won't be fooled. He's

een sniffing around everywhere. When you get out of here, ou should give the boy a tumble. He must be crazy for ou."

Jenna fought back tears. "He's an old, dear friend."

Charlie laughed. "He's a bloody nuisance."

"You said, 'When you get out of here.' When is that?"

"Soon, I hope. You'll be free as a bird."

She didn't believe that. She thought he intended to kill her. But she would pretend to believe his lie, if that was what he wanted.

"How did you get your hooks in the Vice President?" she demanded.

Charlie frowned. "It's a long story, long and nasty."

"I'm all ears."

Charlie yawned. The rain was coming down harder. "Believe me, you're better off not knowing."

Jenna's anger flared. "They'll kill you, you know," she said.

"They? And who might 'they' be?"

"The people you're working for. They'll kill you when you're finished. They'll have to. You know too much. How could anyone hire an assassin to kill a President and then let him live?"

"I'm a hard one to kill," he told her. "I'm not your lame-brain Lee Harvey Oswald, too bloody stupid to see how he's being used. I'm a professional killer."

"So is my father," she murmured.

"What?"

"My father. He flew jets in Korea. Shot down seven MIGs. One on one, and Daddy always survived. So he's a professional killer too."

Charlie smiled. "But he's retired, gone into politics. I'm still active."

"They'll kill you, Charlie. Either the people guarding my father will or the people paying you will. You're just too vain to admit it. Your only chance is to take me to my father, tell him who's paying you, and I'll guarantee that you'll go free."

He shook his head. "Sorry, but I like the challenge."

"If you'd give this up," she said, "and take the money my

father would give you, and get your boat and sail for the South Seas—that's what you want, isn't it?"

"That's the plan, to sail into the sunset."

"Maybe I'd go with you."

He reached out and fluffed her hair. "That'd be nice, Jenna, it truly would be nice. But it can't be."

"Why not? You'd be a hero. I'd be grateful. And we've gotten on well enough, haven't we?"

He stared at her in dismay. He couldn't trust her, he knew that. And yet, since their first night together, he'd wanted to believe her, wanted to think she didn't hate him, wanted to think there was some way to do his job and have her too. She had gotten under his skin. Sometimes he dreamed of sailing into the sunset with her, and sometimes he wished he'd throttled her the first night they met.

"Let me think, let me think," he muttered. "Now, how about one more, before we're off to dreamland?"

She nodded. They would have their drink and then he would return her to her underground cell while he went about his business. But the evening had not been wasted. She knew more now, how he got into the White House, how he planned to kill her father, and if she could only get free there was still time to save him. And she would get free. She didn't know how, but she was sure she would, as sure as that the sun would rise tomorrow.

38

Duke Zeibert's restaurant was a dreary blur of dark-suited lawyers and lobbyists, then in walked John B. Goode, looking like the American flag with his red bow tie, bushy white hair, and bright blue suit.

"You must be Boyle," he declared, as he joined Matt at a table overlooking Connecticut Avenue. "I'm Johnny Goode. What're you drinking?"

They made small talk over their drinks—a vodka martini for Goode, Perrier for Boyle—and finally the older man said, "So to what do I owe this kind invitation, Matthew? You were a little vague on the phone. Not that I mind, if it's a chance to meet the famous media manipulator himself. You're not going to manipulate me, are you?"

Boyle laughed. "I wouldn't even try, Mr. Goode. No, it's no big mystery. I just have some friends with venture capital. They're looking for media investments, and they've heard good things—no pun intended—about the Goode News Bureau. They wondered if it might be available."

Goode nodded to the waiter for another drink. "Not a chance," he said good-naturedly.

"Not even if the price was right?"

Goode grinned contentedly. "Matt, your friends are too late. You want me to tell you why?"

"Absolutely," Boyle said.

The waiter took their order—filet mignon for Goode, a salad for Boyle—and then the journalist told his tale:

"I came to Washington after the war, Matt, a hotshot young reporter for the Chicago *Tribune.* Covered the Hill, got to know Sam Rayburn and Bob Taft, the usual stuff. But after a few years I figured out I was different from other reporters. I got fed up with all the gloom and doom—deficits here, scandals there, tragedy everywhere else. I asked my editor, 'Why don't we ever print any good news?' 'Find some,' he said, so I started looking. Well, by golly, there's good news out there, if you dig for it. So I started specializing in the sunny side of the news. But my editors fought me all the way. They didn't really *like* good news. It was a new concept in journalism. Do you follow me?"

"I think so," Boyle said.

"I was onto something big. America was sick of negativism. Why do you think newspapers kept folding? Because they were trying to sell people something they didn't want —bad news! I decided to open my own bureau, the Goode News Bureau, and report the positive side of the news. Heck, it's not news if a congressman gets caught stealing— what's news is if somebody finds your lost billfold and returns it. It's not news if the President sends the Marines to Timbuktu—presidents have been doing that for a hundred years. What's news is if the President takes time out to see the little March of Dimes girl."

"So your bureau thrived?" Boyle asked.

"The demand for upbeat news was growing fast. I hired a couple of young reporters. There's more good news than you'd think. The White House Easter Egg Roll, neglected for years. National Ice Cream Day, free sundaes and floats at the Senate. Dread diseases being conquered. People living longer. Good news all over the place. My big breakthrough came a few years ago, this fellow comes to see me, says he wants to buy me out. I laugh in his face. But he starts talking numbers and I quit laughing. Man made an offer I couldn't refuse."

"Mind if I ask what it was? My friends would be curious."

"They doubled my salary, paid me $100,000 up front, just for signing, and guaranteed me a fancy pension whenever I want to retire. Plus money for new offices and more staff. Plus a written guarantee of no editorial interference. Shoot, I don't understand it. These tax lawyers today, they make money by losing money. It was like Christmas."

"A nice deal," Boyle agreed.

"You know what they got out of it?"

"What?"

"Instant credibility. The goodwill that I spent thirty years creating. Listen, when a reporter from the Goode News Bureau calls up—the White House, the Senate, anywhere—that call goes through."

"Who are these people, the ones who bought you?"

"Modern Media, Inc. 242 Park Avenue. They're in the book."

"But who *are* they?"

John Goode shrugged. "I talked to a lawyer named Leslie. Beyond that, who cares? Their checks don't bounce."

Boyle already knew that Modern Media had bought the Goode News Bureau four years earlier. One of the papers in the mysterious package Boyle had received the previous Saturday had been a copy of a District of Columbia legal document that recorded the purchase. A second document, from New York, showed that Modern Media was controlled by something called The Hannibal Corporation. A third document, from Georgia records, showed that Hannibal was owned by none other than Masters Enterprises of Atlanta.

So Boyle was talking to Johnny Goode, but he didn't see what this harmless journalist could have to do with Jenna's disappearance. What did they know, really? That Serena Masters indirectly owned the Goode News Bureau. But what did that prove? The woman owned hundreds of companies.

"So these people have treated you right?" Boyle asked as their food arrived.

"Right as rain. They keep wanting to expand the operation. About six months ago they said we ought to have a photographer at the White House, full-time. They recommended a fellow and said they'd pay his salary. Young Englishman. Nice boy."

"You've been in Washington a long time, Mr. Goode."

"Call me Johnny. Yeah, I've seen 'em come and go."

"Ever know a woman called Serena Masters?"

Goode squinted suspiciously. "Why do you ask?"

"Just curious. Somebody from Georgia asked me about her the other day, what she was doing."

"I can't tell you. I remember when she was at the Pentagon. I don't get over there much. Hardest place in town to find good news, take it from me."

After they had coffee, Goode insisted that Boyle visit his bureau's offices in one of the modern boxes that lined K Street.

They stepped out of the elevator across from the Goode bureau. The two o's in Goode encircled little smile faces, and the offices were done in sunshine yellow and sky blue.

"Very nice," Boyle said.

Goode pointed to a row of plaques that lined the corridor. "Look at that," he commanded. "Prizes, citations, awards— people love us. To hell with gloom and doom. Let's have news with a smile!"

Lunch had loosened John B. Goode's tongue, but Boyle didn't know what else to ask him. The man didn't seem to know or care that he was owned by a bizarre billionairess.

"No news is Goode news," the journalist muttered. "Listen, what about Cal Webster? I look at him and I don't see the light side."

The door to the darkroom opened and a big, good-looking, broad-shouldered young man emerged. He and Boyle were eye to eye and bells began to ring.

"Matt Boyle, meet Wes Hillman," Goode said. "Wes is the photographer I told you about."

"Hey, how're you?" the photographer cried, pumping Boyle's hand like a long-lost friend. Boyle, suddenly confused, stared hard at the young man's face, sensing a cold-

ess that the warm-as-toast smile could not quite conceal.
'here had he seen that cold, pretty face before?

He saw in memory a mob of jostling photographers. The
'hite House correspondents dinner, the one he'd taken
nna to two months before. A big, crowded, self-important
fair—Boyle had hated it, except for Jenna, radiant in a
ackless red dress. Now he remembered. When he had es-
•rted Jenna into the hotel ballroom they'd run a gauntlet of
hotographers and this Hillman had caught his eye. Why?
ecause while the other photographers pushed and shoved,
is fellow, for the instant that their eyes met, had simply
ared at them, a bitter smile frozen on his face.

"That dinner at the Hilton," Boyle muttered. "You cov-
•ed it."

"Right you are!" the young man declared. "And got some
ifty shots of you and the lovely Miss Webster. Hey, excuse
e, got to get back—pleased to meet you!"

Hillman ducked into the darkroom. "A nice boy," John
oode said. "A real touch with animals and kids."

Back on K Street, Boyle was bedazzled. Yes, he'd seen the
hotographer at that dinner, and he'd seen him somewhere
se, too, a dim, distant, maddening memory that would not
uite come into focus, until the uncertainty almost made
im scream.

39

Turk Kellerman was on the phone with the President's ma
man, Harry Bliss.

"We started getting calls this morning," Turk said. "W
refer them all to the White House."

"We're not commenting," Harry said. "But he's sure to g
a question on it at his news conference tomorrow. So wh
the hell does he say? That his daughter's been missing tw
weeks and he doesn't know where she is?"

"Don't have a news conference. It's crazy. Dangerous

"It's your job to make sure it's not dangerous."

"We can't strip-search two hundred reporters and photo
raphers. Who the hell knows who all those people are?"

"He's got to have the news conference. The Russians ha
screwed us. The whole disarmament program is falli
apart. He's got to grab the initiative. But now he'll get b
with this Jenna mess. What's he supposed to tell them?"

"There's an old saying," Turk Kellerman said. "When
else fails, tell the truth."

"Wiseass." The President's man slammed down the pho
in frustration.

She paced about her underground cell clutching her wonderful secret in her hand. She'd fooled Charlie. The night before she'd stolen something when his back was turned, stuck it in her jeans, smuggled it downstairs. Would he notice? What would he do to her if he noticed? But he wouldn't! She'd fooled Charlie and it would be her salvation, somehow. But where to hide her treasure? Under the bed? Behind the books on the bookshelf? Where would he look? She slipped into the little kitchen. Cereal, bread, oranges, some milk in the refrigerator. Where, where? She seized the box of Raisin Bran. It was half full. She opened her fist and gazed proudly at her prize, a book of paper matches. Smiling serenely, she plunged her Promethean treasure into the cereal. It would be safe there, until her moment came.

When Wes Hillman emerged from the darkroom later that afternoon, John Goode called him to his office. "I've been getting calls. A story is all over town that Jenna Webster is missing. The *Post* will play it big in the morning, and Webster will get hit with it at his news conference, the poor guy."

"They've got no idea where she is?" the photographer asked.

"That's what I hear."

"Probably nothing to it," Hillman said. "A pretty girl, off on a lark."

"Let's hope so," Goode said. "Anyway, print up your best shots of her and have them ready to move."

"Right, boss," the young photographer said. "Say, that fellow Boyle, what did he want?"

"Who knows? Maybe he just wanted to buy me lunch. He *said* he had some friends who wanted to buy me out. The thing is, Wes, these political types, they've got more angles than a dog has fleas."

The younger man did not smile. "Didn't he used to do Webster's media?"

"That's him."

"I heard he'd gone round the bend."

"How's that?"

"Quit Webster. Turned down a White House job. Dropped out of sight. A bit daft."

"Seemed harmless enough."

"I wonder what he was after. I mean, did he push you on anything?"

Goode laughed indulgently. "What's to push? We talked about the old days. Sam Rayburn, Harry Truman. That was about all. The only strange thing was, from out of nowhere, he asked me if I knew Serena Masters. But you've probably never heard of her, have you? Just get those prints of Jenna Webster ready for me, okay?"

The photographer sprang to his feet. "Sure thing, boss."

"Oh, one other thing. I want you to cover Webster's press conference tomorrow. It ought to be a dilly."

The younger man nodded. "I wouldn't miss it for the world."

Then Wes Hillman withdrew to the darkroom where he thought very hard about Matthew Boyle, for if Boyle was coming around to the Goode News Bureau asking questions about Serena Masters, then he had made himself a matter of the most urgent concern.

After lunch, Boyle dropped by the Class Reunion for a reunion with a half dozen reporters he hadn't seen in months. He was greeted as a political Lazarus, with many toasts and tales of campaigns past. The reporters also passed on the rumors of Jenna's disappearance, and Boyle was glad the word was finally out. He hoped that somehow pressure from the media would finally force the White House to do whatever had to be done to find Jenna.

I'm out of it now, Boyle thought, I did all I could.

The reporters urged Boyle to stay for an early dinner. He called home and asked Zeb if he'd mind spending the evening with the Paynes. Zeb grumbled a bit, but agreed, so Boyle called Jack Payne to make sure it was okay. That settled, he had a fine time with his reporter friends, despite their endless questions about Jenna, her habits, her friends, and her probable whereabouts. When he vowed he'd say no more about Jenna they started grilling him on Webster himself, and how he might respond to the latest Russian duplicity. Was he tough? Was he subtle? Could he walk the razor's edge of an international crisis without blundering into World War Last? Boyle answered as best he could, but who could truly say what any man might do in a nuclear showdown? World War Last would surely come as a vast surprise to everyone, even the fellow who pushed the button.

It was almost nine when Boyle escaped. The reporters grabbed his check, of course. He suspected that his $50 worth of food and booze would wind up on several expense accounts. He was still classified as an official Friend of the President, the kind of Class A Source who never had to pick up a check in Washington, not as long as his friend stayed in power.

During his drive home, Boyle thought about his son, and about the Beatles. Boyle had come of age with the Beatles, in the mid-1960s, at a time when the world had kept getting worse and worse, and their music had kept getting better and better. Boyle loved the Beatles, and was glad his son had grown up loving them. They had been Zeb's Mother Goose; he loved the fabulous world of Mean Mr. Mustard, the Walrus, Mr. Kite, Lovely Rita, Lucy in the Sky, the Yellow Submarine, and all the rest. He was surely one of the few nine-year-olds in America whose favorite album was "Abbey Road," and who could sing every word of it.

The problem was that as Zeb neared ten—double digits, trouble—his musical horizons were expanding, and not in directions Boyle approved. Zeb had discovered Top Forty radio. The radio beside his bed throbbed with strange, sinister sounds, day and night. Worse, when he came downstairs, to play chess or Monopoly with Boyle, he had begun demanding equal time for what he defiantly called "my music." Boyle tried being reasonable but firm: "Son, downstairs, let's listen to *my* music."

This brought the angry declaration: "I don't like your music! Your music's dull!"

Boyle's music, dull? Hank Williams, Billie Holiday, Louis Armstrong, Alberta Hunter, Paul Simon, dull?

The churlish lad added helpfully, "In your music, all they do is sing, 'Oh darling, I miss you, please come home.'" This falsehood was dramatized, with rolled eyes and a falsetto voice, acid satire for a nine-year-old.

Harsh words were spoken, then a compromise reached. When Zeb was downstairs, they would divide their time between the father's music and the son's. Boyle accepted this settlement reluctantly, and only after his son had lectured him on justice and fair play. He feared he had a lawyer on his hands.

Thus were inflicted upon Boyle an endless parade of young howlers who without exception made his head hurt. And, as the final blow, Zeb had begun demanding a "boom box" so he could carry his music with him, wherever he might roam. Boyle hated "boom boxes" and flatly refused to spend a penny for one. Zeb countered that he would buy one with the money he'd earned mowing a neighbor's lawn that summer. There the matter rested.

Such concerns were in Boyle's mind as he turned onto the dark road that led to Harmony. So engrossed was he, that he hardly noticed the lights of the big sedan that pulled in behind him.

There were, Charlie believed, as many ways to kill a man as to make love to a woman: dozens, at the very least. Still, although he believed there were times when innovation was called for, he also thought that, more often than not, the old, familiar ways were best.

The unexplained accident—the car wreck, the fall down the stairs, the drowning in the backyard pool—was to murder what the missionary position was to sex, he thought, and not to be scorned for being commonplace.

Thus, the death of Matthew Boyle must look to all the world like the most mundane of accidents. A bloke's been to dinner in town, had a few too many, and dozes off behind the wheel. Happens all the time.

Smiling, Charlie edged his Buick closer to the Toyota's

aillights. Boyle's snooping had gotten too close for comfort.
He had somehow made the connection between Charlie's
employer, Serena Masters, and his cover, the Goode News
Bureau. Ergo, Boyle must go. A quiet exit, RIP. Then, tomorrow, President Webster would hold his news conference as
planned. His last news conference.

The road curved in and out of the trees, following a small
creek, then straightened. Charlie stepped on the gas.

Boyle was pondering the hard truth that one generation's
music is another generation's headache when the big car
started around him.

"Damn fool," he muttered.

Suddenly the sedan banged against him. He swerved to
the right, onto the narrow dirt shoulder but the sedan
pushed closer. His right wheels were off the road. He fought
the steering wheel. The car was tilting, tumbling into the
creek. Boyle shouted in anger and then the water engulfed
him.

40

Jack Payne puffed on his pipe as he carved on a block of soft pine. Sue was knitting a blanket for their new grandson. Zeb sat on their sofa, a platter of cookies untouched before him.

"Don't you want a cookie?" Sue Payne asked. "Maybe a glass of milk too?"

"No thanks," Zeb said. "I'm full."

"Never heard of a boy too full for chocolate-chip cookies," Jack Payne grumbled.

Zeb didn't hear him because he was thinking about his mother. Why had his mother died? Had God taken her off to Heaven, the way the preacher said? Was there a God? Zeb knew that if there was he hated him. Zeb thought about his father too. Sometimes he wished his father would get a real job like other fathers had. Other fathers went to offices or were farmers or something, but all his father did was stay home and type and talk on the phone and read books. His father was always telling him how books were so wonderful but Zeb thought TV was a lot more fun. He guessed his father was just old-fashioned. He was pretty old, too, getting gray hair, and that was embarrassing because most of his friends had fathers who were young and went bowling and played softball and all. Sometimes Zeb wished his father would get married again but he guessed he was too old for that.

He thought about girls sometimes. There was a girl he sort of liked. She was the prettiest girl in his class at school and sometimes they did their homework together. She'd asked him to a 4-H dance once and it had been fun to dance with her and kid around. His dad was always saying why didn't he invite her over to play but he couldn't do that or all the guys would laugh at him. Some of his friends were older, eleven or twelve, and they were always talking about sex and all this stuff that sounded dumb and ugly. They said grown-ups did that stuff in bed and some of the teenage girls in town did it in cars and barns and other places too. He knew he wouldn't do anything gross like that when he grew up.

But grown-ups were crazy. He knew a boy whose father got drunk and beat up his mother and beat up the boy too and the boy said he'd kill him when he was big enough. His own dad, back when his mom was alive, used to get drunk at parties but all he'd do was act silly and sing songs and dance old-fashioned dances. Zeb used to stay up late at the parties and all the grown-ups would act crazy, except for his mom. She was never silly. So why did she have to die? Old people were supposed to die, not people who were young and pretty like his mother. He dreamed about her a lot. She would be out in a field with wildflowers growing around her and he'd run and run but he could never catch up with her. Or he'd be up close to her and try to talk, but it was like a wall of glass was between them and they couldn't touch or hear each other's voices. That was why Zeb liked TV so much, because on TV things turned out right, on TV nobody died unless there was a reason. There was so much he didn't understand, about girls and bombs and wars and people dying; he wished his mother was there, to explain all those crazy things to him. Sometimes he wished he would die, he missed her so much.

"Zeb, you want to help me carve this duck?" Jack Payne asked.

Zeb looked up and shook his head. "There's a show I want to see. TV Bloopers."

"I'm afraid our TV is dead and buried, pal," Jack Payne said.

"I guess I'll go watch it at home."

Payne frowned. He had a black beard and it was funny to see him frown, mostly with his eyes and forehead. "You sure you won't mind being there alone?"

"I'll be all right. If my dad's not home when the show is over, I'll come back down here."

"Okay, buddy, whatever you say. You know you're welcome."

"Sure," Zeb said. "Thanks."

Charlie eased down the slippery bank to the creek. He had a flashlight in one hand and a small revolver with a suppressor in the other, but he didn't need the flashlight—moonlight poured down, radiant—and he didn't expect to need the weapon either. The Toyota was on its side in three feet of water. Probably Boyle was already dead; if not, he soon would be.

Charlie paused at the creek's edge, cursing to himself—it was a bloody nuisance to get his shoes wet, but it was an occupational hazard. He stepped into the water and was a dozen feet from the silent Toyota when he slipped on a rock. Just then, incredibly, Boyle's head emerged from the car window.

"You son of a bitch," Boyle muttered. He pointed a gun at Charlie and fired.

Charlie threw himself sideways into the water and scudded along the rocky creek bed as far as he could, thirty feet or more, before he leaped up for air. A second shot echoed down the gully and he went underwater again. The next time he came up he scrambled up the bank to the trees.

Boyle, half in the car and half out of it, saw his attacker flee. "You bastard," he yelled at the departing shadow. He sank back into his wrecked car, waist deep in water, not sure he had the strength to save himself.

Turk could hear a piano in the background, cocktail music. He imagined the bar: small, dark, elegant, intimate. Just
the place for a two-star general to entertain a lady who was
not his wife.

"What did you say your name was?" the general was saying.

"Kellerman, Assistant Director of the Secret Service."

"And precisely why are you calling me, Mr. Kellerman?"

"I've got to see you immediately. You've got to authorize
an urgent project. It's . . ."

"Do you know what time it is, Mr. Kellerman?"

"Yes, General, I do, but . . ."

"Then I suggest you call me at my office in the morning."

"In the morning is too late. This is a matter of presidential
security."

"Presidential security? *Your* job is presidential security.
Mine is advanced technological research. Now, if you'll excuse me . . ."

"General, I want you to come to my office immediately."

"And I want you to go straight to hell."

"General, you're there with a lovely young woman. I'm
sure it's hard to leave her. But if you don't get to my office in
ten minutes you're never going to see her again, except
maybe in the newspapers. Do I make myself clear?"

The general sucked air. The pianist played "Laura." Turk
saw Gene Tierney, young and exquisite, glowing in his
memory.

"Where precisely is your office?" the general asked.

Soaked, bruised, furious, Charlie threw open the Buick's
trunk and grabbed a Smith & Wesson Model 34. What the
hell had Boyle been doing with a gun? No matter, he'd finish
the bastard now, once and for all.

But as he moved along the dark road toward the creek, he
saw headlights. One car stopped, then another.

"There's a car down there!"

"Come on, might be somebody in it!"

He heard men splashing in the water. Another motorist
stopped.

"Jesus Christ—look at him!"

"You up there, go call an ambulance!"

Charlie seethed with rage. Boyle must be silenced. But how? Should he follow him to the hospital?

He stood in the darkness, waiting, thinking. He heard an ambulance's siren drawing near. He watched, across a hundred feet of moonlight, as Boyle was carried up from the creek and the ambulance went wailing off toward Leesburg.

By then Charlie had a plan. He climbed into the Buick, and drove slowly into the village of Harmony.

Not so far away, secure behind her gates and electrified fences, Serena heard the distant sirens but paid them no mind. She seized the telephone and dialed.

"Hello?"

"Let me speak to the Vice President."

"May I ask who's calling?"

"No you may not—get him!"

That simpering, drunken cow would soon be First Lady. Serena wondered how much trouble it would be to have Remington divorce her.

"Hello, this is the Vice President."

"I have to talk to you. I'll come to your home at ten in the morning. Do you understand?"

"For Heaven's sake, what is it?"

"Don't waste my time with questions—just be there!"

"Oh, yes, I'll be there," the Vice President said unhappily.

Zeb heard the sirens while he watched the TV Bloopers show. Then he got in bed and looked at a collection of *Far Side* cartoons, his favorite comic strip. He was half asleep when the man spoke to him. He thought it was a dream and then he saw him in the doorway.

"Hello, Zeb."

He was big and good-looking, like somebody in a movie. But he shouldn't be in the house, out of nowhere.

"Who're you?"

"I'm a policeman. Your dad's been in an accident. Maybe you heard the sirens."

Zeb's thoughts spun wildly. Who was this guy? What kind accident? What if his dad was dead? Then he'd be an phan. Would he have to go live with his grandmother in uth Dakota, who went to church all the time? Or with the ynes, who didn't have a TV?

"Is my dad hurt bad?"

"Not too bad. He wants to see you. He asked me to drive u to the hospital."

Zeb stared at the man for a long time. If he was a police-an, why didn't he wear a uniform?

"Why are you all wet?"

"Your dad's car fell in the creek. I helped get him out." The man smiled a lot but Zeb saw something ugly in his es.

"I better call Mr. Payne. He's taking care of me tonight."

"Don't be afraid, Zeb. Here, suppose I show you my dge?"

The man moved toward the bed. He kept smiling but his es were cold and mocking. Zeb wanted to cry out but no ords came.

41

The guards opened the gates and the limousine, sparkling i
the bright moonlight, passed through them, picked u
speed, and after half a mile stopped outside Serena Masters
many-columned Virginia mansion.

The chauffeur leaped out and opened the rear door, and
slender, graceful man in a pin-stripe suit hurried up th
steps. Moments later, Serena greeted the visitor in the bi
library where she displayed her collection of guns, knive
and other weapons.

"Colonel, I do so appreciate your coming," she said.

Colonel Boris Vysotsky, the KGB's ranking official in th
U.S., bowed low over her outstretched hand. His greetin
almost took her breath away, for he was like no Russian sh
had ever seen or imagined, handsome and aristocratic, wit
silver hair that curled back over his ears. He smiled warm1
and said, "And now, madam, to what do I owe the honor
this most welcome invitation?"

Serena pointed him to a chair and took one opposite.
was so strange, she thought; for years she had loathed Ru
sians, denounced them as criminals and barbarians, and ye

w, with the aid of this man, she might bring off her great-
t coup. He was no fool, she could see that, yet she must use
m as she had used so many others.

"Colonel, I believe you know that I, and a great many
sponsible Americans, are deeply disturbed by President
ebster's so-called 'disarmament' plan, just as thoughtful
aders of your government are."

The colonel nodded gravely, his cold eyes never leaving
er face.

"It is in truth a destabilization plan," she continued, "en-
angering the security of our two nations and indeed of the
atire world."

"Just so," the colonel murmured.

"Although we may differ on economic theory," she said, "I
elieve we have much in common. We both recognize the
eed for a strong central government, to assure our internal
ad external security. We both understand that true peace
an only be achieved through strength. We both have a
egitimate need for domination over troublesome countries
a our respective spheres of interest. And we both seek
acreased trade, growth, and prosperity for our nations."

They were sitting on opposite ends of a plum-colored sofa.
he colonel smiled. "I quite agree."

"However," she continued, "we face a common problem.
resident Webster's nuclear retreat has confused and di-
ided both our countries. How can we be respected
aroughout the world if we voluntarily emasculate our-
elves? I fear for the safety, even the survival, of modern
ivilization if this madness is allowed to continue!"

The Russian extracted a Turkish cigarette from a silver
ase and lit it with a flourish. "Madam, as you may imagine,
our views are shared by powerful figures in the Politburo.
he divisions there are bitter and the outcome, I must say, is
a doubt."

"As things now stand, Colonel, your faction—might I call
ou the realists?—seems to have the upper hand."

"We have delayed the dismantling of the second round of
nissiles, yes, but that could change overnight."

"Much could change overnight, Colonel."

Vysotsky sucked on his Turkish cigarette. Serena pause
for a moment, savoring its rich aroma. "As you know," she
continued, "Mr. Webster has a news conference at noo
tomorrow. It is my understanding that he will announce
worldwide alert of U.S. military forces."

"So I am told," the Russian said.

"There are two possible results of such an action, bot
undesirable," she said. "It could lead to war. Or, at the othe
extreme, it could intimidate your government into procee
ing with the so-called disarmament plan, which, I believe w
agree, can only cause worldwide anarchy."

The Russian nodded but did not speak.

"However," she said, "there is another possible turn
events, one that would be to our mutual benefit. I can spea
now only in the most general terms."

"Of course, madam."

"I am confiding in you because I believe the stability
the world depends upon the existence of realistic leadershi
in both our nations. You and your friends in the Politbur
and my associates and I in this country—we speak the sam
language, the language of power, profit, and realism."

"Precisely, madam. And now . . . this other possibility?"

"It is my belief that Mr. Webster may . . . *vacate* his o
fice very soon."

The colonel stroked an errant silver hair back from h
temple. "Vacate," he murmured.

"In that event, of course, Vice President Remingto
would become President."

"I know very little about Mr. Remington."

"There is very little to know, Colonel," Serena said. "Wha
there is, I am about to tell you."

"Please do."

"To begin with, when . . . if . . . Remington become
President, it may be necessary for him to make quite strong
even belligerent statements about the Soviet Union."

The colonel smiled. "Saber rattling," he said.

"Or missile rattling, as the case may be. But your goverr
ment must not be alarmed by whatever he may say."

"That is of course difficult at moments of international tension," the colonel said.

"Yes, and that is why, once Remington becomes President, you and I must be in close communication. I will be, shall we say, a principal adviser to Mr. Remington, and it is my belief that, as soon as possible, a historic drama must be played out upon the world stage."

Her guest smiled approvingly. "Of course. A crisis."

"A most severe crisis," she agreed. "The people of our two countries must believe they are at the brink of nuclear holocaust. Then, and only then, will they understand the need for strong leadership in our two countries, and for more, not less, nuclear weaponry."

Vysotsky nodded thoughtfully. "It is a fascinating plan."

"It is in our mutual interest," she said.

"I must speak to my superiors," the colonel said.

"Of course. But hurry. Time is short."

"If there is anything I can do to be of assistance . . ."

"There is one small matter," she said.

"What is that?"

"I have a young man in my employ. A formidable young man, but troublesome. Here is his picture."

The colonel nodded; he knew this man by reputation.

"Once Mr. Remington is President, it is imperative to our success that the young man be . . . removed. Might you . . . ?"

"Of course," the colonel said. "And now I must leave."

Once again he bowed low over her hand. This time his dry lips brushed her fingers.

Serena stood at the window and watched as Colonel Vysotsky drove off into the night. She thought him a quite reasonable man. Between them, if all went well, they could rule the world. She realized she had been wrong, before, to think you could not deal with the Soviets. She and the colonel understood each other perfectly. The ruling classes, in all countries, came to share a common perspective.

42

Boyle awoke in the hospital and began struggling with the doctors and nurses.

"What time is it? How long was I out? I've got to get home!"

"It's ten-thirty, Mr. Boyle. Please lie down. You've had a nasty . . ."

He broke loose and found a phone. One of the doctors was yelling at him but he ignored him. He called home and let the phone ring twenty times.

Cursing, half mad, he called Jack Payne's number.

"Zeb went home to watch TV," Jack reported. "Hey, are you okay?"

Boyle called home again and let the phone ring endlessly. He's asleep, he told himself. Or he's got those damn headphones on.

"Mr. Boyle, you need stitches . . ."

"I'm leaving," Boyle said.

Leesburg had one all-night cab and by a miracle Boyle found it idling outside the emergency room. As the cab caromed along the road to Harmony he noticed a limousine

aving River Crest Farm but his mind was too jumbled with
onfusion and fear to wonder about it. That afternoon he'd
onfirmed that Serena Masters owned an obscure Washing-
on news bureau. Within hours, someone had tried to kill
im, would have killed him, except that he'd had Jack
ayne's gun to defend himself with. So he was still alive, but
here was his son?

He paid the cab driver and stared at his house, looming in
ie moonlight. He'd lost his revolver in the creek, so he
rabbed the ax from the woodpile beside his house, then
urst in the side door. The door was open of course. He'd
ever gotten around to having new keys made and locking
ie doors, as he'd intended.

"Zeb, Zeb?" he yelled, but only silence greeted him.

He sprinted up the stairs to his son's bedroom. It was the
sual jungle of books, toys, video gear, and dirty clothes. But
o Zeb.

He raced about the big, empty house, calling the boy's
ame, turning on lights, finding nothing.

"My God, my God, my God," he moaned, and flung the
seless ax aside.

A ray of hope speared him. Of course! Zeb had wandered
ff to some friend's house to spend the night. To Derek's
ouse or Bobby's house or . . . Boyle seized the phone
ook. His hands shook so that he had to put the book on the
ounter to read it.

The phone rang.

Boyle grabbed it, expecting to hear Zeb's solemn voice.

"Mr. Boyle, listen carefully to what I have to say."

The voice was slightly accented and maddeningly famil-
ar.

"Who is this?"

"Listen! I have your son. He is alive and well. If you want
im to remain alive and well you . . ."

"You son of a bitch," Boyle whispered. The words sprang
orth on their own, like tears.

"If you want him to remain alive and well, do exactly what
tell you. Stay at home. Do not go out. Do not use the

telephone. Do not speak to anyone. Do absolutely nothir
and your son will be returned to you."

"When?"

"Not long. Remember, I'll be watching. If you speak
anyone, I'll slit the little bugger's throat. Do you unde
stand?"

"Yes," Boyle whispered.

The caller hung up. Boyle fell into a chair. For a while, h
mind buzzed with a thousand schemes. But they all fe
apart in the face of the caller's threat. He felt empty, imp
tent, defeated. Finally he decided the only thing to do was
do nothing and to hope the killer kept his word. Boyle sat
the overstuffed chair in his study, sobbing, broken, waitir
for dawn.

The light awakened Jenna from a deep, dreamless slee
Confused, half-blinded, she heard Charlie say, "I brough
you a roommate."

The door slammed and the boy was in her arms.

"Where are we?"

"Zeb," she cried. "Oh, no, no, no."

His thin body, trembling, pressed against hers. She trie
to pull herself together.

"Don't be afraid," she said. "It's going to be all right. We'r
going to get out of here. Talk to me, Zeb, talk to me."

The boy's face was buried in her thick black hair. "I mi
my mom so much," he whispered.

PART III

The Last News Conference

43

JENNA WEBSTER MISSING
FBI FEARS KIDNAPPING
WHITE HOUSE TO COMMENT TODAY

Charlie adored the headline. Washington was stewing, coming to a boil, and he was the lad turning up the heat. Soon they'd start to panic, making everything easier for the bloke who kept his head. He laughed aloud to think what a bloody disaster Washington would be that afternoon, after Calvin Webster's last news conference.

Charlie was up early that morning; he had a busy day ahead. He unlocked the cabinet that housed his state-of-the-art electronic equipment. He slipped on headphones, punched buttons, and listened as Matt Boyle's recorded voice announced that he was busy, that the caller should leave a message. That message played several times, as excited reporters pleaded with Boyle to call them, but the real-life Boyle never uttered a peep. Charlie had to laugh; the poor blundering sod would sit home trembling all day, afraid that his baby boy might come to harm.

Charlie drank a cup of coffee, then burned some of his

papers in the big fireplace. But he had too many papers, too much gear, far more evidence than he was willing to leave behind. He had to dispose of his gear and he had another problem, too: what to do with his two guests.

He knew what must be done, of course, and yet he hesitated.

Damn you, he thought, are you going soft?

After a tortured, sleepless night, Boyle stepped onto his front porch to claim the morning's Washington *Post*. His eyes swept nervously up and down the street. Framed in the green and gold of early autumn he saw only a neighbor's decrepit dog, an elderly couple out for their constitutional and early morning commuters speeding through the village toward Washington.

No spies, no stakeouts, no mysterious strangers lurking about. Yet in Boyle's imagination, in his gut, someone was watching. He shuddered as he heard again the threat: *If you speak to anyone I'll slit the little bugger's throat.*

Zeb was gone, that was a fact. Boyle had spent the night considering all the things he could do, and he had decided that the only thing he could do was nothing.

He made coffee and looked at the *Post*. The dramatic story on Jenna left him unmoved. All he could think was what a fool he'd been, playing cops and robbers when he should have been protecting the one person who mattered most.

The *Post*'s story told about the homing device on Jenna's car and said she was thought to have been seized while driving to visit a friend in Virginia. Boyle guessed that was why his phone had been ringing, because reporters had guessed he was the friend. But he wasn't answering the phone. If they came and banged on his front door he wouldn't open it. His door was closed, maybe forever.

The *Post* carried a full page of pictures of Jenna, including the one of her and Boyle at the correspondents' dinner, just before she vanished. Boyle remembered the mob of photographers, the confusion in the ballroom, and he remembered the tall young photographer he'd noticed, and he was sure he'd seen him since that night, in the moonlight.

All at once the pieces began to fall into place, too late to matter.

Jenna held him in her arms till he awoke, his brown eyes clear and guileless.

"I dreamed I was home," he said.

"I'm sorry, Zeb. I wish you were."

"Where are we?"

"In the basement of a cabin on a big estate. Not far from our village, I think."

"Is there a big white house with pillars, up on a hill?"

"Yes."

"I know where it is. They said some Arab bought it. They put barbed wire on the fences. That man who brought me here, is he upstairs?"

"He may be. I'm not sure."

"Why is he doing this?"

"I think he wants to kill my father. I think your father was suspicious of him, and he . . . he seized you to make your father leave him alone."

"We've got to get out of here," Zeb said. "We've got to warn the President."

Jenna heard the clang of Charlie's boot on the metal staircase. "He's coming," she said. "Listen to me, Zeb. Here's what I want you to do."

She whispered her instructions. "Do you understand?"

Zeb nodded, his slender face stiff with anger. "We've got to stop him!"

Then the door opened and Charlie was grinning at them.

Turk Kellerman had discovered amphetamines in Vietnam and he still kept a supply on hand for emergencies. He regarded them as the most insidious of drugs, and yet he marveled at the energy, the clarity they could bestow. On the long night before the President's news conference, he gobbled them like peanuts as he marched about the East Room, barking angry questions at the Pentagon's scientists and cursing their endless delays.

Dawn broke unnoticed in the East Room, for the thick

gold curtains were drawn and the heavy doors were locke
and guarded by armed men; soon after dawn the installatio
was complete.

"You'll want to test it now," said a weary army colonel

"I can't test it," Turk barked. "I don't have the weapor
Only a theory."

"That's insane." The colonel was angry at being kept u
all night and told so little. Turk didn't blame him and didn
care.

"Yes, I suppose it is," he said.

Saussy, the FBI agent, drawn and rumpled after the lon
night's work, hurried up to him. "Harry Bliss is outside
boiling mad. Nobody ever kept him out of the East Roor
before."

"Let him in," Turk said.

Alone for a moment, Turk hummed a Cole Porter tune
marveling at how wonderfully clear everything had beer
ever since he discovered the dead pig.

He heard the angry footsteps of Harry Bliss. "What in th
goddamn hell is going on here?"

"I'm trying to save the President's life," Turk said calmly
"His daughter's, too."

Harry Bliss was about to explode. "Explain. Fast."

"I'll explain to the President."

"You'll explain to me. Right now."

Beware the speed freak, Turk thought, for he is fearless
"No," he said. "To the President. It's his life."

One of the Cubans opened the door. There were two o
them, brothers from Miami, Mutt and Jeff, Charlie callee
them. This one was Jeff, a stump of a man with hair as shin
as motor oil and skin the color of peanut butter. Charlie
knew the type; they made brave speeches about the coun
terrevolution, and in the meantime kept busy dealing drug
and breaking legs.

Charlie gave the scowling Cuban a nod and strolled int
the library, where Serena, clad in a chiffon dress, was havin
coffee.

"Today's the day," he said.

She put down her cup. "Are you nervous?"

"Why should I be? It's the other fellow who's going to die."

"I'm glad you came by. I'm just leaving to see the Vice President."

"What does he know?" he demanded.

"Very little."

"He's a fool, remember that."

She arched an eyebrow. "He's my fool," she said.

"The money," he said.

"I have it. All of it, in cash, exactly as specified."

"Good," he said. "Once the job is completed, I'll be back here."

"I'll have the money, in this very room, in a suitcase."

"Don't let your Cubans get their paws on it."

"Luis and his brother are patriots," she said.

Luis and his brother would slit your throat for a pint of rum, he thought, but that was her problem.

"See me to my car," she said.

They walked out of the house and down the steps to her maroon Mercedes. The squat Cuban was behind the wheel.

Serena kissed his cheek. "Good luck, Charles," she said. "Remember, if you need me, I'll always be here."

He wagged two fingers as she drove away, then walked across the dewy grass to his cabin, where his two guests still awaited him.

Only connect, a great writer said.

Boyle was making connections now, a chain reaction. Serena Masters had bought the Goode News Bureau so her assassin, the one who called himself Wes Hillman, could gain access to the White House as a photographer. Boyle had stumbled onto that fact and that was why Hillman had tried to kill him, and, failing that, had seized Zeb to keep him quiet. They planned to kill the President that very day, at his news conference, and make Remington President. It had been Serena Masters who "created" Ben Remington, made him Vice President, and now would make him President.

Boyle burned with frustration. He could foil the plot with

a single call to the White House. But that call might cost Zeb
his life.

If you speak to anyone I'll slit the little bugger's throat.
Boyle could not call the killer's bluff. If he must choose
between the President's life and his son's, it was no choice at
all.

The Vice President was slumped on a blood-red sofa, trying to understand, or perhaps not to understand.

"You could become President at any moment," Serena
repeated.

"If you'd only explain . . ."

"Webster's health is poor. He's tried to keep it secret. He
may resign. Or die. Anything can happen. You must be
ready. Your first hours in office will set the tone."

"I don't *want* to be President," Remington said. "I never
wanted it."

"Nonsense. This is what we've been working toward."

"What *you've* been working toward."

"You were part of the plan. You understood the goal."

"You left me precious little choice," he said bitterly. "I
never wanted to be President. I'm not up to the job."

"That doesn't matter. *I* am! Think of it as a role you must
play." She thrust some papers into his hands. "I've brought
things for you to read. Talking points. Themes. You must be
presidential. Say nothing I have not approved."

Remington skimmed the papers. "My God, I couldn't say
this," he protested. "It'd start World War Three!"

"You'll do as you're told," Serena reminded him.

"Well, how are we this morning?" Charlie said cheerfully.

Jenna leaped to her feet. "How could you involve a child
in this?" she demanded. "It's beneath contempt."

"Had no choice. His father was making a bloody nuisance
of himself."

"That's no excuse."

"An adventure for the lad. It'll all be over soon."

"Over? When?"

"This afternoon. You'll both be free as the wind."

"Damn you, Charlie, look at him."

Zeb lay huddled on the bed, face down, trembling.

"Hey, don't be afraid, mate," Charlie said. "This is a great ace here. When I get back this afternoon, I'll take you up the big house. The lady up there, she's got a regular useum of guns and swords and daggers and all kind of nifty ems. She's even got a dragon that shoots fire out its mouth. Iaybe we'll have a demonstration. Won't that be a lark, eh?"

Zeb began to sob. Jenna said, "Look at him—he's terrified. u can't keep him in this dungeon all day."

"Dungeon? Pretty cosy, I'd say."

"Charlie, please, let us go upstairs."

He shook his head. "Sorry, sweet."

"Why not? The cabin is a fortress—you've told me so your-lf. Let us wait up there. If we're really going to be freed, hat does it matter?"

Charlie had an idea. "Let me think about it. Maybe it'd ork out fine."

Ben Remington paced about his study, studying his lines. "My fellow Americans, at this time of tragedy, we must be rong in resolve, steadfast in unity."

Not bad, he thought. A certain Kennedyesque ring.

"Ben, what on earth are you doing?"

He whirled to find Peaches in the doorway, glass in hand.

"Working on a speech," he told her.

"It sounds like you're declaring war. What is this 'time of agedy'?"

The Vice President melted into a chair. He had to talk to meone, even Peaches. "I'm going to be President," he roaned.

"You're *what?*"

"Webster is a dying man. He could go at any moment."

"Piffle. He's strong as an ox."

"What's that you're drinking?"

"A Bloody Mary. Here." She handed him her glass and estled on the arm of his chair. "Now, what's this all about?" e demanded. "Tell mama."

The cabin had to go, and everything in it. That was easily done; he had an abundance of plastique. He could blow the cabin that afternoon and exit in a blaze of glory.

But what of Jenna? She was a world-class girl, as brave and brainy as he ever hoped to meet. To take her with him had been a lovely fantasy, but the time for fantasy was over. Jenna couldn't be trusted, therefore Jenna must go. It grieved him, but there were always other girls. The boy had to go too, and that fact caused Charlie no pain—the little bugger had bit his arm the night before, drawing blood.

So Jenna could have her wish. She and the boy could come upstairs and spend the day in the cabin. They could have a jolly old time there, right up until the cabin went up in flames. Let Madam Masters explain away their bones, if they were ever found.

Charlie went out and placed the plastique under the corners of the cabin. Then he hurried down to the basement to greet his two guests.

"Guess what? Chez Charlie is all yours, for the rest of the day! Aren't you the lucky ones?"

Senator Ben Trawick sat alone and motionless in the dark shadows of his vast Senate office. Outside his door, in another world, phones rang endlessly and various secretaries and highly paid aides busied themselves protecting his privacy. The senator was not to be disturbed, no matter what.

Amid silence and shadows, the senator brooded, listened, waited, tried to gaze beyond the darkness into the future. He heard whispers, felt tremors that told him something was terribly wrong. The crisis . . . the missing girl . . . they were part of it but not all. He had received a call the night before from a Russian exile he had come to know, a poet who had survived Stalin's slave camps, who now was half mad and yet a kind of genius, and the poet had raved of evil happenings, devils, madness. And the senator, who was in no way mad, believed the poet was right. He felt evil in the air as other men sensed the coming of rain. The question now was, What could he do?

At length he reached out with a trembling hand and

witched on the antique reading lamp on his desk. He
oked up a number and dialed it himself. When Matt
oyle's answering machine responded he cursed that most
ffensive of modern inventions and hung up the phone. He
oured himself a glass of brandy to steady his nerves and
en he dialed again, this time a number that rang a tele-
hone on the President's desk in the Oval Office. The sena-
r was worried and tired; it was time to tell someone not the
ttle he knew but the much that he feared.

Charlie bolted the big front door from the outside and
ocked the shutters in place. As soon as they heard him drive
way they began an agonizing, inch-by-inch search of the
abin. The door held firm against their battering and the
hutters too were unyielding. The walls, ceiling, and floor
eemed solid, and they could find no tool or weapon to aid
heir escape. Zeb peered closely at the big Quaker fireplace,
ut its iron damper was built into the stone and didn't open
ide enough for him to attempt to squirm up the chimney.

They worked in a frenzy. Jenna broke up the table and
hey used its legs to pound in vain on the door and walls. Zeb
rowled the room, tapping the walls, looking for some weak
pot or hidden passage. They shouted, imagining that some
escuer might hear them. But in the end the cabin seemed
s impenetrable as the basement prison they'd left behind.

Jenna threw herself into a chair. "It's hopeless," she cried.

"There's got to be a way out," Zeb said. His hands were
loody from clawing at boards that did not yield.

"Look!" Jenna cried. "The TV. It's plugged in."

It was true. Charlie had ripped the phone from the wall
ut left the television set alone. Jenna switched it on and the
ace of a young black newswoman filled the screen: ". . .
he President will address these and other issues at his noon
ews conference, to be carried live here on . . ."

It was Jenna's first glimpse in an eternity of the world
utside; the news blinded her. "My God," she cried. "He'll
ry to kill him today."

"Who?" Zeb demanded.

"Charlie will try to kill my father at the news conference."

"We've got to warn him," Zeb said, and began clawing a the pine flooring again.

Jenna sank into a chair, fighting back tears. She wanted t be brave, to encourage Zeb, but she felt in her bones tha they would never escape this prison alive. She wondere why Charlie had even let them upstairs—to make it easier t kill them when he returned?

Zeb, digging under the sofa, found the stub of a cigar an threw it across the room in disgust.

Jenna watched, frowned, then exclaimed, "Oh, I forgot t tell you."

"Tell me what?" the boy asked.

She pressed her hand to her eyes. "My memory . . . I'r starting to . . ." She pulled herself together. "The ciga butt . . . it reminded me. I have some matches."

"Matches?"

"A book of paper matches. I stole them from him. Bu what does it matter? We can't burn down the cabin with u inside it."

Zeb leaped to his feet. "Where are they?" he shoutec "I've got an idea."

When Turk Kellerman was ushered into the Oval Office the weary President went straight to the point. "Do yo know where my daughter is?" he demanded.

"No," Kellerman admitted.

"But you have a theory?"

"I think a man is going to try to kill you at today's new conference. We can protect you. The problem is that I thin he has your daughter. The challenge is to save both of you.

"What do you propose?"

"A very dangerous plan," Kellerman said. "A plan yo may not like at all."

"Start talking," the President commanded.

When Kellerman finished explaining his scheme, Harr Bliss leaped to his feet. "Mr. President, it's insane," h shouted. "The risk is too great. He has no right to come in here and . . ."

"Be quiet, Harry," the President said. "Let me think. This is my daughter's life we're talking about."

Zeb stepped into the big fireplace and forced the damper up and down. "It's stiff," he said. "Probably rusted. But it ought to be okay."

He broke up a chair for kindling, piled rags atop it, and yanked a blanket from Charlie's bed. "See, the damper's closed now," he told Jenna. "I'll start a fire. We'll use the blanket to keep the smoke in the fireplace. Then, when it's full of smoke, I'll hold my breath and jump in and raise the damper, just for a few seconds, so a ball of smoke will go up the chimney. It'll be like the smoke signals that me and Derek—Derek and I—make all the time."

Jenna fought back tears. "But who'll see the smoke?"

"Lots of people could. If it works, you'll be able to see it in Harmony."

"What do you mean, if it works?"

Zeb chewed his lip unhappily. "Well, Derek and I, we built a fire on the ground, and held a blanket over it, and that's not exactly the same as smoke going up a chimney. But it might work—it's all I can think of."

She handed him the limp book of matches. Zeb huddled over his pile of paper, kindling, and rags. The wood soon caught and the rags began to smolder. "It's working," he said. "The rags will make lots of smoke."

Jenna watched in awe as thick smoke began to curl up, and then they used their hands and feet to hold a blanket tight across the front of the big fireplace. Despite all their efforts, smoke seeped around the edges of the blanket, filling their eyes and nostrils.

"Hurry," she said. "Do it!"

"Not yet," he insisted. "Hold on a little longer."

The blanket billowed out like a sail. Jenna gasped for fresh air. "Now!" Zeb cried. While she struggled with the blanket, he took a deep breath and leaped into the fireplace, straddling the flames, and pushed the damper open. He held it for a count of five, then let it fall shut again with a mighty clang. He stumbled out of the smoke, coughing and crying.

"It worked," he gasped. "Hold the blanket up, keep the smoke in!"

"Are you all right?" she asked.

"Sure, let's do it again." He grabbed the blanket and it began to fill with smoke again. "That was a good one."

Jenna's eyes were tearing. "It's dangerous," she protested. "There's too much smoke."

"No, it's okay," the boy said. His eyes, too, were red and watery, but his face was rigid with determination. "Someone will see it," he told her.

Charlie stood in line with other reporters and photographers at the Northwest entrance to the White House. The line was a long one, for the President's news conference promised rare political drama. Inside the gatehouse, each visitor went through the metal detector and each photographer's bag was searched. Also, a huge German shepherd was on duty.

"What's the dog for?" asked a pretty blonde, just ahead of Charlie in the line.

"He sniffs out explosives," Charlie said.

"Explosives but not drugs, I hope," the girl said.

Charlie winked. "Might thin down the press corps, eh?"

"This is my first news conference," she said, and they chatted a minute. Charlie enjoyed the diversion, although he never forgot she could be a plant.

When the blonde reached the desk, the guard studied her ID, frowned into his computer, and told her to step aside.

"Hey, I'm in your stupid computer," she protested.

"Routine, miss," the guard said. "You've got plenty of time."

"Rats," the girl grumbled.

Charlie grinned, produced his ID, dropped his camera bag on the table, and strolled through the metal detector. The German shepherd came over and sniffed at Charlie, who watched nonchalantly as one of the uniformed guards slowly went through his camera bag. Charlie knew precisely what was in the bag: a half dozen Nikon and Leica cameras, an abundance of extra lenses, ranging from 28, 50, and 8 millimeters to the 300 and 600 lenses he would need for the news conference; a tripod in a black leather case, to support the camera when he used the heavy 600-mm lens; dozens of packages of extra Duracell batteries; an old German light meter; a Vivitar flash attachment, although he would not need it today because the television lights would fill the East Room; dozens of boxes of Kodak film, including the tungsten film that was needed for today's exceptionally bright lighting; a battery-powered Olympus automatic winder; plus a scattering of personal items that included paperback novels, candy bars, a box of Kleenex, and an old necktie.

The guard methodically opened one after another of Charlie's cameras, then removed his tripod from its case.

"Do you really think he's got a bomb in there?" the girl asked disdainfully.

"Well, miss, he's got everything else," the guard said.

The other guard grinned. "We know he's harmless—he's from the Goode News Bureau," he said. "But, the thing is, some villain might have slipped a bomb in his bag when he wasn't looking."

Charlie laughed good-naturedly. The guard had just held in his hand the device with which he would kill the President, and then put it down because it appeared to be an utterly innocent item, one every photographer carried.

The guard picked up another of Charlie's cameras. "Mind if I click off a round?"

"Be my guest."

The guard pressed the shutter, shrugged, and replaced the camera. "Okay, buddy, you can go."

"Thanks," Charlie said. "Have a nice day."

From time to time Boyle peered out the window, up and down the street, half expecting to see some stranger silently watching his house. More likely his phone was tapped; that would explain a lot of things. Or had his caller been bluffing? *Say one word and I'll slit the little bugger's throat.* No matter, Boyle could not call his bluff.

In midmorning he looked out his window again. A neighbor was mowing his lawn. A plumber's truck was parked down the street. Or were they what they seemed? It was then that Boyle noticed the puff of smoke rising above the trees.

It looked strange, a solitary sphere floating into a cloudless sky. It was not the line of smoke that would rise from burning leaves or trash. Just a solitary ball, whitish-gray against the sky.

Then, incredibly, as the first puff of smoke faded into nothingness, a second rose in its place, off to the east, somewhere over River Crest Farm.

Boyle was frozen; somehow, the unexpected image was hauntingly familiar.

Then he remembered: Zeb and his friend, playing Indian, their smoke signals rising like ragged moons above the village.

Zeb was calling for help.

Jenna clutched the blanket, her eyes pressed shut, her throat aflame. "I can't breathe," she moaned.

"Hold on," Zeb pleaded. "Just once more."

He leaped into the fireplace again and this time stayed longer than before. She heard his fists hammering against the damper, then he stumbled back into the room.

"What's wrong?" she asked.

"The damper. It's stuck. I can't get it open."

Jenna backed across the room in horror as smoke from the smoldering rags began to engulf them.

"I'll try again," Zeb said. This time he took a chair leg to try to force the damper open, only to stagger out, coughing and crying, without success.

"You try," he said. "You're stronger."

Jenna took a deep breath and stepped into the fireplace. She found the damper and pushed upward with all her might. It didn't budge. Soon the smoke forced her back into the room, but the smoke was thick there too.

"I think maybe a brick fell down and jammed it shut," Zeb said.

Jenna threw her arms around him. "We won't be able to breathe in here much longer," she whispered.

Peaches Remington looked her husband in the eye. "They're going to kill the President today," she said. "That must be it."

The Vice President groaned. "I've got to warn him."

"You'll do no such thing," Peaches said firmly. "He can look out for his interests and we'll look out for ours."

"But I don't want to be President. Serena Masters . . . she'll . . ."

"She'll make you her puppet if you let her," his wife said. "But we won't let her."

"You don't understand," he said. "She's . . . she's got something on me."

Peaches seized his arm. "Ben, you tell me the whole story, right this instant!"

He buried his face in his hands. "It's so awful."

"Now, damn you, talk!" she cried.

Ben Remington marched to the bar, downed a shot of bourbon, and pulled himself together. "Just before I ran for governor I went to Atlanta on business," he began. "I stayed at the Hyatt Regency. I was having a drink at the bar—upstairs, that revolving bar—and a . . . a girl started talking to me. I was only being friendly but . . . but she invited me to her room. I'd never done anything like that before, I swear, but . . ."

"For God's sake, Ben, is that all it is? A night with some little chippie in Atlanta? No one cares about that anymore."

"But that's *not* all. She gave me a drink. I must have passed out. When I woke up the next morning . . . Oh God!"

"Go on," Peaches demanded. "What happened the next morning?"

"The girl was beside me in the bed. She was dead. A man was sitting there, smiling at me. He said I'd killed her and he had pictures of us together in the bed. I said, 'Is this blackmail?' He laughed—imagine, *laughed*, with that dead girl lying there—and said, 'Not at all, Mr. Remington. We want to make your life beautiful.'"

"Who was he?"

"One of Serena's henchmen. He said I had a choice. I could be arrested for murdering a call girl. Or I could cooperate."

"What did he want?"

Ben Remington laughed bitterly. "He wanted to make me President."

"That's when you started flying off for your mysterious meetings—with her!"

"That's right. They gave me money when I ran for governor. Gave me speeches to deliver, damn good speeches. It was her man who arranged for me to save that little girl from the river—he planned the whole thing."

"I knew it was faked," Peaches muttered.

"I was terrified. I might have drowned. I begged them not to make me do it. But it was their pet project. They said the publicity would be fantastic. And it was. Then they had my book ghostwritten for me. And set up all those Draft Remington Committees. I just drifted along, doing what they told me to, while they ran me for President."

"It's amazing," Peaches said. "You! You were such a long shot."

"You don't understand," he told her. "I wasn't the only one. She had other candidates. They didn't tell me, but I figured it out. In the primaries last year, she had at least two candidates in each party. People she controlled, the way she did me. It was like she had a stable of horses, figuring that one of them was sure to win the race. Even if one of her people got to be Vice President, that was enough, because all she had to do was . . . kill the President." He began to sob. "Oh, God, I wish I'd never been born."

"We've got to make the best of this, Ben."

"What can I do? I'm at her mercy."

"I'll tell you what you can do. You pretend to play along with her. But once you're President, *you* have the power. The CIA and the FBI work for *you*. When the time is ripe"—she snapped her fingers decisively—"Serena Masters will be gone, just like that. Live by the sword, die by the sword."

Boyle slipped out his back door, raced across the yard, and plunged into the woods that led to River Crest Farm. He carried with him a serrated kitchen knife, his only weapon. He ran through the woods, thinking ahead, realizing he couldn't get past the guards at the gatehouse, that he'd have to find a way over or under the estate's formidable fence. Thinking of the gatehouse reminded him of the time he'd passed it before, when Zeb and his friend had been caught trespassing there that spring, and he remembered the face he'd glimpsed inside the gatehouse and realized it had been Hillman, the photographer, the assassin, and finally the last pieces of the puzzle fell into place. Serena Masters had bought River Crest Farm, not the rumored Arab sheik, and her assassin had made it his hideaway and perhaps it had been hers, too. And now Zeb and Jenna were captives there.

He circled a farmhouse, crouched low as he crossed a cornfield, plunged into thick, shadowy woods, and soon reached the high fence, topped with barbed wire, that surrounded River Crest Farm. He raced along the fence, seeking some tree limb that might overhang it, some creek that might pass under it. Flies buzzed about his face; branches tore at his arms. The fence seemed impenetrable. Why hadn't he brought pliers? Should he go call the police? And tell them what—that he'd seen a smoke signal? He plunged on, bleeding, panting, almost empty of hope, when he noticed a hole beneath the fence, barely big enough for a fox to slip through. Desperate, Boyle fell to his knees and began tearing at the soft earth with his hands.

Colonel Vysotsky summoned his agents, bulky men in ill-fitting suits. They worked in the embassy motor pool when not on special assignment. They were cattle, he thought, creatures without poetry or wit. But useful. "You will go to the Masters estate," he told them in Russian. "In the afternoon this man will arrive"—he gave them a long look at Charlie's photograph. "The Masters woman wants him dead. But bring him to me alive if possible. Do you understand?"

"Don't kill him unless we have to," one of them muttered. The colonel nodded stiffly and dismissed them.

They staggered about the cabin, pounding on shutters and doors, desperate for air. They banged at the damper again and again but it wouldn't open. Zeb poured water on the smoldering rags but that only brought forth more smoke. There was no stopping the smoke; it filled the cabin like a rising tide. They dropped to the floor and tried to suck air from under the front door but they only took in more·vile, toxic smoke with each painful breath. Jenna held tight to the boy; that was all she could do.

"I'm sorry," he whispered. "I thought it would work."

"I love you, Zeb. Your mother and father love you."

"We did our best," the boy said.

"Don't talk," she whispered, and held him close as the smoke billowed around them.

Serena spent the morning thinking about the future, the glorious future. Soon Webster would be gone and she would have the power she'd dreamed of and schemed for. Soon after that Charlie would be gone, too, which grieved her, for he had given her much pleasure, but she could never rest easily while he lived. The important thing now was Remington, that he be carefully controlled, that he take office smoothly, that he be neither too good nor too bad a President, for in Serena's scheme of things he was only a caretaker. President Remington's most important task would be to appoint his own successor. And was not the moment ripe for a woman Vice President? Clearly it was and clearly there was no more perfect choice than Serena herself. Once she was Vice President her image could be expertly rehabilitated. She had learned from her past mistakes; she would watch her words, and her new image could be created, out of money and guile, as a new car was created or a new missile. Then, when she was widely beloved and respected, Ben Remington could be removed, one way or another.

President Masters!

Charlie and some other photographers were slumped in
easy chairs at the rear of the White House Press Room.
Charlie feigned sleep, one hand atop his camera bag, while
the others talked about cameras, women, and sports, in
roughly that order. Various big-name reporters paced about
the Press Room, trying to look important but unable to hide
the sorry fact that they had nothing at all to do except await
the President's pleasure.

"Hi."

Charlie opened his eyes and saw a pretty face. He let his
smile unwind. "So they let you in," he said.

"Finally," she said. "You don't look very excited."

"Why would I be?"

"The rest of the world is. It's a White House double fea-
ture, the Missing Daughter and the Red Peril."

Charlie shrugged. "Daughters are always running off and
the Bolshies are always acting nasty. I just take pictures."

"You're cute," she said. "How about a drink, later?"

"Not unless you tell me your name," he said. He thought
that she, or her car or her apartment, might possibly prove
useful.

She gave him her card—her name was Libby and she
worked for a Cleveland paper—and then an officious Assistant Press Secretary arrived to shepherd the media mob up
to the East Room.

Charlie gave the girl a parting wink. Be pleased to give
you a tumble, sweet, but first I've got to banjo your President.

The Press Secretary looked at his watch nervously. "Five
minutes, Mr. President," he said.

Cal Webster stared out the window at the sky, wishing he
were up there, where things were simpler. He had faced
death too many times as a fighter pilot to worry much about
He guessed the odds were in his favor, if what the experts
said was true.

Harry Bliss approached him. "Please," he said. "It's too
dangerous."

"I don't want to hear it," the President said. "You fellows go on. Give me a minute to myself."

Harry walked to the East Room, packed now with reporters, photographers, and TV camera crews. Most of the photographers crouched on the platform at the back of the room; a few were kneeling up front, near the big podium with the presidential seal. The podium was new; Harry wondered if anyone would notice.

Boyle emerged from the trees onto a bluff overlooking a long valley. Serena Masters's mansion was up the hill to his right, her maroon Mercedes parked before it. Across the valley, half hidden in a stand of oak trees, was a sturdy log cabin with a big stone chimney. Farther down the hill, almost out of sight, some bulldozers were at work, clearing the land for a new barn.

Boyle studied this silent tableau, looking for the puffs of smoke he had followed like a star. He stared at the cabin's chimney, hoping for a sign, then he saw smoke rising not from the chimney but from the eaves, as if the cabin were leaking smoke. He gazed at the wisps of smoke in confusion then with a cry began to race across the valley.

As he came closer he saw smoke pouring from under the eaves and oozing through cracks in the cabin's walls and under the door. He tried the door but it would not open. He tore loose one of the nailed-down shutters and through the bars that covered the windows saw a room dark with smoke. Gazing into the gloom he thought he saw a body on the floor.

"What's going on, mister?"

Boyle whirled and found a lean man in work clothes and a yellow hardhat.

"Someone's in there. I can't get the door open."

"Come on."

Together, they crashed against the wooden door, two, three, four times. Finally they felt it start to give; foul smoke seeped out around its edges.

"Stand back," the man said. He gave the door a powerful kick with his booted foot and it crashed open.

Boyle plunged into the darkness and found Zeb and Jenna
conscious on the floor, their lips purple, their faces ashen.
"No, no," he cried, and he and the stranger dragged them
t into the crisp, pure morning air.

The President took his place at the podium and waved the
porters back into their chairs. Secret Service men flanked
m and lined the walls. A reporter sprang to his feet to ask
e first question. On the big platform at the back of the
om, most of the photographers had their cameras set on
tomatic, so the air hummed with a ceaseless *swick-swick-
ick*. The only other sound was an occasional muttered
rse when someone's camera jammed.
Charlie was taking pictures too; he was relaxed and in no
rry. He glanced now and then at the tense young Secret
rvice men, whose eyes relentlessly scanned the room,
oking for the unfamiliar face, the unexpected act. Their
gilance did not worry him. His face was familiar, his ac-
ns routine. He changed lenses, adjusted his tripod, and
ot off more pictures.
Swick-swick-swick.

The man in the yellow hardhat was the foreman of the
ew that was working down the hill. He and Boyle
etched Zeb and Jenna out on the grass. Both were uncon-
ious, ashen, but breathing.
"We've got to get them to a hospital," Boyle said.
"I'll get my truck."
"Wait! We can't go out the front gate. The guards . . ."
"No sweat. There's a back gate we use."
The man brought up his pickup truck and they lifted Zeb
d Jenna into the back of it. The foreman went and peered
the foundations of the cabin.
"Did you see what's under there?" he asked.
"What?"
"Enough explosives to blow that cabin to the moon."
They roared out the back gate and went flying toward
eesburg.

"There's nothing I can add about my daughter," the President told a persistent reporter. "An intensive investigation is underway. Her mother and I are hopeful. Beyond that, I cannot speculate."

Serena paced before her television set, feeling a mixture of anxiety, impatience, and something like guilt. Part of her remembered the teachings of her girlhood, that it was wrong to kill, and doubly wrong to kill a king. Yet Webster's was perverted authority, she told herself; he must die so others could live in peace.

But where was Charlie? Webster spoke on. It was twelve-eighteen. "Do it, blast you!"

They wheeled Jenna and Zeb into the emergency room and gave them oxygen. She was still unconscious. The boy opened his eyes.

"President Webster," he said. "Did Charlie . . . ?"

"Just relax," Boyle told him.

A nurse told Boyle he'd have to wait outside. He tried to protest but she eased him out to the waiting room, where a soap opera was playing on an old TV set. The clock on the wall said twelve twenty-two. Boyle switched the channel. Calvin Webster's drawn face filled the screen.

Boyle dashed to a pay phone, dropped in some coins, and called the White House.

Swick-swick-swick.

The platform hummed with excitement as the photographers tried again and again, with only minutes remaining, to find the perfect shot.

Charlie, smiling contentedly, reached into his camera bag and pulled out an automatic film winder and snapped it onto the bottom of his camera. It was an L-shaped, black plastic device, powered by four AA batteries, that enabled the camera to shoot continuously, three frames a second, *swick-swick-swick*. Charlie's winder looked identical to those almost all the photographers were using, but in fact one of its batteries was his miniaturized laser weapon, capable of

ending a tremendous burst of energy across the East Room
and felling Cal Webster in an instant. Charlie had made
certain slight adjustments to the winder, so that when he
aimed his camera he was also aiming the laser's fatal beam.

Charlie focused on the President's right eye. He could not
miss from this distance.

The President, with only seconds remaining in his news
conference, was talking passionately about peace.

Charlie had him perfectly framed. The moment at last
had come. The amazing thing, he thought, was how easy it
had been.

"White House, can I help you?"

"Give me the Secret Service," Boyle cried. "It's an emergency!"

"One moment, please."

While he waited, second after agonizing second, Boyle
watched the President's face on the TV screen across the
room.

"Hello, this is Agent Barr," a man said. "What's the trouble?"

"The President," Boyle said. "Someone may try to . . ."

Then he stopped, for on the TV screen Calvin Webster
suddenly threw up his hands and pitched forward across the
podium.

Peaches Remington leaped to her feet. "Ben, you're President now!" she cried.

The Vice President stayed in his chair, unable to move.
"Oh God," he said. "I wish I was dead."

44

An instant of silence gripped the East Room as Calvin Webster crashed to the floor.

Then a woman screamed, and a team of Secret Service men surrounded the stricken President.

"What happened?" the reporters demanded. "Is he alive?"

"Keep back," the agents warned.

Amid the confusion, the photographers worked on. *Swick swick-swick*. When the agents began carrying Webster's limp body out of the East Room, Charlie carefully removed his lethal film winder from his Nikon and dropped it into the camera bag of the man next to him, a bearded, surly fellow from a French news agency. Then he started snapping pictures again.

Boyle collapsed in a plastic chair in the hospital's waiting room. The TV screen showed reporters milling around in the East Room, forbidden to leave by the Secret Service while an announcer talked excitedly: "No official word yet

. . possible stroke or heart attack . . . carried out uncon-
cious . . ."

I didn't save him. I might have but I didn't.

"Mr. Boyle, you can see your son now."

Boyle got up, dazed. "How is he?"

"Much better."

"What about the young woman?"

The nurse stiffened. "You'll have to ask the doctor about
that."

Furious reporters demanded that they be freed from the
East Room. Finally a senior Secret Service official stepped to
the podium. "Ladies and gentlemen, you can leave now," he
said. "Each of you must show identification as you leave and
go through a security check."

"Why? What's happening?" the reporters cried.

"I have no comment."

"How is the President?"

"No comment at all."

Grumbling, the reporters pushed toward the door. Charlie fell in line, inwardly exulting. It had gone like clockwork.
The doctors would be working over Webster now, trying
vainly to revive him. If ever an autopsy caused them to
suspect foul play, it would be days from now, and he would
be long gone.

The stocky Cuban knocked, then opened the door.
"What's wrong?" Serena demanded.

"The cabin, there was a fire. A big mess."

Serena glared at him. Perhaps Charlie had tried to burn
the cabin, to destroy evidence. How damnably crude. But
Charlie would learn his lesson soon enough.

"I expect him back soon," she said to the Cuban. "Is the
suitcase prepared?"

The Cuban flashed a smile. "The suitcase, it's all ready,"
he said.

Charlie hurried from the White House back to his new bureau, unaware that he was being followed. Johnny Good greeted him the moment he entered the office.

"Isn't this terrible?" he exclaimed. "You get any decen art?"

"Some great stuff," Charlie assured him, and disappeare into the darkroom.

Across the hall from the news bureau, a young woma sitting at a receptionist's desk picked up the telephone. "H just went into the darkroom," she said softly.

Down on K Street, Kellerman and Saussy were sitting i an unmarked black Mercury. Saussy had the car's phon pressed against his ear. "You've got a clear view of the dark room door?" he asked.

"Perfect," said the woman, who was one of his best agent

"Call me the moment he comes out."

"Count on it."

"He's in the darkroom," Saussy told Turk Kellerma "We've got men in the lobby, in the alley, and watching h car. I figure he kills some time here, printing his picture letting things die down, then heads for his hideout. An leads us to Jenna."

Kellerman shook his head. "This boy is clever."

"Not clever enough," said the FBI agent.

"We'll see," Kellerman muttered.

Forty minutes after the President's collapse, the Whit House Press Office issued this statement: "The President ha suffered what his doctors describe as a mild stroke. He resting comfortably." Despite protests from reporters, th Press Secretary refused to elaborate on the President's co dition or to comment on precisely who was piloting the shi of state during his disability.

Serena smashed her champagne glass against the fir place. "He's supposed to be dead!" she cried. "Dead!"

Saussy kept up a running commentary on everyone wh left the building: "A big ole sloppy fat gal in red pants, look

ike a fire truck . . . A skinny little black kid with headphones on . . . A damn Arab in his robes, the suckers are
verywhere . . . A gal with a face'd stop a clock, looks like
ny first wife . . ."

Kellerman said, "I don't like it. He's taking too long."

"Dammit, Turk, he's still in the darkroom, snug as a bug in
rug. What's his hurry?"

"I don't like it," Kellerman repeated. "Go check it out."

Saussy took the elevator up and went into the law office
cross from the news bureau. The receptionist whispered
nat the door to the darkroom had not opened since the
oung photographer went in.

Saussy stepped into the news bureau and entered Johnny
Goode's office. Goode was perplexed; they'd told him his star
hotographer might have a problem with his green card. "It
eems like he ought to be out by now," he said and went and
ounded on the door of the darkroom. "Hey, Wes, how
bout those prints?"

There was no reply. Goode pounded on the door and
elled again. When there still was no response, he yanked
e door open.

After a moment he turned back to Saussy, wide-eyed.
He's gone!" he said. "He's just flat vanished!"

The doctor was telling Boyle how smoke killed people.
The carbon monoxide keeps oxygen from getting to the
ood cells," he said. "The body gets starved for oxygen."

"Can . . . can the carbon monoxide cause permanent
mage?"

"In some cases. Your son seems fine. The young woman
. I can't say."

"Can I see her?"

The doctor shook his head. "She's not conscious."

Boyle called the White House and got Doris Webster on
e line. He told her where Jenna was and she thanked him
arfully. But when he asked about her husband she stam-
ered and said she had to go.

Boyle found Zeb propped up on some pillows watching a
me show on TV. He asked, "How do you feel?"

"Pretty good. I still cough up this black stuff and my che
hurts. How's Jenna?"

"I don't know," Boyle admitted. "Zeb, tell me what ha
pened."

Zeb sat up in the bed, brimming with excitement. "Th
guy Charlie, he came to our house and said he was a polic
man and threw a blanket over me and locked me in t
trunk of his car and took me to this basement where he h
Jenna. She said he was going to try to kill the President. T
morning I pretended to be sick and he let us go upstairs
the cabin. He locked us in there but Jenna had som
matches and we sent up smoke signals. The trouble was, t
damper got stuck and the cabin filled up with smoke. D
you see our smoke signals?"

Boyle nodded. "That's how I found you. You did a gre
job. Now I've got to go somewhere. You do what the doct
say and I'll be back as soon as I can."

Zeb's face darkened. "Where are you going?"

"To find Charlie," Boyle said.

"He'd cut a hole in the darkroom wall," Saussy explain
"and put a panel over it. He could squeeze through the h
into the storage room next door."

"Where his disguise was hidden," Kellerman said bitter

"What disguise?"

"He was the Arab who walked right past us," Kellerm
said. "His car, what about his car?"

"It's still in the garage."

"He had another one. Or stole one."

"Well, what now?" Saussy asked.

Kellerman did not reply directly. "I blew it," he said.
told the President that if he'd buy my plan the assas
would lead us to his daughter."

"Turk, whatta we *do?*"

"You're in charge now," Kellerman said. "I'm turning
my resignation."

Harry Bliss pushed his way through the reporters in t
Vice President's waiting room and stormed into his offi

What the hell do you mean, calling a news conference?" he demanded.

"What do you mean, barging in like this?" Peaches Remington replied.

"I'll handle it," Ben Remington said. "Harry, the reporters e about to break down my door. I've got to say something."

"All you've got to do is keep your mouth shut!"

"All sorts of rumors are flying about, that the President is ead, or a vegetable. We must have leadership. The whole orld is looking to me, Harry."

"You idiot, when the President recovers, we'll have your ead on a platter!"

"My loyalty is to the nation," Remington declared. "Only I and between America and anarchy."

My God, he believes it, Harry thought, and retreated from e office.

Inside, Peaches Remington straightened her husband's e, murmured words of encouragement, and sent him forth meet the press.

Charlie stopped his rented Oldsmobile at the forbidding on gate. He'd traded his Arabian robes for jeans and a tan ush jacket. A Colt Commander .45 automatic with an ght-inch suppressor rested in his lap, and the pockets of his ush jacket contained other means of destruction. He onked impatiently until the tall Cuban, eyeing him suspiously, came out and opened the gate.

"Hey, mate, is the dragon lady home?" Charlie called.

The Cuban muttered in Spanish. Charlie smiled and leved the Colt at his chest. "Adios, amigo," he said. The Colt ade a muted pop, a kissing sound, and the Cuban tumbled ver backward. Charlie dragged his body into the trees, en drove slowly toward the mansion. He thought they ight have gone for him there, a crossfire at the gate, but ow it seemed they had something cuter in mind. Which as their mistake. To be cute in killing was always a mistake.

Serena saw him stop before the house. "Do exactly as I ld you," she told the stocky Cuban.

The Cuban opened the front door and found the Co[
pointed at his gut. "Hey, no sweat man, she got yo[
money," he said. Charlie pushed the man ahead of him in[
the library.

Serena stood before a TV screen in the corner of the roo[
The mounted heads of a lion, a bear, and an elephant dec[
rated the wall above her. Charlie walked past the pricele[
Chinese dragon and confronted her. She glared at him, i[
different to the weapon in his hand. "He's alive," she rage[
"They say he's alive!"

"They lie," Charlie snapped.

Ben Remington's solemn face loomed on the TV scree[
He stood on the White House lawn, Peaches at his sid[
facing a tangle of reporters and TV cameras. "I am in co[
mand now," he declared. "In this hour of crisis, we mu[
have vigorous leadership. To our adversaries, we say . .

"Fool," Charlie said and cut off the TV. Then, to Seren[
"Where's my money?"

"There," she said. A belted, calfskin suitcase rested at[
her desk. "Count it if you wish," she added.

Charlie glanced at the suitcase, then at the Cuban and t[
hint of a smirk on his face. Charlie felt the tremors, the on[
that had saved him before. "You," he said. "Open the su[
case."

The Cuban's fat lips undulated but no sound emerge[
Charlie jabbed the Colt at him. "Move," he said. "Cho[
chop."

The Cuban inched toward the desk. His eyes darted b[
tween Serena and the suitcase. "Charles, really," she sai[

"Open the suitcase, you ape, or I'll blow your ugly hea[
off."

The Cuban seized the suitcase and tried to hurl it at Cha[
lie. Charlie fired and the suitcase exploded, blowing t[
Cuban to bits. Serena was thrown to the floor by the bla[

"Get up, bitch," he said.

She rose unsteadily to her feet, her eyes fixed on him.
didn't know," she said passionately. "I swear."

"No, you didn't know," he said mockingly. "It was t[
Cuban's idea to give old Charlie a suitcase full of newspape[

l a bomb. So when Charlie tries to count his money he
s his pretty head blown off. You do try my patience, luv."
You must believe me," she pleaded.
Where's the money?"
In the safe."
How much?"
A million cash. Maybe more."
Open it."
Ie poked the Colt at her and she sleepwalked to the wall
ide the fireplace. She pressed a concealed button and a
el slid back, revealing a sturdy wall safe. With trembling
gers, she started to spin the dial. "Truly, I didn't know,"
whimpered, but he ignored her. She pulled out bundles
housand-dollar bills and dropped them on the sofa. Char-
found another suitcase in the closet and loaded the
ney in it. When the safe was empty she turned to him
vously.
I have more," she said. "Tomorrow I can get you ten
llion. Twenty."
I'm not greedy," he said. "But you are. Your kind always

I was wrong," she said. "I didn't trust you. But now Rem-
ton is President, don't you see? Together, we can rule the
rld."
Not bloody likely," he said.
Ier dark eyes cut toward the door. He glanced away and
grabbed her purse. Amused, he let her draw her tiny,
d-plated pistol before he shot her. Serena sank to the
r, her face twisted in disbelief.
But who will save America?" she whispered.
Not me or thee, luv," he said, and fired again, this time to
ish her.
Charlie knew he had at least a million dollars from the
e, but it was far less than she owed him. He thought of her
vels, in the safe in her bedroom, worth at least another
llion. He hesitated, then bolted up the stairs, the Colt in
hand, the suitcase in the other. But when he reached the
ding and looked out the window and saw the black Lin-

coln in the garage that did not belong there, he cursed a
froze in his tracks.

Boyle raced from the hospital, flagged a ride to a
station that rented cars, and soon was speeding back to Ri
Crest Farm. The radio was full of reports of conflict betwe
the Vice President, who had claimed power, and the Pr
dent's staff, who said Webster would soon make a stateme
Senate leaders were demanding to see the President so th
could reassure the nation. Constitutional scholars gave c
flicting opinions. Boyle cut the radio off. He wasn't int
ested in the White House melodrama. He thought of
smoke-filled cabin, the explosives underneath it, and he
gripped by a venomous passion to find the man who
almost killed his son.

Charlie guessed the Lincoln was an embassy car, proba
Russian, but where were the bloody Russians and how m
of them were there? It was his instinct to seize the initiati
so he eased up the window and reached into the pocke
his bush jacket. He took out a round, shiny object that loo
like a Christmas tree ornament; it was in fact a Ladyl
Three, the most modern and lethal of hand grenades.
pinched the timer pin and flung the French-made gren
out the window. It was an expert toss: The grenade ro
under the Lincoln and exploded. The car lifted off
ground like a toy, and pieces of the garage flew hundred
feet. The Russian who had been hiding behind the gar
staggered into view. The blast had blinded him and set
clothes afire. "Ilya, help me," he cried. Charlie hoped
would be fool enough to show his face but he did not. S
the burning man fell to the grass and lay still.
Charlie went back downstairs, thinking about Ilya, thi
ing he was probably somewhere on the left of the d
hidden behind the boxwoods. But was there a third Russi
He heard a sound, a whimper, close at hand. He thr
open the door to the hall closet and found Serena's you
Peruvian maid cowering there. He slapped her and m
her put on a raincoat and hat he found in the closet.

ced her to the front door and said, "You run or I shoot you.
mprende?" He jerked open the door and jabbed her with
e Colt. The girl crossed herself and began to run. She had
y reached the steps when there was a popping sound and
e fell in a heap.

Charlie saw a flash of light where he had expected it,
ong the boxwoods, and he emptied the Colt at it. He was
varded with a howl of pain. A dying man stood up, tried in
n to raise his weapon, and pitched forward onto the grass.
arlie's eyes swept back and forth across the elegant
unds of the estate. All was quiet again. If he was lucky,
t would be all of them.

Boyle left his car on the road and approached the gate-
use on foot, amazed to find no one on duty. He searched
e gatehouse and found a small revolver taped under the
le. He seized it gratefully and set out for the mansion.

Charlie reloaded the Colt and bounded up the stairs to
ena's bedroom. The safe was behind a Monet. He tossed
e picture aside; it was worth a quarter million but he
ldn't sod around with it. He broke loose the plaster
und the safe and applied some plastique. Then he backed
t of the room, took cover behind the doorway, and fired at
e explosive. The wall exploded and jewels glittered among
e debris. He filled his pockets with them and eased back
wn the stairs. He was trying to decide if he should take
ae to blow up the cabin, and his two prisoners with it,
en he was startled to hear a familiar voice say, "Drop it,
u son of a bitch."

The federal agents overran the hospital and surrounded
na's room. Soon two of them entered the room where
b was watching a Carol Burnett rerun and breathing pure
ygen from a plastic mask. He studied their faces with
erest. One was lean and pockmarked and the other was
ge and had strange, shadowy eyes.
"Where's your father?" the lean one asked.
"He went to find Charlie."

"Who's Charlie?"

"Are you blind?"

"Yes. Who's Charlie?"

"The man who kidnapped Jenna and me."

"Do you know where he is?"

Zeb nodded. "I think so."

"Will you tell us how to get there, Zeb? It's importan

The boy's eyes gleamed with excitement. "If you'll ta me with you," he said.

Charlie made the life-or-death decision in an instant. could spin and fire and hope the man behind him was a b shot. Or he could play for time. If the man had been professional he would have risked it, knowing he was pro bly dead whatever he did. But he recognized Boyle's voi knew he was an amateur, his head filled with silly notio and that meant other options were open. He let the C drop to the floor. "Easy, now," he said. "Don't get trigg happy."

"Put your hands up and turn around," Boyle said.

Charlie turned and found Boyle standing in the libra beside the Chinese dragon, a revolver clutched in be hands.

"Come in here, slowly," Boyle said. Charlie moved f ward, his hands slightly out from his body. The room wa shambles.

"I ought to kill you right now," Boyle said.

Charlie thought, No, you'd rather jaw about it, like in movies.

"Kill me? Why would you do that?" He measured distance between them. One of the grenades in his pocl would do the job nicely.

"You were going to kill Zeb and Jenna. I saw the exp sives."

"Me kill them? I saved them from the dragon lady."

He was thinking that he hadn't much time, that if Bo had blundered in, the Secret Service could be along at a moment. "Listen, I've got a million dollars cash. Not to m

n a pocketful of diamonds and rubies. Suppose we divvie
? All's well that ends well, eh? Here, take a look."
He eased his hand toward the pocket of his bush jacket.
Vatch it," Boyle warned.
"Not to worry. All slow and easy, eh? No tricks." Charlie
pped his hand into his pocket and brought out a handful of
arkling gems. Grinning, he tossed them at Boyle's feet.
:ompliments of the house."
Still smiling, he lowered his other hand toward the pocket
th the grenades. "Lots more where those came from,"
aarlie said in a sing-song voice. "Pretty little gems like you
ver dreamed of."
Boyle felt himself trembling. He hated this man, and
ared him too, and yearned to shoot him now and be done
th him, yet he hesitated, held back by the sheer inability
kill a man in cold blood. He watched tensely as Charlie's
ght hand eased into his pocket.
Both of them were startled by the apparition that sud-
nly appeared in the doorway, a bloody hulk of a man, his
sh torn, his clothing in tatters, his eyes wild, who waved a
volver at Charlie while muttering incoherently in Russian.
Charlie knew at once who he was: the third Russian gun-
an, wounded but not killed by the grenade that blew away
e garage.
The intruder swayed back and forth in the doorway, try-
g with trembling hands to aim the revolver at Charlie. In
instant, Charlie saw Boyle's confusion, his indecision. You
ol, he thought, you bloody fool.
He threw himself at Boyle and in midair he flung a gre-
de at the Russian. The room blazed with light. Boyle,
aggered by the blast, fired blindly, but Charlie was atop
m, knocking his gun across the room.
"Get up, you poor sod, I'm taking you with me."
The assassin yanked Boyle to his feet. His Colt was pressed
ainst his head. Yet somehow Boyle was supremely
afraid. He felt pure, whole, invincible. With a cry of rage
slapped the Colt aside and wrestled Charlie to the floor.
ey rolled about, atop jewels and debris, until Charlie
nerged upon Boyle's chest, pounding his face. Boyle's legs

snaked up and flipped the Englishman onto his back. Then Boyle was banging Charlie's head against the floor, screaming "You tried to kill Zeb!"

Charlie broke free and stumbled across the room toward his Colt. Boyle tackled him and the two men pounded each other furiously. Charlie gave Boyle a vicious karate chop to the throat, one that dropped him to his knees, gasping for breath. Charlie turned and grabbed for his revolver, which lay on the floor beside Serena Masters's huge, bejeweled Chinese dragon. As Charlie bent down to seize the weapon, Boyle, fearing all might be lost, lunged forward and shoved the dragon toward his foe. The dragon tipped, then toppled heavily, falling atop Charlie and pinning him to the floor.

"Bloody hell," he cried, flailing with his arms and legs. Somehow his struggles tripped the dragon's fire-making mechanism, and a jet of flame shot from the creature's mouth, engulfing the trapped Englishman.

Boyle stumbled through the doorway. Seconds later, the flames reached the grenade that remained in Charlie's pocket; after the explosion, little remained of either dragon or assassin.

Boyle, sobbing and bleeding, lay helpless on the hallway rug. He didn't move when he heard car doors slam outside, and he looked up indifferently when men with drawn guns rushed through the front door.

"Where is he?" they demanded.

"Dead," Boyle told them. "Everybody's dead."

The men advanced into the smoldering ruins of Serena Masters's library. One of them whistled. "My God," he said. "He wasn't kidding."

The men gave Boyle water and dressed his wounds. "We have to take you to Washington," one of them said. "The President wants to see you."

Boyle almost laughed. He wasn't even sure who was President now; nor did he greatly care. "No," he said. "Just take me to the hospital in Leesburg, where Jenna and Zeb are."

One of the agents went to the door and called to someone. A moment later, Boyle thought himself delirious as Ze walked slowly into the wrecked mansion. They embraced; Boyle fought back tears, then surrendered to them.

"I love you, Dad," the boy said.

Boyle couldn't speak.

"Did you kill Charlie?" Zeb asked.

Boyle pulled himself together. "Not really," he said. "He killed himself."

Turk Kellerman knelt beside them. "Mr. Boyle, the President wants you, as soon as possible."

Boyle began to laugh. It was all too much. "I look like hell," he said. He thought he might be in shock. A visit to the White House at this moment seemed quite hilarious.

"Please," Kellerman said. "It's all right."

Too dazed to argue, Boyle hobbled out of the ruined mansion, holding his son's hand for support.

45

Saussy drove with Kellerman riding shotgun and the Boyles, father and son, in back. Red lights flashing, they covered the forty-odd miles to the White House in under thirty minutes.

Halfway there, Boyle asked, "What's happened? I don't know if Cal Webster is dead or alive."

Kellerman said, "Mr. Boyle, if you don't mind, just wait till we get there."

"Then tell me how Jenna is."

Kellerman shook his big head. "I honestly don't know." They rode the rest of the way in silence.

A cluster of Secret Service men met them at the door and ushered Kellerman, Boyle, and Zeb into the Oval Office.

Cal Webster rose to greet them. He'd never looked healthier. Doris Webster was there too—she ran to Boyle and embraced him—and Harry Bliss, Senator Ben Trawick, and the Attorney General, a chain-smoking Alabaman named Hewlett.

The President greeted Boyle and Zeb with bear hugs. "Come in, the both of you," he roared. "Thank God you're all right!"

The new arrivals settled in chairs facing the President's huge desk. "Mr. President," Boyle stammered, "I thought you were . . . I mean, I saw you collapse on TV."

Webster beamed. "I know, I know. I'm going on television in a few minutes to explain all that. But first, tell me what you know about this affair. There are a lot of loose ends that still don't fit."

Boyle explained what he had learned, about Serena Masters's control over Remington, about Remington's faked heroism, about Charlie's cover job as a photographer, and about the smoke signals that had led him to Jenna and Zeb.

"By Heaven, that's one brave young man," Webster declared. "Zeb, would you come and sit with me?"

Blushing, Zeb went to the President, who scooped him up on his lap. "We now have an honorary presidential grandson," he declared. "And you, Matt, Jenna wouldn't be alive now except for you. If there's anything at all I can do for you . . ."

"Sir, the thing I want most is for you to explain what's going on," Boyle said.

"Of course, of course. How's our time, Harry?"

"You're on the air in eight minutes," Harry Bliss said.

"Then I'll be brief," Webster said. "First of all, we had some important help from Senator Trawick."

The Senator shook his head. "Very little help, in truth," he said. "Matthew, I sent you the documents that linked the Masters woman with the news bureau where, I'm told, her assassin worked."

"So that was you?" Boyle exclaimed.

"Yes. There was no one I trusted more to get to the bottom of things."

Boyle was moved. "That's a great compliment, sir," he said.

The President, frowning as the senator took center stage, said, "Well, to continue, I've accepted the Vice President's resignation, Matt. He confessed everything—that wife of his is the tough one—and the Attorney General is advising me about possible criminal charges. If what Remington says is true, that Masters woman was using her money to try to corrupt the entire political system. She'd buy candidates, or blackmail them, thinking that if she fielded enough of them she'd elect a President in time. But I understand she's no longer a threat."

"That's right," Turk Kellerman said. "Her assassin, the Englishman, killed her. Then Mr. Boyle—acting with tremendous courage—disposed of the Englishman."

"Good riddance," Harry Bliss added.

The President said, "You see, Matt, once we realized Jenna had been kidnapped, Turk suspected it was tied to an assassination plot. Perhaps you'd better explain, Turk."

Kellerman nodded gravely. "Once I found out that Dr. Lamb had been working on a miniaturized laser weapon, I realized that he himself had been killed with it, out on his farm. But we didn't know who had the weapon. I'd been worried for years about a laser attack on the President. It was so obvious, if you could make the device small enough, to conceal one in a camera. What else can you point at a President and not be shot down immediately? But how could we examine every camera without scaring off the assassin? Then we received evidence that this photographer, the one who called himself Hillman, might be the assassin."

"How did you find that out?" Boyle asked.

"Senator Trawick passed onto us the same information he sent you. But you found Hillman faster than we did."

"Only because he tried to kill me," Boyle said.

"Well, once we suspected that Hillman—or Charlie, or whatever you call him—would try to kill the President at today's news conference, we faced a hard decision. We could have grabbed him. But we were afraid that if we did we'd never get Jenna back alive."

The President broke in impatiently. "Turk laid it on the line. Our best hope of saving Jenna was if the assassin thought he'd killed me and then led us back to Jenna. It wasn't foolproof but it was the best shot we had."

"The plan failed," Kellerman said bitterly, "because I let the assassin slip through my fingers. Mr. Boyle's the one who saved your daughter, sir."

"There's plenty of credit to go around," Webster said.

'And, incidentally, I've torn up that resignation you sent me. Now, why don't you explain how we tried to trick the assassin?"

"The Pentagon has spent billions on laser research," Kelerman said. "The question was whether they'd developed any sort of a defense to a hand-held laser weapon. I found out last night that they've been experimenting with one. In layman's terms, it's a maser, interacting with an electric field, to form an invisible shield. When the laser beam strikes that shield, it's diffused into harmless beams of light. Or so we hoped. We didn't know the precise nature of the assassin's weapon, so we couldn't be sure our defensive shield would handle it. But the President was willing to take the risk."

"Of course I was," Cal Webster said. "What sort of man would I be if I hadn't? Not worthy of this office, at the very least."

Doris Webster tried without success to choke back a sob. The President hurried to her side and took her hand.

"Two minutes, Mr. President," Harry Bliss said.

"To wrap this up," Webster said, "Turk had the maser equipment installed last night, built right into the podium. He had them attach a tiny red light that would flash when the laser beam struck our field, so I'd know when to fake my collapse. It meant misleading the nation—the world—for a few hours, but it was worth it to save Jenna and to give Remington a chance to show his true colors."

The President stood up. "I spoke moments ago to the Soviet Premier, who's as outraged by this as I am. Communist or capitalist, heads of state don't like assassination plots. He's in full control now. The demolition of the second round of missiles will start tonight, and he's ready to move ahead on the third round. I'll announce all that on TV."

"Mr. President," Harry said anxiously. "We've got to . . ."

"Matt, I wish you'd stay and brief reporters after I make my statement. In fact, why don't you and Zeb stay for dinner and spend the night? I believe the Lincoln Bedroom is made up."

"Neat-o," Zeb murmured.

"And Matt, don't get the idea you've heard the last of my job offer. I still think we can work it out, the three of us."

With that, Cal Webster marched out to meet the press for the second time that day. Most of the men hurried after him.

Boyle stayed where he was, too exhausted to move. Doris Webster came and took his hand. "Why don't you two come upstairs with me?" she said. "We can watch Calvin on television and have a bite to eat."

"Can they fix me a cheeseburger?" Zeb asked.

The First Lady smiled. "I think so."

They took the elevator up to the family quarters. When they emerged from it, Doris turned to Boyle and said, "There's someone who wants to see you both."

She led the way to a small bedroom where Jenna, in blue pajamas, was propped up on a pile of pillows. A nurse hovered at her side with oxygen equipment. Jenna smiled and held out her arms to them. "You two saved me," she said.

Boyle took her hand. "It's all over now," he said.

"Are you okay?" Zeb asked.

"I swallowed a lot of gunk, but I'll get well."

"You can't stay," the nurse said. "She must rest."

"When you're well, will you come see us?" Zeb asked.

Her pale face seemed to glow. "If you want me to."

"We want you to," Boyle said.

Jenna shut her eyes and smiled.

A Selected List of Fiction Available from Mandarin

While every effort is made to keep prices low, it is sometimes necessary to increase prices at short notice. Mandarin Paperbacks reserves the right to show new retail prices on covers which may differ from those previously advertised in the text or elsewhere.

The prices shown below were correct at the time of going to press.

☐ 7493 1352 8	**The Queen and I**	Sue Townsend	£4
☐ 7493 0540 1	**The Liar**	Stephen Fry	£4
☐ 7493 1132 0	**Arrivals and Departures**	Lesley Thomas	£4
☐ 7493 0381 6	**Loves and Journeys of Revolving Jones**	Leslie Thomas	£4
☐ 7493 0942 3	**Silence of the Lambs**	Thomas Harris	£4
☐ 7493 0946 6	**The Godfather**	Mario Puzo	£4
☐ 7493 1561 X	**Fear of Flying**	Erica Jong	£4.
☐ 7493 1221 1	**The Power of One**	Bryce Courtney	£4
☐ 7493 0576 2	**Tandia**	Bryce Courtney	£5
☐ 7493 0563 0	**Kill the Lights**	Simon Williams	£4
☐ 7493 1319 6	**Air and Angels**	Susan Hill	£4.
☐ 7493 1477 X	**The Name of the Rose**	Umberto Eco	£4.
☐ 7493 0896 6	**The Stand-in**	Deborah Moggach	£4.
☐ 7493 0581 9	**Daddy's Girls**	Zoe Fairbairns	£4.

All these books are available at your bookshop or newsagent, or can be ordered direct from the address below. Just tick the titles you want and fill in the form below.

Cash Sales Department, PO Box 5, Rushden, Northants NN10 6YX.
Fax: 0933 410321 : Phone 0933 410511.

Please send cheque, payable to 'Reed Book Services Ltd.', or postal order for purchase price quoted and allow the following for postage and packing:

£1.00 for the first book, 50p for the second; **FREE POSTAGE AND PACKING FOR THREE BOOKS OR MORE PER ORDER.**

NAME (Block letters) ....

ADDRESS ....

....

☐ I enclose my remittance for ....

☐ I wish to pay by Access/Visa Card Number ☐☐☐☐☐☐☐☐☐☐☐☐☐☐☐☐

Expiry Date ☐☐☐☐

Signature ....

Please quote our reference: MAND